A TASTE OF HEAVEN

Reilly turned to leave. "We'd better get back to the house."

Sam took hold of her arm and pulled her to him. "No, not yet. This is the first time we've had a chance to be alone. We should take advantage of it."

As Sam lowered his head to kiss her, Reilly turned her head and his lips brushed her cheek. "No, someone might see us."

"It's a sorry gambler who never takes a risk," he said, cupping her chin and turning her to face him.

Reilly gazed up at Sam, her soft mouth parting as he lowered his head and kissed her. Too long they had denied themselves this pleasure and what had started as a gentle touching of mouths turned to greediness and fierce possession. Passions flared up between them and, clasping the back of his head, she pressed her mouth firmly and eagerly against his own . . .

DANA RANSOM'S RED-HOT HEARTFIRES!

ALEXANDRA'S ECSTASY   (2773, $3.75)

Alexandra had known Tucker for all her seventeen years, but all at once she realized her childhood friend was the man capable of tempting her to leave innocence behind!

LIAR'S PROMISE   (2881, $4.25)

Kathryn Mallory's sincere questions about her father's ship to the disreputable Captain Brady Rogan were met with mocking indifference. Then he noticed her trim waist, angelic face and Kathryn won the wrong kind of attention!

LOVE'S GLORIOUS GAMBLE   (2497, $3.75)

Nothing could match the true thrill that coursed through Gloria Daniels when she first spotted the gambler, Sterling Caulder. Experiencing his embrace, feeling his lips against hers would be a risk, but she was willing to chance it all!

WILD, SAVAGE LOVE   (3055, $4.25)

Evangeline, set free from Indians, discovered liberty had its price to pay when her uncle sold her into marriage to Royce Tanner. Dreaming of her return to the people she loved, she vowed never to submit to her husband's caress.

WILD WYOMING LOVE   (3427, $4.25)

Lucille Blessing had no time for the new marshal Sam Zachary. His mocking and arrogant manner grated her nerves, yet she longed to ease the tension she knew he held inside. She knew that if he wanted her, she could never say no!

LINDSEY HANKS

NEVADA ECSTASY

ZEBRA BOOKS
KENSINGTON PUBLISHING CORP.

ZEBRA BOOKS

are published by

Kensington Publishing Corp.
475 Park Avenue South
New York, NY 10016

First printing: October, 1992

Printed in the United States of America

Chapter 1

Castletown, Nevada
1881

A brisk wind played teasingly with the merchandise displayed along the weathered boardwalks. Signs creaked on rusty hinges, and a piece of newspaper weaved and bounced through the main thoroughfare like a drunk in search of a drink. The afternoon sun beat relentlessly against the storefronts, its heat undulating from the hard-packed ground.

In the narrow alley running behind the shops on Main Street, Reilly Reynolds placed her hands on her slender hips and pondered the draped figure of the corpse laid out before her. Her sun-browned face was flushed and her sky-blue eyes sparkled with resentment. She was mad as hell. She could stomp and fume and sputter until she was blue in the face, but it wouldn't do any good. Sam Chandler was dead.

That morning, the bank had been robbed and the head teller killed. The sheriff and his rag-tag deputies had left town in hot pursuit of the robbers. Sheriff Murdock had returned with Chandler's body, telling an outlandish story about Chandler being the leader of the gang. Then Oscar, one of the deputies, had come to her studio to inform her that she would be photographing the outlaw. Words of accusation had risen to Reilly's throat, but she'd quickly swallowed them back. No telling what would happen to her if she called the sheriff a liar.

Reilly flipped her long blonde braid over her shoulder and bit her lower lip as she frowned down on Chandler's ashen face, still handsome even in death. Wiping her sweaty hands on the seat of her baggy pants, she picked up her camera. Sauntering around the body, she paused every few feet and took a bead on her subject through the lens of her camera.

From the corner of her eye she saw her friend, Susan Waters, step from the back door of the mercantile store.

"Damn," Reilly mumbled as the wind whipped a cloud of dust between her and the corpse. Pulling a soft cloth from her pocket, she cleaned the lens.

Susan curled her lips in distaste and stepped back in the shade, yet she couldn't take her eyes off the proceedings. A chill swept through her as she turned her attention to her friend's camera. A wide board was wedged against a support post which held the lifeless body of the sheriff's latest triumph. Susan watched Reilly adjust her camera and peer through the lens.

"Reilly?" Susan called softly.

"Huh?"

"How can you bear to do that?"

Reilly snapped the shutter. "You don't have to whisper, Susan, he can't hear you. He's dead."

"I know that. It just seems somehow sacrilegious to take his photograph. After all, like you said, he's dead."

"As a door nail," came Reilly's dry reply as she turned toward her friend.

Her petite figure clad immaculately in yellow gingham, Susan inched her way slowly through the

6

alley, and her green eyes narrowed apprehensively as she neared the body. "Doesn't it bother you? The other pictures you take are so beautiful, but these are so—"

"Lifeless?"

"Well . . . yes."

As Reilly straightened and stretched her back, Susan swept her eyes appraisingly over her friend's tall, willowy figure. How she wished she could convince Reilly to occasionally wear dresses instead of always wearing those horrid baggy pants.

Reilly interrupted her musing. "I have to admit this one has been harder than most. I suppose it's because I knew who he was. Still, I have to do this; it pays the bills and keeps me in supplies. You know my uncle only works when he's in dire need of funds to purchase a bottle, or when his conscience moves him to go on the wagon for a spell."

"My mom says no one can build a finer piece of furniture than your uncle when he sets his mind to it."

"It's just a shame that he doesn't set his mind to it very often."

"Well, it's a disgrace the way you have to work," Susan said, rearranging an auburn curl the breeze had mussed. "And another thing. If the sheriff didn't puff up like a rooster over his killings, he wouldn't want pictures taken of dead men. He may say it's to discourage other outlaws from lingering in his town, but everybody knows it's for his own personal glory. He catalogs his photographs as if he was a mother placing the births of her children in the family Bible."

Reilly had her own thoughts about the sheriff, but it was his money that paid her.

She positioned her camera again and snapped the shutter. Trying to ease the turmoil roiling within her, she said flippantly, "One thing's for sure, Mr. Chandler won't complain if I don't get his best side."

"Oh, Reilly, I can't believe you said that," her friend groaned.

"It's the truth. If you had to deal with some of the people I do, you'd believe it. They think I can turn a prune-faced old maid into a blooming beauty. I'm a photographer, not a magician. Besides, the camera doesn't lie."

Susan laughed. "And I suppose you've told them this?"

"I have, on occasion," Reilly admitted as she approached the corpse. "He was a handsome man, wasn't he?"

Working up the courage to look at the corpse, Susan squeaked, "Yes," as Reilly took a step closer, then another.

Indeed, he was a very handsome man, Reilly thought. His hair was a blue black as the sun glistened off it. His brows were thick and well-defined. Heavy and slightly curled, his lashes would be the envy of any female. He had a slender nose, but his lips, swollen and parched, looked out of place in comparison to his other features. His face was a network of planes and angles. High sharp cheek bones jutted from smooth, darkly tanned skin, although now his complexion was more gray than tanned. He needed to shave, Reilly thought absently as she noted his stubbled face.

"He doesn't look like your run-of-the-mill bank robber, does he?" Susan said.

Reilly shook her head furiously as Susan continued her perusal.

"I truly don't know what I expected a bank robber to look like, but it wasn't like this," Susan stated. "I never would have thought it of him, he being a city slicker and all. I guess it takes all kinds."

8

"He didn't do it," Reilly whispered.

"What?"

Reilly looked at her friend. "He didn't have anything to do with the robbery."

"You're sure?"

"Positive, and I have the proof."

"Oh, my God, Reilly," Susan gasped. "Do you know what you're saying?"

Reilly nodded her head. "Yes, I know."

"What's your proof?" Susan asked.

"I have photographs of the robbers."

Susan clasped her hand over her mouth in astonishment. "Oh, my God, you're going to get yourself killed. Does anyone know?"

"Just you. I was there this morning when it happened. I had my camera set up when they rode into my line of vision. Afterwards I went straight to the studio and developed the pictures. I was so excited when I saw them. I knew I had something the newspaper back East would buy. I had just returned from mailing the pictures when the deputy came and told me the sheriff wanted me to photograph Chandler."

"What are you going to do?"

"What can I do? We're looking at a dead man, and dead men don't talk. It just makes me so angry that this happened and nothing will be done about it."

"Then the sheriff framed him?"

Reilly nodded. "He's an evil man, and he never leaves any witnesses."

"It wouldn't be the first time. I've heard things, Reilly. Bad things."

"So have I, but it doesn't matter. I can't do anything. Can you imagine what would happen if I approached the sheriff?" She sighed. "I can see it now." Reilly made her voice deliberately high and feminine, batting her eyelashes. "Oh Sheriff, a

9

terrible mistake has been made. Your men have killed an innocent man, and I have the picture to prove it." Reilly returned to normal. "He'd lie his way out of it and make me look like a fool. It makes me sick, Susan, but my hands are tied."

When Reilly began tugging on the sheet, Susan covered her mouth and watched in fascination.

The sheet slipped from his chest and the man's arms fell limply to his sides. Susan gasped. "He's not naked, is he?"

"No, I don't think so," Reilly admitted, afraid to move the sheet any lower. "No, they left on his pants. I see the waist band." She couldn't resist the temptation to let her eyes drift over his bare chest. His death call had been a bullet just beneath his collarbone. Around his neck lay a limp, black string tie. Dried blood crusted the mat of hair covering his chest. As she stood there, his injury welled with fresh blood and ran across a large brown nipple, down his side, and dripped slowly to the ground.

Reilly gasped and jumped back.

Susan grabbed her and whispered urgently, "What is it?"

"I thought he groaned."

They looked at each other in astonishment, fright building in them. Hesitantly, they turned their heads toward the corpse.

He was perfectly still, yet as they watched they could see his eyes rolling wildly beneath closed lids.

Reilly grabbed the sheet and threw it over his face. He groaned, and they both heard it as plain as day.

"Oh, my Lord, he's alive!" Reilly exclaimed.

"No question about it—he's alive," Susan agreed, wringing her hands. "What are you going to do?"

"I don't know," Reilly pointed to the side of the building. "See that pine box in the wagon?"

Susan lifted her head. She hadn't noticed the

10

rickety wagon or the coffin. A lop-eared nag stood dozing in the shade of the building, his wiry tail swishing like a pendulum to ward off flies.

"When I finished taking the photographs, that was supposed to be his destination," Reilly explained. "My uncle left it when he brought the body. He'll be back in a little while to load the body for burial, if he isn't drunk. He was on his way to really tying one on when he brought the body. I don't know what to do. I can't send for the sheriff."

Susan gave Reilly a knowing look.

"If you do, you know what the sheriff will do, don't you?"

"He'll manage to kill him, one way or another," Reilly admitted softly.

"W-Water," came a mumbled plea.

The girls reached for the sheet in the same instant, then like a well-oiled cog, their eyes swept around to see if anyone was paying them any attention. The alley was clear. They eased the sheet from his face. Deep brown eyes rolled in the man's head. "W-Water," he whispered.

"I'll get it," Susan replied, taking off in a dead run.

The moment Susan left several events happened at the same time, reinforcing Reilly's decision not to turn Sam over to the sheriff.

She lifted her hand to his brow, the unnatural heat emanating from his body scorching her fingers. For an instant he opened his eyes, and this time they were clear, yet deeply puzzled. "Don't cry," his gravelly voice scraped before his eyelids drifted shut.

Her heart hammered wildly at his words. She hadn't known tears were rolling down her cheeks. When she lifted her hand from his brow, strands of his thick black hair brushed her knuckles. Her stomach fluttered strangely and a spiral of pleasure curled through her. She wiped her tears away and

11

adjusted the sheet. Again she noticed the fresh blood staining the cloth. Her heart almost stopped. He would bleed to death if she didn't do something. With trembling hands and a rushing heart, she tore strips from the bottom of the sheet.

Reilly worked diligently, trying to staunch the flow of blood. Susan returned with a cup of water and followed Reilly's instructions nervously. Now was not the time to be squeamish. They began to feel like criminals themselves as they worked over the unconscious man, watching anxiously over their shoulders for an uninvited attention.

They bound his wound and swabbed his swollen mouth with water. It didn't shock Susan when Reilly informed her that she was taking him home with her. There weren't any other alternatives. Working as quickly as possible, they prepared to move him.

Reilly had to threaten, cajole, and threaten some more to get the ornery nag to leave his comfortable spot in the shade. Backing the wagon was a task indeed, yet her determination didn't fail her and eventually she maneuvered it into position.

When they lifted the body from the slab, the dead weight almost jerked their arms from their sockets. His head barely missed cracking against the end of the wagon. They strained and grunted and groaned until they wrestled him onto the rickety bed. After a short rest, they picked him up once again and lowered him into the coffin. This time his groan was laborious and loud. Susan pretended a coughing fit to cover any discernible sounds coming from the pine box. They cocked the lid over the opening so he wouldn't smother. Reilly jumped onto the wagon seat and jerked the reins. The piebald, unaccustomed to such rough treatment, bolted forward, and a muffled groan emerged from the box as the anxious women departed.

"What if he dies?" Susan asked hesitantly. She was struggling to be brave and have the courage her friend had in such abundance.

"He won't." Reilly shook her head, enforcing her edict. "I won't let him." A queer pain rippled through Reilly's insides. She didn't want him to die. Suddenly, keeping him alive was the most important thing in her life.

Chapter 2

Reilly guided the wagon through town, trying to think of anything other than the possibility of Sam Chandler dying. Seeing him debilitated was contradictory to every vision she'd had of him. And she'd had plenty. She didn't know him personally. Nice girls didn't know men like him. Still, she'd watched him from afar for weeks. Imprinted in her memory was the day Sam Chandler arrived in Castletown.

On that day, dark, low-hanging clouds blanketed the summit and a misty fog rolled through town. Continuous rain had turned the streets of Castletown into a quagmire and tested the patience of its residents.

The saloons were doing a roadhouse business, and the professional gamblers soon routed the unwary social gambler, leaving him with little more than pocket change.

Reilly was hurrying through the drizzle when old Number 7's whistle pierced the gray mist, hanging like a high note for several long seconds. She came barreling through the fog like some prehistoric monster.

Reilly stopped just beneath the awning of the depot and watched the large wheels as they screamed and sparked. The train belched to a grinding halt before the depot. While it took on more wood, the passengers had a few moments to stretch their legs, and those at their journey's end gathered their belongings.

She watched as the porter swung to the ground and offered an arm to those disembarking. That was when she saw the stranger. He ducked as he made his way through the portal and lifted his hand to place a bowler on his dark curling hair. He was nattily dressed in a black cutaway coat, his shirt a crisp white. A narrow string tie rested smartly against his starched collar. He wore a double-breasted waistcoat with shimmering threads woven through the fabric. A watch chain was draped neatly from his vest pocket. His coat was of the same dark fabric as his britches, fitting his long legs as though they'd been tailor stitched for him. Reilly noticed several things at once—he wasn't wearing a gun and on his feet he wore soft leather shoes. Shoes! How odd. Since coming west with her father, she hadn't seen men who weren't wearing boots of one form or another. His appearance screamed tenderfoot.

When he reached the platform, he took his time removing a small dark cigar from his breastpocket. He looked unaware of his surroundings until he flipped the head of a match and applied the flame to his smoke. Then Reilly saw his hooded eyes as they made a brief inspection of the men loitering on the boardwalk. His eyes lit on her lightly, then returned to peruse her at his leisure. She felt the flush staining her cheeks, and when she would have turned away, his eyes trapped hers, and he nodded ever so slightly. She shifted the package in her arms and nodded in return. His smile was barely discernible, yet it sent the butterflies in her stomach into flight.

The idle roustabouts and miners, sheriff's deputy,

and the like who were handy to the depot, watched in eager anticipation for an easy mark. They, too, noted the stranger as he got down from the steamcars and decided to take him.

Reilly saw the men converging on the stranger like wolves on a fresh kill. She wanted to warn him of their intentions. Everyone knew they were a worthless lot when left to their own nefarious pursuits. Instead, she shook her head sadly and turned away. It was none of her business.

The next day she heard the most amazing thing. The stranger had indeed known what he'd been about, and the miscreants had miraculously got their due. Although city slicker that he was, he'd played them for the fools they had taken him to be. He was a gambler, and a good one. He'd left with their every cent in *his* pockets; his opponents in shopworn shape on the floor. And Neal, the foul-mouthed deputy, had the back of his hand ventilated by the stranger's gleaming blade when he dared to slip an ace from his sleeve.

Sometimes Reilly caught a glimpse of him—Sam Chandler was his name. More often than not one of the soiled doves from the Pleasure Palace would be hanging on his arm. Once, she'd even seen him with a girl on each arm. Her heart had done crazy things. She admitted with defeat that this kind of man would never look twice at her. Besides, why would she want him to? He was a fancy man with fancy ways. She was a hard worker, trying to make her way in this world on her own merit. She had more calluses on her hand than the local smithy. Sam Chandler probably didn't even know what a callus was, much less have any on his smooth gambling hands.

She knew a lot more about him than anyone would ever dream possible. When she set her mind to it and used her camera the way her father had taught her, she could tell a story with her pictures. And . . . she had a story on Chandler.

Yes, Reilly thought with a wistful smile, she had been taught by the best, her father, Morgan Reynolds. He'd been an adventurous soul, and he and Reilly had traveled the country together. He had worked for one of the eastern newspapers, chronicling the growth of the West. He had been well respected for his work. Reilly didn't have the flair her father had possessed, but she had a growing talent. Her father had been a pioneer in his field, and his work was grabbed up by the hungry Easterners.

Reilly was continuing her father's trade, sending work she thought was particularly interesting to the paper her father had worked for. Sometimes she got lucky and they bought from her. But times had changed and the field of photography was no longer as scarce as it was when her father had begun his career. She was convinced there was a photographer behind every tree, though that was not the case at all. If she were a man, she would think nothing of taking off on her own. But being a female didn't lend itself to traipsing across the country alone. Being tied to a small town limited her in getting photographs that would sell. But nonetheless she tried. The sheriff was as crooked as a dog's leg, and everyone knew it. The gossip was rampant. Still, that didn't produce salable photographs.

Reilly flicked the reins and coaxed the horse with the promise of an extra helping of oats.

She had a shred of hope that her luck was about to change. The pictures she'd taken early that morning should garner a good price. It was just by happenstance that she'd been out at that particular time. She normally scheduled portraits in the morning hours, but this day her time was her own. She'd made the most of it by working on her newest brainstorm. She was doing a history of a mining town and its inhabitants. As luck would have it, she had her camera set up just across the street from the bank when the outlaws robbed it. Trying to look like a lump of scenery, she'd taken her pictures and then made herself scarce. It had been unbelievable when later her uncle had brought the sheriff's latest *prize*— Sam Chandler.

Reaching the outskirts of town, Reilly handed Susan the reins. "If you'll take us up to the house, I'll ride back here and keep the box steady."

Climbing over the bench, Reilly dropped beside the coffin and, looking around to make sure no one was watching, opened it halfway and checked the patient. His color was not good and he was sweating profusely. The coffin had become a virtual oven in the hot sun, but mercifully Sam Chandler was unconscious.

Turning in her seat, Susan looked down on their patient. "Is he still alive?"

"Yes, but honest-to-God, I don't know how. Just take it real slow, Susan. The road's full of holes and too much bouncing around sure won't do him any good. Also I'd hate to break the axle and have to carry this coffin up the hill."

Slapping the reins against the horse's rump, Susan proceeded up the rutted road. Situated at the top of the knoll within a grove of nut pines was Reilly's home. The house was a mismatch of rooms, as though the builder had had no idea of what he wanted when he started, or had randomly added rooms as he had needed them. The kitchen jutted from the side as though it was an afterthought. The rock chimney leaned precariously and the porch roof sagged in the middle. Still, Susan could see Reilly's hand in fixing up the place. Flowers filled the window boxes that she'd coaxed her uncle into

19

building, and a rosebush struggled from the hard-packed ground, lending its beauty as it climbed the porch banister.

Susan recalled the first time she'd seen Reilly. Reilly had come into the mercantile store to purchase a pair of denims. Dressed in grubby britches, jacket, and boots, her hair invisible beneath a hat, Susan had first thought she was a young boy. Reilly'd laid the denims on the counter to pay for them and looked across at her. Susan found herself staring into the most striking blue eyes she had ever seen. Clear and bright, they reminded her of a light blue sky mirrored on a glittering lake. As Reilly'd turned and walked out the door, Susan got the shock of her life. A long thick tail of blonde hair tied with a ribbon scaled the center of the retreating back.

Several days later, Susan had seen Reilly again on the boardwalk, and they'd struck up a conversation. After introductions, Susan learned Reilly's father was a photographer, his work taking them all over the West. While visiting his brother here in Castletown, he'd told her he just wasn't up to traveling anymore. He'd decided to open a photography studio in the vacant building next door to the mercantile store.

Two months later, Morgan Reynolds died and the grief-stricken young woman continued to run her father's business. With their businesses next door to one another, they quickly became good friends, visiting one another frequently when business was slow.

Castletown was a mining town where the cost of a drink in the saloons gauged the town's prosperity. When the mines produced, everyone in town benefited. Even during slow times, the mercantile store managed to do well because they carried necessities. But the photography business suffered. Even in the best of times, Reilly was always scraping the bottom of the barrel, trying to stay in business.

Reilly was the most wonderful thing that had ever happened to Susan. She had never had a best friend. She was shy and bookish, and she'd always felt that she made people her own age uncomfortable because she was always reading. Reilly didn't mind at all. Sometimes Susan would take her book and Reilly her camera, and they would go on short photography excursions. But instead of reading, Susan found herself watching in fascination while her friend worked. Susan discovered that Reilly's clear blue eyes didn't miss anything; they were curious and investigative eyes, finding pleasure and beauty in objects that most people took for granted. Her photographs were beautiful, yet Reilly confessed she made little money from them, only enough to keep her going during the rough times.

In the year that Susan had known Reilly, only one time had she seen her dressed in anything besides men's clothing. That had been at her father's funeral. Susan had helped her pick out the garment. It had been stark and simple. She'd also volunteered to arrange Reilly's long wavy blonde hair in a more becoming style. Reilly had stubbornly refused, telling her she wasn't out to impress anyone with her looks, but to attend her beloved father's funeral.

Still, it frustrated Susan that Reilly took such pride in producing beautiful pictures, yet ignored her own beauty. Finally, she'd asked Reilly why she insisted on hiding her femininity. As always, Reilly had a reasonable answer for everything. She wasn't hiding anything. She couldn't hike through woods, up mountainsides, and into mining camps to take pictures, wearing bothersome dresses that would only get in her way. While at her studio, her customers didn't care about her attire, only the fine quality of the pictures she took of them. Besides, the solutions she used in developing the pictures sometimes missed her apron and splattered her clothes.

After that, Susan decided that arguing the issue was as futile as beating a dead horse. Surely, someday something other than photography would spark her friend's attention and she'd take a long hard look at herself and take pride in being a woman.

Chapter 3

Susan drew the wagon to a halt at the back of the house. The small shed where Reilly's uncle made furniture blocked the view from anyone who might come down the hill behind them. With a lot of grunting and heaving, they managed to lift their patient from the coffin and get him inside the house.

After placing him on the trestle table, Reilly pressed her ear against Chandler's chest. "His breathing's shallow, but at least he's alive." She straightened and placed her hands on her hips. "He's also burning with fever. We've got to get that bullet out of him soon or he's history for sure."

Reilly rummaged through cabinets and drawers, brought her supplies to the table and set them on the bench. She chuckled lightly when she removed his string tie. "He won't be needing this for a while." She took her scissors and cut through the wrapping that bound his chest, gingerly peeling it from his wound.

Susan stared worriedly at the blue-black puncture that had begun oozing blood again. "Maybe I ought to go find Dr. Watson."

"No. You know how he talks. We can't take that chance."

"But Reilly, I don't know anything about treating gunshot wounds."

"I do. I dug a slug out of my father once."

"Someone shot your father?" Susan asked, appalled. "Who?"

"An Indian," Reilly said nonchalantly as she pressed a bandage against the wound to staunch the flow of blood.

"An Indian!" Susan echoed.

"Yes, but he was a friendly Indian," she answered, glancing up at her wide-eyed friend with a smile.

"An Indian shoots your father and you call him friendly? I sure would hate to run into a mean one."

"It was an accident, Susan," she said, picking up a bottle from her tray. "Pa had taken pictures of several Indians and one young buck got all excited when he saw his own photograph and dropped his rifle. The gun went off and the bullet struck Pa in the leg."

"Well, why didn't you say that in the first place?"

"Because you're so much fun to tease," she quipped, dabbing carbolic acid around the wound. "But—this is a bit more serious than Pa's leg wound. You're going to have to hold him down, Susan. Though he's unconscious, he'll probably still jerk when I begin probing. Do you think you're strong enough?"

"Who helped you get him in and out of that coffin?" Susan countered as she moved to the other side of the table. Taking a deep breath, she leaned over him and placed her hands on his shoulders.

"Ready?" Reilly asked, her mouth suddenly going dry.

Susan nodded.

Picking up a knitting needle she had sterilized with alcohol, Reilly confronted the task before her with apparent steadiness. Yet her body raced with fear. And as she gently probed the wound, her heart beat hard and fast as she glanced at Sam's sweat-laden face. His mouth suddenly tightened into a thin grim line and an agonizing cry tore from deep inside him.

His shoulders suddenly jerked up off the table and Susan firmly pressed him down. She talked soothingly to him, her eyes on his handsome face rather than on Reilly's working hands. If she fainted, she'd be no help at all. Yet, she couldn't quell the churning in her stomach.

Hearing his moans, tears pooled in Susan's eyes and spilled over the rims, the droplets falling and mingling with the moisture on his face. "Oh hurry, Reilly, *please*," she choked out.

Reilly took a deep breath. "Hold tight, Mr. Chandler," she urged as much to herself as to her patient. "Ah . . . I feel it." Seconds later, she extracted the bullet, dropping it and the needle on the tray.

Susan's face turned white as death and she thought she was going to be sick. "Oh, my Lord, look at all the blood!"

Reilly grabbed a piece of cloth and pressed it gently against the gaping hole. "Don't worry, the bleeding cleanses the wound. The bullet wasn't deep and didn't puncture a large artery. Our main concern now is infection." She placed a small square of cloth over the wound and then a larger one. Taking a strip of fabric, she wrapped it around his neck and beneath his armpit to hold the bandage in place.

Righting herself, Reilly walked over to the washbowl and cleaned the blood from her hands. "I need to take the coffin to the cemetery. Can you stay with him?"

Susan was clutching the table for support, watching the erratic rise and fall of Sam's chest. "W-What if he d-dies? Then we w-won't have anything to bury him in."

"Susan," she said in exasperation, "we can't wait. If I have to, I'll build another one myself. Now, will you stay with him?"

"Yes, I'll stay," Susan said softly. "But Reilly, don't you think Digger will notice how light the coffin is?"

"Yes, that's why I'm going to fill it with firewood. He weighs close to two hundred pounds, wouldn't you say?"

"At least," Susan said with a groan, aware of an annoying ache in her lower back. "Just tell me what to do while you're gone."

"There's vinegar in the larder. Mix it with warm water and bathe his face and upper body. They should help his fever. If he wakes up and is in pain, there's a bottle of Uncle Chug's whiskey under the dry sink. Give him all he wants. I shouldn't be gone long if everything goes well."

Chug. Susan had forgotten all about him. Because of his habit of drinking, he'd gained the nickname of Chug. "Oh Lord, he is still living with Lois, I hope?"

"Yes. I don't see him much except when he needs money to buy his liquor. He must be drunk, or he would've returned to take the coffin."

"Where are you going to put Mr. Chandler?"

"In my bed."

"But where will you sleep tonight?"

"On a pallet in the room so I can keep a close eye on him."

Reilly moved behind Sam and gripped him beneath his arms. Susan picked up his feet.

"I won't be able to get out of bed for a week," Susan grumbled.

The graveyard basked beneath a simmering sun atop a grassy meadow. Tombstones of various shapes and sizes rose from the dark earth, contrasting sharply with the snow-covered peaks behind them.

Reilly's wagon neared the outlaw burial ground that was located on a gentle slope at the far end of the cemetery. She supposed the people of Castletown thought the bad blood in these thieves and murderers

26

would run downhill, and therefore wouldn't contaminate the blood of the good souls lying peacefully on the hill above them. She sadly noted the unkempt graveyard where several weathered tombstones slanted heavily like weary celebrators. Included among these were recently-covered graves, causing a chill to quiver through her. Were all these men outlaws as Sheriff Murdock claimed when he'd killed them?

The wheel hit a rut and the firewood rumbled in the coffin. *Damn! Double damn, triple damn!* She thought she'd packed it tight enough so that wouldn't happen. She had no earthly idea how much the box weighed, probably more than three times Chandler's weight. How could she explain it to Digger if he asked about it? She doubted he'd believe her if she said they were burying his horse with him.

Digger Davis, the local grave digger, leaned on his shovel, gazing down in the grave. Hearing the wagon approach, he squinted up at Reilly as the bright sunshine pierced his eyes. Drawing the wagon to a halt and putting on the brake, Reilly leaped down.

"Chug must be chuggin' agin, right?" Digger asked, wiping the sweat from his brow with a dirty sleeve.

"Isn't he always when there's work to do?" Reilly returned, an edge of mock sarcasm lacing her voice. This time she was glad to be doing her uncle's job. "But I'll help you."

Digger studied the slender woman. This wasn't the first time he'd faced this situation with her. Just wait until he saw Chug again. He'd give him what for, yeah he would. "Wal' . . ." he drawled, scratching his stubbled chin, "all right then. But once we get it on the ground, I'll take it from there. Ain't fittin' you doin' a man's work, Miss Reynolds. Your daddy'd roll over in his own grave if'n he saw the way you work."

"Somebody's got to do it," she added quickly.

"Yeah, but it still don't make it right," he grumbled.

"Please, Digger," she pleaded, "Let's just bury the wood—the man—" she quickly corrected, "and get it over with."

"Humph," he snorted and climbed into the wagon.

She moaned and groaned to drown out any sounds that might come from the coffin if the wood shifted, as she helped Digger. After they finally got the coffin off the wagon, Reilly knew she'd overshot Sam Chandler's weight.

Digger brushed his hands off on his heavy denim pants. "Heavy son-of-a-gun. You didn't put that gold he robbed in there with him, did you?" he teased with a grin splitting his weather-beaten face. His teeth reminded Reilly of a yellowed picket fence missing most of its slats.

"What would be the use? I once heard a preacher say that gold goes in at any gate except heaven's," Reilly quipped.

Digger chuckled. "Don't think that varmint's heaven-bound anyway."

Anxious to get the whole mess over and done with, she moved to the end of the coffin. "Ready?"

"Ain't no need in your helpin' none now. I'll take it from here with the hoist. Guess you're gonna read him his final rites like you usually do, ain't you?"

"Of course," Reilly said, thankful to have a good excuse to stay. She wouldn't relax until that box of firewood was buried six-feet in the ground.

"Suit yourself, but I'll never understand what you expect them dead outlaws to gain from it. Them fine scriptures don't mean nothin' where they're goin'."

While Digger secured the rope around the coffin and rigged the pulley, Reilly gathered a bouquet of deep pink shooting stars that grew in abundance in the meadow. She returned as Digger started lowering

28

the pine box to the bottom of the pit. Her heart tripped several beats when the coffin hit bottom. She quickly looked over at Digger, wondering if he'd heard the shuffling sound coming from inside the box.

When he didn't mention it and dropped the first shovel of dirt atop the coffin, Reilly relaxed and scattered the wildflowers over it. Opening her prayer book, she began reading the burial rite, and after a few minutes ended it with: *I commend thy soul to God the father almighty, and thy body to the ground, earth to earth, ashes to ashes, dust to dust* . . . Reilly closed her book and silently explained to God her desperate situation and begged his forgiveness for the mock ceremony.

Leaving Digger to finish his job, she bid him good day and stepped up into the wagon. Releasing the brake, she slapped the reins against the horse's rump and the wagon moved slowly up the hill. Her eyes drifted to her father's tombstone in the distance. Surely Susan could take care of Mr. Chandler a few more minutes. It had been over a week since she had put fresh flowers on her father's grave.

Leaving the wagon at the side of the road, she trudged up the hill, gathering wildflowers along the way. Several family plots were ornately fenced and bordered with wildflowers and native shrubs, while scattered here and there rested those poor souls who'd had no family to grieve their passing.

Walking to her father's grave, she knelt beside it. Removing the dead flowers, she replaced them with the fresh ones. Settling back on her haunches, she read the marker: *Morgan Tate Reynolds, born 1824, died 1880. Beloved husband of Martha Reilly Reynolds.* She would have liked to have buried her parents side by side, but her mother was buried in Philadelphia, Reilly's own birthplace. Her only consolation was that in death her parents were finally united and nothing could separate them again.

Sadness and despair rushed through her. Would the pain ever go away? Eight months had passed since her father's death and still it seemed like only yesterday. Sometimes the loneliness was more than she could bear.

Reilly had been fourteen-years-old when her mother had died. Fortunately, her father had been at home instead of out West. After the funeral, he'd confronted her with their dilemma. They had no close relatives she could live with, so she would have to go with him. Reilly had thought he didn't want her, thinking he had no choice but to take her with him. She'd run to her room and burst into tears. She had missed him terribly all her young life, their times together so rare. It had not been her fault that her mother had died, yet she felt guilty in putting her father in such an awkward position.

Tears sparkled in her eyes even now when she recalled him coming into her room and sitting beside her on the bed, stroking her back and trying to soothe her. He began telling her things her mother had never explained to her. When he'd married her mother, they'd planned to go West together. The trip had fallen through when his wife found herself with child almost immediately. After Reilly was born, her mother refused to take an infant into such a wild land. The newspapers wrote horror stories about the living conditions, the Indians, the outlaws, and the corruption. He couldn't argue with her because the newspapers had printed the truth. So instead he went alone, returning to Philadelphia at short intervals to be with his wife and daughter. If it wasn't too late, he wanted to make up to her all those years he had missed with his daughter.

From that moment on, they were inseparable. Morgan Reynolds had become not only a father to her, but her friend, teacher, and mentor, a constant presence and peace in her life. And she'd thanked God everyday for giving them those wonderful ten years together before He took him away.

Reilly stood and walked to the precipice that overlooked the town. Castletown appeared buried beneath a veil of silver as the bright sun glinted off the tinned roofs. Snow-capped peaks rose like watchtowers and clinging to the upper sides of the ridges were the residences of the wealthy citizens, while beneath them smaller houses dozed in shady seclusion. In the distance was a large crystal lake nestled within a dense forest of evergreens. On a partially denuded hill were the smoking smelting plants, refineries, and stamp mills. Slowly winding around the base of the mountain, she saw the train nearing the depot; it always let off more passengers than it took on.

A picture-perfect town, she remembered her father calling it when he'd taken a photograph from the same place she was standing now. But after living there only a short time, they discovered the picture was deceiving.

Castletown came into existence with the discovery of silver. When the mines no longer produced, many prospectors left to find a new outlet. Then three years ago, the discovery of several rich lodes of gold brought another swarm of people into the town. Investors bought into the mines and built a spur to connect with the Central Pacific Railroad to transport the ore. Soon after, outlaws, murderers, and swindlers rolled like a tidal wave into town to prey upon the citizens. Illicit activities, wanton slayings, and robberies became commonplace.

Floyd Murdock had breezed into town playing his charm and his fast gun in the name of justice. The citizens of Castletown had been duped completely by the fast-talker. Thinking he was the answer to all their problems, they convinced him to run for sheriff. They elected him hands down, giving him free rein over their town. The improvements they had expected never materialized. Slowly but surely to the citizens' horror, conditions had worsened. Oh, the sheriff brought in the criminals—or people he said were criminals—but they were all dead. It was his word against theirs. And everybody knew a dead man had no voice in the matter.

There were rumors that he was a crime boss, the leader of an outlaw gang. Proving it was a difficult matter. Actions spoke louder than words and Floyd Murdock had put the fear of God into the townspeople. No one would go against the sheriff.

Reilly knew that Sam Chandler was no more an outlaw than she was. As she walked back to her wagon, she vowed, *Now that I've saved his life, I'll be damned if I let the sheriff try to take it again.*

Chapter 4

Reilly wiped the sweat from her face and smoothed the hair from her brow. She knew she looked like she'd been caught in a wind storm, but there was nothing she could do about it. She'd gone at a break-neck speed to get back to check on the patient. Lord, it had been some day, she thought as she jumped down from the wagon. What was supposed to have been an easy day had turned into a race against the clock. And she wasn't through yet.

As she darted through the front room, she noticed that Susan had cleaned up the mess from the doctoring. When she entered her bedroom, she came to a jarring halt. In all her wildest dreams nothing had prepared her for the sight of Sam Chandler in her bed. She thought for a moment that her heart would leap from her chest.

He dwarfed the four poster. His black hair was curled wildly against her pillow. His skin gleamed darkly against the white bandage wrapping his chest. His arms lay limply at his sides with his bare feet crammed against the foot board. Reilly swallowed rapidly several times as she watched him sleeping before turning to Susan.

"Well, he's buried," Reilly said. "It went off without a hitch."

"I was worried sick. I could just see all that firewood rolling to one end."

"Let me tell you, the possibility was never far from my thoughts either. My mind was in a whirl the whole time trying to think of a plausible excuse for the corpse to be making such a racket, if the firewood suddenly shifted. I didn't think Digger would believe me if I told him that it was only the ghost of Christmas past."

Susan laughed. "I'm glad it's over."

Shifting her attention back to the bed, Reilly smiled. "He's a big man, isn't he?"

Before Susan could answer, Sam Chandler sat straight up in the bed, "Get the son of a bitch!" he bellowed.

The girls jumped and darted to his side. "Hold him," Reilly shouted.

"Do you think he's having a bad dream?" Susan whispered, her face as pale as their patient's.

"A nightmare's more like it."

Reilly gently eased the patient back to the pillow, talking softly until he quieted. His face was marred with a frown and the muscles in his jaw worked furiously. She smoothed the rumpled hair from his brow and tested the heat of his face.

. . . Something wonderfully cool was stroking his face. Don't stop, please don't stop, he wanted to plead, but he couldn't make his mouth work. He felt like he was swimming in muddy water, and the faster he swam the faster the mud sucked at his legs and arms, impeding his progress. He could hear voices from a distance, soft, feminine voices. Maybe if he lay very still, he could make out what they were saying.

"He's not as hot as he was earlier. It was probably from being closed up in that coffin that caused him to be so feverish . . ."

Coffin! I was in a coffin? His fever-struck mind screamed.

"Yes, I wish we could've brought him up here faster, but the bleeding would have been worse."

Up here? Up, as in heaven? What bleeding? His befuddled mind couldn't get a grasp of what was happening.

The coolness once more soothed his face and a gentle voice assured him. "You're safe, Mr. Chandler. No one will look for a dead man."

She knows my name. Oh God, it is me and I'm a dead man! She's talking to a dead man? How can that be?

Sam's eyes rolled wildly beneath his lids as he struggled to open them. Suddenly bright, jarring light pierced his skull. *Heavenly light?* he wondered fleetingly as he adjusted to the brightness. *How ironic,* he thought. He never figured he'd make it to heaven. Not in his line of work.

When he could focus his eyes, the first thing he saw was two angelic faces smiling down at him. They appeared very happy about something. The one with her cool hand resting on his brow had golden hair that was pulled back from her face and tied with a blue ribbon. The ribbon matched her sparkling eyes and a smattering of freckles danced across her nose. Something about her was vaguely familiar. The other had happy green eyes and a tumble of auburn hair that draped shoulders swathed in butter-yellow fabric.

Why were they so damn happy? He sure as hell didn't have anything to be joyous about. He'd been killed before he finished his job.

He moved his eyes to encompass his surroundings. Where were the pearly gates and the streets of gold? All he saw was plaster peeling from the walls and a ceiling that dipped and swayed like the back of a mule. *Heaven? This can't be heaven. It looks like hell.*

And that was another thing. Didn't angels have

wings? If they did, he saw no evidence of anything resembling wings. And halos? He'd always heard that angels had halos. Well, there was nothing that remotely smacked of a halo.

He puckered his brow. Something was definitely wrong with this picture. He'd never given much thought to heaven one way or another, but he was sure angels didn't wear blue ribbons in their hair and have freckles. Nor did they wear dresses of butter-yellow gingham.

Reilly noticed his sudden alarm and tenderly combed her fingers through his hair. "You're going to be fine, Mr. Chandler. The worst is over."

"The worst," he croaked. *What the hell could be worse than being dead?*

"Yes, I got the bullet out," Reilly assured him.

Bullet? Before her eyes, he paled even more. Then he wasn't dead and this wasn't Heaven. He just couldn't make any sense of what was happening to him. He'd finally decided he was lying in someone's bed. His body was screaming with pain. He felt like he'd been run over by a team of mules.

"Someone shot you, Mr. Chandler."

God, the story was getting worse all the time. He had to think, to remember. Before he could put his thoughts into action, blessed sleep claimed him.

"He'll be all right now, won't he?" Susan questioned, drawing the sheet over his chest.

"He'll be fine."

"I still can't believe we're doing this. If we ever get caught—Lord help us. When they brought Chandler's body back to town, you'd have thought the most notorious man alive had just been killed. The sheriff's got a list a mile long of crimes Sam Chandler was supposed to have committed."

"Murdock has more nerve than anyone I've ever seen. If Chandler had died, his body wouldn't have been cold before the sheriff was cleaning the slate of every unsolved crime in this town. The sheriff is trying to make himself look good." Reilly pointed to Sam. "How could this man spend all his time gambling and still be the leader of a bunch of outlaws?"

"He didn't spend all his time gambling. I saw him too many times with a woman clinging to his arm." Susan blushed, then giggled. "You know what I mean."

"I know what you mean. I've heard the gossip. He's a real ladies man."

"You don't think he'll try anything with you—when he gets better?"

"He won't be here that long," Reilly vowed. "I know one thing, he's got to have some clothes. Do you think you could get in his room at the Claiborne hotel and get his belongings?"

"Oh Lord, Reilly, I can't do that!"

"Sure you can."

"They've probably already moved his things out."

"Well, you won't know until you check it out."

Susan wrung her hands together. "Why me? I can take care of Mr. Chandler while you go."

"No, if Sheriff Murdock sees me going inside, he'll think I'm snooping around and taking pictures."

"All right," Susan said with a sigh. "Just tell me how to go about it."

"I don't know, make up something. Use your womanly wiles."

"Womanly wiles, my foot." Susan released an exasperated sigh. "Oh, I'll give it a try. But so help me, Reilly Reynolds, if I'm caught, you'd better think of something quick to get me out of this mess."

Reilly's tinkling laughter followed her from the room.

This is no laughing matter, Reilly thought a moment later, a frown suddenly stealing across her forehead. Had she acted too hastily in sending

Susan on such a mission, perhaps pushed her into a situation she couldn't handle? Surely not. As meek and timid as Susan might be, she had come to Reilly's aid when she'd needed her, her courage overriding her fears. Still, Reilly wouldn't rest easily until she heard from her.

Sam lay quietly, his mind reacting to the sudden silence in the room. Between bouts of consciousness, he had heard part of the women's conversation. What he could remember of it made no sense at all—something about removing his things from his room.

Was he alone? He struggled to open his eyes. Through the thin line of his vision, he saw a woman standing beside him, her back to him. Damn, she was wearing britches! Visions of another woman he'd seen dressed in britches flashed through his mind. Her name came to him as his eyes drifted shut. Reilly Reynolds.

Was this her house? He remembered one of them saying he had been shot. Had she removed the bullet? Why hadn't a doctor taken care of him? God, he was so confused and his head hurt like hell. Suddenly a pain shot through his chest and he cried out.

Reilly whirled around as Sam's arms shot up from his sides, his hands gripping the top of the bandage as though to rip it off.

Quickly grabbing his wrists, Reilly held him with all her strength as he pulled against her. "Darn it all, stop it, Mr. Chandler!" she ordered, relieved when she finally felt his hands loosen and his body relax.

She continued holding his wrists, her eyes fixed on his full, well-defined lips. How would it feel to have him kiss her? Releasing him, she hesitated, then daringly brushed the tip of her finger over his pale mouth. Unconsciously, she licked her lips as they tingled expectantly.

His mouth parted as he emitted a soft sigh. Reilly

jerked her hand away, appalled that she had behaved so indecently. Good Lord, if just thinking about him kissing her was driving her to such distraction, what would happen to her if he actually did?

Her emotions in an upheaval, Reilly sat down on the bed beside him. He looked so boyish, so innocent in his sleep. Yet she knew better. She also knew she was going to have a hard time nursing him back to health while fighting her attraction to him in the same breath.

Reilly hoped that his unconscious mind might absorb her words. "I'm going to make you well, Mr. Chandler," she vowed.

Sam wasn't asleep. He'd been lying still as a statue while she had tenderly stroked his mouth, wishing it was her mouth exploring him instead.

Reilly couldn't prevent her hand from lifting and brushing an unruly lock of dark hair from his forehead. "I might not be a doctor, but you're in good hands."

Yes, her hand felt pretty damned good, he wanted to tell her. He imagined there were other parts of her that would feel good too. She must have heard his carnal thoughts because she removed her hand.

"I know you can't hear me, but I'll tell you anyway." She cleared her throat. "I know your reputation with women, and I've also seen the kind of women you keep company with."

Sam waited expectantly, his mind lingering on her words.

"I thought I'd better warn you that I'm not that kind of woman," she finished adamantly.

Well hell, Sam swore silently as he lost consciousness again.

"Come back real soon, honey," called the sultry voice.

"Darn tootin' I will, Liz," the miner returned with a toothless grin. "See ya next payday."

Hearing the exchange, Susan kept her pace brisk, her back stiff as an iron poker, and her eyes straight ahead.

"Hey fellas'," the syrupy voice called out again, "come on in."

Susan's curiosity getting the best of her, she looked across the street where several miners were mingling on the boardwalk. Above them, a soiled dove was leaning out the window of the two-story brothel. She wore a sheer red wrap with black feathers scaling the front.

"I'm new in town," she said, pushing aside her wrap. "How about me showing you a good time."

Susan's mouth gaped and her eyes widened in shock. The woman had completely bared the largest breasts Susan had ever seen, though she readily admitted the only ones she'd ever seen were her own. Her eyes fixed disgustedly on the whore, the toe of her shoe struck an uneven board on the walk. Tripping forward, she fell into a miner staggering out of the saloon adjacent to her.

Grabbing her around the waist, he flashed her a grin through a mouth circled with a thick, bushy mustache and beard. "Hey, little gal, you're some looker. You from the Pleasure Palace?"

His whiskey- and tobacco-laden breath and sweaty smell smacked her in the face. "No," she hissed, shoving him away from her. Her heart racing in her chest, she matched its pace to her feet and hurried down the boardwalk.

She had taken a shortcut from Reilly's house to save time and had somehow found herself in the red-light district. Although there were brothels on Haynes Street, the main thoroughfare in town, those were considered the classy brothels. She'd never seen the prostitutes who lived there ply their trade in such a vulgar fashion.

Relieved when she'd made it to Haynes Street, she headed toward the Claiborne Hotel. The town was bustling with activity. Thirsty miners and gamblers kept the doors swinging as they entered and exited the saloons that lined both sides of the street. Other labor-stained miners drove their heavily laden wagons of ore toward the depot.

Outside the hotel, Susan paused a moment to gather her courage and still her racing heart. With quick accustomed fingers she whisked her reddish gold locks into place.

Now what do I do? Her finely manicured thumbnail was quickly becoming a memory as she worked it between her teeth. She pondered the books she'd read and the dilemmas of her favorite characters. How would they deal with this situation? Lie through their teeth—that was the only reasonable conclusion she could come up with.

As a plan formulated in her mind, she adjusted her dress and stiffened her back. She took one step, then another, composing her features. Now if she could keep a straight face and her train of thought, everything would work out fine. She rehearsed her lie once more. *Mr. Chandler bought some clothing from me on credit and planned to pay me today. Since he was killed, I need to get the items from his room. Good, Susan,* she thought with a smile. *Surely they won't deny me my own merchandise. Reilly will be so pleased with my womanly wiles.*

Opening the door, she slowly entered the crowded lobby. Other than herself, there wasn't another female in sight. All heads turned toward her and openly appraised her from head to toe. It suddenly dawned on her why she was drawing so much attention. Claiborne Hotel was known as a *men's only* hotel, frequented mainly by affluent businessmen and gamblers. They were probably wondering why a lone woman had come into their domain.

Susan smiled nervously as she approached the desk, waiting expectantly while the clerk took care of a customer checking in. She knew most of the people in town, but she'd never seen this clerk. Although it was no wonder. There were so many people continually moving into town, seeking to make their fortune in the mines. The clerk kept glancing at her curiously.

When the customer left, the clerk looked over at her. "Good afternoon, Miss. May I help you?"

As Susan stepped forward, the room suddenly became very quiet. "Uh . . . yes." She cleared her throat. "I'm Susan Waters. I need to ask you about Mr. Sam Chandler, one of your guests? I was wondering—"

"I'm sorry, Miss, he died earlier today," he said, shaking his head slowly.

"I heard. That's why I'm here."

He clucked his tongue. "He appeared to be a fine man, yes indeed. I just can't believe he was an outlaw, but I guess looks can be deceiving. Did you know him . . . well?"

"Only slightly, but he owed me some money."

She heard a few chuckles from the men behind her. *My lord, what did I say that was so funny?*

The clerk smiled. "And you've come to collect?"

"Yes. He planned to pay me today, but now he's dead. And my father will be terribly angry with me for giving a man credit when I barely knew him."

Again the men chuckled, but this time more heartily.

Susan gritted her teeth and leaning forward, whispering, "I don't know what these men find so amusing, but there are several items of clothing in his room that belong to me and I must get them."

"I see," the clerk said, his gaze sweeping the fullness of her breasts.

What was this man's problem? Was her dress stained?

The clerk leaned forward and whispered, "The sheriff was here earlier and checked the room. He told me we could dispose of Chandler's belongings, but we've been so short on help, the maids haven't had time to clean it yet. I guess it's all right for you to remove your . . . things."

Susan straightened and sighed with relief. "Thank you, I promise I'll only take what's mine."

The clerk fished a key from the wall of hooks behind him and handed it to her. "Room 210 at the end of the hall. Just leave the key inside on the wash stand when you leave."

When Susan reached the stairs, she couldn't resist a peek over her shoulder at the men. As she turned her head, one of the men had lifted his arms and was drawing the shape of her body with his hands. She snapped her head toward the stairs before they could see the blush crawling up her neck. Still, their laughter and back-slapping accompanied her up the stairs. It was a crying shame, but a decent woman just wasn't safe in this hotel.

Chapter 5

Susan walked down the wide corridor until she found room 210. When she unlocked the door and entered, an eerie feeling of intrusion swept through her. The window facing the street was open and the curtains stirred in the gentle breeze. The room bore the results of the sheriff's investigation . . . or his greed. Drawers were thrown open and clothes were hanging out in disarray. The bedcoverings were scattered on the floor and the mattress was askew on the bed. The contents of a small night stand were tossed hither and yon. A book with its binding carelessly broken and an old newspaper littered the floor. Chandler's carpetbag was opened and the inside was turned wrongside out. The doors on the wardrobe were standing ajar and the fancy suits, vests, and shirts that had been inside were scattered over the room.

As only a woman can, Susan began to search the room for anything the sheriff might have missed. She picked up a red garter trimmed with black lace and studied it with disgust, wondering if it belonged to the woman, Liz, she'd seen hanging out the window. It did match her dressing gown. No, she didn't know Sam Chandler personally, but she knew his women were a touch above the whores on Liz's street.

Besides, she didn't know if men brought women to the hotel. She was truly naive when it came to the goings on of men and the women that sold their bodies to them. Still, she couldn't help wondering what the woman that the garter belonged to looked like.

As she prowled, she folded the rumpled clothes neatly. After punching down the carpetbag, she placed his clothes inside. She found shaving gear and toiletries carelessly strewn across the floor and under the bed, and placed them in the bag. In the wardrobe, pushed to the very back, she saw a dark mass. After she pulled it out, she saw that it was another carpetbag, but quite heavy.

She chuckled. "Fancy that. The sheriff missed something."

Opening it, she saw a red union suit lying on top. Suddenly she heard voices outside the door and became scared. She'd be in a fine mess if the sheriff returned. Hurriedly, she closed the bag and picked up the other one and left the room.

"Now that's using your womanly wiles," she said with a proud smile.

Looking down the corridor, she saw a side door and hastened to it. Opening it, she found a way out of the hotel without having to go through the lobby again. Without further ado, she descended the outside steps, carrying Chandler's bags with her.

From there, her journey was a cinch. Fortunately, the hotel and her store were on the same side of the street, so she took the alley running behind the shops. After listening through the back door of her store and hearing her parents voices, she lugged the bags up the outside stairs to their apartment and shoved them beneath her bed.

She knew she had to let Reilly know that she had successfully completed her mission. But how? If she was away much longer, her parents would start worrying about her. Before everything had happened, she'd told them she was going to the dressmaker and get fitted for a new dress. More than enough time had passed for her to complete her errand.

Her only choice was to send a message to Reilly, and the only person she could think of to deliver it was Toby. Everyone in town felt sorry for the young man because he was slow. He went from store to store, doing odd jobs for the owners, if they needed him.

Yes, Toby would do it for her. She hastily scribbled a note using only one word: *Done!* Reilly would know immediately what it meant, but should Toby lose it, no one else would.

Reilly was groggy from lack of sleep. Her patient had slept the night through, but she had been up and down all night checking on him. She'd made herself a pallet at the foot of his bed so she could hear him if he chanced to wake. She worried because he was sleeping so deeply. But there was nothing she could do except watch over him and be there if something happened.

Thank God, she didn't have Susan to worry about too. If there'd been any other way to handle the situation, she wouldn't have asked Susan to do it. She smiled, recalling Susan's message *Done!* Had Toby been able to read, he would've asked, "Done whut, Miss Reynolds?"

Reilly rushed through her household chores, then went outside to feed the chickens, gather the eggs, and milk their only cow. The swayback nag grazed, but she liked to treat him with a scoop of oats each day.

It was a shame that her uncle had let the house get in such sad shape. If he'd put as much thought into the state of the house as he did in his attempts to have a drink, both their lives would be better. Reilly could never figure out what made her uncle turn to drink. The women liked him, and as Susan said, he built wonderful furniture when he set his mind to it. At present he was involved with a hard-working woman. He had just up and moved in with her, and that suited Reilly just fine. When he lived at home, he wasn't much help when he was drinking. She could never depend on him when he went on a spree, sometimes staying away for days at a time. And it made him furious when Reilly hid his liquor.

Still, she'd tried to turn his ramshackle house into a home. With the addition of curtains and a rug here and there, the appearance had changed dramatically. And when she was really industrious and had the time, she gathered wildflowers and placed them throughout the house.

But today she didn't have the luxury of extra time. As soon as Susan came to relieve her, she had to get Chandler's photographs developed. The sheriff would be anxious to see his latest victory.

Reilly wasn't sure yet what she would do with her information. Maybe when Chandler was on his feet again he would know what to do. Yet it did her heart good to know that if she wanted to, she could prove the sheriff was a liar and had shot an innocent man.

Susan had slept no better than her friend. That night her sleep had been invaded with dreams of danger that the discovery of the previous day brought on. With the light of day, however, her fears fled and she was eager to get on with their deception. She couldn't get to Reilly's fast enough. Determined to avoid the red-light district, she cut through a familiar alley, a longer route, but one where she'd be less visible while lugging the carpetbags. By the time she finally reached Reilly's house at the top of the hill, she was exhausted.

When she entered the bedroom, Reilly was sitting on the bed beside Chandler, wiping his face with cool water. She turned toward Susan and smiled when she saw the bags. "Toby delivered your message. Did you have any problems?"

"Not a one," Susan replied proudly. "I lied. I told the clerk Mr. Chandler had bought some clothes on credit at the store, and asked if I could get them since he wouldn't be needing them."

"I'm proud of you. It seems we've adjusted smoothly to our life of crime."

"It's a good thing the clerk couldn't see my knees. They were knocking like loose boards." Susan thought a minute, her smooth brow etched with a tiny frown. *I still wonder what I said that made the men laugh.*

"Is something the matter?"

"No, not really. It's just something that happened yesterday while I was at the hotel that's puzzling me," Susan admitted.

"I thought you said everything went well?"

"It did, as smooth as clockwork. That's not what's bothering me."

"Then what is it?"

"The men in the hotel laughed at me."

"Whatever for?"

"I don't have the slightest idea. Their first chuckles came when I told the clerk that Mr. Chandler owed me money. Then when I mentioned that I'd given him credit after only knowing him slightly, I thought they would roll on the floor."

"Did you tell them that you were from the mercantile store?"

"Well . . . no, I just assumed they knew it."

"Susan, do you think they thought it was *your* clothes that you wanted back?"

"Why would they think that? I plainly told them—oh my goodness! I told the clerk there was clothing in the room that belonged to me. Those men *did* think I was talking about my clothes." Susan's face blanched, and she nervously fidgeted with the lace cuff at her wrist.

"Reilly, those men thought I was a—" Susan couldn't bring herself to say the word. "You know, a woman with loose morals, like one of those women living on Haynes Street."

Reilly had already figured out what the men at the hotel thought. But Susan in her innocence had no earthly idea that anyone would think something like that about her. All her clouds had silver linings.

"Don't worry about it, Susan. At least one of them didn't offer to accompany you upstairs."

"Well, they would've had a corpse on their hands for sure, because I would have died. I can't believe I didn't know what was going on. But I might have known I'd do something wrong."

"Don't be so hard on yourself. You did fine." Reilly hugged her.

"I wish I could be more like you," Susan admitted.

"And I've always wanted to be like you."

"You have?"

"Look at me and then look at yourself. You're everything a woman is supposed to be."

"Maybe we can help each other," Susan volunteered. "But I'll admit you've helped me a great deal. I have more courage than I ever thought possible. Imagine me marching into a hotel full of men a year ago. I could never have done anything like that."

"Yes, you could've too."

"We both know better. You have a lot more nerve than I do. Papa always told me I was afraid of my shadow." She smiled brightly. "Wonder what he would think of his scaredy-cat daughter now? Harboring a criminal."

50

"I imagine it would take some getting used to," Reilly admitted dryly.

Susan laughed, unafraid. "So much for my great adventure, if Papa finds out what I did." She picked up the bags she'd lugged from town. "Where do you want me to put these?"

"I guess the wardrobe is as good a place as any."

After Susan placed the bags inside, she covered them with a blanket and closed the doors tightly. "His clothes and grooming items are in the bag on top. There's more clothes in the other one, if you need them. You should have seen his room at the hotel. The sheriff had turned it upside down."

"I've heard Mr. Chandler made a lot of money at the gaming tables. You didn't find any of it, did you?"

"No. If he didn't keep it in the bank, I'd say the sheriff has it now."

Reilly shrugged her shoulders. "Well, a lot of good money in the bank would do a dead man anyway. He'd sure have a hard time withdrawing it."

Walking to the other side of the bed, Susan stared down at Sam. "His coloring is much better today. Has he woken up yet?"

"No, he slept the night through. I don't know if that's natural or not."

"Reilly, you'd better get to the studio. The sheriff will be beating down your door to see the photographs. I'll watch Mr. Chandler."

"Thanks, Susan, I couldn't have done this without your help."

"Yes, you would have figured out something," Susan said with a smile as her friend left the room.

Sam lay quietly, his mind reacting to the sudden silence in the room. Between bouts of consciousness, he had heard part of the women's conversation. What

51

he could remember of it made no sense at all—something about removing his things from his room and men laughing at her.

Was he alone? He struggled to open his eyes. Through the thin line of his vision, he saw a woman standing beside him, her back to him. The sight only lasted a few seconds before his eyes drifted shut. *Who were these women and where the hell was he?* He remembered one of them said he had been shot and she had removed the bullet. *Why hadn't a doctor taken care of him?*

He heard a chair squeak beside the bed and then a soft hand gently stroking his face.

"You're going to get better, Mr. Chandler," she vowed. "Reilly's just as good as any doctor who might have tended to you. Probably a lot better when you get right down to it. Yes, you're in good hands."

Chapter 6

The townspeople were going about their business as on any other day. They nodded or passed a few words with Reilly as she made her way to the studio. She couldn't help feeling guilty, though she knew no one could tell by looking at her what she'd done. Still, it didn't ease her conscience any. Before she got her door open, an old man approached.

"Missy, ain't you the picture taker?"

"Yes, I am."

He turned toward the street and spit a stream of tobacco juice, then wiped the ragged cuff of his jacket across his mouth. "Would ya take my picture?"

"I'd be happy to, if you'll just step inside."

"I can pay ya," he boasted, holding up a bag of what Reilly assumed was gold nuggets.

"Bein' it's all the same to you, I'd like to have Sal in the picture too. He's been with me fer a long time. We've been through some hellacious times together."

Reilly didn't see anyone with him. "Do you need to get him?"

"Yeah, just a minute." He lifted his hand and placed his thumb and forefinger just inside his mouth and gave a piercing whistle. From down the street, a lop-eared mule began its ponderous trek to his master. The mule was loaded down with pots and pans, pickaxes, shovels, and some items Reilly couldn't identify. With every step the animal took, he sounded like a one-man band.

"Well, ya took your sweet-ass time gettin' here. Don't you know it's bad manners to keep a lady waitin'? We're goin' to have our picture took."

The mule swished his tail and nosed the miner's hand.

"I'll get my camera. We need to do this out here. Sal might not appreciate it if we tried to get him inside."

"No, that's a fact. He's an ornery cuss at the best of times."

When Reilly returned with her equipment, the prospector had poured his gold nuggets into a pan and was carrying on an animated conversation with the mule.

Every time Reilly got the pair positioned for the shot, the miner began talking, and he couldn't talk without waving his arms. She was very patient with the man because she soon realized he was hungry for conversation. He told her about his adventures and how he and Sal had been trapped in a cave for weeks on end when a blizzard caught him unaware. When Reilly asked him how long he'd been mining, he'd told her seven years. As he talked it became apparent he wasn't as old as she'd first thought. He'd made his dream come true, with hard work and loneliness. He was giving up mining and settling down. He had enough gold to buy himself a small spread and send back East for his wife. He was going to send the photograph to her, to show he was still alive.

Eventually, he wound down and she got her picture. He would pick it up later in the day. When he and Sal rattled off down the main road, Reilly was left with a warm feeling inside. She loved hearing about good things that happened to people.

She entered her studio and set up her equipment. She could always gauge her business on the prosperity of the town. It was an expensive profession she was in, her equipment and supplies were costly. Having a photograph made was to most people a luxury. And when there was extra money, they wanted their picture taken or their children's. Photographing miners was nothing new to her. In her short career she had taken some outlandish pictures.

Reilly's shop was small, but she put every inch to good use. Her craft had changed so much since her father had started in the business. When he was traveling across the country, he'd had to carry along an absurd amount of equipment for the wet-plate process. Regardless of where he was, he had to set up a dark room and develop the plates immediately. With the development of the dry plates it became possible to do away with all the ponderous machinery. Now, she could buy the dry plates ready prepared and could keep them for months before use, and for months again after exposure before she had to develop them.

Her father had taught her that the secret of making good pictures indoors was the lighting, managed by the photographer. Outdoors, nature took care of it.

Reilly had created a small photography area draped with white lengths of fabric. The windows coming within the range of her lens were partially covered until a sufficient exposure was given to the rest of the room. Weather conditions played greatly on the movement of the drapes. But she had it down until she could rearrange the fabric with a few quick flicks of her wrist.

Other areas of her studio were covered with her

55

work and her father's. Her dark room was a tiny cubicle, emitting only light that passed through a tiny window framed with amber glass. The odor of various solutions lingered in the room. Trays of water and other mixtures were placed in order on the long table. Her father had gone to the additional expense of having an indoor pump so they'd have running water in the dark room. Lines were strung across the space for drying photographs.

She was behind in her work and eager to get caught up. Before she went into the dark room, she examined her pictures of the robbery again, this time studying them closer to make sure she was right. A thrill of pure pleasure coiled through her. Indeed, Sam Chandler was not among the robbers. In no way did he remotely resemble any of the three men. She had one shot of the robbers as they crossed into her line of vision on their way to the bank, and another, when they left the bank with their bandannas covering their faces. It frightened her to know she held the identity of the outlaws in her hand. But no one would ever know—at least not right now. In a week, Bud Corbett of the Philadelphia Times would have the picture of the holdup. If he bought it, it would bring a good price. She also hoped it would bring someone to Castletown to help rid it of the corruption. She had almost sent the picture that showed the men's faces, but had decided to hold onto it, hoping it would bring even a bigger price.

She locked the front door and entered the dark-room. She wanted to make more pictures of the robbery, and she would process the miner's picture along with the one for the sheriff. She waited for her eyes to adjust to the darkness. She knew the small space like the back of her hand.

When she'd finished, she studied the wet negative. Seeing Sam lying on the slab with the sheet wrapped around him caused a lump to form in her throat and tears to sting her eyes. Knowing he was safe and sound at her home didn't help. It was a miracle that he was alive.

What had happened? Why would someone shoot him? Had they known he was innocent and set out to frame him? So many questions and no answers. She'd have to wait on Sam to recover and hope he had the answers.

Knowing the sheriff was anxious for the photograph, she hurried through the rest of the process until she had his photograph of Sam. She took it to the jail immediately, hoping to leave it with the deputy. Pausing just outside the opened doorway, she was disappointed to see the sheriff sitting behind his desk. She studied him briefly. The shape of his head was noticeably more wide than long, as though it had been pressed between a vice. Between his thin grayish hair and heavy jowls was a face ugly as sin. His expression seldom changed, so no one ever knew what was going on in his head or his mood. His dense unruly eyebrows met over his bulbous nose, and a permanent line crossing his forehead gave the appearance that he was always frowning. His small eyes were black as coal and barely discernible through his half-closed lids. He wore a thin mustache above his thick lips. His torso was thick and wide, his legs long and thin in comparison.

Reilly had not lived here when the people had elected him as their sheriff. She could only assume they thought his appearance alone would scare the outlaws from the town. Yet Reilly had learned that Murdock was as shrewd and calculating a man as she had ever met.

"I was just thinkin' about comin' to see you. Do you have my picture?"

"Yes," she answered, carefully removing the picture from the folder she was carrying with her. She handed it to the sheriff.

He straightened in the chair and studied the picture greedily. "Damn, you're good."

"Thank you."

"He looks like he might just sit up any second."

Cold chills scaled Reilly's back. *He almost did,* she thought promptly.

"Look here, Oscar, don't he look like he's just asleep? I'll give him credit—he was a hard bastard to kill." He quickly realized his blunder and clarified what he said. "I mean hard to catch in the act. If we'd been a few minutes later, he would've been gone. His gang might've got away with the money, but we got their leader. We were just lucky he didn't kill one of us."

"I didn't know Mr. Chandler wore a gun."

The sheriff stiffened in his chair and Reilly could tell she'd hit a nerve when he snapped, "There's a lot the people of Castletown didn't know about Chandler. He was very clever the way he worked his way into being a member of this community. But he didn't fool me for one second, no siree."

Reilly had to bite her tongue from telling the sheriff he had just described himself rather than Chandler. Instead she said as sharply as she dared, "I guess we're very lucky to have you protecting us, Sheriff."

"Damn right. Ain't no amount of money worth facin' the likes of a Sam Chandler. He was as cunnin' as a cat and as deadly as a strikin' snake."

"Well, you won't have to trouble yourself with him any longer."

"Oh, there'll be another one come along to take Chandler's place. There always is."

"For the sake of this town, I hope you bring in his

gang. Then the people of this community can breathe easier."

Neal Holt, one of the deputies, swaggered into the office and tossed a dirty cloth sack on the sheriff's desk. The sack hit the desk with a thud. "A little present for you, Sheriff."

Reilly couldn't help notice the gleam that jumped into the sheriff's eyes when he leaned forward and gripped the sack. He reminded her of a miner she'd once seen caressing the breast of one of the saloon girls. The sheriff squeezed the sack, then his fingers stroked the fabric, then he squeezed again.

Reilly thought she would be sick if she didn't get out of his office. Then it dawned on her that the sack was familiar. It was the same one she'd seen that morning—the one the prospector had so proudly showed her.

Before she could stop herself, she stepped forward. "Where did you get this?" She turned a hard glare to Neal.

The sheriff picked up the heavy bag and shifted it from one hand to the other.

"Some ol' man. He was mouthin' off at the saloon, totin' that poke around, tellin' everybody he was retirin'. He claimed he's spent seven years gettin' rich and now he was ready to send fer his little lady. We all knowed he was lyin'. Where would somebody like him get that much gold? When I asked him to see it, he pulled a hog-leg on me. I figured if'n he'd been tellin' the truth, he wouldn't've pulled no gun on me. It was a fair fight."

Reilly thought she would smother. The hatred welled up in her like a bubbling fountain. Neal had killed an innocent man in order to bring his boss a gift. A blood-stained gift.

"Did it ever occur to you that if he had gained his wealth by ill-gotten means, he would never have said

59

anything about it?"

"Are you sayin' I killed an innocent man?" he asked harshly.

Reilly knew she'd said too much. The prospector was dead. There was little she or anyone else could do for him now. "I'm saying you used very poor judgment in getting your boss a little present."

"I have witnesses."

"I'm sure you do." Before she got herself in anymore trouble with the sheriff, she decided it was time to make herself scarce. She didn't need any trouble. Any other time she wouldn't care, but now it was different, especially when she was harboring a criminal. But Sam was no more a criminal than that poor prospector. It took all the control she could muster not to call the sheriff and his deputies liars and murderers.

"If you men will excuse me, I have appointments." In her own subtle way she insulted them by refusing to call them gentlemen.

"Bitch," Neal called to her back as she made her way up the street.

"A smart bitch just the same," the sheriff added as he picked up the photograph of Sam Chandler. "Here, Neal, have a look." He handed him the picture.

The evil grin that encompassed Neal's mouth pleased the sheriff. "Hell, boss, we made Chandler famous. Too bad he didn't live long enough to 'preciate it."

His belly laugh drifted outside and pedestrians turned their heads toward the jail, wondering what had made the sheriff and his deputies so happy.

Reilly was furious; her long stride indicated as much. The tears that burned her eyes made her mad.

60

She was angry that a man could be killed so carelessly for a bag of gold, and no one tried to help him. She was angry that she cared when apparently no one else did. And she was angry because they didn't. She was so angry that she marched right inside the Gold-Dust Saloon and up to the shiny bar. Heads turned, mouths gaped, and a few of the more well-known citizens of Castletown tried to duck their heads behind the saloon girls. But Reilly didn't care what anyone thought, or what they were doing. She had a purpose and she intended to carry it out if hell froze over. And from some of the looks she was receiving, that was quickly becoming a possibility.

The bartender swiped his rag her way. "What can I do for you, Missy?"

"Is this where the prospector was killed?"

He lowered his head and his voice. "I'm ashamed to say it is."

"Do you know what happened to his belongings?"

Suddenly the bartender's face turned hard and his manner became brisk. "What business is it of yours? You looking for the gold?" he asked, eyeing her with disgust.

"No. I know what happened to the gold. I thought he might have had an address in his belongings. Earlier today I took his photograph. He mentioned sending it to his wife so she would know he was still alive. I thought I would send the picture and tell her of his death. She deserves to know what happened to him."

The bartender's face softened and once more his manner became pleasant. "Sure. His things are in the back. After Neal killed him, he emptied his pockets and took everything that was of any value. The only things left are a couple of old letters. I'll get them for you."

"Thank you."

The letters were worn, and where they had been folded repeatedly, the papers were torn. It broke her heart to think about how many times the letters had been carefully unfolded and read. Too bad others didn't care for the welfare of their fellowman the way the prospector had cared for his letters from home.

Willis Norman—that had been his name. She shook her head sadly. "What a tragedy."

"I knew the prospector was a dead man when he pulled his gun. Neal had been biding his time waiting for the old man to do something. He couldn't take his eyes off that pouch of nuggets. There wasn't a damn thing anybody could do."

"He had a mule. Do you know if anyone took it?"

"I don't guess anyone knew about it. If you want me to, I'll see if George down at the livery'll buy him. I'll try to get enough so we can give the man a decent burial."

After she described what he could expect from Sal, she left the saloon.

Her fingers trembled as she composed the letter. How did you tell someone their loved one was dead, that their hopes and dreams had been shattered by an uncaring hand? By the time she finished the letter, tears were streaming down her face. Still, a smile tugged her mouth when she looked at the picture of Willis and Sal. In the midst of her weary smile, her anger renewed and a determination to see justice done reared its head. She didn't know how yet, but someday, someway . . .

Suddenly the image of Sam Chandler came to her as clear as the day when she'd seen him step down from the train car. Would he have the courage to help her? Damnit, he owed her . . . or he would if he lived. He was a gambler, and from what she'd heard, a good one. Maybe he would take a gamble on her. And if there was one thing absolutely sure about Reilly Reynolds—she was not bashful. She would ask him at the first opportunity. He was her only hope. She was sick to death of the evil ways of the men running Castletown.

Chapter 7

Evening shadows soon blended, bathing the house in darkness. A soft glow of mellow light fell from the window attracting moths and other night creatures. Inside, Reilly stepped from the tub and toweled her body dry, then coiled the cloth around her wet hair and donned fresh clothes. When she had started supper, she'd put water on to heat for her bath. She'd been so hot and dirty, she had decided she'd have her bath, if she didn't have time for anything else. Now she felt human again and refreshed enough to finish her chores.

She strained broth from the thick stew she'd made and placed it on a tray with a couple of fluffy biscuits. Carrying it into the bedroom, she placed it on a small table and lit a lamp. Her patient had kicked the sheet away and was sleeping partially on his side. For a moment she stood glued to the floor, experiencing the most delightful sensations as she studied him at her leisure. His back was sleek and corded with muscle. His deeply tanned skin was marred in several places with scars. She fisted her hand to keep from reaching out and touching the imperfections. Scolding herself for her thoughts, she moved around the bed. She was hesitant to wake him, but he needed nourishment.

Sitting gingerly on the side of the bed, she folded her hands in her lap. "Mr. Chandler, I've brought you some food."

He shifted in the bed and rolled toward her, his pelvis curling around her back like the handle on a cup, and a hairy arm flopped into her lap.

Reilly's back popped in three places as she snapped into a rigid position. "Oh, my Lord," she whispered, the breath catching in her throat, "Mr. Chandler? Can you hear me?"

He smacked his mouth and moved against her.

Now she was in a fine mess, trapped by her own ignorance. She could feel his hardness against her buttocks. His heat branded her, and she was afraid to move an inch, lest she hurt him. Her flesh became alive with sensitivity from the tips of her toes to her scalp and all the places in between. His hand moved, drawing her attention. For a time she studied his long fingers and the neatly-trimmed nails. Hesitantly, she lifted her hand and traced the length of his fingers and the width of his palm. His hand jerked and his fingers closed around her hand. It was startling, but not unpleasant. His hand was warm and strong, not soft like she'd thought a gambler's hand would be. When she tried to ease her hand from his grasp, he tightened his grip. Now she was truly and completely trapped.

"Mr. Chandler, I've brought your supper. If you'll let go of my hand, I'll help you eat."

Sam could hear the gentle voice. It played through his mind like a soothing melody. He struggled with druglike sleep until an understanding of what she was saying penetrated his fog-filled mind. She was saying something about eating. If she was talking about food, what was she doing in the bed with him? What kind of food did she have in mind? He could feel her pressed against him. He blinked his eyes until he could focus. Well, maybe she wasn't in the

66

bed with him, but she was on the bed with him, and to beat it all he was holding her hand. Had he missed something while he was sleeping? God, he hoped not.

She was a real beauty. What was that thing she had wrapped around her head? It looked like a cone. He slipped his free hand up her back, bumping each vertebra as he scaled the soft fabric until he could reach the towel. He'd figured out what it was the moment his hand began its journey. Was she scared? She was as stiff as a poker. She'd turned her head to face him. Their eyes locked. Hers, a frightened blue. His, a questioning brown. His fingers tugged the fabric and the towel slid from her head. An abundance of wet golden hair cascaded down her back. She shook her head and mopped the loosened hair from her face.

"Damn, you smell good."

"Mr. Chandler?"

"Sam," he said hoarsely, moving against her back.

"Would you please let me up?"

"Why? This is so nice." He released her hand and wrapped his arm around her waist.

"I've brought you some supper," she repeated. "Aren't you hungry?"

"Not for food. It's not everyday that I wake up to find someone as lovely as you in my bed."

"It's not your bed. It's mine and I'd appreciate it if you'd keep that in mind."

"That's even better." His hand moved up her stomach until his thumbs stroked the fullness of her breast.

Fresh from her bath, Reilly wore nothing beneath her shirt and with his first stroke, Sam knew it too.

"You ungrateful bastard, let me go." She slapped his hand and tried to get up.

"Hey, what do you mean ungrateful? If you'll give me a few minutes, I'll show you just how grateful I am." He rocked against her back, his hardness throbbing with every beat of his heart.

"I should have let the sheriff have your worthless hide."

That got his attention.

"The sheriff? What's he got to do with any of this?"

"Everything!" She really didn't want to hurt him, but he'd left her little choice. Pulling back her elbow, she let go and jabbed him in the stomach, then leaped from the bed.

She instantly regretted her action when she saw him rolling in pain. "Will you be still? You're going to start bleeding again, and if you do, I'll have to send for the doctor. The first person he'll tell is the sheriff."

"I thought you wanted the sheriff to have me," he groaned.

"You're supposed to be dead. How will I explain why you're not?"

"Surely he can see for himself that I'm not dead."

"But I buried you and everything."

"You did what? My God, every time I open my eyes you're here telling me the most ridiculous tales I've ever heard. What's going on? Have I lost my mind or have you lost yours?"

"Look at your chest. Do you think those bandages are some kind of game?"

He did as she asked. "I don't know what's going on, but it hurts like hell."

"Someone shot you. I brought you home with me and removed the bullet."

"Thanks, I think. Who shot me?"

"I have no idea. The sheriff brought you into town. He said you were the leader of the men that robbed the bank yesterday."

Instead of clearing his mind, he was becoming more confused every moment. "What in God's name are you talking about? What bank?"

She held up her hands in supplication. "Okay, wait just a minute. I know you're confused."

"That's putting it mildly." He grimaced and tugged at the bandage.

"Let me help you get comfortable and I'll tell you what I know." She fluffed his pillows and held his shoulder as he eased against the headboard.

Instead of sitting on the bed, she pulled a chair up beside it and sat down. "The bank was robbed yesterday. After the robbery, the sheriff and his men took out after the gang. Several hours later he returned to town with you slung across your horse's back."

"I didn't rob any damn bank."

"Please let me finish before you blow up."

He nodded his head stubbornly.

Reilly couldn't help noticing the way the light reflected off his rumpled hair when he moved his head. "Okay. The sheriff told everyone that you were the leader of the gang. The rest of the gang got away with the bank's money."

"That figures," he muttered, not pleased at all with the picture she was painting.

"The sheriff and everyone else in town thinks you're dead."

"How did you pull that off?"

"The sheriff sent your body to me to be photographed."

He smiled. "You're the one who takes pictures. I thought I recognized you."

"Yes." Her heart slapped against her chest. He did know who she was.

"I've seen some of your work."

"When?"

"The sheriff is mighty proud of his killings. He shows off the pictures to anyone who'll look at them."

"I know how he is. As I said, I was to photograph

69

you. While I was working, I discovered you were still alive."

He smiled. "I bet that got your attention."

She smiled at the memory. "It did. I was scared to death. I didn't know what to do."

"So you brought me here. My very own angel."

"Not if we're found out."

"Why did you do it?"

"I guess I knew if I turned you over to the sheriff, you wouldn't live. He would see that you didn't."

"I'll be forever in your debt."

"But then I made my crime even worse. I buried you."

"This I've got to hear."

"Well, I didn't have a choice. The arrangements had already been made, the grave dug. I had to produce a body."

His eyes sparkled with mischief and he sighed deeply. "I'm afraid to ask."

"It was firewood. I put firewood in the coffin."

"Very clever. Still, weren't you afraid it would roll around?"

"It did shift a little. But I grunted and groaned so loud that Digger couldn't hear it for all the racket I was making."

He studied her for several seconds before asking, "Reilly? Isn't that your name?"

"Yes, how did you know?"

"I have my ways. How could I forget you? You were the first person I saw when I got off the train."

There went her stomach again. She probably needed to eat something.

"Is this your house?"

"My uncle's. Chug's his name."

"I know who Chug is. I've bought him a drink on occasion."

"Just what he needed, I'm sure," she replied softly, getting to her feet. "Are you hungry now?"

70

"Starving. I could eat a sow and seven pigs."

She laughed. "I don't have any pork, but I've brought you some beef broth and biscuits. You should eat before it gets cold." She saw the grimace that passed across his face when he moved. "Can you manage?"

"I think so."

She placed the tray on his lap and began picking up around the room until his bellow of pain spun her around.

"What is it?" she asked.

"My head. It hurts like a sonofabitch."

She ignored his language and rushed to his side. The pillows had slipped and his head had cracked against the headboard. She pulled the pillows up behind him and touched the back of his head. To her astonishment, there was a lump the size of a goose egg on the back of his head. "No wonder it hurts. You've had quite a lick. How did you do this?"

"Beats the hell out of me. It must have happened when I was shot."

"That's probably the reason you've slept so long."

"Come to think about it, it probably saved my *worthless hide*."

Reilly had the grace to blush.

How pretty she was with her cheeks stained a rosy glow. Hell, she was pretty anyway. "The sheriff thought he'd killed me, when all along I was just knocked out cold."

"Where were you?"

"I don't remember."

"But why would someone shoot you?"

He shrugged his shoulders and dodged her eyes. He had a vague recollection of what had happened, but he wasn't ready to share it with anyone just yet. Was this some kind of trap? Reilly was probably as honest as the day was long, and everything she'd told him was on the up and up. Still, he had to be careful.

71

He'd bide his time until he knew what was going on for sure.

"So you believe I didn't have anything to do with the robbery?"

"If I'd thought for one moment that you would do anything like that, I wouldn't have brought you home with me."

"Thank you." He broke a piece from the biscuit and dipped it into the broth. "Hmmm . . . good."

She couldn't take her eyes off him, sitting there in her bed, eating the biscuits she'd made. His chest was naked except for the bandage. His long legs were still encased in the expensive black britches, and his fine leather shoes were peeking from beneath the bed with his socks tucked inside . . . she couldn't get over it. His face was darkly shadowed with whiskers and his hair looked like it had been run through a sausage grinder. Still, he was a handsome man.

"Think I might have seconds?" He handed her the bowl.

"Yes, there's plenty. Would you like a cup of coffee?"

"If it's not too much trouble."

"No, none at all. When you finish your supper, you might like to bathe. I mean if you feel like it. I have water heating." She felt awkward discussing his personal grooming habits.

"I don't want to put you out any. I know I've been a lot of trouble all already. But a bath would be nice."

"I need to change your bandage anyway. I'll remove that one, and when you're finished bathing I'll put on a fresh one. Let me get you something else to eat right now."

What's in this for you? he wanted to ask as she left the room, but didn't have the heart. She seemed so genuine in her offer of help. He'd never met anyone yet who would give of himself like she appeared to be doing without having an ulterior motive. He figured he'd find out when she was ready to tell him.

When she returned and handed him the tray, the bowl of broth was not strained. This time it was full of chunks of potatoes and carrots and tender mouth-watering beef. "Mr. Chandler?"

"Yes."

"I have your things here. My friend, Susan, went to the hotel and got your belongings. They're in the wardrobe. You might want to go through them to see if anything is missing. The sheriff was there before she got there, but he left your clothes."

She saw the frown marring his brow. "Oh, don't worry, Susan won't say anything. She's the only one who knows about you. She helped me get you here."

That was part of the conversation he had heard that hadn't made any sense. "How did she manage to get my clothes?"

"She told the desk clerk that you still owed her father for the clothes, and since the sheriff had killed you, you wouldn't be wearing them. You see, her father owns the mercantile store."

"You have more schemes than a dog has fleas. The sheriff had better watch out. You'd be better at his job than he is."

"The sheriff doesn't do his job, not that of protecting the people he serves. He only serves himself," she snapped.

"Why do you take his pictures for him if you dislike him so much?"

"I don't have a choice. I have to pay to stay in business just like everybody else. Oh, he pays me for the pictures. But then his deputy always makes the rounds to collect a monthly protection fee."

"Protection from what?"

"Everything. Theft, vandalism, fire."

"My God, that's his job. Does anyone else pay this protection fee?"

"I believe everyone does. No one likes it, but

73

they're afraid of the consequences if they don't pay. A few have resisted and either lost their business or their life."

"The sheriff sounds like a charming man," he said tightly.

"Very," she answered in the same vein.

For some reason she told him about the prospector. She didn't hide her pain or her anger as she related the story. Sometimes tears sparkled with the telling; other times her face glowed with anger. Finally, she admitted sadly that she'd written his wife and told her of his death. When she was spent, she smoothed the edge of the sheet she'd twisted and said, "Uncle Chug took time off from his drunk to build the coffin. I'm surprised all that hammering this afternoon didn't wake you."

"Out of curiosity, just how are you going to keep my presence here from your uncle?"

"Fortunately, he doesn't live here anymore. He's staying with a woman in town," she admitted shame-faced.

At last she said tiredly, "While you finish your dinner, I'll get the tub."

When she returned dragging the tub, her bed was empty, "Mr. Chandler?" She rushed through the house. "Mr. Chandler?"

The front door creaked open and Reilly jumped a foot. There he stood with his britches riding low on his hips, bare feet and all. "Mr. Chandler, you've scared me to death."

"I didn't mean to frighten you, but nature called."

She hoped the dim light hid her blush. Nervously, she pushed her hair away from her face and turned toward the bedroom. "Uh . . . I'll have your bath ready in a few minutes."

He followed at a slower pace admiring the sway of her trim bottom. "Nice," he whispered. "Very nice."

She stopped stone cold. "What did you say?" She

knew good and well what he'd said. He was a womanizer through and through.

"Mice, do you have mice? I've heard in town that mice are causing all kinds of problems this year."

"No, I don't have a problem with mice. But you have a young lady taking care of you who'll take your head off if you don't behave yourself." With that, she turned smartly on her heel and entered the bedroom. She couldn't let him get away with his little off-color remarks, not if she was going to be taking care of him. She must never let him know how his presence sent her heart to pounding.

Sam smiled at Reilly's remark. He clicked his bare feet together and lifted his hand to his head, saluting her retreating figure jauntily. "You got it, young lady."

Reilly busied herself cleaning the kitchen, rattling the pots and pans in rhythm to the tune Sam Chandler was belting out. If Reilly Reynolds had nothing else, she had a vivid imagination. And right now it was turning cartwheels in her head as she heard the splashing water and his off-key lyrics.

Chapter 8

The morning light splashed across the rumpled bedclothes and caressed the handsome features of the occupant. Sam shifted in bed, but the sunlight continued to pursue him. He yawned loudly and his eyes fluttered open. Bowing his back and linking his hands, he stretched until his bones were popping like green firewood. He could stretch a mile if he didn't have to walk back. The light of day hadn't improved his first impression of the room. It was shabby in the most generous of terms. But it was clean, and the bed linen was crisp and smelled like fresh air. He'd slept like a baby and felt like a new man.

He picked up a framed photograph from the bedside table. It was a picture of a man and a young girl. He recognized Reilly immediately. She must have been about thirteen or fourteen at the time. Her hair was in long braids and she was wearing britches and a loose shirt. What struck him most was the laughing smile on her face. She looked happy and carefree. The man's hand rested on her shoulder and her own was covering his. There was a marked resemblance between the pair. Sam ran his hand over the image of Reilly. She had a mischievous, capricious look about her. It was evident even then that she would be a beauty.

He set the picture down and stacked his hands behind him. His eyes drifted around the room. Reilly's presence was evident. Her photographs decorated the walls and a vase of wild roses sat atop a dressing table. Hairpins and ribbons were neatly separated in glass containers on the dresser and a hairbrush was turned on its side. A queer feeling spiraled through him when he realized this was her room. Her bed. She'd given up her bed for a stranger. But why? Had she done it to protect him as she claimed? In his line of work he had trouble believing anyone would do anything just out of the goodness of their heart. Especially when that act would place their own life in danger.

But then Reilly was like no one he'd ever encountered. She was the first person he'd laid eyes on when he stepped down from the train in Castletown. There she had stood, clutching a package to her chest, boldly appraising him. He had returned her appraisal. Right off the bat, he was shocked that she was wearing britches. When he saw the jaunty way she walked and tilted her head just so, he'd known if anyone could carry off wearing men's britches she could. The pain of that memory stirred his loins even now. He'd become hard just watching the sway of her bottom. He'd wanted nothing more than to pull her to him and fondle her gently rounded buttocks and let nature take its course. Of course that hadn't happened.

Instead, a group looking for an easy mark had approached him. Acting, as they'd expected him to act, had garnered him a tidy sum and an enemy for life. Neal Holt expected everyone to bow and scrape to him because of his position as deputy. Hell, Sam hadn't known him from Adam's house cat, and he sure as hell wasn't going to sit quietly while the loudmouth fleeced him out of his money. Neal's hands hadn't proven quicker than the eye either, and

Sam had called his hand at cheating. Well, maybe he hadn't exactly called his hand, but his toad-stabber had quickly got Neal's attention—it had gotten everyone's attention within the confines of the saloon. Sam had seen to it that it would be a while before Neal held a hand of cards comfortably. But he'd messed up not knifing his gun hand. If he had, maybe the prospector would be alive today.

The fight that had broken out afterward would take some doing to surpass. But it had been worth it, even if it had cost him half of his winnings. God, he'd felt good when he left the saloon. Nothing like a good knockdown, dragout to clear the cobwebs from your head. The doors had no sooner shut behind him when a pretty little blonde had approached him. He'd known exactly what she'd had on her mind. And it hadn't been a bad idea. He'd still been aching from the memory of the britches-clad young woman.

The blonde had accompanied him back to his hotel room, where they'd spent several delightful, passion-filled hours together. Damn, what that little blonde could do with her tongue was amazing. As he thought about it, he couldn't discount her toes either. She had been incredible.

Sam's second day in town, he spied the young woman he'd seen at the depot. She'd set up camera gear on the boardwalk and was taking pictures of a group of miners. Curious about her, he'd subtly asked one of the shopowners a few questions about her and learned her name was Reilly Reynolds. She and her father had opened a photography studio, then he'd died a short time later. The people of Castletown admired her. Miss Reynolds made her own living and her reputation was tarnish free. She might wear pants, but she wasn't some britches-clad, snuff-dipping, gun-toting female that was always sticking her nose in everyone's business.

Sam had decided right off he'd better stick to

79

women like the pretty little blonde instead of a woman with a tarnish-free reputation. Still, he'd see her frequently in town taking her pictures and he couldn't help staring at her. A few times, he thought she might even be sneaking a glance at him too.

And now . . . here he was in her house . . . alone with her. Hell. Of all the willing women in town, he would wind up in the bed of a beautiful, desirable woman with a damned tarnish-free reputation. Had his own tarnished past caught up with him and this was some form of punishment? Who'd ever believe he'd be living in hell with an angel?

His nose twitched and his stomach growled. Was that food he smelled? No sooner had the thought made its way through his head than Reilly was standing in the doorway with a platter of food.

"Good morning. Are you hungry?"

"Yes, I could—"

"I know. You could eat a sow and six pigs."

"Seven pigs," he corrected.

"Will some side meat, eggs and biscuits do? I also have a jar of apple butter."

"Sounds good. I'll just eat the sow a little at a time."

She laughed and placed the tray on the nightstand. "How is your head this morning?"

"Believe me, I know it's there. But it doesn't throb quite as bad."

She watched as he ate his breakfast. His manners were exemplary. And she knew about manners. After her mother died, her father had set the same stringent standards in her upbringing. His only concession was her wearing pants because the places his work took them was not conducive to dresses and all the paraphernalia that entailed. She'd never thought much about it before, but now she wondered what Sam Chandler thought about her wearing pants. Whatever, good or bad, it was too late to think about it now. She'd already made a first impression. Besides, she might have fanciful thoughts about him, but when it came right down to it, he was out of her league. And regardless of what she wore, they could never be a pair.

"Did you sleep well?" he asked after he set the plate aside and wiped his mouth.

"Yes, did you?"

"Like the dead," he chuckled. "Are you still upset about the prospector?"

"I've come to grips with it. I'm only one person against a crowd of many that accepts whatever happens. There's not a lot I can do."

He studied her for several moments in silence before asking, "If you could do something, what would you do?"

"I would prove without a shadow of a doubt that not only is the sheriff stealing the people of this community blind, he is also murdering innocent people. Then he claims they are criminals to make himself look good, so he can squeeze more money out of us."

"Sounds like a tall order to me." *Was she for real?* He wondered yet again.

"You think I'm crazy, don't you? Well, I can back up what I say." She rushed out of the room before he could question her further.

A shiver of anticipation ran up his spine. What was she up to now?

She returned, carrying a case that she plopped down on the bed. She sat down beside him and opened the case. Next, she started slapping photographs in his lap, unaware of where the material was landing.

He grunted and moved up in the bed.

"Look at those and then tell me I'm crazy." She snapped her hands to her waist so fast Sam found himself dodging.

81

"Hey, I'm on your side."

That seemed to soothe her ruffled composure. She took a deep breath and let it out slowly.

"I'm sorry. I didn't mean to snap at you. Just look at the pictures."

He looked down at the picture. Before him was the corpse of his own body. A breathless fear swept through him. He couldn't believe it. Sure, she'd told him, but for him to see his death picture—my God, what an attention-getter. He swallowed loudly.

"It's true then?"

Reilly's mouth dropped in astonishment. Her eyes bored holes into him. "You doubted me?"

"Damnit, Reilly, don't look at me like that. Hell, I know I was shot. I've got the hole and the pain to prove it."

She shook her head sadly.

"Now just a minute, you'll have to admit that your story sounded a bit farfetched."

"Farfetched? I've told you nothing but the truth. What reason would I have to lie?"

"I don't know, you tell me?" he asked softly.

Her head snapped around so fast that her hair swirled in a blonde wave. "My God, that lick on the head has scrambled your brain. And another thing, don't you dare think for one second that I'm in the habit of carrying strange men home with me. I don't, or I never have before. Everything I've told you is the truth. If you don't believe me, then just show your face in town and see how long it takes before the sheriff locks you up. That is, if he even bothers to lock you up. He'll probably shoot you on sight." Her voice caught on a sob and she jumped up. "I thought I was doing you a favor."

"Come here, angel."

"No." her chin came out and her lips trembled.

"Please." He patted the spot beside him.

Reluctantly, she did as he asked.

"Can we start over? Will you give me another chance?"

What choice did she have? She nodded.

"Let's look at the pictures." He picked up the photograph of himself and studied it. "Ugly bastard, isn't he?"

"Don't say that. You look very good for a corpse. But I'm glad you weren't dead," she admitted.

He flipped through the photographs. They were all of dead men. "These are all the sheriff's victims?"

"Every last one. He likes to build himself up in the eyes of the community so everyone will think he's doing them a favor by keeping their town clean. The first time he asked me to take a picture of a gunslinger he'd killed I didn't think too much about it. He claimed it was to discourage other unsavory characters from lingering in his town. *His town,* mind you.

"Well, that was just the beginning. You have no idea how many men he's killed. And with each killing his stories became more outlandish. I became skeptical, so I started keeping pictures of each man he killed. There's no way on earth these men could have all been guilty of the things he said. If it was true, the town would be crawling with United States marshals."

He didn't want to voice his doubts. He didn't want to upset her again because he recognized how passionate she was about her ideas. Yet he had to point out the one thing she lacked. "You've worked hard and you're probably right about the sheriff. But you don't have any proof." He flipped through the pictures. "These men aren't talking."

A smile of pure triumph lit her face. "Ah ha, that's where you're wrong." She began going through the case again and slapping pictures onto the bed.

In her excitement she'd moved until she was against his legs. He could feel the heat of her body

83

and smell a hint of lavender. Only with extreme control did he keep his hands in his lap, when all he wanted to do was bury them in the thickness of her hair and draw her mouth down to his. God, he hoped she didn't notice the sheet. It looked like someone had pitched a tent under it. He pulled up his knee and redirected his attention.

"See," she said.

"What am I looking at?" he asked as she placed a photograph before him.

"Those are the men who robbed the bank," she explained.

Sam knew a moment of panic as he stared at the photograph. In fact, his heart stopped beating for several seconds as he recognized one of the outlaw's faces. He recomposed his shocked features before he lifted his head. "They're ah . . . quite clear."

"Yes, they rode right into my line of vision. It's very clear that you're not part of the gang. This one right here was their lookout."

"By lookout, I guess you mean he never went into the bank."

"Right."

Thank God for that, Sam thought relieved. "Uh . . . did you get a good look at him?"

"I think I would recognize him if I ever saw him again."

Sam almost groaned aloud.

"But if I'd known a robbery was taking place inside the bank, I would've checked him over more thoroughly. Do you recognize any of them?"

He shrugged and kept a blank face as he lied. "No, do you?"

She shook her head. "I hate that. I thought maybe one of these men might have been the one that shot you." She handed him another photograph. "Now, look at this one. I took it when they were coming out of the bank."

"But their faces are covered."

"I don't care. You can still tell that none of these men are you. They're all too short. But there's something else. Don't you see it?"

He studied the photograph, then shook his head.

"They're all holding their gun in their right hand. You're left handed. I noticed it last night when you were eating."

"Well, I'll be damned, you're right."

Reilly clapped her hands together and said excitedly, "I knew it."

"You're a very good detective." Too damn good, he thought to himself. "What do you plan to do with the photographs, Reilly?"

For a moment she debated whether or not she should tell him she'd already sent one of the pictures to the newspaper. But she didn't know him well enough to predict his reaction. "What can I do? I sure can't show them to the sheriff."

"Have you told anyone besides me about these pictures?"

"Only Susan . . . but I haven't shown them to her yet."

"Then don't. The fewer people who know this, the safer you are."

"All right." She studied him a moment and weighed her words carefully before she spoke them. "Sam, since these pictures prove that you had nothing to do with the holdup, and the sheriff accused you falsely, I was wondering—"

"Reilly, you're jumping to conclusions. I don't know who actually shot me, remember?"

"Maybe so, but you can bet Murdock was behind it, regardless whether or not he pulled the trigger."

"Just what are you leading to?"

"I want you to help me prove the sheriff is a murderer."

He ran his hand across his bristled face and shook

his head. "Hey, angel, you've got the wrong man. I'm a gambler—a lover. Now if you wanted me to take somebody down to the shirt on their back, I could do it." He trailed his hand down the length of her spine. "Or if you wanted to make love all night long I could oblige you. But proving the sheriff is a murderer . . . my God, you'll get us both killed."

She jumped from the bed in absolute mortification. She couldn't believe he'd actually said what he had. Make love to her, the very idea! She'd known he was a womanizer, but to out and out admit it! Well, it was just unbelievable.

"Then you won't help me? I should have known better. I just thought since I saved your life and put myself in danger to do so, you'd be more agreeable."

"Reilly." His brows shot up and his tone warranted caution.

"Well?"

"Do you realize what you're asking?"

"Yes, but someone has to do something, or it's just going to get worse."

"Why have you set this task for yourself? You have a good business."

"Not for long. The people may not stand up to the sheriff, but they'll move away. Some already have left."

"What do you propose to do?"

"I don't know. I was hoping you might have some ideas on the subject."

"Why in God's name would I have any ideas? I told you I'm a gambler and a—"

"I know, I know, you're a lover," she tossed over her shoulder as she paced the room.

"You say it like it leaves a bad taste in your mouth."

She frowned at him.

"Come here, Reilly."

Cautiously, she lowered herself to the very edge

86

of the bed.

His voice was low and sultry as he acknowledged, "It's apparent you've never made slow, hot, wet, sweet love until you were weak from pleasure." As he talked, he twirled a thick blonde tress around his hand.

His words sent spirals of pleasure rippling through Reilly's belly. She knew she should be angry and call attention to his crudeness, yet she just couldn't work up the strength. More than anything, she wanted to know what it would be like to have him make slow, hot, wet, sweet love to her until she was weak from pleasure. Except when she did let it happen, she wanted more than a night—she wanted it to last a lifetime. She wanted a deep and abiding love, someone to share all that she had to give. And she knew without a doubt that Sam Chandler desired no such commitment. He was like a strong wind that whirled through causing chaos, then leaving as quickly as he'd appeared, giving no thought to the disruption he'd caused.

"You're right, and I have no plans to do any such thing." She pulled her hair from his hand and stood up. "I have work to do, and I'm sure you can find something with which to entertain yourself. Oh, I almost forgot." She pulled a brand new deck of cards from her pocket and tossed them to him. "I didn't want you to get out of practice."

As she started through the door, his words stopped her. "If you ever change your mind—I'm your man."

She snorted and left the room.

He had more gall than anyone she'd ever encountered. But she guessed he had every right. He was something to look at and aroused feelings in her beyond those that she had known before. What was a girl to do exposed to his company the way she was?

Chapter 9

Sam was going out of his mind. The walls were closing in on him. If he had to spend much longer in bed, he would be a raving lunatic. He was so bored he'd even reduced himself to cheating at solitaire. He palmed the deck of cards then released them. They sprayed the bed.

What in the world was he going to do about Reilly? She was hellbent on exposing the sheriff. She didn't know their purpose was the same, but he couldn't tell her. Not yet.

Reilly wasn't the only one interested in proving the sheriff was up to no good. The man had stepped on one too many toes. He and his deputies—hired gunmen, that's what they really were—moved from one town to another playing the same game. Well, the game was up—or it was as far as the United States Marshal's office was concerned. Now Sam's assignment was to provide unquestionable proof against the man.

It puzzled him that the sheriff had picked him as a target. Sam knew his cover was airtight. He knew the sheriff had no idea that he was a marshal. He had worked the town, and he knew the bad guys from the good guys.

Reilly's photographs of the robbery had really

taken him aback when he saw his partner, Mason Womac, among the outlaws. Mason had been trying to gain the trust of a man he suspected was a member of the outlaw gang. His plan had evidently worked and he'd joined the gang. Now he knew why their scheduled meeting had never taken place. Mason had been robbing the damn bank. Hell, there was no way around it, he had to get answers.

On the morning they were to meet, Sam had had a lot to tell Mason. He'd waited around for him and when he hadn't shown up, he'd headed back to town. That was when he was bushwhacked.

Slowly he'd remembered things—after his head quit pounding so bad and his memory had become clearer—and he'd bet his last dollar that it was members of the same gang that had shot him. It still galled him that they'd caught him unaware that day. He rubbed his hand over the pump-knot on the back of his head. It was as though they'd seen him and sat in wait. He'd become the perfect cover-up for the job they'd just completed.

What really bothered him was the fact that Reilly had had a good enough look at Mason to know he was one of the outlaws if she should happen to see him. His only consolation was knowing that she wouldn't run to the sheriff with her information.

One thing was for sure, he had to get out of the bed and get word to Mason that he was all right and warn him that Reilly could probably identify him. Mason had a short fuse on the best of days, and by now he'd know his partner had been killed. No telling what he'd do. And if Miss Reilly Reynolds didn't calm down, she could get herself killed. Lord, he had his work cut out for him and here he lay in the damn bed. Yet how could he leave the house to search for Mason when he never knew when Reilly might return home? Her work hours were erratic, and he didn't know how long it would take him to get in touch with Mason. He certainly couldn't stroll non-chalantly into town and look for him. His only hope was that Mason was still using the same place where they'd held their secret meetings and had passed messages back and forth between them.

He and Mason had been partners for years, and they were very good at their job. He couldn't think of another person he would trust guarding his back. Mason was as mean as a coiled rattler; he was a hard worker, hard drinker, and hard to get to know. He was a no-nonsense man. That's why Sam always went into town as the gambler. Mason didn't have the tolerance to fool with people; he was a Loner with a capital L. In all their years together, Sam knew very little about the man, yet he trusted him implicitly. Once when they'd been drinking, they got to talking about marriage. Mason had said something about almost getting married once. There had been a bitterness about the way he'd said it. He didn't volunteer any more information and Sam hadn't asked.

The women found Mason irresistible, probably because of his careless attitude. But he had formed no lasting relationships with anyone. They worked together, but when they had time off, they went their separate ways.

Sam had so many things rolling around in his head he couldn't bear lying in bed. He got up and paced the room.

What was he going to do about Reilly? He had to continue his work, and at the same time try to keep her out of trouble. If anyone ever found out about the photographs, she wouldn't be safe. He couldn't help admiring her spunk, even if at the same time he wanted to strangle her. There was no way on earth she could take on somebody as ruthless as the sheriff. The man wouldn't think twice about killing a woman if she interfered with his plans.

Sam ran a weary hand through his rumpled hair and groaned into the silence. "Lord, just what I needed . . . a female with a conscience."

Susan checked the door to make sure it was locked. It had been a busy day and she was looking forward to a long soak in the tub and finishing the book she was reading.

Her father teased her about reading all the time. He told her she should quit dreaming about the characters in her books and live life. He said there wasn't any people like the ones she was reading about anyway. She knew he was wrong. As for experiencing life, she was. Hadn't she helped save a man's life? Hadn't she marched right into the hotel like she owned the place and lied like a dog? She still couldn't get over doing that. If anyone had questioned her, she would have run screaming from the place in mortification.

It didn't matter what people thought about her. She didn't care if everyone thought she was spoiled and fast becoming a spinster. Why didn't they think Reilly was going to be an old maid? In all honesty she knew the reason. Reilly was outgoing and had enough determination for half a dozen people. Reilly would probably meet someone and have a house full of children.

Well, Susan had determination too, and she was determined that she didn't want any of the men in town. She wanted excitement and adventure. She just wasn't quite sure what *kind* of excitement and adventure. But there wasn't a doubt in her mind that she would find it. It would come and she would be ready.

Her books had opened up new worlds for her. People might think she was bookish and shy, but on the inside she was like a match waiting to be lit. She didn't want a tobacco-chewing, spitting, bushy-faced man that couldn't carry on a conversation without scratching his crotch. When she met him—the man of her dreams—she would know it. He had to be clean shaven, and she really liked blond hair and sparkling eyes—the color didn't matter. Still, she wanted someone that would appreciate her mind . . . someone that actually read books.

She moved up the walkway, mulling over a passage in one of the plays she'd recently read, "'Romeo, Romeo, wherefore art thou?'"

"He sure as hell ain't standing here," came the exasperated voice as she and a large body fell against the side of the building.

The voice grunted and Susan struggled to right herself. A dusty black hat dropped between them, its brim catching between their bodies. She looked at the hat cocked against her stomach and the man's belt buckle. A lavender ribbon, her lavender ribbon, lay across the brim dipping into the bowl of the hat. She jerked her ribbon from the hat and lifted her head. Angry green eyes slammed into flashing midnight blue eyes.

"Why the very idea! If you saw me coming toward you, why didn't you get out of my way?" She raised her arms and with a few quick tugs replaced the ribbon.

He grabbed his hat before it hit the ground and watched with appreciation as the fabric of her bodice stretched across her breasts.

"I wasn't looking at you. I was looking over my shoulder for the fellow you were hollering at."

"I do not holler. I was saying aloud a passage I read from Romeo and Juliet."

"Well, for heaven's sake, why didn't you say so? With all the caterwauling you were doing, I figured whoever you were hollering at had disappeared down the street."

"This is a ridiculous conversation. I have better things to do than stand here like a fool trying to tell you who Romeo is."

"I know who Romeo is."

"You do?" she was dumbfounded.

"And Juliet," he answered smartly.

"Who?" She didn't believe him for one second.

"They were lovers and died at the end of the story."

Now she was speechless. She looked him over from head to foot. He was tall and well-muscled. His hair was thick and an odd mixture of light brown heavily streaked with blond. His eyes were so blue that they took her breath away. The lines of his face were stark and unrelenting, and she wondered if his beautiful mouth ever smiled. His shirt was black as was his pants, and slung low on his hip was a leather holster housing a gun with a pearl-handle grip. Susan didn't know the first thing about guns, but if they could be pretty, his was. And she would bet every book she owned that he would have no qualms about using the gun. He looked like a cowboy, a roughneck, a drifter—but definitely not someone who actually knew who Romeo was.

"Who was Capulet?" she ventured, not completely satisfied that he knew what he was talking about.

"Only to humor you, I will play your game. Capulet was Juliet's father."

"You're right," she breathed in amazement.

"Now it's my turn."

"To what?"

"To ask the questions."

She looked at him blankly. "What are you talking about?"

"Tell me about Sam Chandler."

Her mouth suddenly dried. "I . . . I don't know anything about him."

"You're lying."

She turned as though to walk away.

He grabbed her arm and pain rippled through her.

He didn't know it, but she wasn't going anywhere. Her legs were too weak to carry her. The name Sam Chandler crossing the man's lips had been the last thing she'd expected. A terrible fright filled her. Lord, what would she do? What would Reilly do in this situation? She could feel what little courage she had seeping out through her pores as her hands became damp.

"He's dead," she croaked.

"I know. But there's more, isn't there?"

"W-What do you mean? What more can there be? The man is dead. He was a bank robber." She was going to cry. She blinked her eyes to quell the tears.

"You're not a very good liar. You're too tender-hearted."

She swallowed loudly. "I didn't know him personally."

"That's not the story I heard."

Oh Lord, what's he talking about! Has someone been spreading untruths about me?

"I admit Sam's taste ran more to whores and one night stands. Easy come, easy go."

"I wouldn't know," she said stiffly.

He lifted his hand to her face and brushed away a strand of loosened hair. "But you know more than you're telling me."

"No, I don't."

"Then what were you doing in his room the night before he died?" He saw her face turn white as a sheet. "You did go to the hotel the next day to get your things out of Sam's room, didn't you? Well, some of his belongings are missing too."

His question threw her into a panic. Her blood turned to ice. Reilly was right. Everyone in that hotel had thought she was a . . . a . . . w-whore. She had to do something. She couldn't let him believe she was that kind of woman.

"You've got everything wrong. I went to Mr. Chandler's room only to take the things he had charged at our store. They were still brand new, so I put them back in stock." The lies were beginning to flow like honey across her lips. "The sheriff had been there before me. The room was turned upside down."

"You didn't see any of his personal belongings?"

"Well yes, they were scattered all over the room. But I had no reason to go through them. I'm not a thief, Mr.—"

"Womac, Mason Womac. And I'm not calling you a thief. It just strikes me as odd that you went in search of the things he'd purchased from your store."

"It wasn't odd at all. It was good business. My father knew he hadn't paid for the things so he sent me after them."

"Maybe I should speak with your father then."

Oh Lord, there was no way she could let him speak with her father. Her father would have a fit if he ever found out what she had done—because Sam Chandler had never charged anything, but had always paid for his purchases. Her lie was growing by leaps and bounds. She twisted her hands nervously. "I'll do what I can to help you, Mr. Womac, but I don't know anything."

Mason knew he'd hit a nerve. She was lying about something, and he planned to find out what and why. There were too many loose ends. First of all her story didn't fit with what he'd heard at the hotel. Yet, this woman didn't exactly fit the image of the kind of women who'd frequent men's hotel rooms. Also, she didn't look like the kind of woman Sam would fool around with either. Damn, nothing made any sense. He couldn't imagine the reason for the lie unless she was involved with the sheriff. Somehow, she didn't look like the sheriff's type either. But the good Lord knew he was no expert on women. What man was?

Suddenly the image of Sam came to mind. Mason smiled inwardly. Maybe Sam was the one exception. His smile faded. Hell, it made him mad to think Sam had been killed so senselessly. Damn it, he wanted to hit something.

"Look, I'm just trying to get the facts straight surrounding his death."

"Why don't you ask the sheriff then?"

"I did," he lied. "He was no more cooperative than you are. But I did see the picture that Miss Reynolds, the photographer, took of Sam after his death. The sheriff was showing it to everyone in the saloon one night. I've been by her studio several times, but I've missed her."

"Uh . . . yes, t-that's right. She's been very busy." How could she warn Reilly that this man was looking for her?

"Well, I'm sure to catch her around sometime. I'll be in touch." With that final parting remark, he turned on his heel and sauntered up the walkway.

When he was out of hearing, Susan curled her lip and mimicked, "I'll be in touch. Well, you can bet your blue eyes I won't lose any sleep over it."

She was lying through her teeth and she knew it. Her show of bravado was only for her own benefit. She would never have the nerve to say something like that to his face. He scared her when he just looked at her with those probing midnight eyes. Had he known she was lying? She had to get in touch with Reilly. Reilly wouldn't put up with his hatefulness. She'd spit in his eye.

Mason stopped just out-of-sight, then back-tracked. From across the street, he waited and watched the studio. He didn't have a long wait. In a flurry of lace and petticoats, Susan Waters whirled down the street, glancing over her shoulder every few steps.

Mason knew it. He could smell a lie like most

people smelled fresh baked bread. Damnit, he knew something was going on. And he knew Susan Waters was his link to the truth.

Susan was beside herself with worry. As Mason Womac had said, Reilly was not at her studio. She contemplated whether or not she should go to Reilly's house, but was afraid she might run into Mason Womac again. He could very well be on his way up there now to talk to Reilly.

That night she didn't sleep a wink, worrying that she had fouled up everything. The next morning, she met Reilly at the door and anxiously followed her into the studio.

"Oh Lord, Reilly, you won't believe what's happened."

Closing the door behind them, Reilly turned to her friend. "Susan, sit down before you fall down."

They both sat down on the divan.

"Has . . . has Sam ever mentioned a man named Mason Womac?" Susan asked.

"No, why?"

"Yesterday, after I'd locked up and was going home, I . . . ah . . . ran into him . . . literally."

"What did he say?" Reilly urged, noticing Susan's nervousness.

"Well, to make a long story short, right out of the clear blue he asked me about Sam Chandler. He knew about his death." Now Susan began getting very fidgety. "Oh Reilly, he must have asked the clerk at the hotel what had happened to Mr. Chandler's belongings. He knew everything that had gone on and thought like everybody else that I had spent the previous night with Mr. Chandler. He wanted to know what all I'd taken from the room."

"Oh Lord, what did you tell him, Susan?"

"I . . . ah . . . stuck to my original story, but he

didn't act like he believed it. I even told him to ask the sheriff because he was in the room before me." Susan twisted her hands nervously in the folds of her skirt. Her eyes were fearful when she added, "He said he had already asked him and learned nothing."

"Oh God, Reilly, what if he told Murdock I'd been in the room that same day and Mr. Chandler's bags were missing? The sheriff might wonder himself what I was doing prowling around in that room and ask me about it."

"Susan, did anyone see you when you left the hotel with Sam's bags that day?"

"No, I don't think so. I left by the side door upstairs."

"Well, the question is: Why is Mason Womac interested in Sam?"

"Oh Reilly, I hope I haven't ruined everything."

Reilly patted her hand. "We're probably getting upset over nothing. I'm sure Sam can clear all this up."

"What did this Mr. Womac look like?" Reilly asked so she could describe him to Sam.

"Oh, he was . . . ah . . . handsome in a rugged sort of way. He had the most piercing blue eyes. They reminded me so much of yours, except darker. His hair was brown and streaked with blond. And he's surprisingly well read."

The bell over the door tinkled as Reilly's first customer walked in, putting an end to their conversation.

"Oh, I'd better be leaving." Susan leaned over and whispered, "Tell me later what Sam says."

"I will. Thanks."

And when Reilly returned home that evening, she told Sam what had happened to Susan.

"Damn, will the bastard never give up? He's followed me everywhere I go. I won a pile of money off him one night and he didn't like it. He thinks I

99

cheated him, which I didn't, and wants to collect his money."

Reilly released the breath she had been holding. "Oh, I'm so relieved. I'll tell Susan first thing in the morning. He scared her to death."

"Don't worry. He's probably already left town since he can't collect from a dead man."

Reilly's information helped relieve Sam's mind too. Mason knew something fishy was going on and was trying to get to the bottom of it. Somehow, Sam was going to have to let Mason know he was alive. But how was he going to keep Reilly out of the house long enough so he could do it?

Chapter 10

Reilly dug deeply into the cabinet until she reached the hamper. She stood at the counter and filled the basket with crispy fried chicken, fresh-baked bread, deviled eggs, fruit, and hard cheese.

When she glanced out the window, her hands stilled in motion. Propped against a wild peach tree, Sam surveyed his surroundings. She knew he shouldn't be outside where anyone might see him, but she could understand his boredom and need for fresh air.

He broke a limb from the tree and stripped away the leaves. She watched as he pulled a knife from his pocket and applied it to the limb. His arms were strong and supple, his strokes sure and smooth, as the shavings fell to the ground.

A funny fluttering set up in Reilly's stomach as she watched him, the food forgotten. He propped one leg against the tree and continued to whittle. She couldn't take her eyes off him. He was so handsome and so unattainable. Oh, he talked a good talk and hinted at untold pleasures that sent her blood into a dangerous heat, but never once had he mentioned ever settling down. Reilly knew he was restless. His injury was healing, and he was eager to move on. She could feel it in her heart. She didn't want him to leave. Not yet.

She had never put much thought into the idea of marrying. She would be lying to herself if she denied that she had never thought about it. She had, but never to this extent. The idea had always been in the back of her mind. She'd just assumed that someday she'd meet someone and fall in love, and the natural order of those things would follow. But until her encounter with Sam, she'd always thought she didn't have time to fall in love. She had so many things she wanted to accomplish. Photography was changing by leaps and bounds and she wanted to be a part of that change. Or so she had thought, until a brown-eyed gambler had entered her life. She had to get a grip on her thoughts; she was behaving like a pea hen.

She called through the window, "Sam, would you like to go with me this afternoon? I have food."

"What kind of food?" His eyes sparkled with mischief as he pushed away from the tree and sauntered toward the window.

She lifted the basket for his inspection.

He eyed the food and licked his lips.

"I know you're bored to death," she said. "Would you like to accompany me this afternoon?"

"Where're you going?"

"To the lake."

"For what?"

"Sometimes I need to get away. I thought we could have a picnic."

"In the woods?"

"I have a rowboat we can take out. It's beautiful out on the lake, and no one will see you. And right in the middle of the lake there's a small island. We could have our picnic there."

Well, so much for his plan of getting a message to Mason today, Sam thought with a frown marring his brow.

Reilly saw his frown. Didn't he want to go with

102

her? "I know the beauty of the lake can't compare to the wonder of a smoke-filled saloon crowded with unwashed bodies. But I thought you might enjoy getting out for a while."

"Don't get your feathers in an uproar. It sounds good to me. I've never been on a picnic."

Sam hitched up the swayback and helped Reilly put the boat in the wagon. His brow hiked up in disbelief at the boat. "Are you sure this thing will float?"

"It will. I take it out all the time. If you'll get under the boat until we're out of danger of anyone seeing us, you'll be safe."

Famous last words, he thought later as he bumped along, his head vying for the same space as the narrow seats in the boat. Once more he was folded like a slice of bread in narrow confines. He made a mental note to do something about Reilly's penchant for dark places. If he wasn't careful, she would end up smothering him. It seemed to take forever before she pulled the wagon to a halt. He unwrapped his long legs and climbed onto the seat beside her.

They rode along in silence, enjoying the peace and beauty of their surroundings. Sam had to caution himself to remain callous to the outdoors he loved so much. He was a gambler and should have no appreciation for the sweep of the land, or the mountains that played host to an abundance of wildlife; and he had to remember that. Yet he couldn't control the sparkle that entered his eyes when deer lifted their heads from nibbling the thick lush grass that grew along the water's edge, then scampered into the protection of the woods.

Reilly let the horse have his fill of water before she looped the reins in the shade. Sam couldn't help appreciating her thoughtfulness for everything she met, even the lazy horse.

Before he could reach her side, she was dragging

the boat out of the wagon. Was there no job too tough for her? "If you'll give me a minute, I'll help you."

"I'm sorry, I didn't think. I'm used to doing it by myself."

"Well, you shouldn't. And another thing, do you always take off by yourself into God knows where?"

"Yes. Is there any reason I shouldn't?"

"Do you ever think of the danger you could encounter?"

"I can take care of myself. I'm not completely unprotected." She pulled a revolver from beneath the bench and waved it through the air. "I'm not that foolish."

"Do you know how to use it?" Sam asked, reaching for the Colt.

"I do." She lifted the gun and took a bead on the distant limb of an alder. The shot rang through the air and the limb fell to the ground. Sam didn't think he'd be able to hear anything for a week. His head rang with vibrations.

"Would you like to shoot it? I can show you how."

He lifted the heavy gun awkwardly and took a bead just like Reilly had. He missed the tree. He looked at her sheepishly. "I'm not much of a marksman."

"I noticed." She smiled sweetly at him. Couldn't this man do anything? This man of her dreams?

They pulled the rowboat to the water's edge and placed the basket of food inside with her gun and a blanket. All the while Reilly cautioned him to be sure and get the oars. When they were all set, he griped about having to get his feet wet to push off the boat. Reilly sighed deeply and shucked her boots and, rolling up her pants, jumped from the small craft and pushed them off. So much for her Prince Charming, she thought. Sam wouldn't even get his feet wet for her. How could she expect him to protect her if anything serious happened?

"Would you like me to oar?"

If he oared the way he used a gun, no telling what would happen to them. But she didn't say that, instead she insisted, "No, you need to take care of that injury. We wouldn't want you to pull something loose."

"Is that a polite way of saying thanks, but no thanks?"

She smiled sweetly again and took the oars in hand. "Oh, what a glorious day," she said to the bright blue sky.

"A little warm, if you ask me," he said, wiping the sweat from his brow.

The water was as smooth as glass, and the small rowboat skimmed the lake with little effort from Reilly. Sam leaned against the side and studied her. The warm glow on her face was indicative to her surroundings. It was a beautiful day. The lake was still except for the gentle ripple the boat created. And the only sound was the oars as they sliced through the water. If he could be true to form, he'd strip off his clothes and dive deeply into the cooling depths and take her with him. Instead he rubbed his stomach and reached for the picnic basket. Lifting the lid off the basket, he rearranged the food. At last he took a deviled egg and popped it into his mouth. "I haven't had deviled eggs since I was a child. It was a favorite of my mother's with Sunday dinner."

Odd, Reilly thought. She'd never imagined Sam having parents.

"Is your mother still living?"

"Yes, both my parents are in good health, as far as I know. At least they were the last time I was home."

"Where is home?"

"The Blue Ridge mountains of Georgia. Where the pines grow so thick and tall they have to pump sunshine in."

"When was the last time you were there?"

"In the spring."

105

"Do you have any brothers or sisters?"

He smiled. "Both."

A melancholy smile tilted the corners of Reilly's mouth. "I think that's wonderful. I always wanted a brother or sister."

"I've never thought about it. I guess it was. I'm the youngest of four children, so I always had more bosses than I thought fair."

"How did you ever end up so far from home?"

"I was the restless one. I don't like staying in one place too long."

"Why not?"

"Because you develop friendships and relations. They become more important to you than the job you've set for yourself."

"Is that so bad?"

"Not if you want to be a butcher all your life."

"God forbid that you ever become a butcher. You'd cut your fingers off. But what's wrong with that, if it's what you want to do?"

"My father is a mountain man first and foremost, but he's also the town butcher. He always wanted to travel, to see this great country. But instead he fell in love and married. When my mother began having babies, his chances of doing what he'd always dreamed about went up in smoke. Now that we're all grown he's too old, so all he does is talk about what could have been."

"If he's happy with his life, does it matter?"

"I'm afraid I don't have the answer."

"Maybe someday you'll understand," she answered softly.

"You sound like you have the answer for me."

"Not I. It's hard enough to try to understand the things happening in my own life. I don't presume to know what's happening in others."

"Now that's not completely true. You're ready to take on the sheriff and his cohorts."

She wrinkled her mouth in distaste. "That's different; he's not a nice man."

"Neither am I."

"I think you are."

"Good. It matters to me what you think."

"It shouldn't. I have some very farfetched notions."

"Open wide," he said, leaning toward her with a deviled egg.

She took a small bite and chewed slowly. Sam popped the remainder into his mouth.

Reilly swallowed with difficulty. There was something so intimately disturbing about sharing food.

Right there in the middle of the lake with the sun shining down brightly on them, they had their picnic. Reilly's hands lay idle on the oars as the small rowboat drifted aimlessly. Sam fed her at his leisure, tempting her with the food she'd prepared. He patted her lips with a soft napkin when the peach he fed her dribbled onto her chin.

Their laughter blended and lifted above the high flying birds that called the region home. Raccoons, foxes, and muskrats watched the strange goings on from their positions along the bank of the lake. Sam and Reilly were unaware of all the attention they were getting as they enjoyed the food and each other's company.

Sam leaned back in the boat and closed his eyes. But sleep was the farthest thing from his mind. The warmth and wit, the softness and gentleness of Reilly was weighing heavily on his heart, and he didn't want it to.

"We're almost there." Reilly pointed to the island that loomed closer and closer.

Sam shifted his body to look at the island they'd been in no hurry to reach. It was small with a wide beach until it was swallowed up by the density of trees. When he shifted his body again, the boat rocked wildly.

"Be careful, you'll turn us over." Reilly shrieked, grabbing the sides of the boat.

He smiled wickedly and lifted his hand from the water. The crystal droplets of water dripping from his fingers caught his attention. The devilish curl of his mouth should have warned Reilly that he was up to mischief. He plunged his hand beneath the water again. When he brought his hand to the surface, he flipped his fingers at Reilly, spraying her with water.

Less delicate than he, she closed her fingers and scooped a handful of water that she splashed on him. The water fight was on. Her shirt became damp; his was soaked. Her hair lay wet and limp on her shoulders; his own curled and sparkled with droplets of water. They laughed and scooped until he discovered the container that had held the deviled eggs. He filled it and threatened to dump it on her head. She screamed and retaliated with the warning that she would hit him with an oar. The boat rocked wildly as they faced off against each other, daringly.

Never one to pass up a challenge, Sam dumped the water on her. She playfully swung the oar. He dodged the paddle and the boat tilted to one side. Before he could right himself, he fell smoothly into the water.

Reilly was mortified at what she'd done.

She leaned over the side of the boat. "Sam!" She didn't think she'd actually hit him.

"Sam!" she called frantically.

He surfaced, spitting and churning the water.

"Sam, are you okay?"

"No!" he managed to say before his head disappeared beneath the water.

"Sam, this is no joking matter," she shouted as he surfaced again.

"No one's laughing," he sputtered, slapping

toward the boat.

She picked up the oar she'd tossed down in fright and extended it toward him. "Here, grab this."

"I got it."

Relief surged through her. She pulled the oar, dragging Sam toward the boat. "Aren't you a swimmer?"

"I told you I'm a gambler and a lover," he sputtered.

"Sam," she warned in her harshest tone.

When he was out of danger, she smiled. "I'm sorry."

"That's just not good enough, Reilly." He jerked the oar.

Reilly tumbled over the side of the boat with a very brief, unladylike epithet.

Sam draped his arm over the side of the boat and waited for her to emerge.

"You're all wet, angel," he mocked when she came up sputtering.

As she joined him, hanging from the side of the boat, she questioned, "How did you know I could swim? I might've drowned."

"I wouldn't have let you. Besides, you do everything else so well I just assumed you could swim. Someone who couldn't swim wouldn't venture out in a boat just for the hell of it."

"Okay, now tell me what we're going to do? We can't possibly climb back in the boat without turning it over."

"We're not that far from the island. Can you make it?"

"Yes, but what about the boat?"

"I'll take care of it."

Suddenly, a fine leather shoe popped to the surface, then its mate. He grabbed his shoes and poured the water out before he tossed them in the boat.

Reilly laughed.

He then removed his socks and his shirt.

"Here, if you can lift your legs, I'll remove your boots," he suggested.

While clinging to the side of the boat, she lifted one leg at a time, watching as he tugged the water-logged boots and socks from her feet and tossed them beside his in the boat.

She swam beside Sam, ready to help if he became tired.

He'd wrapped the rope from the bow around his good shoulder, and he and the small boat were moving smoothly toward the shore. He beached his burden, then carried their things to a grassy knoll.

Reilly gathered small pieces of wood for a fire when she could take her eyes off Sam's broad back and rippling muscles. He was so different. He seemed right at home out in the open. Oh, he was a rascal all the time, regardless of where he was. But there was a look about him that left her breathless.

Of course, after he brought their things from the boat, he plopped down on the ground and stretched out, while she built the fire. Still, she thought several times he was going to tell her how to do it, but he didn't. Who was the real Sam Chandler? Was he only a gambler and a lover as he proclaimed to be, or was there more to him than he was willing for her to see?

Right now, he was hoping there was less of him for her to see. He was doing all he could to control the lust soaring through him. His wet pants clung like a second skin and his arousal was as plain as the nose on his face.

He tried to picture unpleasant things to take his mind off of Reilly's trim buttocks and pebble hard nipples, outlined perfectly beneath her wet clothes. Oatmeal. He would think about that; he hated the slimy, slick stuff with a passion. It only made his pain worse as he thought of Reilly's slick, wet body joined with his. So much for the oatmeal. He would think about snakes. He hated snakes, the way they coiled up waiting for their victim. But that only conjured up a picture of Reilly's legs coiled around his as he plunged deep inside her. Oh well, maybe pleasant thoughts would change the course of his thoughts.

Whiskey should do the trick. He really loved a shot of smooth-aged whiskey. Its rich color and keen bite was an adventure for the tastebuds. And the heat of the liquor when it slid down his throat and settled in his stomach, sending its warmth throughout his body, was pure pleasure. Lord, that thought failed miserably. For once again his imagination had a field day with his thoughts. The warmth of the whiskey couldn't compare to the heat that surged through him when he chanced to touch Reilly. His overworked imagination and celibate state did little to control the throbbing in his loins. Swearing soundly, he jumped to his feet and paced vigorously.

Reilly watched him cautiously. What was his problem? "Are you hungry?"

"No," he growled.

"Cold?"

"No."

"Then what's your problem?"

He turned on her and hooked his thumbs in the pocket of his pants. *Nothing ventured, nothing gained,* he thought stubbornly. "Do you really want to know?"

"Yes, yes I do."

"I need a woman."

She gasped.

"You asked," he supplied sheepishly.

"My mistake." She knew her face was wreathed in glowing color. There was nothing she could do but delicately try to change the subject. Her fact was hot, yet suddenly her body began to shiver with cold.

111

Sam was quick to get the blanket and wrap it around her shoulders. She huddled before the fire, but nothing eased the chill that had beset her body. Was it his words or her wet clothes that caused her body to shiver? It was a mystery to her. The feelings coursing through her were so new to her that they frightened her.

Sam could have kicked himself. He regretted his admission. He was a man of few words, but he should have held his tongue. Now he had probably scared her to death.

As they packed up and loaded the boat, they talked of inconsequential matters. A great yellow moon cast its light across the still lake as the boat skimmed its glassy surface. Reilly tried to count the stars in the heavens and compare that number to the times she'd wished that Sam would take her in his arms. There was no way she could put a number to either one.

Chapter 11

Tap . . . tap . . . tap.

Sam groaned and, rolling to his side, folded his pillow over his ears. Half asleep, the muffled sounds continued seeping through the pillow until he came awake with a start and bolted straight up in bed. At first he thought it was the blood pounding through his ears until he finally recognized that the sound was a hammer banging on the roof. He looked up and saw small pieces of plaster dropping from several places on the ceiling. Outside the window, he saw the muted pastel shades of dawn spreading across the horizon.

"Chug," Sam grumbled, plowing his hands through his sleep-tousled hair. From the looks of the ceiling throughout most of the house, the roof had been leaking for months and, of all times, Chug had decided to repair it now. Well, it was for damned sure, he couldn't leave the house now and find Womac.

The hammering stopped, and Sam heard the roof top squeaking beneath Chug's weight as he walked across it and started hammering again.

Dragging himself from bed, Sam walked to the wash stand. Cupping his hands into the bowl of cool water, he doused his face. As he patted his face dry with a small towel, he studied the thick growth of whiskers. He had decided a beard might come in handy at some time in the future, so had not shaved since he'd come to Reilly's house. It surprised him that she had not called this fact to his attention. He looked worse than most miners he'd seen. Now it was at the stage where his face itched all the time. Being a smooth-faced gambler was more to his liking, but if he was going to risk leaving the house the first chance he got, maybe no one would recognize him.

He heard a loud expletive coming from above him.

"Good God, that's not Chug, it's Reilly!"

Sam rushed to the window and raised it, feeling the cold morning air sting his damp face as it rushed into the room. "Damn fool woman," he muttered. Placing his hands on the sill, he leaned through the window and shouted, "Reilly!"

She didn't answer him, but kept pounding away on the roof. The next time he yelled louder and the hammering stopped.

Reilly made her way cautiously to the edge of the steep roof and, lying on her stomach, peered over the eave. "Good morning, Sam. Sorry I woke you up, but I wanted to patch the roof before the sun hits it."

"You shouldn't be up there. Come on down and I'll fix it."

"Thanks for the offer, but someone might see you. Then we'd be in a fine mess, wouldn't we?"

"Yeah, but we'll be in a finer mess if you fall off and break your damn neck. Why not let Chug do it?"

She rolled her eyes. "Sam, I gave up on my uncle a long time ago. When the rainy weather starts, I'm going to be ready for it this time. Besides, the biggest leak is right over your bed. If I don't fix it, you'll have to sleep with a bucket between your legs," she said with a teasing smile.

Realizing nothing he said would sway her de-

114

cision, he asked, "How much longer is it going to take?"

"Oh, I can't finish it all in one day, so I'll quit soon and fix us some breakfast."

"All right, Reilly, but please watch your step," he pleaded.

"Don't worry. I've climbed steeper heights than this. Pa used to say I was a regular mountain goat," she returned boastingly.

Sam muttered beneath his breath as he moved back inside and closed the window. He put on his clothes and, his nerves on edge, anxiously paced the small room, listening to the sounds above him. He prepared himself for the worst. If she fell off, he'd have to risk going into town and get Susan's help. She could get a doctor up here to tend to Reilly . . . that is, if the little fool survived the fall. The next time he saw Chug, he swore he'd ring the bastard's wiry neck.

When he heard the hammer banging away over the bed, he left the room. He needed something to do, anything that would take his mind off his worries. An idea came to his mind. Reilly was forever doing something for him, so he'd fix breakfast for her this time.

Shortly, Reilly came through the back door. She couldn't believe her eyes when she saw Sam standing at the stove, flipping a flapjack in the skillet.

When he turned around, he saw her mouth drop open in astonishment. As added entertainment, he picked up the platter and positioning it behind his back, he flipped the flapjack high into the air and turned to catch it on the platter. It missed and landed on the floor.

Reilly burst out laughing.

Clucking his tongue and nodding his head, he said with a grin. "I wanted to impress you."

"I'm impressed," she admitted.

Picking up the flapjack, he discarded it and turned back to the stove. "Hungry?" he asked over his shoulder.

"Starved," she said, walking over to stand beside him. She watched as he poured a perfectly round circle of batter into the skillet. "My goodness, what a surprise." She nudged him playfully in the ribs and teased, "Not only are you a gambler and a lover, but a cook also. Hmmm, I'm definitely impressed."

"Whoa there, angel. None of which you've sampled, I might add, so hold off on the praise until you do," he returned with a devilish wink.

Her mouth twitched in amusement. "You know, Sam, you're really something."

He chuckled. "Yeah, that's what I've been trying to tell you for days."

"Would you please stop that and tell me what I can do to help?"

"Nothing. The table's already set and the coffee's made." He wiped a smudge of dirt from her chin. "This is my treat. I had a great time on our picnic yesterday. The least I can do is cook our breakfast."

"Then I'll go wash up and be right back."

Reilly left the kitchen with a broad smile spanning her face. When she returned, Sam was scooping up another flapjack and stacking it atop several others.

"Only a couple more and we're ready to eat. I hope you have some butter and syrup."

"No, but I've got honey," she called over her shoulder as she went into the larder. Bringing out a jar, she set it on the table, then fixed them both a cup of coffee. Sitting down on the bench, she sipped her coffee as she watched him cooking. She smiled as she reminisced. "When my father and I used to camp, he cooked flapjacks nearly every morning over an open fire."

"You aren't tired of them, I hope."

"No. It's been a while since those days."

116

Sam brought over the platter and joined her, then piled four large flapjacks on her plate.

"I'll never eat that much!"

"You wouldn't want to hurt my feelings, would you?" Sam said, handing her the honey.

"Oh, all right," she said laughingly.

Removing the lid from the jar, she drizzled the thick golden honey over the flapjacks. She sliced through the stack and slipped a bite into her mouth, chewed slowly, then swallowed. She looked across at Sam. He was watching her expectantly. "They're really good, Sam."

"As good as your father's?"

"Yes, as good as my father's," she said with a smile. "You'd better eat before yours get cold."

A short while later, Sam had already finished his second stack before Reilly could eat half of hers. He poured them another cup of coffee and then sat back down. Reilly was so full she was about to pop, but to appease him, she continued eating. She pushed the last bite through the honey and plopped it into her mouth.

Her mouth glistening with honey held Sam spellbound. His finger idly circled the rim of his coffee cup as he mentally stroked her lips with his tongue and imagined their sweetness.

Reilly laid down her fork and looked up, finding him staring at her. "Do I have honey all over my face or something?" she asked curiously.

"Just on your mouth," he said hoarsely.

"Oh!" Her tongue snaked out and sliced across her lips. After wiping her mouth with her napkin, she asked, "Is it off?"

"Yes," he said, his gaze still lingering on her very kissable mouth.

"Well, guess I'd better get back to work," she said, starting to get up from the table. "Thanks, Sam."

"Hey, not so quick," he said, taking hold of her

wrist as she laid her napkin on the table. "Have another cup of coffee with me. The roof can wait for a little while."

"Of course it can. Here you've just fed me a wonderful breakfast and I jump up from the table like it didn't mean a thing." Shamefaced, she lowered her head. "I'm sorry. That was very rude of me."

As Sam poured them another cup of coffee, he said, "You aren't rude, Reilly, you just don't take time to relax."

"I can't help it. I guess I'm restless like Pa."

Sam set her cup in front of her then sat back down across from her. "Have you ever thought that that may be the reason he died?"

Her heart skipped several beats. "Yes, and I told him the same thing time and again. It's hard to break a habit you've lived with for years. We lived a rigorous schedule, Sam. Pa knew three months in advance where we were going. He'd figure how much time to spend in each area and we abided by that rigid schedule like it was the golden rule. If something happened that threw us off, he'd work himself into a frenzy to get us back on schedule again."

"I notice you don't have much of a schedule in your photography business. The only time I'm sure you'll be here is at noon."

"I know. My father and I traveled to where the business was. Here, I have to wait for it to come to me."

Sam took a sip of his coffee and leaned forward, resting his elbows on the table. "You've never mentioned your mother. Didn't she go with you?"

She shook her head, a sad smile on her face. "My mother died when I was fourteen. We lived in Philadelphia, clear across the country from where my father spent most of his time. With no close relations to keep me when she died, he took me with him." She took a sip of her coffee, then added, "I'm sure it would've been easier on him if I'd been a boy. He had his work cut out for him trying to teach me everything from scratch." She chuckled. "All I knew how to do was sew on a button, darn a sock, and stitch up a split seam when it was necessary."

"It must've been hard on a young girl losing her mother and then finding herself uprooted from her home and her friends."

Reilly's heart suddenly tightened. She gazed ruefully at Sam as memories of her lonely childhood flitted through her mind. No one, not even Susan, knew the pain of those years. She had locked them away in a secret chamber of her heart and had tried to keep them there. Now, for reasons unknown to her, she wanted to tell Sam.

Finally she spoke, trying to keep her voice from quivering. "Yes, losing my m-mother was devastating, as it would be to any child. In t-truth, she was the only friend I had. She . . . she understood why I was—" she gulped back the tears forming in her throat.

Sam reached across the table and clasped her hand and said softly, "I'm a good listener, angel. But if you don't want to talk about it, I'll understand."

Her eyes were bright with unshed tears. "I do, but it's . . . it's hard to tell someone that . . . that you drove off your friends," she blurted out. "I behaved so horribly, no one wanted to be around me."

"Then you were not the Reilly I know now. Just what thing did you do?" he urged, lightly squeezing her hand.

"I was eight-years-old when the War Between the States was over. Most all my classmates' fathers came home, except of course, those who had died during the war. Pa came home only on rare occasions. While my friends would talk about the things they'd done with their fathers, I seldom got to go anywhere or do anything with mine." She sniffed. "Well, I started

119

bragging about how famous my father was, that he was making all this money out West, that one day my mother and I were going to move out West and live with him. He was going to build us this big house with lots of land around it. Later, I'd feel ashamed of myself for lying, but it didn't stop me from doing it again and again.''

"Reilly, you were only a child. You felt different from all your friends and that was the only way you knew to . . . well . . . even the score, you might say.''

She gazed across the table at him and said, "Well, one day my mother overheard my outlandish tale as I was talking with a schoolmate in front of the house. Mother talked to me about it, and we shed a barrel of tears together. She had always wondered why I never brought children home to play with me and then she understood why.''

"Shortly after that mother-daughter talk, Pa came home. One evening while we were having supper, out of the clear blue, my mother said she'd decided she was ready to move out West. Pa was so happy, I thought he'd burst the buttons off his shirt. For the first time in fourteen years, we were going to be a real family.''

Now the tears she had been holding back, spilled over the rims of her eyes. "Then Mother got sick. Each day, her condition worsened and she was wasting away right before our eyes. And then she died, and with her, our dreams of being a family. I convinced myself that this horrible event in my life was my punishment for lying to my peers. I never had a chance to win back their friendships, and I wanted to, I really did. But there wasn't time. We left almost immediately.''

Sam's voice was raw with emotion when he asked, "Did you tell your father what was happening to you emotionally?''

"No. When Mother died, I knew his hopes and

dreams had been shattered just like mine. If I'd told him about those terrible lies, he would've felt worse than he already did. He was feeling guilty about abandoning me all those years and wanted to make it up to me."

Sam saw a sudden glow spread over her face. It was like sunshine breaking through a cloudy sky.

"And he more than made up for our lost years. He left me with ten wonderful years of memories that I'll cherish forever."

Sam left his seat and came around the table and stood behind her. Placing his hands on her shoulders, he gently kneaded them. "You know, Reilly, it sounds to me like you really were a family. You just shared your love and lives at separate times."

She swung her legs over the bench and, looking up at him, she smiled softly. "That's a beautiful way of looking at it, Sam. Thanks. I feel better already just talking about it."

He cupped her chin, his thumb stroking her lower lip. "As I said, I'm a good listener."

Reilly's pulse quickened. She was unaware of the compelling, wistful expression in her eyes as they lingered on his full mouth. Sam watched her carefully, his eyes glittering with expectation, the desire he saw surfacing from their warm liquid depths causing a deep quiver of need to rush through him.

Sam slowly pulled her to her feet and his hands closed around her waist. As he drew her near him, Reilly knew he was going to kiss her, but her restraint dissolved and vanished. As his mouth slanted over hers, she felt a slow weakness steal over her. She savored the feel of his full, warm lips pressed against her own, his demanding and persuasive touch evoking a deep yearning from her heart and mind that she had never known had existed within her. This emotion both frightened and fascinated her.

And then from some far corner of her mind, a voice called a warning to her.

Gently, she broke the kiss. Her breathing unsteady, she stepped from his arms and turned from him. She folded her arms around her shoulders as though a chill had suddenly claimed her. But it wasn't a chill sweeping through her, but a heat so intense, it consumed her.

Sam drew a mask of iron over his face to hide the turmoil going on inside him. "Well hell, at least you liked my flapjacks," he said in his usual cocky manner.

His response caused her to smile and helped ease the tension inside her. "Yes, I liked them very much."

"Then what can I do to make you like my kisses too?"

"Sam," she said, turning to face him, "we're living together under unusual circumstances. When I brought you here to my house, my concern was to save your life because I knew you were innocent. We've been together a lot as a result of this. But believe me when I say that I did not have in mind an intimate relationship with you."

Sam shifted his weight from one foot to the other. He rubbed his bristled chin. "Would you like me better if I shaved? Some women find whiskers annoying."

Reilly couldn't believe what she was hearing. It was as though he hadn't heard anything she had just told him. "Your whiskers have nothing to do with what I just said." She paused. "You admitted yesterday that you ah . . . well, you know, needed a woman. What I'm trying to beat into your thick head is that I am *not* that woman."

"Only time will tell," he said with a cocksure grin.

"Well, right now I don't have time to argue with you. I need to go to the studio."

"I thought you weren't finished on the roof."

"I'm not. I just think it's better that I spend more time away from you."

"Running from me, huh?"

"With the mood you're in now, darned right I am."

She lifted the kettle of water from the stove that she had started heating before she'd gone up on the roof. "I'll have my bath now and fix yours next."

While Reilly bathed, Sam cleaned up the kitchen. Reilly had said it was better that she spent more time away from him. Well, she had given him the first opportunity to get word to Mason that he was alive. But he needed more time than just a couple of hours.

An inkling of an idea started forming in his mind. He knew exactly how he was going to gain that time.

Chapter 12

Sam watched Reilly from the bed as he idly shuffled his cards. Her britches pulled tightly across her buttocks as she bent over and tossed her hair forward until the long wavy tresses grazed the floor. As she vigorously brushed the underside, the morning sun splashed through the window, striking her hair with its golden brilliance.

Sam was racked with guilt about what he had in store for her. Reilly was a lady, regardless that she didn't dress like one. He respected her and enjoyed her company. He had only teased her about lovemaking because her response was so delightful, though in truth being around her so much and trying to keep his hands off her was driving him insane. She was honest and trustworthy and she trusted him. Now he might ruin it all, but he saw no other way to handle his dilemma. She was going to be mad as hell at him, but business was business—he had to contact Mason.

Straightening, Reilly brushed over her hair again, then picked up her ribbon. As she gathered the thick mass at the back of her head and started to tie it, Sam's hand on her wrist startled her. "Don't go into work today. Stay here with me. I'm sure we can find something to do to pass the time," he said, then slyly looked toward the bed.

His remark flew all over her. "No, Sam. You're perfectly capable of taking care of yourself now, and I need to spend more time at work."

Sam released her wrist. "Well, you can't say I didn't try." He walked back to the bed and sat down, picking up the deck of cards again.

"I'll get your bath water. It should be hot by now."

After quickly tying back her hair, she started toward the door.

"Would you mind making sure it's hot? It hasn't been hot enough the last few times."

His demanding attitude caused the hair to rise on the back of her neck. She whipped around to face him. "You can fix—" She saw him grimacing as he massaged the area around his wound. Was he really in pain, or was it an act? As she walked toward the bed, he looked up at her and smiled tightly.

"Is it hurting?" she asked suspiciously.

"Oh, every once in a while, I get a twinge."

"Hmm . . . maybe I ought to have a look at it," she said, sitting down on the bed beside him. "Did you knock it when you fell out of the boat yesterday?"

"I don't know." He watched her closely as she gingerly removed the bandage, breathing in the clean scent of her bath soap as it wafted from her body. As she lightly touched the area around the wound, Sam shuddered, not from the pain, but from the gentle touch of her warm fingers.

Reilly felt him flinch. A faint redness circled the wound, but it wasn't from infection, just part of the healing process. "I don't think you need the bandage now. After you bathe, just pat it dry." She rose from beside him. "I'll get your water now."

The water Reilly had started heating earlier, one kettle on the hearth and one on the stove, were both hot, as was her temper. She knew exactly what he was up to and she was so mad she could bite nails. So, he wanted her to stay home and entertain him in bed all day. She should have known it would come to this. After all, he was an extremely virile man, positively reeking with sexuality, and obviously used to having his way with women. Well, here was one woman he wouldn't have.

So he wanted his bath water hot. Well, she'd give it to him hot! Reilly waited until both kettles of water came to a rolling, bubbly boil, then one kettle in each hand, she carried them to the bedroom.

Sam fixed his eyes on Reilly's rounded buttocks as she poured the hot water into the tub. Desire shot like a flaming arrow to his loins. Gritting his teeth against the pain, he picked up his cards.

As Reilly turned to leave she glanced toward Sam as he lay on his side, playing his usual game of solitaire. Her eyes roamed the length of his muscular body. He looked so handsome, so thoroughly male with the blanket draping only his lower body. She wondered if he had removed his clothes and was naked beneath the blanket. That thought played havoc with her senses.

She quickly averted her gaze to his face and their eyes locked. He gave her a naughty, provocative grin. Damn his hide, he knew he was getting under her skin. And that got her dander up. Reilly turned on her heel and quickly left the room, hearing Sam's laughter behind her.

Finally, Reilly had filled the tub to within a few inches of the top. Her arms aching and her face sweaty from the steam rising from the tub, she fixed her hands on her hips and glared at him. "From now on, Sam, if you want a hot bath, you can fix it yourself. Your arm could use the exercise." Her cheeks a vivid red, she hissed, "If you find it too strenuous, then forget the bath. You don't need one every day anyway when you don't even break a sweat."

The grin still tugging the corners of his mouth, he said, "I'm sweating now, angel. Just watching you flit around in those pants makes me hot all over."

Reilly shot him a go-to-hell look. "That does it!"

"Does what?"

"I'm leaving," she snapped, heading toward the door. She whirled around, her eyes shooting fiery sparks. "And when I return at lunch, you'd better behave yourself. I won't put up with this foolishness much longer."

Damnit, he could never get back here by lunch, Sam thought. He laid the cards on the nightstand. He had hoped it wouldn't come to this, but she had left him no choice. He'd never met a more difficult woman to deal with in his life. Whipping back the bedcovers, he rose from the bed.

Reilly was so relieved to see him wearing his pants that she didn't notice him walking slowly toward her until he asked gruffly, "Behave myself? I think I've been doing a damned good job. Do you realize that in the whole time I've been here, I've only kissed you once."

Reilly gulped and started backing toward the door. "Stay away from me, Sam. I'm warning you!"

"Warning me about what? That you'll kick me out?"

Her heart racing in her chest, she said breathlessly, "Yes . . . yes, I might do just that!"

"Might?" he asked with a crooked smile. "Then I'll take my chances."

Reilly gasped as Sam grabbed her arm and dragged her against his broad chest. Lifting her from the floor, his arm scaled under her buttocks to support her while his other hand jerked the ribbon from her hair. He ran his hand beneath the heavy tresses and, holding her head firmly, his mouth came down on hers. It wasn't the gentle kiss he had given her earlier, but a feverish, ardent, possessive kiss that filled her with frantic, impotent fury. Squirming against him, she tried to wrench her mouth free, pushing her small hands against his chest.

Sam softened the pressure of his mouth against hers. He wanted so much to pleasure her, not to scare her so much she would never want him to touch again. Reilly's breath quickened as his teeth playfully caught her lower lip and gently tugged it, the tip of his tongue stroking and coaxing her lips until they parted. When his tongue slipped between her lips and explored the soft recesses of her mouth her world exploded into a thousand sensations. She should have felt shock at such an intrusion, instead desire built like a growing flame.

Then a sense of fear began replacing her desire; no matter how much she wanted to experience the wonder of making love with this man, she knew she had everything to lose if she surrendered. She wanted more than he was willing to give. She squeezed her eyes together as though she could shut from her mind what his mouth was doing to her.

Sam felt her body stiffen and breaking the kiss, looked down at her. Her eyes were closed so tightly, he could barely see her eyelashes peeking out from under them. He brushed his lips across her eyes. Sam knew his own body could not stand much more torment. He wanted her so badly, he hurt all over. Make her angry . . . *now*, his inner voice warned. "What're you hiding in there, angel? White hot passion?"

His remark had the desired effect. Her eyes shot open. "Don't flatter yourself, Sam. Now let me go."

"Why? I like this."

"You'd like it no matter who was in your arms," she returned hotly.

"I wouldn't say that."

Reilly shoved him from her. "Well, I would. You're just like a tom cat; you have no morals.

Believe it or not, I've got more important things on my mind right now other than your sexual prowess," she lied. "I've got to get to work. Enjoy your bath . . . your hot bath," she added slyly as she walked toward to the door.

"See you at lunch, angel," he called.

"Over my dead body," she returned.

Sam's insides were turned wrongside out. He was ashamed of his behavior. If anyone had come out the loser, he had. Still, he let out a sigh of relief that she wouldn't be returning for lunch.

He walked to the window and peered outside. Even from this distance, he could see Reilly's anger as she stomped down the road, her back rigid, her stride long and brisk, and her arms swinging stiffly at her sides. He smiled. She hadn't kicked him out . . . yet. He could only hope he would gain favor in her eyes again.

He grabbed his pants and shirt from the chair and dressed quickly, then going to the wardrobe, he brought out the carpet bag that held the belongings of the real Sam Chandler. Opening it, he lifted out his boots and tugged them on. He studied his Colt 45 a moment, wondering if he should take it. Yes, he had to be prepared in case someone recognized him, but he'd keep it hidden, he thought, slipping it inside his waistband. Finding a pencil and paper in the drawer of her nightstand, he wrote his message to Mason. In the kitchen, he plucked a worn slouch hat and a jacket that was hanging on a peg near the door. Probably Chug's, he thought as he donned the items.

He hurried to the small barn where Reilly kept her wagon and horse. Seeing a worn, dust-laden saddle settled over the rail, he hoisted it over his shoulder. Gathering the rest of the gear, he looked through the open space at the back of the barn and momentarily eyed the swayback piebald that was dozing lazily in the fenced area. Now this is going to be interesting, he thought as he strolled toward the animal.

A while later, Sam was gritting his teeth, thinking he would have made better time walking than riding this decrepit nag. Added to this, he was taking a much longer route to avoid any well-traveled roads. At the rate he was going, he hoped he'd riled Reilly enough so she wouldn't return until supper.

Finally arriving at the place where he and Mason always met, he dismounted and walked through the woods toward the abandoned mining shaft. He brushed aside the overgrowth of wild shrubbery that hid the entrance and stepped inside. Striking a match against the heel of his boot, the flame wavered, casting eerie dancing shadows on the rock wall. In the corner behind a pile of fallen rocks, he saw a leather bag containing several stacks of crisp bills. After examining it, he figured this was Mason's cut from the holdup. He breathed a sigh of relief that his friend was still using the same hiding place. He laid his hastily scrawled note on top of the bag and left the shaft.

Sam was about halfway back to the house when he heard the rapid beat of a horse's hooves approaching from the direction of town. Reining his horse off the path, he hid behind a boulder. As the rider passed, Sam immediately recognized him. Oscar. He frowned. Now why was the sheriff's henchman way out here? There was only one way he would find out . . . follow him. Hell, fat chance he could keep up with him on this horse. Still, he wouldn't know anything if he didn't at least try.

Sam managed to keep the deputy in sight until he suddenly disappeared into a crevice cutting through the boulder-strewn mountainside. Ordering the recalcitrant nag to get a move on, he reached the area several minutes later. He studied the narrow path, flanked by high walls of granite for as far as he could see. He couldn't risk taking his horse in, especially *this* horse. He hid the piebald behind a cluster of mammoth boulders and tethered him to a scraggly scrub growing between the rocks.

As he scurried up the trail, Sam took note of several crevices and large boulders where he could hide if a rider approached him from either way. Ahead of him, he saw a small hill and the blood began pulsing madly through his veins; he knew he was on to something. When he reached the hill, he glanced to his right and saw the trail that Oscar had taken. Crouching, Sam climbed to the top of the hill and, stretching out on his belly, peered below him. A blue ribbon of water curled its way through the small valley and cattle and horses grazed peacefully on the high grass. Sitting amidst the panorama was a one-story house with a porch running the width of it. Surrounding the house were numerous outbuildings and a corral that contained at least three dozen horses.

Sam noted a few men milling around on the front porch. Several horses were tethered to the railing. He was too far away to recognize any of the men. Had he come upon the outlaw hideout or was this a legitimate ranching operation?

His question was answered as he felt the barrel of a rifle digging into his back. The gravelly voice standing over him said, "Keep your face to the ground and don't make any sudden moves, pal."

Sam complied, his hands curling into tight fists in front of his face.

"Now, who are you and what're you doing up here?"

"I could ask you the same question."

"Don't get smart-mouthed with me, feller. I'm the one holdin' the gun. Now answer me."

"I just stumbled onto this place."

"You're lyin'," he said, jabbing the gun harder into Sam's back. "You follered that man in here, or

132

you woulda' been ridin' a horse. Yeah, I'd say you was spyin' on us. That's bad, pal, real bad. We got ways of takin' care of spies . . . permanently. I'd do it now but the boss'll want to ask you a few questions first."

"If he's going to kill me anyway, why should I tell you anything?"

Sam felt the toe of the man's boot scrape along his right side, knowing he was looking for a gun holstered to his hip. Moving to Sam's other side, he repeated the process. Sam waited tensely for the man to lift his jacket . . . which he did. He chuckled. "Knowed you'd have one on you somewhere."

Placing one heavy foot on Sam's back and holding the gun at his head, the man leaned down to retrieve the gun at Sam's waist.

Knowing he'd be a dead man anyway if taken captive, Sam rolled quickly to his side and in the same instant, grabbed the barrel of the rifle. The man was straddling him, trying to take aim at his head. Their eyes met and locked.

"Hey, I know you!" the man growled.

"Damn, I wish you'd never said that," Sam ground out.

Sam held on to the barrel and shoved it to the side of him just as the man squeezed the trigger. The bullet cut the ground mere inches from his head. Sam lunged forward from the waist and ducked his head and shoulders between the man's spread legs. Feeling the sudden surge of strength that flows through a man's veins when he's fighting for his life, Sam came to his knees, hurling the man over him toward the cliff. Behind him, he heard the man's screams echoing off the high walls as he fell to his death.

Sam had no time to waste. He looked quickly over the cliff and saw the outlaws running for their horses. Plucking his hat off the ground, he quickly settled it on his head and hurried to the bottom of the trail and on to the cluster of rocks. Untethering the horse, he mounted, hearing the men's excited voices above him. They would expect him to make a run for it, which he would have done if he was sitting on a spirited horse. Instead, he stayed where he was, knowing he could never escape them on Reilly's horse. Peering around the boulder, he looked for Mason among the outlaws riding out after him, but he didn't see him. The instant they were out of sight, Sam cut across the path behind them and struck out for the woods.

By the position of the sun, he could tell the hour was well past noon. As he rode back to the house, he hoped Reilly hadn't returned to the house.

Regardless of the fact that he had almost gotten himself killed, Sam felt more alive than he'd felt in weeks. He was back at work and had had a most productive day.

Chapter 13

At two o'clock, Reilly locked the door to the studio and walked along the boardwalk toward home. She'd had only two appointments scheduled for the day and the last customer had never shown up. Since her mind had not been on her work, but on her dark-eyed, handsome gambler, she had left several negatives in the solution too long and had ruined them. Now she'd have to ask the family to come in for another sitting. With several small children in their group, she knew what an inconvenience her accident would cause them.

Darn Sam anyway! All she'd thought about was how wonderful it would have been if she had stayed home from work and let him make love to her. It frustrated her that he could so easily arouse her with just a kiss. For the first time in her life she had experienced a woman's passion, and these sensations had made her feel uncertain and scared. Would she react to any man's kiss in that way, or only Sam's kiss? The only thing that had kept her from losing her control had been her thought that she was merely a diversion for him. She was grateful that her parents had instilled strong morals in her, or she would have surely yielded to his undeniable charm. Yet, she found adhering to these strict principles a difficult task to undertake when he was living in her house. If she had any sense at all, she'd send him on his way as she had threatened. But how could she do such a thing when Murdock or his men would surely kill him if they spotted him?

Unconsciously, she jutted out her lower lip in determination. From now on, their relationship was strictly business. Either Sam helped her get evidence against the sheriff, or she'd find another way.

Sam was exiting the barn when he saw Reilly walking up the hill toward the house. "Oh hell!" he cursed, dropping flat on the ground, hoping she hadn't seen him. Drawing up slightly, he crawled quickly toward the back door. When he was out of her sight, he stood up and ran pell-mell for the house. Throwing open the door, he barely took time to close it behind him before he took off at a breakneck speed for the bedroom. Halfway to the bedroom, he remembered the hat and jacket he was wearing and dashed back to the kitchen, hanging them on the peg. Returning to the bedroom, he tugged off his boots and shoved them into his carpet bag. Pulling the gun from his waistband, he set it on top of the boots and closed the bag. Hastening to the wardrobe, he placed it beneath his other bag and closed the door.

As he started to get into bed, he noticed the tub of clear clean water. It was obvious he had never bathed in it. The washcloth and towel were still folded neatly on the chair beside the tub with the dry bar of soap resting on top of it. Hearing the creak of the back door as Reilly entered, Sam didn't bother with unfastening his shirt, but yanked it over his head, sending buttons flying through the room. In record-breaking time, he removed his pants and union suit, and stepped into the tub just as Reilly knocked on the door.

"Sam, I'm back."

Sinking quickly into the cold depths, a shuddering chill swept through his body. "Hey, angel," he called, grabbing the soap and cloth and quickly working up a lather.

Just moments ago, Reilly had had the shock of seeing Sam dismounting from her horse, a horse that as far as she knew had never had a saddle on him. Hiding behind a tree alongside the road, she'd waited until he came out of the barn before she started for the house. She could have sworn he'd tried to hide from her. One second he was there and then gone the next. It hadn't taken her long to determine where he had been on his outing.

He'd gone to another woman . . . a willing one. Yet she knew Sam wouldn't risk going to one of the brothels. No, he had to have a lover he trusted enough to keep his secret and who also would take care of his insatiable appetite. Reilly knew she ought to be feeling relieved that he wouldn't desire her now, but instead she felt hurt and angry. It only clarified her earlier thoughts. He just needed a woman . . . and any woman would do.

"We need to talk," she said, a sharp edge to her voice.

"Later. Right now I'm having my bath."

Sam looked up in surprise as Reilly opened the door. She'd never come into the room while he bathed. She didn't blink an eye as her eyes roamed over him. Had she seen him sneaking back to the house after all? Well, he'd know in a minute. Devilment was sparkling in her eyes.

"A little late taking it, aren't you?" she asked.

He lifted his arm and shivered visibly as he dragged the cold soapy cloth over his armpit. His teeth chattered as he said, "Y-Yeah, the water was t-too hot earlier. I f-fell asleep waiting for it to cool off."

She narrowed her eyes at him. "I see." Then she

swept into the room.

Ignoring him, she calmly went about the room, gathering up his strewn clothing. "This room looks like a tornado hit it."

As she was folding his shirt, she noticed the buttons missing and the sleeve was torn from the shoulder. Her back to him, she grinned. "It looks like it got a hold of your shirt, too."

"I-It's o-old. J-Just fell apart," he said, noticing his skin was turning blue.

"Well, old or not, you don't have that many." She saw the buttons scattering the floor and picked them up. "I'll fix it."

Sam watched as she opened a drawer and brought out a needle and thread. "N-Now?"

"Yes, now. While I'm mending it, we can talk. But first, I need to open the window. It's so stuffy in here I can't breathe."

She strolled by him and raised the window. A blast of cold air whipped against his wet neck and shoulders causing goose bumps the size of hail stones to pop out all over his body.

"Ah . . . much better." *Revenge is so sweet,* she thought smugly. Her eyes on the road, they widened as she saw a horse break through the clearing. "Oh my God," she whispered as she recognized the bulky man's figure.

Sam's body was shivering so violently, the water threatened to slosh over the rim of the tub. "W-What?"

Reilly whirled around. "Sheriff Murdock's on his way up here."

Sam's first thought was that one of Murdock's men might have followed him here. "A-Anyone with him?"

"No, he's alone."

Murdock was too much of a coward to come after him without his henchmen. "He's p-probably just s-shot . . . another outlaw and w-wants you to t-take a picture of him."

"I don't trust him. Get out of there and get dressed."

Sam would love to oblige her and waited for her to leave, but she lingered by the window, peering outside. *Well hell, if she doesn't care, then I don't either.* Unhurriedly, Sam braced his hands on the sides of the tub and started to lift himself up. The cool air rushing into the room sent him back down into the tub.

"W-Would you p-please close the damn window f-first?"

Reilly lowered it. The sheriff was almost there. More concerned with protecting him than with his nakedness, she hurried over behind him. Grabbing him under his arms and clasping her hands in front of him, she yanked up on him.

"For G-God's sake, I can get out by myself."

"Well, you're not doing it fast enough!"

As he stood up, Reilly's arms slid down his wet cold body and locked like a silken vice around him. Glancing down, Sam saw her warm hands clasped below his navel, so close to his manhood that he could almost feel her stroking him, her small hand enveloping him . . . As she pulled against him, he felt her breasts pressing and rubbing his back and her pelvis grinding against his buttocks. The blood suddenly shot like hot lead through his veins and settled in his loins. It was the strangest sensation. The only part on his body that wasn't cold was his manhood.

As he lifted one foot out of the tub, Reilly tugged again, and Sam lost his balance. Feeling himself falling backward, he quickly turned his body, and brought his weight down on his hand to keep from crushing her beneath him.

He forgot all about being cold, his body on fire as

139

he gazed down into her shocked face. A northern wind sweeping through the room wouldn't have affected him. Their bodies positioned for making love, his powerful legs between her spread thighs, Sam could not have kept himself from growing hard with arousal if his life had depended on it. Dropping his gaze to her breasts, he noticed the outline of her hardened nipples beneath her wet flannel shirt. God, how he wanted to put his mouth there, swirl his tongue around the delectable little nub, then draw it inside his mouth and suckle it until she was mindless.

Reilly felt the power and strength of his body against her, and realized how potent a weapon it was. He could easily force her if he wanted. For a moment she stared up at him, the naked desire in his dark eyes causing her blood to vibrate through her veins. Her face flamed with embarrassment as she realized her hands were laying on his buttocks. Lifting them quickly, she placed them against his chest, her fingers entwining within the crisp hair.

She heard the sound of the sheriff's heavy-booted feet on the front porch, followed by a sharp knock on the door.

"Sam," her voice squeaked, "he's . . . he's here! I have to hide you."

His eyebrow shot up. "Why? He has no reason to come into your bedroom."

"Please Sam, just do as I ask," she pleaded, pushing against him. "I won't be able to stop him if he wants to come in here!"

Sam didn't like the thought that suddenly struck him. He cupped her chin and held it firmly. "Has he been in your bedroom before?"

"What's that supposed to mean?"

He studied her closely. "You said you and the townspeople have to pay him for protecting your businesses. What happens if you don't have the money, Reilly? He hasn't forced you to share your bed with him, has he? Because if he has, so help me, I'll kill the bastard right now."

Reilly was too stunned to even speak; the expression on Sam's face was changing drastically. His eyes, once burning with desire had turned hard and feral; his mouth had thinned into a grim line of contempt. In that moment, he actually looked as though he could kill a man without blinking an eye.

Then she remembered his insult and she shrieked with rage. "If that's what you think, then I'll be damned if I'll try to save your measly bones. When Murdock walks through that door, Sam, you're as good as dead."

At that moment, Sam's aroused member moved against her belly. He gave her a slow, lazy grin.

The flame heightened in Reilly's face.

The sheriff knocked again, this time louder. She pushed him away and rolled from beneath him. Coming quickly to her feet, she threw him a towel, not daring to look at him.

Sam wrapped the towel around his waist. "All right, damnit, hide me."

Reilly ran to the wardrobe and, throwing open the door, she ordered, "Get in here."

Sam surveyed the short, narrow interior where a few of her garments were hanging, but below them, the floor space was taken up with his bags. "Only a contortionist could fit in there," he growled. "Why in the hell are you always doing this to me?"

The sheriff knocked and called her name.

"I'm coming," she called.

She'd lost patience with him. "It's either there or with the sheriff. Take your pick, Sam."

"Oh, what the hell," he cursed, shaking off her hand. Sweeping aside her garments, he ducked his head and stepped inside. The towel getting in his way, he tossed it outside to the floor. She gave him a

141

few seconds to position his body, then closed the door, cringing at his muffled oaths.

Rushing to the front door, she took a deep breath and asked innocently, "Yes, who's there?"

"Sheriff Murdock. I need to talk to you, Miss Reynolds."

After wetting her dry lips and wiping her damp palms on her pants, she opened the door and pasted a pleasant smile on her face. "Good afternoon, Sheriff. I'm sorry it took me so long to answer the door. I was . . . ah . . . taking my bath."

His beady black eyes lowered to her breasts.

Reilly's eyes followed his gaze. She caught her breath as she noticed her rigid nipples pressing against her wet shirt. His power was in his ability to intimidate people, but she'd be damned if she'd let him frighten her with his leering stare.

Squaring her shoulders, she asked, "What brings you up here?"

"May I come in?"

"Yes, of . . . of course," she said, stepping aside for him to enter.

He gave the room a quick perusal, then he turned to her. "I have something for you."

"What is it?"

Reaching inside his jacket, he brought out a folded slip of paper and handed it to her. "A wire from a newspaper in Philadelphia."

Reilly opened it, her heart beating at an alarming speed as she read the message. *Photograph of the robbery great. Send more if you have them.*

"Why didn't you tell me you took pictures of the robbery?" His voice was quiet, dangerously quiet.

"You had no business reading my wire," she returned hotly. "What are you doing with it anyway?"

"Answer me, Miss Reynolds," he demanded gruffly.

She stiffened her back and not blinking an eye, stared him straight in the face. "When I took the picture, the outlaws were running out the door of the bank. Their images were blurred, so I knew the picture wouldn't help you identify them."

"Why didn't you let me determine that? After all, I might have seen something you missed."

"Quite frankly, Sheriff Murdock, I didn't want you telling me I couldn't send it to the newspaper. Being at the scene of a crime with camera in hand is a dream come true for a photographer. And," she added, "the money's good for a picture like that."

"You took only *one* picture?" he emphasized.

"Yes."

"You're sure?" he asked as though he didn't believe her.

"Of course, I'm sure," she snapped.

"I'd like to see it," he demanded.

"It's at the studio. If you'll come by in the morning, I'll show it to you."

"Very well, Miss Reynolds." He started to leave, but turned and said, "Oh, just a warning. The agent at the telegraph office is a big talker. It won't be long before everyone in town knows you took that picture. You do understand what that means, I suppose."

"No, what?"

"If the outlaws are still in these parts, they'll hear about it too. They just might think you can identify them."

Reilly didn't flinch. "You'll see for yourself tomorrow there's no way I can."

"I'm not talking about the photograph. You were still an eyewitness."

She paled visibly. "But I didn't see anything."

"For your sake, I certainly hope not, Miss Reynolds. Whatever, if I was you, I'd keep my mouth shut if someone's face did happen to click in my mind. But of course, you can tell me."

He touched the brim of his hat. "Good day, Miss Reynolds."

After Reilly closed the door, she leaned back against it, absorbing everything the sheriff had said. Had he believed her lie about having only one photograph? She doubted it. And then there had been his warning about her being a witness. Her mind had been so occupied with the photograph that would identify the outlaws that she hadn't even thought about being an eyewitness. Lord, she was getting deeper and deeper into this mess. And now, she needed Sam's help more than ever.

Sam swiped the shirt from his face. *Damn, what's going on out there? Much longer in here and I'll suffocate. But I guess there's worse ways to die than smothering in a woman's sweet clean smell.*

But this woman seemed to have a penchant for boxes in one form or another. First, she'd put him in a coffin, next beneath a boat, and now here he was stuffed in a closet, his feet flat against the wall, his knees crammed beneath his chin. He at least had his carpetbag beneath his butt—which might be comforting—if it wasn't opened and his shaving brush wasn't standing straight up in the mug and jammed against one cheek. Thank God, it was the soft bristled end. What bothered him was the razor that he knew was close by.

"Sam, are you all right?" Reilly called on the other side of the door.

"Sam, are you all right?" he mimicked. "Hell, open the damn door and see for yourself."

Reilly's hand paused on the latch. Still miffed with him, she decided she'd teach him a lesson in gentlemanly behavior. "You're still naked."

"Well, I for damned sure can't dress in here."

He waited. Nothing. "Reilly, you still there?"

144

"Yes," she answered.

He could swear he heard her chuckling. "Would you open the door?" he asked nicely although his heart just wasn't in it.

"Why should I do you any favors after you accused me of sleeping with that horrid man?"

"Look, I made a mistake, all right? Nothing to get all up in arms over."

"You also made a mistake manhandling me," she returned.

"I'm sorry about that too, angel."

She placed her hands on her hips, bunching them into fists, and glowered at the door. "I doubt you've ever been sorry about anything, Sam Chandler."

He grinned devilishly. "I'm sorry I stopped."

Nothing. No turn of the handle. Nothing but complete silence. God, he'd really made her mad with that remark. When would he ever learn to keep his foul mouth shut? Now she'd probably leave him in here until she cooled off. Busting down the door was his only way out. *Sure, Chandler. Just how the hell can you turn around in this tiny space and get your feet against the door? And do you dare try it when there's a shaving brush close to impaling you, and a razor that might castrate you?*

"Reilly, I'm waiting and not too patiently either."

"You can wait until hell freezes over."

"So help me, if you don't let me out of here, I'll—" the string of epithets and vile words that followed got results.

The door flew open, the sunlight nearly blinding him. Reilly had vowed she wouldn't look at him, but she couldn't help it. Also she couldn't help her sudden burst of laughter. A mistake . . . a big one.

Reilly's eyes flew toward his face. The dark scowl on his face caused her to take several steps backward. She watched as he put one long hairy foot on the floor, then shifted her gaze toward the door that was

145

only a foot or so from the wardrobe.

His hand clutching the top of the frame, Sam slowly raised his cramped, sore body and emerged from the closet. He didn't have time to work the kinks and numbness from his body before his tormentor fled toward the door. As she opened it, his hand snaked out and hauled her back against him. Reilly kicked at his shins and tried to wiggle from his arms. Sam gnashed his teeth together as the rough fabric covering her buttocks grazed his manhood.

"Sam, let me go!" she shouted. "You only got what you deserved."

Not quite *all* you deserve, she thought as she brought her booted heel down hard on his bare foot.

Sam let out a yowl as he grabbed his injured foot, and balanced himself on his other.

Keeping her eyes diverted from his nakedness, she jerked open the door. "In case you've forgotten, the sheriff was just here. When you want to hear what he had to say, I'll be in the kitchen fixing supper."

She slammed the door noisily behind her.

His toes were throbbing like a son-of-a-bitch. "Hellfire, she's probably just broken my damned foot," he growled.

Chapter 14

She had every right to tell him to leave. He couldn't leave . . . yet. Nor did he want to.

Sam raked his hand through his hair in frustration. Damn, he had never been this uptight about a woman, nor felt as helpless. She had him swinging about like a weathercock in the March wind. Damnit, having her in his life had only complicated matters, his desire for her taking precedence over the reason he had come to Castletown in the first place. He should have known better than to try to mix business with pleasure. But . . . in truth . . . she was business. If she hadn't taken that photograph, he would have left days ago and wouldn't have found himself in this damnable situation, he reflected almost savagely.

He had no choice but to make amends for his reckless behavior, though now he didn't feel as guilty as he had at the time. She might have fought him, but by God, she had liked his kisses whether or not she would ever admit it.

Sam finished dressing and, leaving the bedroom, walked to the kitchen. Reilly had drawn the curtains over the windows and lit a fire in the hearth, making the room all nice and cozy. He stood quietly in the shadows and watched her prepare their evening meal.

She slammed the lid on the kettle. "I'm a damned idiot. I ought to kick him out. Then what would he do?"

What I should be doing . . . working instead of lusting, Sam mused.

As she made the batter for cornbread, Reilly ruminated aloud, "What surprises me is why he's stayed here this long when he has another woman who'd gladly give him what he wanted."

Sam raised his eyebrows in question. What the hell was she talking about? What woman?

"Well, that's just fine and dandy with me!" She poured the batter into the skillet and slid it into the oven. "If he wants to risk his fool neck just for that, then let him. But I'll be damned if he'll ride my poor broken-down horse to get there."

A broad smile broke across Sam's face. *Well, I'll be damned! She did see me!* And from the sound of her voice, she was jealous. That made him smile even broader. Well, let her think he had another woman. Sam almost laughed outright with sheer joy.

He waited a minute, then walked into the kitchen. "Smells good."

Reilly jumped and barely glancing at him, said, "Supper'll be ready in a minute."

He took his place at the table and waited for her to speak. She busied herself at the stove and avoided looking at him. "Are you ready to hear what the sheriff had to say now?"

"Yeah, I'm ready."

She turned around and crossed her arms over her chest. "He knows I have a picture of the robbery."

The color drained from Sam's face. "Good God. How?"

"Well," she hedged, dreading the outburst from him that would surely come. "I ah . . . sent one of them to a newspaper back East where my father used to work and—"

Sam jumped to his feet, almost upsetting the bench. "You what!"

She reached inside her pant's pocket and brought out the folded message and held it out to him. "The newspaper sent me back this telegram. The sheriff read it and brought it to me."

Sam scanned the message, then sat down again. Pressing the heel of his hand against his forehead, he closed his eyes and emitted a long sigh. "Angel, do you realize what you've done?"

Her heart pounding, she said, "Yes, I'm afraid I do." Unable to stand a moment longer, she slumped on the bench across from him. "I mailed it before the sheriff brought your body to me to photograph."

Sam stared at her, dreading to ask, "Which one did you send?"

"The one that wasn't too clear. I wanted to stir the newspaper's interest first and then I'd planned to send the other one together with your death picture later."

"Damnit, Reilly, why did you do such a fool thing?"

"I needed the money. Also, I hoped it would bring us some outside help. I sent the photograph and a brief report about the numerous unsolved crimes in our town."

"I'm sure the sheriff would like to see that written up in the paper. Whew, you've really got yourself in a mess, woman. What'd Murdock say?"

Reilly told him most of the conversation. "I don't think he believed I took only that one photograph. He also said the agent at the telegraph office would probably tell everyone about the wire, and it wouldn't be long before the outlaws heard about it."

"He's right. News like that travels fast."

"He wanted to see the picture, but I told him it was at the studio. He's coming to see it in the morning. I almost told him I didn't have a copy, and that I'd

149

accidentally ruined the negative. But I decided it'd be better to show it to him so he'd know I couldn't identify the outlaws." She let out a long sigh. "Then he took me by surprise when he mentioned that it didn't matter. I was an eyewitness anyway."

For a long moment Sam didn't say anything. He had to do something and do it fast. "How good an actress are you, Reilly?"

"Actress? I don't know. Why?"

"Tomorrow when he comes to the studio, you've got to convince him that if you saw any of those men in town, you would never recognize them. If he's the mastermind of this gang, he wouldn't have any qualms about killing you to save his skin. The only other thing I can suggest is to get out of town."

"You mean hide?" she asked aghast.

"Yes, hide. Do you have anyone you could stay with for a while?"

She shook her head. "No. Besides, I don't want to run. I have a better idea. Why don't we take your death photograph and the ones of the robbery to the governor? It would prove you're innocent, and it would show him the corruption in our town."

"It wouldn't show him corruption, Reilly. It would show him a bank robbery taking place. You have no proof against the sheriff."

"Then what about the United States Marshals? Couldn't they do something?"

Hell, I am the marshal, he wanted to shout. *God, what a mess,* he thought raking his hand through his tousled hair.

"Look, first you need rock-hard evidence against the sheriff. All we have is speculation and rumor. The sheriff's guilty of charging the business owners a protection fee, but unless the people are willing to press charges and stand behind those charges, the law's hands are tied."

"How would you know?" she smarted off.

"I just know, damnit. Besides, Reilly, if the sheriff finds out that you have another photograph that's clear enough to show *I* wasn't involved, he'll know it's also clear enough to identify his men. Then he'll come after you for sure."

"Well, if you won't help me, who will?" she snapped.

"Looks like you have only me, angel."

Reilly's heart skipped several beats, but she played down her excitement. "You said you didn't want to help me before. What changed your mind?"

"If I don't, I'm afraid you'll get yourself killed."

"I might get you killed, too, you know."

He smiled. "I'm a gambler, remember?"

And a lover, she started to add. "All right, then what next?"

He shrugged his broad shoulders. "Hey, hold on a minute. This isn't exactly my line of work. I need time to think things through. First, we'll see how it goes tomorrow with Murdock and then make our decision on how to handle it. In the meantime, you go about your business as you always do."

And I'll go about mine, he concluded.

He leaned forward, resting his elbows on the table. "Now. Before the sheriff came, you said we needed to have a talk."

"Yes, but I hope it isn't necessary now. You've volunteered to help me and I'm grateful, really I am. But from here on out, Sam, our relationship is strictly business."

"Sorry, but I won't agree to your terms, angel."

His reply stunned her. "What's that suppose to mean?" Then realization sudden dawned. She jumped up from her seat and fisted her hands on her hips. "I will not . . . *will not*," she stressed emphatically, "trade my body for your help. Why, that's blackmail!"

"Oh, don't get your dander up, Reilly. I'm not

151

asking for a trade. What I'm saying is this." He let his eyes drift slowly over her. "You're a very desirable woman, and I'm a hot-blooded man. You'd die before you'd admit it, but you've got a fire raging inside you too. It would be damned near impossible to work together and keep our desires from exploding." He paused. "Now, if you still want me to help you, I will."

He sniffed the air. "Smells like the bread's burning."

"To hell with the bread! And to hell with you, too, Sam Chandler!"

"I can't do you any good down there . . . business or pleasure," he countered with a crooked grin.

Reilly was still fuming the next morning as she walked along the boardwalk to her studio. She'd had no choice but to accept Sam's help. Darn his arrogant hide! Who was he to tell her about a fire raging inside her? Well, it would be a cold day in hell before her pride would let him know just how much truth there was in his words.

Reaching the studio, Reilly unlocked the door and entered. She immediately went to her desk to put the robbery picture in the file drawer. At first glance, she noted nothing out of the ordinary. Then she discovered someone had rifled through the drawer. She kept her files in alphabetical order and several were out of place. Fortunately, she had hidden her pictures and negatives of the robbery at her house in case something like this should happen.

The search could only mean one thing. The sheriff hadn't believed her and had broken in sometime during the night to hunt for more pictures. Since the front door was locked when she arrived, she assumed that he, or one of his men, must have entered through the window in her storage room. She had planned to fix the lock, but had forgotten to do it.

She withdrew the photograph from beneath her shirt and laid it on the desk instead of placing it inside the drawer. The sheriff would wonder how he could have overlooked it and might become suspicious.

Sheriff Murdock opened the door; the bell above it tinkled. He walked on into the room and came right to the point. "I'd like to see that picture now, Miss Reynolds."

"Yes, I have it right here." She picked it up and handed it to him.

He studied it closely, then said, "I want to keep it."

"Of course," she agreed. She had another print and also knew she could easily make more if she needed them. "As you can see, there's no way I could possibly make an identification. They are also wearing bandannas over their faces, so even as an eyewitness, I can't help you."

"You didn't see them riding in?"

Sam had said to elaborate, so Reilly did. "No, I'd just gotten there. But I did hear the gunfire as I snapped the picture," she added, pretending to sound helpful. "This must be Sam Chandler here." She pointed to the blurred image of an outlaw backing out the bank door. "He had to have fired that shot at the teller as he was leaving."

"It's a shame you didn't get a picture of their horses. Sometimes that can be a dead giveaway."

Her eyes suddenly brightened. "Oh! I do remember one of them. Maybe it'll help you."

"What?"

"One of the men rode away on a brown horse."

"A brown horse, huh? Miss Reynolds, do you know how many brown horses there are in this town?"

"No, I've never paid much attention to horses."

"You don't remember any distinguishing marks

153

. . . white feet, blaze on the forehead, anything like that?"

"No, as I said, it all happened so fast."

He nodded, but the frown he always wore, deepened. "If you do think of something else, you will tell me, won't you?"

"Oh yes . . . definitely," she said, briskly nodding her head.

"Clarify one thing for me. You did say you heard the gunshot as the robbers fled the bank?"

Uh-oh, Reilly thought. Had she made a mistake and he was trying to trap her? "Yes . . . I think so."

"You can't be certain? It's very important, Miss Reynolds . . . because your story doesn't match the head teller's story."

"It . . . It doesn't?"

"No ma'am. You see, before Mr. Franklin died, he told me that the outlaws practically followed him into the bank when he entered it, and immediately ordered him to open the vault. Chandler shot him the second he unlocked it. So, there was a time lapse between gathering up the money and fleeing the bank. And . . . there was only one shot fired, which means, you had to have been standing across the street pretty close to the time the robbers entered the bank to have heard that shot."

Lord, she'd lied herself into a corner. "Maybe I made a mistake, but Sheriff Murdock, I did not see those outlaws until they ran out of the bank."

"Miss Reynolds, you must come clean with me so I can protect you. These men are dangerous. They might have even seen you with your camera. Actually, I'm surprised they haven't already made an attempt on your life, or at least given you a warning." He smiled, but it never reached his eyes. He briefly scanned her studio. "You have a nice little business here. I'd sure hate for something to happen to it. I could have someone watch it around the clock, if

154

you'd like . . . of course for an additional fee."

"The fee I'm already paying you is more than I can afford as it is." She couldn't keep the bitterness from her voice. "Now, if you'll excuse me, I have work to do."

She walked to her desk and purposely opened the drawer that had been searched the previous night. She knew he was watching her. She leafed through her files and brought out one folder, laying it on her desk.

"Do you have a busy day ahead of you?"

She had a nagging suspicion of the purpose behind that question. "Yes, I'm expecting my first appointment in an hour or so," she lied. Then as an afterthought, she added, "Oh, I just remembered."

"What?" he asked, thinking she might finally confide in him.

"I left the special lens at the house that I'll need." She stood up from behind the desk. "If there isn't anything else you need, Sheriff, I'd better hurry home and get it."

"No, Miss Reynolds. Just be careful," he warned as he closed the door behind him.

Reilly didn't linger. After locking the door, she snatched up her camera case and left through the back door, stepping through the side door of the mercantile shop. Fortunately there weren't any customers in the store and Susan was busy setting out merchandise. She saw Mr. Waters in his office at the back of the store studying his ledger.

Susan looked up from the long table where she was arranging kitchen items. "I'm glad to see you. Goodness, you don't ever come in anymore."

"I don't have time to visit, Susan. Right now, I need to ask a favor of you. Can you watch the studio for a little while?"

"Sure, no problem. Mother's supposed to be here in a few minutes."

"Good. I've left the back door unlocked. Someone might come by to pick up pictures or schedule an appointment. If anyone comes in, please tell them I had to run an errand and to come back later."

"All right. Is something wrong?"

Not wanting to frighten Susan, she called back, "No. I'll explain everything when I get back."

Chapter 15

Reilly rushed through the door of her bedroom. "Sam, you won't believe what's just happened."

Sam was just finishing a game of solitaire on the bed. For the first time, he was winning without cheating. "Calm down, Reilly," he said, raking up his cards and setting them on the table. He got out of bed and lightly gripped her shoulders. "The sheriff came, I gather."

"Yes, and he's coming up here . . . I hope."

As Reilly talked, she restlessly paced back and forth from one side of the room to the other. When she mentioned the sheriff's threat about her studio, Sam frowned. "Do you think he'd burn it?"

"No. A fire could destroy the whole town. Then where would he be? No, it's my equipment he'd destroy. He knows I can't afford to replace it." She laughed crisply. "Of course, then he wouldn't have anyone to take the pictures of his dead outlaws.

"Just before he left, he asked about my schedule today. I told him I was very busy, so I've given him the perfect chance to search the house and be done with it. When he doesn't find anything here either, maybe he'll leave me alone."

"He might have sent someone to follow you."

"No, I told him I had to return to the house to get a

lens I'd forgotten."

She opened her case and removed her camera. "Do you know how to use a camera?"

"No, why?"

"You're going to have to learn. If we get his picture breaking into my house, that's evidence, isn't it?"

"Yes, but I can't guarantee you a good picture."

"It isn't all that hard. Just focus on his face and keep the camera still. Any picture you take I can enlarge."

"All right, give me a quick lesson, and I'll hide somewhere and do my damnedest to get your evidence."

Her eyes lit up brightly. "I know the perfect place. The outhouse."

He quirked an eyebrow. "Are you *sure* you can't think of a worse place? Now think hard, Reilly."

"Hmm," she replied thoughtfully, tapping a slender finger against her cheek. "No. It's close to the back door and you should get a good shot of him. If you're lucky, maybe you won't have to stay in there too long," she said with an impish grin.

"Revenge, huh?"

"Now why would you think that?"

"Yeah, why would I think that?" he returned cajolingly. On a more serious note, he said, "If he's that anxious to search your house, we'd better get started."

She opened her case and removed the camera. After inserting the lens into the tube in front of the camera, she showed him how to adjust the lens. Next, she slid the frame into the groove. "Just remember these steps and you should get a good picture. Keep this sliding screen down until you're ready to take the picture. When you have your subject focused, remove the lens cover and lift the screen. The frame holds two plates."

"Looks simple enough. After I get his picture, I'll

158

bring the camera to the studio. Do you really have a heavy day?''

"No, I don't have any appointments. I just told him that so he'd know I wouldn't catch him." She gave him a quick once over. "You can't go traipsing through town in broad daylight wearing those clothes."

Reilly thought a moment. Yesterday, she'd seen Sam wearing her father's coat and hat when he'd been sneaking back to the house. She had a whole trunk of his clothing. "While you're gathering up your belongings, I'll go find you something to wear."

Sam took his carpetbags from the wardrobe. After placing his belongings and the deck of cards inside the bag, he closed it.

Reilly entered, her arms laden with clothes, boots, a jacket, and a hat, and laid them on the bed. "These belonged to my father. You'd better hurry and get dressed."

"I'll change after he leaves."

"Fine. When you come into town, take the back way. There's an alley behind my studio. Don't knock on the back door, just open it enough to see if I'm alone."

"Oh, I'd better take my other photographs and negatives with me." Beneath a loosened board in the bottom of the wardrobe, she removed the package and slipped it inside her shirt.

Sam couldn't help commenting, "Angel, that's the first place a man would look if he had a notion to search you."

"All men aren't like you, Sam," she shot back.

"Touché," Sam said laughingly.

She handed him the key to the back door and smiled. "No sense in making it too easy for him to get in. Please be careful, Sam," she said as she left the room.

Before she walked outside, Reilly looked through all the windows around the house, slowly canvassing the area around her. Not seeing anyone, she opened the door and walked toward the road. Hearing nothing but the usual chirping of birds and the chattering of squirrels, she felt assured no one was watching the house. When she entered town and walked along the boardwalk, she noticed the sheriff and several of his men mounting their horses. They looked her way. She nodded and smiled pleasantly, feeling their eyes on her as she made her way toward the studio. Were they on their way to her house?

Reilly found Susan alone in her studio. She collapsed in her chair, her gaze immediately falling on her open appointment book. Her eyes nearly popped out of their sockets. "Oh my God, what's happened?" She looked at the date, thinking she was on the wrong page. She wasn't. "There weren't any names on here when I left."

"I know. Several people came in and asked for an appointment. Since your book looked empty and I knew you needed the money, I scheduled them for you," Susan said proudly.

"Oh, thanks, Susan," Reilly said dismally.

Susan's smile faded. "I don't understand. Aren't you glad that business is picking up?"

"I am, but not today."

"What's happened, Reilly? Has Mr. Chandler taken a turn for the worse?"

Reilly almost laughed aloud. "Oh, he's taken a turn for the worse all right, but his health is fine."

Susan looked at her perplexed.

"But that's the least of my problems right now. You'd better sit down, Susan."

She went on to tell Susan about what had happened. She kept her word to Sam and did not show Susan the photograph that identified the outlaws' faces. There was no sense in frightening

160

Susan anymore than she was already. And then she brought her up-to-date on Sam's remarkable recovery. But she did not tell her everything.

Not about the excitement she always felt when Sam looked at her with fire in his eyes.

Nor about the tremors of pleasure that flooded through her body when he touched her.

Nor the sweet, liquid heat that churned inside her when he kissed her.

She didn't need to tell Susan a thing. The soft and sometimes dreamlike expression on her face as she talked about Sam told Susan all she needed to know. "You love him, don't you?" she asked softly.

Susan's question startled Reilly. "Lord, Susan, you've been reading way too many love stories. No, I don't love him. He's the most crude, overbearing, unscrupulous man I've ever met."

"Still, he must care for you, if he's wanting to help you."

Oh yes, he wants to help me, but he has a price, she wanted to tell her friend. Instead, she said, "Don't forget, Susan, he wants to save his own neck too. In helping me, he hopes to find out who shot him too. So, it's all business and no love about it."

"Whatever you say, Reilly. It's none of my business anyway." Susan stood up. "I'd better get back to the store and help Mother. If you need me again, just let me know."

After Susan left, for a long moment, Reilly pondered her friend's words. Was she falling in love with Sam? If so, she had to put an end to that emotion soon or she was in for a heartbreak for sure.

Inside the outhouse, Sam waited for his quarry to appear. He found a loose board at eye level in the wall and lifted it slightly so he could get a good shot of the sheriff's profile when he stepped upon the stoop.

161

The interior wasn't completely dark. Narrow shafts of sunlight filtered through the boards in the roof and the cracks in the walls. He practiced focusing the lens on certain objects around the back door until he felt comfortable with the camera. As he and Reilly had predicted, he didn't have a very long wait. Hearing footsteps, Sam peered through the crack and saw a tall, stout man step upon the porch. Disappointment washed over Sam's face. It wasn't Sheriff Murdock, nor had he ever seen the man before. Sam watched him pick the lock.

Carefully positioning the camera, Sam focused the lens on his subject. When the intruder turned the knob, he snapped the picture, the click of the doorknob blending with the clicking sound the camera made. After the man entered the house, Sam waited anxiously. It seemed like an eternity before his subject finally slipped back outside. Sam took another picture of him as he closed the door and relocked it with his pick. Looking quickly around him, the intruder ran toward the woods.

Sam emerged from the outhouse and went inside the house. He made a quick survey of each room, noticing the intruder had taken great care in returning everything to proper order so no one would ever suspect the house had been searched.

After setting his bag on the bed, he undressed, then began donning the clothes Reilly had given him. Though the pants were long enough, the waist was too small and the coarse denim hugged his thighs tightly. The buttons on the plaid shirt barely met across his broad chest. Trying to tug on the boots was made more difficult because of his tight pants. When he'd finally finished dressing, he put on the worn black slouch hat and viewed his smooth face in the mirror. He shouldn't have shaved this morning, and his face was too clean. Going to the hearth, he collected some ashes and smeared them on his face, hands, and clothing.

Since the house was no longer under surveillance, he saw no reason in taking his bags with him, so he placed them back inside the wardrobe and closed the door.

A low voice coming from behind him said, "Put your hands up, or you're a dead man."

Chapter 16

Sam grinned with relief and raised his hands. "How can you kill a dead man, Womac?" Slowly, he turned around with a broad smile on his face, his eyes twinkling with amusement.

"Good God, it's you!" Mason Womac said, holstering his gun. Pushing back his hat with his thumb, his eyes roamed over Sam. "What're you doing dressed in that getup?"

"It's a disguise. I was getting ready to go into town, but I'll tell you all about that later. We have a lot of catching up to do, pal."

"Damned right, we do," Mason said, pulling the makings for a cigarette from his pocket. Rolling one, he struck a match against the sole of his shoe and lit it. "Want one?"

"Sure. It's been a while," Sam said.

Mason gave him the one he'd just lit and rolled himself another. Sam went to the window and raised it, knowing Reilly would immediately smell the tobacco smoke lingering in the room.

"I found the message you left me. Why'd did you wait so damned long to tell me you were alive? I've been going out of my mind trying to find out who killed you. Guess you know since you aren't dead."

"No, I wish to hell I did. Never even got a glimpse

165

of him. I took a hard lick on my head, probably hit a rock when I fell off my horse. That's probably what saved my life. He thought he'd killed me. The sheriff even had Reilly take my death picture."

Mason took a long draw on his cigarette and exhaled the smoke slowly. "Yeah, I saw it. The bastard was showing it off to everyone in the saloon one night. You looked dead enough to make a believer out of me. I even went to the cemetery to pay my final respects."

Sam laughed. "I'm sure the firewood appreciated it."

Mason cocked his head and blinked. "Come again?"

"You heard right. Have a seat and I'll tell you all about it."

Mason sat down in the chair. Sam remained standing, his pants too tight to sit comfortably. Propping one hip against the wardrobe, he draped his arm over its top and told Mason about Reilly and Susan bringing him to the house and removing the bullet.

Mason smiled. "I met her friend, Susan. Scared the hell out of her, too."

"Yeah, Reilly told me. What made you think Susan knew something about my death in the first place?"

"I was in the hotel, trying to figure out a way to get into your room without raising anyone's suspicion. I'd already seen the sheriff come through the lobby. He wasn't carrying anything that belonged to you that I could see. I hoped he hadn't found the bag that had your guns and badge inside it. Those items he could have concealed on his person."

Mason chuckled. "Anyway, this woman comes bouncing in, tells the clerk she needs to pick up some things that belonged to her that were in your room, and goes right in there just as pretty as you

166

please. I thought she'd spent the night with you . . . like everybody else in the lobby. I heard the clerk tell her to leave the key in the room, so I knew I could get in after she left. I gave her time to get her things, but she never came down. I went upstairs and caught a glimpse of her leaving by a side door, carrying both of your bags. That bugged the hell out of me. And when I really started thinking about it, she didn't look like a whore; she was too prim and proper-looking. I remembered her name and found out her father owned Waters Mercantile store.

"A few days later after watching her, I waited until she closed the store then approached her on the boardwalk. Well, you know what happened there. I didn't believe her story about you charging those things at her store. You make too much money gambling to charge anything. Besides, she was acting so damned flustered, I knew she was up to something."

"When we parted, she went straight to the studio, but Miss Reynolds wasn't there. Later, I came close to asking Miss Reynolds a few questions about you too, but decided to watch both women's movements for a while. I thought they were in cahoots with the sheriff."

"Well," Sam said, "I had to cover your story with one of my own. I told Reilly you'd been following me around for months trying to collect a gambling debt that you thought I owed you. That seemed to placate her."

Sam flipped his cigarette out the window, then turned toward Mason and asked casually, "Now, would you mind telling me how you got yourself tangled up in that bank robbery?"

Mason jerked. "How'd you know?" he choked out, quickly catching the long ash from his cigarette in his palm before it dropped on the floor.

"Reilly just happened to be across the street from

167

the bank with her camera. You and your outlaw friends came riding into town just as she snapped her picture. Your ornery face was plain as day."

Mason's jaw went slack. For a moment he couldn't speak. "My God, Sam, has she shown it to anyone?"

"Just me." Sam folded his arms across his chest. "She has two pictures, but the one that shows the men running out of the bank is blurred."

"Are either of them clear enough to prove you weren't part of the holdup?"

"Yeah. Your companions aren't as tall as me, and they're holding their guns in their right hands. I'm left-handed. Reilly has an eye for detail and picked up on that almost immediately."

"Damn, this sure would blow a hold in Murdock's story that you had been the leader of the gang and had killed the teller."

"Who did kill him, Mason?"

"Cord Lillard. His bandanna didn't completely cover his birthmark. It's a big red blotch that damn near covers one side of his face. He was afraid the teller noticed it, so did away with him." Mason sighed. "Miss Reynolds will find herself in a heap of trouble, if Murdock ever learns about those pictures."

Grim-faced, Sam replied, "He already has."

Alarm shot across Mason's face. "But you just said she hasn't told anyone but you about them."

"She hasn't. Let me explain. Reilly got excited about the pictures and mailed the blurred one to a newspaper in the East. She'd planned to mail the other one later with hopes of getting more money for it. This happened before Murdock brought my corpse to her to photograph. Anyway, the newspaper sent her a wire, asking for more pictures if she had them. Murdock got hold of her telegram and read it."

Sam then told him about the string of events that had

immediately followed. "So-o-o, we decided to set Reilly's camera, hoping to get a picture of Murdock breaking in here. Instead, I got two pictures of a man I've never seen. If they turn out all right, I'll give you a copy. Maybe you'll recognize him.

"Now, tell me how you worked your way into the gang?"

Mason got up and flicked his cigarette through the window. "I haven't yet, not completely. Still, I've made some headway. Pryor, the other outlaw who robbed the bank with me and Cord, wants me in the gang. I'd say he was testing me when he asked me to take part in that bank job. After it was over, they gave me my share, then we split. He told me he'd get back in touch with me and let me know if I was in.

"Last night was the first night I've seen Pryor since the holdup. I walked into the saloon and he motioned me to join him at a table. I thought I'd have my answer then. Instead, he told me about an incident that had happened yesterday that had the gang worried. A few of the men were at the hideout when they heard a gun shot. Looking up, they saw Striker struggling with some man on the cliff. In the next instant, the man pushed Striker over the cliff. Some of the gang went after the man, but never caught him. Pryor said Striker was a mean son of a bitch and wouldn't be missed, but no one liked the idea that someone had found their hideout."

Sam smiled to himself and didn't comment.

"Then Pryor let it slip out that the stranger must have followed Oscar in from town. He was so worried about their predicament that I don't even think he realized he'd mentioned Oscar's name. Well, I jumped on it like a flea hopping on to a dog's ass. I told Pryor that I killed Striker."

Mason saw Sam's startled expression. "Hey, don't worry. It couldn't have worked out better if we'd planned it. Anyhow, I told Pryor I happened to be in the area and saw Oscar riding by, and thought it strange he'd be out that way. So . . . I followed him and found their hideout. Since weeks had gone by and Pryor had never contacted me, I decided to take my chances and ride on in. That's when I had my run-in with Striker. The bastard tried to shoot me. We fought and I pushed him over. I got scared that the men might not like me killing one of their own, so got the hell out of there. Pryor said this would certainly relieve everybody's mind. Before he left, he told me he'd meet with me tonight and probably have some good news for me." Mason smiled broadly. "So, if everything works out, I'll know where the hideout is."

"I've already found it, Mason. I killed Striker," Sam said simply.

Mason's mouth dropped open.

"After I left my message to you at the mine yesterday, I saw Oscar and followed him. Striker caught me spying and recognized me. We fought and . . . well, you know the rest of the story."

"Damnation, Sam, here I've worked my butt off for weeks, trying to find that place, and you just happened to run upon it."

Sam grinned. "Like you said, it couldn't have worked out better if we'd planned it."

Mason rubbed his chin thoughtfully. "Yeah, and now that we know Oscar's the sheriff's messenger, we're bound to get something on Murdock soon. When I'm in town, I'll keep a closer eye on the jail."

"Good idea, but Mason, you've got to be doubly cautious. If Reilly sees your face, she'll connect you immediately with the outlaw in her picture. She hasn't shown Susan the pictures, but she told her about taking them. I asked her not to show them to her or anyone else. But I can't guarantee she'll follow my advice."

"Looks like we've got a real sticky situation here,

partner. Maybe we can come up with a way to use those photographs to ferret out Murdock without endangering Miss Reynolds.''

"No way, Mason," Sam said adamantly. "I've already suggested she hide out somewhere, but she refused. Besides, those pictures don't prove Murdock's part of the gang. We'd have to arrest Cord and Pryor and then try to get them to testify against Murdock.''

"Yeah, and while we're trying to convince them, Murdock would find out about it from the other outlaws and fly the coop. Then we'd have to track him down again.''

"Right. As I see it, all we can do is hope they'll accept you into their gang tonight. Then we'll know how many outlaws we have to deal with. When they make plans for another job, you can tell me. Maybe we can catch Murdock with them when he meets with them to distribute the money.''

"Murdock might send Oscar or Neal to pick up his share.''

"As greedy as Murdock is, I doubt it. He'll probably be waiting for them right after the job to make sure they don't double-cross him.''

"You're probably right. I'd say Murdock was waiting somewhere nearby the day I rode with them.''

"I've thought of that myself. It's possible that after I left our meeting place and was on my way back to town, Murdock saw me. After all, I was in the general area of their hideout. He shot me, then set me up to make himself look good.'' Sam raked his hand through his hair in frustration. "Sometimes I start remembering things, but then it completely leaves me.''

"Well, we can't arrest him for attempted murder until you do remember. There's still Neal to consider as a suspect too. He could've come after you for stabbing his hand."

Sam sighed. "I know. Whoever the man was . . . he took my damned knife too. I feel naked without it."

Following a long moment of silence, Mason asked, "Are you going to continue staying here?"

"Yeah, for the time being. Reilly's very headstrong and independent. She needs watching every moment, or she could get herself killed."

"Tell me, Sam, are you sure that's the only reason you're staying with her?" Mason commented, lifting a dubious brow. "She sure fills out those britches mighty nicely. Looks to me like while I've been grieving over the death of my partner, he's been up here fooling around with a good-looking woman."

"She isn't that kind of woman."

"Yet," Mason stressed with a chuckle. "Unless, of course, you've lost your touch." He saw the scowl on Sam's face, but added daringly, "Giving you a hard time, huh?"

"It's none of your business," Sam warned.

"You're wrong, partner. Anything, anyone involved with this case is my business. In the seven years we've worked together, we've been very careful in our dealings with women. Occasionally, we've had to use a woman to gain important information, but that was as far as it went." Mason paused and, fixing his eyes on Sam's face, added, "Until Miss Reynolds came along."

"What are you talking about?"

"I probably know you better than my own brother, Sam. It's for damn sure I've spent more time with you. Just listening to you talk about her and watching the expression on your face, tells me your feelings for Reilly Reynolds run deeper than you're willing to admit . . . even to yourself."

Sam rolled his eyes. "Sure, I care about her. For God's sake, Mason she saved my life!" He tried to calm himself. "Look, I don't have any plans of

172

establishing a lasting relationship with Reilly, and she isn't expecting any such thing either."

"I know, but—" Mason started to say more, but instead removed the pouch of tobacco and paper from his pocket and rolled another cigarette. "Want another one?"

"No. Go ahead with what you were about to say."

After lighting his cigarette, he turned from Sam and walked toward the window. As he gazed outside, the vision of a woman's face started forming in his mind. He said quietly, "I didn't plan a relationship either, but it happened. Her name was Elizabeth."

"Elizabeth?" Sam asked puzzled.

"I've never told you about her. Nor have I told you about my partner before you and I teamed up. Burt Strong was his name." Mason turned and propped one booted foot on the sill. "He was murdered while we were working on a case." He paused, pain evident in his eyes as he continued, "Burt and I were trying to get evidence against this crooked bank president, John Crenshaw. His woman, Elizabeth Baker, was a widow and ran a ranch outside of town. Burt and I hired on as cowhands, hoping we could learn something about Crenshaw's activities through her. To make a long story short, I fell in love with her and thought the feeling was mutual. Burt tried to tell me she was as crooked as her lover, but I wouldn't believe him.

"Late one night, I was up when the banker came riding in and entered her house. I crouched below Elizabeth's opened bedroom window and listened in agony while they made love. Afterward, I heard Crenshaw tell her that a rancher he'd tried to swindle in some land deal that evening had threatened to report him. Crenshaw had killed him. He'd already robbed the bank vault and asked Elizabeth to leave town with him.

"She agreed to go with him . . . just like that,"

Mason said with a snap of his finger. "She was giving up a damned good ranching operation to take off with that bastard."

"Well, I went into a blinding rage. A few moments later, I burst into her room, gun drawn, and presented my badge. Crenshaw jerked Elizabeth's gun from under her pillow. I dove to the side as I fired." He took a deep breath before he choked out. "Burt rushed into the room as I hit the floor. Two more shots rang out. When it was all over, the only person left alive in that blood-splattered bedroom was me."

Sam hated to ask the question. "Who killed Elizabeth, Mason?"

Mason leveled his eyes at his partner. "I did. I saw her throw herself in front of her lover as I fired. Burt and Crenshaw caught each other's bullets. They died instantly."

A long moment of silence followed until Sam finally spoke. "God, Mason, I'm sorry."

Mason shrugged his shoulders. "Yeah. Wasn't a very pleasant story to hear, was it?"

"No, and I know why you felt compelled to tell me, Mason. But even you have to admit my circumstances with Reilly are different. She's not Murdock's woman; nor am I sleeping with her."

"True, but she's constantly on your mind. In this business, that can get you killed, partner. Do you think I would've run into Elizabeth's room that night if I'd been thinking straight? Only a man in love would find himself doing such a damned fool thing."

"I'm not in love with her, damnit," Sam argued.

"Maybe not yet, but you're mighty close. She's different from most women you've known. She won't let you in her bed at the drop of a hat." Mason clucked his tongue. "And you say she isn't on your mind? I know you, Sam. You're wondering how long she's going to make you wait until she lets you into her bed.''

"Now, wait just a damned minute," Sam said, throwing up his hands. Then he dropped them to his sides. "Hell, what's the use? Let's forget it, all right?''

Mason threw back his head and laughed. "Damn, this has to be a record for you, Sam. God help the poor whore that gets you when you finally break loose. She won't be able to get out of bed for a month.''

"Shut up, Mason," Sam warned.

Mason held up his hands in defense. "All right . . . all right, partner. Sorry I hit a nerve.''

"Yeah, well watch it from now on." Sam picked up the camera. "Look, I need to get this camera to her. Can you meet me tonight? I want to give you the pictures of the bank robbery and these I just took.''

"Sure, where do you want to meet me?''

"Behind that shed out back shortly after midnight. When Reilly's asleep, I'll slip out.''

"I'll see you then," Mason said, tipping his hat. "It's nice having you back, partner.''

Reilly anxiously paced back and forth in the studio, awaiting Sam's arrival. He should have arrived ages ago, she thought, if the sheriff had started his search when they had predicted. Her worst fear was that they'd found him in the outhouse, or had recognized him on his way to the studio and had killed him. If he wasn't here shortly, she'd have to return to the house.

She went to the back door once again and looked down the alley. If she hadn't known her father's clothing, she would have never recognized Sam as the man she saw limping towards her. She almost shouted with joy. Why was he limping? Then it

175

dawned on her that he was wearing her father's boots. He was used to wearing soft leather shoes.

Sam stopped. Not realizing Reilly was peering at him from around the door frame, he tugged at the crotch of his pants and a strained, painful expression gripped his features. As her eyes scanned him, she noted every thick muscle in his long, strong legs. Then she realized Sam's problem. Her father's pants were too small for him.

Sam looked up and saw her watching him. He limped towards her, a scowl on his face. As he stepped through the door, he handed her the camera. "I got your pictures."

"Lord, I was afraid something had happened to you. I saw the sheriff and several of his men mounting their horses in front of the jail right after I got back to town. I figured they were on the way to the house. That was over an hour ago."

"The man who searched your house wasn't the sheriff."

"Oh darn, I just knew we'd catch him in the act."

"Well, let's develop the damned things so I can return to the house and get out of these clothes."

"I'm sorry, Sam. I had no idea that my father was that much smaller than you. The only other clothes I had were Uncle Chug's and his clothing wouldn't have come even close to fitting you."

"If those pictures turn out, and you recognize the intruder, I reckon it'll be worth my misery."

"You didn't have any problems, did you?"

"No, everything worked smoothly. You wouldn't know by looking inside your house that a search had taken place at all." He rubbed his hands together. "Ready?"

Reilly smiled lamely. "It will be a little while before I can get to these. I'm expecting a customer at any moment."

"I thought you said you didn't have any appoint-

176

ments," he countered in disappointment.

"I didn't. But Susan saw my book and felt sorry for me, so she scheduled several appointments while I was away this morning. I can't get started in the darkroom until I have time to stay with it. Once we're in there, we can't leave until fixation is complete. Any light at all coming into that room would ruin the negative."

"How long does that take?"

"It varies. Sometimes only a few minutes, sometimes more."

A knock on the door interrupted their conversation.

"That must be my appointment now. Just wait in the darkroom," she said, opening the door. "I won't be long."

Sam complied and stepped into the darkroom, closing the door. He hadn't had time to look around the room and had no idea where anything was. How was it that since he'd met Reilly, he always seemed to end up in the dark? A faint glow came through the tiny tinted window, but not enough for him to see well. He ran his hand along one wall and found nothing in his way. Leaning against it, he crossed his ankles and folded his arms over his chest. Fixation . . . hmm . . . He smiled, almost ashamed of his thoughts. He could think of several pleasant ways to pass the time. Yes, the darkroom was sounding better and better, especially when she couldn't leave.

His mind drifted back to the previous day. Though he had angered Reilly with his overzealous actions, he was sure he was making progress with her. He'd sensed an emptiness inside her that cried out to be filled, yet she stubbornly refused to admit what her body was telling her. Trying to break through her armor of restraint was no easy conquest and Sam was not accustomed to taking things slow and easy; it just wasn't part of his nature. In his job, he never knew from one day—or one hour—to the next if he'd be alive. So he'd always lived hard and fast, determined to experience the splendor of every moment as though it was his last.

And damnit, he wanted to share at least one moment of splendor with Reilly.

Chapter 17

The day was turning out to be the busiest day Reilly had had in months. Already, she'd taken pictures of a newly-married couple, two families, and a little girl with her new kitten. Between all this, people kept coming in to either make appointments or pick up their pictures. And there was still a couple of hours before closing. She was ecstatic thinking about all the money she was making, but she wasn't ecstatic about facing Sam. He had expected only a short wait and he'd been in the darkroom for more than two hours. It was well into the afternoon, and she knew he must be hungry, but she hadn't had time to leave and get him something to eat. Maybe things would ease off in a little while so they could get around to developing those pictures. If not, she could always stay after closing and finish them. She was sure Sam would understand.

Sam was so miserable and bored, he thought he might go stark-raving mad in the dark, airtight room. He didn't know if his stomach was nauseated because it was empty or from the lingering odor of chemicals. Long ago, he'd removed Reilly's father's boots and had found painful blisters all over his aching feet. He couldn't move freely around the small room for fear of bumping into something, and though he had found a chair, he couldn't sit down comfortably because of his tight pants. It mattered little that he'd unbuttoned the fly; they still pulled tight across his crotch. And on top of it all, he needed to relieve himself.

With her day going like it was now, no telling how much longer he'd have to spend in here.

He cracked the door and listened. Reilly was instructing someone how to pose. He heard her camera click several times before he closed the door. Damn, the first chance he got he was getting out of here and returning to the house.

A while later, Reilly approached the darkroom warily. As she opened the door, light flooded into the room, nearly blinding Sam. "It's about time," he growled.

She saw Sam propped against the wall, perspiration rolling down his face. "I'm sorry, Sam, this is the first free moment I've had to come back here. It's the best day I've had in months."

"Yeah? Well, it's been my worst," he countered acidly. "Believe me, I'd take the outhouse any day over this damned place. How do you stand it in here?"

"I don't stay in here that long," she admitted.

"Then you should try it sometime and see if you like it. Are we ready to get started on those pictures now?" he asked expectantly.

"Uh . . . not yet." She would have sworn she saw steam coming from his ears.

"Then I'm out of here. We'll do the pictures another time."

"Oh, don't leave yet! I only have one more appointment scheduled, and they aren't due for another thirty minutes. I'll go get us something to eat. That should make you feel better."

"What will make me feel better is to get out of this mole hole."

"I'll lock the front door so you can come out and move around. After the Morris's leave, we'll see if we can start developing the pictures."

Sam raked his hand through his hair and waved his hand in dismissal. "Then go on. Hell, I've waited this long."

As Reilly left the darkroom, Sam heard the tinkling of the bell over the door. Thinking she'd left the studio and had locked the door behind her, he started to step out when he heard Reilly say, "Why, ah . . . good afternoon, Mr. and Mrs. Morris."

"We finished our errands in town early, Miss Reynolds. If you aren't too busy, could you take us now?"

"Oh, of . . . of course. Please be seated."

Sam ground his teeth together and drew his hands into tight fists at his sides.

"Just heard about outlaws holding up the train this morning. They killed the guard, then made off with the mining company's payroll," Mr. Morris said. "The sheriff and his men rode back in a while ago."

Reilly frowned. That must have been where they were going earlier when she'd thought they were going to her house. "Did they catch them?"

"No, but I didn't expect them to, did you?" Mr. Morris grumbled. "Oh, we heard someone at the post office say you got a picture of those robbers that held up the bank. Probably the same bunch."

Though Reilly thought she was going to be sick, she forced herself to smile and said, "Yes, I gave it to the sheriff, but I doubt if it will be any help to him. It wasn't a good picture."

"Do you think you could recognize them if you saw them again?" Mrs. Morris asked.

"No. They were on their horses and gone before I

181

got a good look at them."

"I just don't know what's to become of this town," Mrs. Morris said ruefully. "The senseless killing of that poor prospector by one of the sheriff's own deputies was terrible . . . just terrible."

"Martha and I have decided to sell the barber shop and move to another town," Mr. Morris piped in. "It just isn't safe living here anymore."

"I know what you mean," Reilly said with a long sigh. "But I hate to see you give up everything here and have to start all over somewhere else. If you could just wait a while longer, maybe we'll get some help."

When the subject came to a close, Sam was glad to have something else to think about besides his misery. If Mason had known about the train robbery, he would have mentioned it this morning. He'd said he would know something tonight. Pryor, no doubt, had to check with the sheriff first. He hoped like hell Mason pulled this thing off. That way, Sam would know in advance when and where they were going to strike next.

He suspected Oscar was on his way out to the hideout yesterday to give the outlaws Murdock's orders. Murdock must have known the time the train was expected into Castletown with the miners' payroll. Reilly had told him several days ago the mining company had hired on more men recently, so the payroll would have been big.

After her customers left, Reilly told him she'd get them something to eat. Sam finally came out of the dark room and took a deep breath of fresh air. He had noticed a privy in the alley and darted across to it, at that point not caring if someone happened to see him.

When he returned inside, he moved around the room, studying the pictures on her walls. He noticed her father's signatures on most of them. Some were pictures of towns Sam had frequented in the past,

182

and occasionally he thought he recognized some-one's face, probably a man with whom he'd played cards or had shared a drink.

He noticed a photography book lying on her desk with the initials "M.T.R." Her father's book, he thought as he picked it up and slowly leafed through it. Through the pictures, he watched Reilly grow from an infant into a beautiful young woman. Some of the pictures showed Reilly's mother at close to the same age that Reilly was now. Both had been blessed with the same golden hair, an effer-vescent smile, bright clear eyes, and the same tall, willowy frame. It tore at his heart when he thought of Reilly losing her mother at such a young age. He also wondered how her father had bore that pain and managed to rear a daughter on his own.

One particular section held him spellbound. They were all pictures taken within an Indian camp. Reilly, around eighteen or so, was pictured in each, wearing Indian attire. He looked from one photo-graph to the next, seeing her playing Indian games with the children; another, posing with a bow and arrow, the string pulled taut as though she was ready to release it; and another, sitting bareback on a pony, one long shapely leg draping the pony's side. One picture he studied longer than the others. She was standing beside a young squaw, holding a papoose in her arms, and the smile she bestowed on the babe brought a smile to his own mouth. One would think she was the child's mother.

Mother? he wondered with a gentle smile. What kind of mother would Reilly make? Probably a damned good one. She had to be blessed with patience and understanding. After all, few women would have put up with him in their house this long.

Why had she never married? She needed a good man to take care of her. She was barely eking out a living in this photography business, and he hated seeing her working so hard and gaining so little.

She deserved a home of her own with flower gardens surrounding it. She was a good housekeeper, keeping her uncle's house as neat and clean as possible. Though she didn't have the money to prepare elaborate dishes, she was a good cook. Yes, she'd make some man a fine wife and a wonderful mother to his children.

Suddenly a restless longing stirred his heart. It was a damned shame that man couldn't be him. Sam groaned, wondering where that foolish notion had come from. Marriage to Reilly was the last thing he should be thinking right now.

It aggravated him to no end that Mason might be right about his feelings for Reilly. Just how did one determine whether it was love or lust he was feeling? To his way of thinking, you couldn't love a woman if you didn't lust for her too. But on the other hand, you could lust for her and not love her. He ought to know—he'd lusted over enough women to last him a lifetime.

"Hell," he swore, passing a restless hand through his hair. The more he tried to untangle his thoughts, the more confused he became. "I just want Reilly, pure and simple . . . with no strings attached," he added.

He'd thought he might have sounded convincing when he said his thoughts out loud. He was wrong.

As Reilly made her way back to the studio, she spoke to pedestrians and shop owners along the way, hearing them whispering as she passed. As the sheriff had predicted, everyone knew that she'd taken that darned picture. Her eyes darted anxiously here and there at the many strangers in town. Any of them could be part of the outlaw gang. She felt as though a hundred pairs of eyes were watching her, waiting for the opportunity to gun her down. Lord, how she wished she had never sent that photograph to the newspaper. No amount of money was worth losing her life.

Reaching the studio, Reilly unlocked the door and opened it.

"Hey, Reilly!" someone shouted.

Her mind on the outlaws, the voice startled her and Reilly's packages went flying over her head. She turned around and saw a drunken Chug weaving and reeling towards her, one hand on the wall of the building to keep himself afoot.

Sticking her head inside the door, she saw Sam and whispered loudly, "My uncle's coming! Hide."

"Been watchin' the studio all day tryin' to get a word with you, but there was always somebody around," Chug said, leaning against the door frame for support as Reilly picked up her packages.

Righting herself, she said, "Yes, it's been quite a busy day." She walked on into the room and set her packages on the desk, her eyes shifting to the door of the darkroom.

"Musta' made a lot of money, huh?" he asked, staggering in behind her.

Reilly knew what was coming up, so she hedged. "Not yet. I get paid when they pick up their pictures, not when I take them, Uncle Chug."

He scratched his scraggly gray beard and screwed his mouth from side to side. "I was hopin' you might spare me a coupla' dollars."

"Let's see what I have," she said, opening her small leather pouch. She scooped out the last of her change and handed it to him. "That's all I have left after going to the market, Uncle Chug."

He eyed the small change, maybe enough for a bottle of whiskey. "Thanks, Reilly. I'd borrow some from Fred, but outlaws stole the payroll so he didn't get paid. Guess you heard about that, didn't you?"

"Yes, I heard." She thought about the woman he was living with and asked, "Can't Lois lend you some money?"

"She ain't here. Her sister's ailin', so she left today to go to Virginia City for a while and help her brother-in-law with the children."

Reilly's heart skipped a beat. "Are . . . are you planning on staying at the house tonight then?"

"Nah . . . she told me I could stay at her place over the restaurant. She ain't openin' up until she gets back and asked me to keep an eye on it for her."

Reilly breathed a deep sigh of relief. Lord, what would she have done about Sam if Uncle Chug had decided to come home? "She's such a nice person, Uncle Chug. Why don't you marry her?"

"I asked her once," he said sheepishly. "She . . . ah . . . said she would if I quit drinkin'. Well, I decided I'd just stay a bachelor for a few more years. Fifty's too old to get hitched anyhow."

Reilly shrugged her shoulders sadly. "So you'd rather stay hitched to the bottle instead."

"Yeah, we've been friends too long to part now."

Chug hitched up his pants and said, "Wal, guess I'll be on my way. Thanks for the loan."

Loan? Reilly mused dismally. Her uncle had yet to pay her back the first cent she'd ever lent him, but she'd never said anything. After all, he wasn't asking her to pay for living in his house, so how could she even suggest such a thing?

"There probably won't be nothin' much happenin' in town tonight since a lot of the miners didn't get paid. I'll just get a bite to eat and hit the sack early."

"See you later," Reilly said, knowing later meant at the end of the week when she collected the money from her pictures.

Following her uncle, she locked the door behind him and, leaning forward, rested her head against it, saying a quiet prayer that all would go well.

Then turning around, she saw Sam padding toward her in his stocking feet. He stopped in front of her. "Does he hit you up for money often?"

She sighed. "Only at the end of his drinking spree when he's running low on money. I'd say tomorrow he'll have to go back to work to pay for his next one."

"Does that mean he'll be hanging around the house?"

"Could be, so you'd better stay inside."

Damn, Sam swore silently.

"Tell me, if he had been living there, how would you have handled this situation?"

"I could've managed, since he never goes into my room. But *you* wouldn't have managed so well. At least you've been able to roam freely around the house. As long as Lois feeds him, gives him a roof over his head, and shares his bed, he'll never leave her."

"Like me, huh?" he drawled lazily, his naughty eyes slowly raking her body. "Except I'm not sharing your bed."

"Exactly." Unable to meet his steady dark stare a moment longer, she brushed by him and started to open the packages of food. "I think . . . we'd better eat while we have the time." When they heard the knock on the front door, Sam rolled his eyes. "Damn, I'm not believing this."

"Me either," she said, picking up his food and taking it into the dark room. Turning, she smiled up at him. "Come Friday, when I get paid, we'll celebrate my good fortune."

Brushing her hair aside, he leaned down and whispered, "Yeah, with a good steak and a bottle of good whiskey, and then . . . well . . . who knows how the celebration might end?"

His wicked innuendo caused Reilly to very nearly melt into a puddle on the floor. Before she lost complete control, she stepped quickly around him. "If you'd like some light while you're eating, there's a gas light over my work table. You can't see the glow from beneath the door," she said, closing the door behind her.

After spending two damn hours in the dark, now she tells me there's a light in the room.

His stomach rumbled as he eyed the packages of food. Food wasn't his biggest craving right now, but at least it was a craving he could satisfy. And the other? It might take a little more time, but he was a patient man. He had a feeling he wouldn't be waiting much longer.

Chapter 18

Sam fumbled around on the shelf for matches so he could light the lamp. "There has to be some around here somewhere," he mumbled impatiently.

His hand knocked against a bottle, and as he tried to steady it, he hit another one, setting off a chain reaction on the shelf. One bottle after another tumbled to the table below, crashing against each other and rolling in all directions. Quickly grabbing for them, his arm struck a metal tray, sending it clattering to the floor.

Outside in the front of the store, the camera froze in Reilly's hand. The two elderly sisters sitting on the sofa bounded to their feet. "What on earth was that?"

"A rat . . . a big one," Reilly said quickly. "I saw it earlier in my darkroom. But don't worry, the door's closed and it can't get out." *Lord, I hope it doesn't come out!* Reilly had no idea what was happening, but she wouldn't dare open the door to find out. Had Sam gone into a rage and destroyed her darkroom?

Sam stood nailed to the floor, not trusting himself to move or even breathe, fearing another disaster if he did. He could just imagine the mess he'd made of Reilly's darkroom. Damn, all because of a simple match. When no one came storming into the room, he relaxed and let out the breath he'd been holding.

He couldn't risk stepping on everything and making more noise, so he knelt and found the tray and bottles, placing them quietly on the table.

That mess taken care of, he felt around on the table for his food. A shard of glass pierced his finger. "Son of a bitch," he hissed, sticking his injured finger in his mouth.

He had almost given up even trying to eat when the enticing aroma of cinnamon wafted up into his nostrils. He remembered smelling his mother's apple pies as they had baked in the oven when he was a boy. Very gingerly, he patted the table here and there until his finger sank into something soft. He licked the sweetness from his finger. Breaking off a piece, he plopped it inside his mouth and chewed slowly. He didn't notice the bitter taste until he swallowed. Chemicals! His body broke out in a cold sweat. Good God, had he just poisoned himself?

A few minutes later, he was still alive, but the accident had completely destroyed his appetite and, if possible, had worsened his temper.

He opened the door and heard a woman remark, "I hope you catch that big rat, Miss Reynolds. But do be careful, dear. They can be quite vicious. One actually reared up on its haunches, hissed, and bared its teeth at me."

Sam felt like baring his teeth and hissing. He'd be damned if he stayed in this room another minute.

"Oh, I can handle the varmint," Reilly replied. "Thank you for coming in, ladies. I'll have your pictures ready Friday."

The bell tinkled, announcing their departure. Finally, finally, he was getting out of here. He saw Reilly placing something in her desk drawer as he marched through the room.

Reilly turned and saw him streak by her toward the door. "Sam, you can't leave!"

"This *varmint's* locking the blasted door," he said,

pulling down the shade and then turning the key in the lock. Next, he reached behind the shade and flipped the sign to *Closed*. Whirling around, he faced her with a furious scowl. "Anybody else who wants their picture taken can damn well have it done tomorrow."

Reilly slammed the drawer shut. Leaning forward, she splayed her hands on the surface of her desk. "Now, you listen to me, Sam Chandler. I needed today's work in order to pay my bills. Sure, it came at a bad time for you, but it was great for me, and it'll put food on the table." She walked around her desk and came to stand in front of him. "You have no money, Sam, at least none that you can get at the moment. I don't make as much money as you do gambling, but it's all we have to live on."

Sam passed a restless hand through his thick black hair. "And I hate like hell living off you." He suddenly felt terribly guilty over the problems he was causing her. If he could just get his money out of the bank, he could help her. What did a bank do when a person died and they didn't know who or where to send the money? In this case, he wouldn't doubt that the sheriff hadn't found a way to take it all for his own personal use.

He leveled his eyes on her. "I promise you, Reilly, when I can get us out of this hellacious mess, I'll pay you for my upkeep. Then I'll be out of your life for good."

. . . *be out of your life for good.* Reilly's heart sank at his words. For the past few weeks, he *had* been her life, his presence adding an excitingly sweet spice to her days and nights that had been flavorless before his arrival into her life. Regardless that he provoked her anger time and again, she found she enjoyed their verbal battles. Her deepest regret was that she didn't know how to deal with the myriad of emotions he released inside her when he touched her. After he left, she would never experience these emotions again, for she doubted she would ever meet another man who affected her in this way.

Reilly tried to look cool and natural, though inside she was falling apart. "I don't expect you to pay me back, Sam. All I want to do is put the sheriff behind bars. Maybe together we can do it."

Fisting his hands on his hips, he said, "Well then, for starters we can get those pictures developed."

"Dare I ask what went on in there?"

"Are you sure you want to know?" he ground out.

"Oh no, you . . . you didn't wreck everything, did you?"

"Close," he hissed. "If you'd told me where you keep the matches, none of that would've happened. I broke several bottles of solution trying to find them. Then to top it all off, the solution spilled on my food."

"I'm sorry . . . really I am."

"Sorry enough to close for the day and find out who broke into your house?"

"Yes, Sam," she acquiesced. "That is, if I have a darkroom left to work in."

"Good, then that's settled," he said, feeling relieved for the first time all day.

Not to be outdone, Reilly remarked, "But, Sam, it means staying in the darkroom again. If you'd like, you can wait out here."

"No. What's a few more minutes after spending hours in there?"

"Very well, then let's get to it."

Sam followed her into the darkroom and leaned against the door jamb, watching as she went to the sink and pumped water into a measuring container. Next, she took a couple of bottles from the shelf that he had miraculously not broken, and after measuring them, poured the solutions into the water. She cleaned off the table where he'd made the mess and arranged the trays.

Picking up the metal box that held the plates, she said, "While we're at it, I'm going to do today's pictures too and a couple more of the robbery. You can close the door now. I'm ready."

"Yeah, me too." The moment he'd waited for all day was finally becoming a reality. Unless she wanted to ruin those negatives, she had no choice but to stay in here with him.

He could barely see her with only the soft amber glow lighting the room. "How can you know what you're doing when you can't see?"

"By feel and instinct."

"Feel, huh?" he asked, imagining his mouth on hers while his hands stroked her satin skin.

He didn't know what she was doing, but heard her movements as she went about her work.

"I guess you heard Mr. Morris ask me about the picture of the bank holdup."

"Yes, you handled it well. But you'll have to be extra careful now, Reilly. If you ever think someone's watching you or following you, let me know."

"I will, but I don't know what you can do about it."

"We're going to *have to do* something about it. Mr. Morris also mentioned the train robbery this morning. As he said, it was probably the same gang that robbed the bank. If I'm going to find evidence that the sheriff's behind all this, I can't stay holed up in your house all day."

After a long pause, she said, "Sam, I want to ask you something and I'd like you to tell me the truth."

"Haven't I always?"

"Maybe, but I don't think you've told me everything, have you?"

"Like what?"

"You slipped out of the house the other day. I saw you when you were returning, so don't deny it.

Why?" There. She'd said it. If he was with a woman, she'd . . . she'd . . . Lord, she wouldn't do anything. It was his own business.

Sam scratched his chin. "Hmmm . . . I had no idea you saw me. You were acting mighty damned cocky when you returned. So, you want to know what I was up to," he hedged.

"Yes."

"All right. I'll tell you. I rode out to the place where I was bushwhacked. You see, I lost my knife and thought I might find it. Well, I didn't. I guess the bastard took it."

"Why didn't you just tell me instead of being so sneaky about it?"

"I would have . . . if you'd told me you'd seen me. I didn't want you to worry about me."

His story sounded reasonable, but she just wished she could see his face as he'd told it. Still, she'd much rather hear that explanation rather than the one she had dreamed up. "Well, I guess I'll have to believe you . . . for now. It's time to pour the solution over the plates."

"Fixation?" he asked, trying to hide the eagerness in his voice.

"Yes. Now comes the boring part . . . the wait."

"Boring? Not on your life, angel."

His husky voice gave him away. Reilly's heart beat a rapid staccato. Darn, she should've expected this from him. She quietly moved from his side and began making little noises doing this and that, nothing in particular. "Uh . . . why do you gamble, Sam?" she asked nervously, hitting the first subject that leaped to her mind, anything to keep him at bay.

The question was so off the wall from anything they had been discussing for the past several days that Sam knew what she was doing. He decided to placate her. They'd run out of conversation before too long . . . he'd make certain they did. "I make good

194

money doing it—a helluva' lot more than I would've made being a butcher, and the work's not half as messy."

"Oh, I don't know about that. I heard you put a knife through Neal's hand when you caught him cheating. That sounds a bit messy to me."

He chuckled. "Fortunately, I don't have to do that often."

"I've heard gamblers are notorious for carrying a derringer beneath their sleeve."

"Not this gambler. Me and my pigsticker do pretty well. At least we did. Damn, I wished I could've found that thing," he added for good measure. He chuckled. "As far as hiding a derringer up my sleeve, what good would one do me in a tight fix? I'd probably blow my foot off."

The conversation came to an end and Sam moved closer to Reilly, reaching out into the darkness for her arm.

Reilly jumped when she felt Sam's hand touch her, then slide slowly down to her hand where he enfolded it with his own. "I can think of better ways to pass the time than talking, can't you, Reilly?"

"Uh . . ."

"Uh?" He grinned. "Don't know?"

She flinched as she felt his other hand softly stroking her cheek. Feeling trapped, she bit the inside of her lip to keep it from quivering and tried to swallow past the lump in her throat.

He stepped in closer to her. "I have an idea you do. I warned you it was going to happen sooner or later."

"Yes, but I had expected *later*, not the day *after* your warning, Sam," she said hotly.

"Come on, Reilly, I only want to kiss you," he urged softly. "Since yesterday, I've thought of little else. Admit it, you've thought about it too."

"Oh, I thought about it all right," she snapped, "and I don't like you backing me into a corner. How can you expect me to allow you such liberties with my person when I hardly know you?"

"Hardly know me?" He laughed softly and drawing her into his arms, brushed his lips across her brow. "Tell me, Reilly, have you ever spent this much time with another man before?"

She heard her heart pounding in her ears. "Of . . . of course not."

"Me either."

"I should hope not," she cajoled, trying to sound flippant to cover up her nervousness.

"Damnit, Reilly, you know what I mean. You've seen the good side of me and the bad, and needless-to-say, I've seen yours too. Relationships have come about on less than that, I can assure you."

"You aren't talking about a relationship, Sam. You're talking about proving to me what a lover you are. Well, I don't need to know. You've given me enough clues to have satisfied my curiosity." That was as blatant a lie as she'd ever told, but he needed his ego dropped a notch or two.

His hand found her face and he gently stroked her cheek. "Why remain curious when you could experience the wonder of it all, feel the little death that claims you in that final moment of ecstasy?"

"Little death? You should've been a poet," she grumbled. In all the times she had been around miners while taking pictures, she had never heard that glorified description before. And she had heard an ear full; they would forget she was around and boast about their recent conquests, describing the carnal act in vivid detail.

"Yes, little death," he replied, glad he'd finally gotten her attention. He placed his hands on her shoulders and said softly, "But when I make love to you—and I will, angel—it won't be in a place like this. For now, all I want is to taste your sweet mouth again."

His desire for her mounting within him, Sam drew her between his hard thighs and, with a groan that rose from deep inside him, he held her head gently between his hands. Reilly's blood rushed through her body as panic seized her. Feeling his warm breath caress her mouth, she quickly turned her head, causing his kiss to fall on her cheek.

Reilly brought her hands up between them, pushing Sam away from her. "Stop it!"

"Well, hell."

"Ditto," she echoed, then said, "I think it's time to see if we've got a picture."

Sam got the picture all right. And her refusal cut clear through the bone. What was he doing wrong? He'd never spent this long a time trying to woo a woman into submission. She couldn't be real . . . she had to be an angel. If she was a real flesh and blood woman, he could have brought her to her knees with just one kiss, begging him to make love to her. But not Miss prissy picture-taking, britches-clad Reilly Reynolds.

The rest of the day and late into the evening, Reilly worked diligently in the darkroom while Sam paced the floor of the studio, wondering what he had done to deserve her rejection. If she didn't need protection from the sheriff, he'd be long gone by now. The only matter they seemed to see eye to eye on was getting the bastard. He was caught between a rock and a hard place . . . the hard place being between his legs and aching like a son of a bitch.

Reilly came running from the darkroom. "You did good, Sam," she said excitedly.

But not good enough, he thought as he turned around to face her.

"Look at these two pictures."

Reilly placed the photograph Sam had taken next to the one she had taken of the outlaws.

Sam looked. "So?"

"So? Is that all you can say? This man—" she pointed to the middle man in her picture—"is the same man here in your picture. Now we know for sure the sheriff's in on all this. See?"

"I see."

She was taken aback. "You don't sound very enthusiastic."

"Sorry." He looked across at her. "I know it and you know it . . . still, we can't prove the sheriff was in on it."

"Why not? He's the only person who knew my schedule today. Why else would this man break into my house?"

"It's still not enough. I'd like to keep these, if you don't mind, and study them. Also I'd like the pictures of the robbery if you have some extras. Maybe when I begin my investigation, I'll recognize the men around town."

"Sure. I made a few more pictures in case we need them."

"Can we go back to the house now? I'm about ready to collapse."

"Me too. We can sleep late in the morning. I finished today's work."

Good for you, he thought glumly.

"Sam, we can't leave here together." She glanced at her wall clock. "Why don't you wait until later and return?"

Sam glanced at the clock. He'd told Mason to meet him shortly after midnight. This would work out perfectly and he wouldn't have to make any excuses for Reilly about going out, if she happened to still be up. "Sure, but I'll need a key to lock up here."

She opened the drawer of her desk and took a key, handing it to him. "It fits the back door. I'll try to stay awake until you return, but if I should fall asleep, do you still have the key to the house?"

198

"Yes." He hesitated. "Reilly, are you carrying a gun?"

"No, it's at the house."

"I don't like you walking alone at this hour."

"I'll be all right. After such a busy day, no one will think it's unusual that I worked late. Besides, the sheriff and his men have had a busy day too. They've probably been asleep for hours."

"Still, don't let down your guard."

"I won't," she said as she extinguished the lantern in the studio and departed.

Mentally and physically exhausted, Sam sat down on the sofa and laid his head against the cushioned back. As he closed his eyes, he tried to block the vision that was slowly forming in his mind—Reilly lying beneath him on the bed, her eyes dreamy, her mouth swollen from his kisses, her pert rosy nipples . . . her thighs parted and welcoming him into her tight silken sheathe. He heaved a desire-ladened sigh.

Chapter 19

Shortly after midnight, Sam left the studio. Turning up the collar of his jacket and lowering his hat over his brow, he slipped through the alley. Drifting through the back door of the saloon were the sounds of tinkling piano keys and drunken voices. Deep guttural moans and passionate sighs escaped through the open windows of the brothel. Sam remembered when he'd been a frequent patron of such places. Those days had passed. Now he doubted any of those women could quench the desire that throbbed inside him. He only wanted one woman, the woman who'd sowed the seeds of this infernal ache; he wanted Reilly Reynolds.

At the end of town, a dog's sharp bark startled Sam from his reverie. Suddenly a screaming cat streaked in front of him with the yelping dog close on its heel. Sam watched until the pair disappeared into the night, then struck out for the road that led to Reilly's house.

Sam used the sparse light from the twinkling stars and the pale glow of the sickle-shaped moon to guide him. Staying close to the woods, he crept from shadow to shadow, hearing the small nocturnal animals scurrying into the underbrush.

Nearing the house, he paused and waited, his ears

alert to the sounds around him. Mason should be here by now, he thought as he quietly approached the back of Chug's shop. Coming around the corner, he saw the glowing tip of a cigarette in the darkness.

"That you, Sam?" came the whispered question.

"Yeah. I brought you the pictures. Reilly and I have already identified one of the outlaws that rode with you. Keep an eye on him. Who knows, he might be the sheriff's most trusted confidante within the gang."

They discussed the train robbery and, as Sam had thought, Mason had not known about it until after the fact. But Mason had met with his outlaw friend and was now a full-fledged member of the gang. Before they parted, Mason said he'd let Sam know the next time they were planning a job.

Sam fished the house key from his pocket. Getting ready to insert the key to unlock the door, he discovered it was already unlocked. The hair rose on the back of his neck. Something was wrong. Not having a weapon of any kind, Sam picked up a large rock sitting beside the stoop. Cautiously, quietly, he opened the door and listened. Not a sound broke the quietness.

Taking one step forward, something rolled beneath his foot. His feet went out from under him and the rock went flying from his hand. With a hard thump, his rear end hit the floor, ramming his teeth together.

Hearing a moan, at first Sam thought it was his own, then he heard it again, coming from directly behind him. Easing his hand back, he touched a slender shoulder. Good God, it was Reilly! And she was hurt, he thought, his heart suddenly pounding in his chest. Turning around quickly, his hand came down on a bottle. Picking it up, he caught the odor of strong whiskey.

He heard a hiccup and then another. Hell, she

wasn't feeling any pain at all; she was drunk! He had never known Reilly to drink, but with everything that had happened today, anyone could be driven to drink.

He smiled in the darkness as he stroked her arms soothingly. He shouldn't be thinking the thoughts that came sneaking like a thief into his mind. Alcohol lessened inhibitions. No . . . he couldn't. If he took advantage of her when her mind wasn't her own, she'd hate him later. As it was, he was having a hard time gaining any ground with her. Still, he knew she liked his kisses, so why not arouse her just enough to make her want those kisses again?

His hand slid down her arm and came to rest on her hip. "Angel?" he whispered softly.

She grunted, then hiccuped again.

He leaned in closer and inadvertently, his hand came to rest on her buttocks. He almost removed it, but noticed she didn't feel quite right. As he gently squeezed and kneaded her, he frowned. Where was the softly rounded flesh he'd expected to feel? She felt downright bony.

"Oh darlin', feels so-o-o good," came the slurred, gruff voice.

Sam jerked his hand back and cocked his head in puzzlement at the sound of her voice. As he leaned over her, starting to touch her face, her hands suddenly locked behind Sam's neck and pulled his head down. The breath that invaded Sam's nostrils would have lit a fire, but the rough, thick beard that scraped his face and the wet, thin lips that seized his mouth caused his stomach to lurch.

At that precise moment, Reilly lit the lantern and light spread throughout the room. Aiming her revolver towards the pair on the floor, her eyes widened in disbelief. "What in the world is going on?"

Sam wrenched his head free and dragged the back

203

of his hand across his wet mouth. "You drunk son of a bitch," he growled.

"Come 'ere, sweetie-pie," Chug protested, his hands grabbing for Sam as Sam rolled to his feet. "Jus' luv me a little."

"Like hell I will."

Chug's eyes drifted open. He stared fuzzy-eyed at the image towering over him. Leaning up on an elbow, he blinked his watery eyes several times then said, "Lois?"

"Hardly," Sam said nastily.

Chug rubbed his eyes and they nearly shot out of their red-rimmed sockets. "You ain't Lois . . . yore— no, you cain't be. Yore dead!"

Reilly knew she had to do something fast. The situation was getting totally out of hand. "Uncle Chug, what are you talking about? I'm not dead."

Chug's eyes darted wildly around the room and lit on the blurred image of his niece. "I know yore not . . . but he is. I oughta know. I brung him to you deader'n' a door nail."

"Who, Uncle Chug?"

"Whadaya' mean, who? Sam Chandler. He's standin' right there. See," Chug said, pointing a trembling finger at Sam.

"There's no one here but you and me," Reilly said with an exasperated sweep of her hand.

"No, he's there, plainer'n all get out."

Reilly stepped around the table and with her hands on her hips, shaking her head sadly. "Uncle Chug, you've got a hold of some bad liquor. Sam Chandler's dead. I took the coffin to the cemetery and watched Digger bury him."

Chug's Adam's apple wobbled up and down in his long thin neck. "He ain't dead, I'm tellin' ya!"

"For goodness sake, Uncle Chug, stop this nonsense. I've warned you that someday alcohol would drive you mad. Well, it's finally happened."

"B-But I . . . I kished him!"

Sam looked at Reilly and winked before he replied, "Yeah, Chug, and if I wasn't already dead, a kiss like that would've killed me for sure."

Chug looked beseechingly toward Reilly. "Y-You had to have heard t-that!"

Again Reilly looked at him and shook her head sadly.

"Chug, only you can see or hear me," Sam said quietly. "I'm a ghost, you see."

That did it. Chug picked up another bottle and uncorked it with his teeth.

As he tilted it to his mouth, Sam said, "Take it easy, that stuff'll kill you. And then you'll be just like me, Chug," he added dryly.

Chug drained the bottle. He clutched it tightly as though it were his last link to sanity. "They ain't no sech thing as . . . as ghosts."

Sam clucked his tongue as he shrugged his shoulders. "I didn't believe in them either until I became one myself. And I wouldn't be here now, if I didn't have some unfinished business to tend to."

Chug frowned. "What kinda unfinished business?"

"Actually, it's with you, Chug. And I won't rest in peace until I've settled it."

Chug's face paled. "M-Me? We ain't n-never started nothin' to finish, Chandler."

Sam scratched his chin. "Yeah, Chug, you made me mad. You did a damned sorry job on that coffin. You left a lot of nail ends exposed and every time I moved, the damned things stuck me. Hurt like hell."

Reilly was having a hard time controlling her laughter. How did Sam think up crazy things like this so quickly?

"D-dead people don't move . . . o-or feel pain."

"You ever been dead?"

He gulped. "Uh . . . 'course not."

Sam only nodded. "You know, Chug, we poor

205

souls are put there to rest for all eternity. The least you could do is make us comfortable."

Chug looked at him in drunken wonder. "I'd be g-glad to build you a-another one."

Sam grinned. "No, I just wanted to warn you to be more careful in the future."

"Oh, I w-will, I will. You can bet on it. C-Can I g-go now?"

"Sure. Here, let me help you up," Sam said, offering Chug his hand.

"No!" Chug screeched.

Seeing two full bottles of whiskey, he grabbed them and tucked them under his arm. Taking hold of the table, he hoisted himself up and stumbled through the doorway.

Sam and Reilly followed him and stood outside on the stoop. His drunken vow drifted back to them. "Tomorrow, I'm quittin' the bottle, I swear to God I am."

Stepping back inside the kitchen, Sam and Reilly broke into fits of laughter. They laughed so hard they had to hold onto one another to keep their balance.

"Poor Uncle Chug," Reilly said with tears sparkling in her eyes.

"Poor Uncle Chug, hell. Poor me. I'll probably have nightmares the rest of my life about him kissing me."

"So will he, I'm sure. He thinks he kissed a ghost. So, how did you get yourself in such a mess?"

Sam picked up two empty liquor bottles from the floor. After setting one on the table, he juggled the other between his hands. "The door was already unlocked when I got here. After I came in, I found Chug on the floor. I thought he was you, and was afraid that someone had attacked you."

"Oh," she said, her heart lurching in her chest.

"While I was at the studio, I was worrying about you up here all alone anyway." He chuckled. "My mistake. I should've learned by now you can take care of yourself."

Reilly placed her hand on his cheek and smiled softly. "No, not always. Even so, it's nice to know someone worries about me occasionally. Thank you, Sam."

Turning her hand, he kissed her palm, then slid his tongue slowly across it. Reilly's legs went all rubbery and she grabbed his arm to right herself. "Are you hungry?" she blurted, her voice scoring several octaves.

She saw the devilment in his eyes and immediately added, "I saved supper for you."

He chuckled knowingly. "Sure, if it's not much bother."

"It isn't. All I have to do is reheat it."

"Then fine, I'm starved," he said, sitting down at the table.

A few minutes later, Reilly placed a plate of stewed chicken with biscuits and gravy in front of him. She sat down across from him and rested her chin in her hands, watching him with a smile on her face. Lord, there was never a dull moment when he was around.

Sam hadn't realized how hungry he was until he took the first bite. They talked very little while he ate and, after finishing a second plate, he leaned back and rubbed his full belly. "That hit the spot. Thanks."

"A very empty spot, I'd say. You haven't eaten since early this morning."

Pushing his plate aside, he leaned forward and took her hand in his, lightly stroking the back of it. "I don't recall ever telling you, but you're a good cook."

"Thank you. I haven't cooked very much since Pa died and Uncle Chug moved out. Being alone, it seems like such a bother to do much cooking." She paused and, shyly lowering her head, she admitted,

207

"It's wonderful having someone to share meals with again."

"Yeah, it is . . . I enjoy it too. Most meals I eat are in hotel dining rooms, either alone or with strangers." He paused and studied her briefly before he said, "What surprises me, Reilly, is that some man hasn't already snatched you up and led you to the altar."

Her heart beat a rapid tattoo. "I haven't met anyone with whom I'd want to make such a commitment. In all those years I spent with my father, we moved around so much, I never even thought about marriage."

"But he's been dead nearly a year now. And honestly, Reilly, I don't know why every unmarried man up here isn't beating down your door to ask you to marry him. Hell, there aren't but a handful of decent, good-looking, unmarried women in this town. You and Susan come to my mind immediately. Aren't you lonely? Don't you sometimes wish you had a man to take care of you?"

Reilly felt uneasy with the turn of the conversation. She got up and took his plate from the table.

Sam knew he'd hit a nerve. "Sorry for interfering, angel. It's none of my business."

"You're right," she countered, washing his plate. "But in answer to your question, Sam, I don't need anyone to take care of me. Sure, this place is a hovel and I don't make much money, but I manage. Work is all I've ever known and I enjoy it. I don't want some man to tell me I can't do it."

Whoa, Sam! his mind warned. Her independent, stubborn nature was rearing its head. Yep, she'd put him in his place. Admittedly, times were changing. More women were working outside their homes and still managing to take care of their husbands and children. If they could handle it, why not let them try?

Still, he couldn't help thinking that women needed protection too. Reilly in particular right now.

A shadow suddenly passed over his face and he said seriously, "Reilly, this incident tonight with Chug. We might have laughed too soon."

She turned and frowned. "You don't think we fooled him?"

"I wouldn't count on it. When he sobers up, he might start thinking differently. Does he talk a lot when he's had too much liquor?"

"He never shuts up, drunk or sober. If you want to know the latest gossip, just ask Uncle Chug. He thrives on that and liquor. But I really don't think he'd ever talk about what went on here tonight because he'd be too embarrassed to mention it. People would think he was crazy for sure."

"I hope like hell you're right." He got up from the table and stopped in front of her. "Still, for your own safety, I think I'd better leave early in the morning."

"Leave!" Reilly's heart slammed against her chest. Her mouth set in determined lines. "You can't. Where will you go?"

"Oh, I'll be around, I assure you. I told you I'd help you and I won't run out on you."

She couldn't keep from asking. "W-will you be coming back . . . here . . . at all?"

"Do you want me to?" he dared to ask.

"Y-you do what you have to do, Sam." Feeling the tears spring up in her eyes, she quickly turned her back on him.

But it wasn't quick enough. Sam saw the tear that slipped over the brim of her eye. He placed his arms around her waist and pulled her back against him, clasping his hands just beneath her breasts. He felt the shudder that coursed through her. "Thanks, I needed that," he said softly.

"Needed what?" she returned with a sniff.

"To know you'll miss me." He turned her around in his arms and stared down into her tear-filled eyes. "But I'd like to hear you say it, Reilly."

She smiled tearfully. "All right, damnit, I'll miss you."

"Good." He pulled her into his arms and rested his chin on the top of her head. He gently kneaded her back as he said, "I'll miss you too, angel. While I've been here, I've given you a hard time." He chuckled lightly. "But you've put me in my place, I'll give you that. Yeah, you're some woman, Reilly Reynolds."

"You . . . you will let me know you're all right from time to time, w-won't you?" she choked out.

"Sure. Like I said, I'll still be around."

Reilly's immediate impulse was to move from his embrace. Yet she lingered, feeling irresistibly drawn to the undeniable tenderness of his hands as they gently stroked her back. With her cheek pressed against his chest, she heard his heart beat in rhythm with her own. It felt so right having him holding her. She wished the moment would never end. She'd known this day would come and thought she'd prepared herself for it. She hadn't. And though he had said he would keep in touch, she knew there was no guarantee that he would . . . or could. Her only hope was that one day the sheriff wouldn't bring his body to her again to have his picture made.

Sam's blood sang through his veins as his senses became acutely alive with her nearness. He relished the wonderful feeling of her full breasts crushed against his hard chest and her slender legs resting intimately between his muscular thighs. His body was tormented with longing for her. Only by exercising extraordinary self-control was Sam able to release her from the circle of his arms. "It's getting late."

"I'll fix you breakfast before you . . . leave."

"You don't have to do that."

210

"I want to," she said. Then on tiptoes, she surprised him by kissing him lightly on his mouth. "Good night, Sam."

As she turned from him to leave, he almost dragged her back into his arms. Instead, he watched her walk from the kitchen, hungrily staring at her slender figure and heaving a deep-drawn, quivering sigh.

Chapter 20

Reilly turned restlessly in bed. From the kitchen she could hear water dripping. The dripping kept time with the beat of her heart. Her sad heart. She couldn't imagine coming home to an empty house any longer. Sam had only been there a short time, but she'd grown accustomed to his presence. How did she convince her aching heart that it didn't matter, when in truth it mattered more than anything? She wanted to experience all the pleasurable things Sam had hinted at. He was a gambler and a lover. She had no reason to doubt him for he'd told her so many times.

Could she take a gamble and love him, let herself be loved by him? In her heart she knew it would only be the joining of their bodies, not their hearts. Not his anyway. And she feared it was too late for hers; she'd lost it when she discovered he was alive.

The bed creaked when she sat up and swung her legs over the side. She pushed her tangled hair from her face and, before she lost her courage, she padded from the room. A mellow light splashed under the door of Sam's room. She took a deep breath and placed her hand on the doorknob. As she stood there the knob turned in her hand and the door opened. Standing before her was Sam. She looked up into his haggard face.

"Please," she whispered, tears sparkling in her eyes.

Her plea wasn't questioned. All that mattered was that she was there, and that they both wanted the same thing. She stepped into his open arms. Enfolding her in his warmth, Sam buried his face in Reilly's hair, delighting in the feel of her. They stood in each other's arms for what seemed like an eternity, savoring the pleasure of their embrace.

Sam lowered his mouth to Reilly's and cautiously flicked his tongue against the fullness of her lips. When she sucked in her breath, the air tingled between them. He placed his hands to the sides of her head, his thumbs stroking her temples as he tilted her head upward. His lips teased and tantalized until hers opened in fevered response, moving with urgency against his, the hot wet heat of their mouths claiming any doubts they might have harbored. His tongue tangled with hers, leaving her breathless, yet eager for more. His hands roamed her body, settling on her bottom and dragging her against him. Reilly felt the evidence of his arousal and answered the pressure as she strained against him.

Before she knew what he was about to do, Sam scooped her up into his arms and carried her to the bedroom. Her bed groaned in protest when they collapsed atop it and Sam rolled her onto her back, immediately applying his mouth to the sleek column of her neck. Her hair framed around them, the glorious silken strands luring his hands to its thickness. As his mouth made its journey across her face, exploring her features with skilled intent, it left a fiery path in its wake.

She was breathless with anticipation and the beating of her heart accelerated with Sam's every touch. The blood singing through her veins made even her fingertips ache with longing. She clasped his back and let her hands explore the width of muscled smoothness; her fingers tangled in the hair at the nape of his neck and trembled along his stubbled jaw. She mimicked his play as her tongue traced the curve of his lips. He groaned into her mouth and joined their lips firmly together.

As she absorbed the effect of Sam's kisses, his hands were busy with the buttons that scaled the front of her gown. When his warm fingers slipped beneath the fabric to cup her breasts, she became immobile. The sensations flaring through her body took her breath away. Her breasts felt heavy and swollen as Sam palmed their fullness and coaxed her nipples to throbbing life with pliant fingers. She absorbed the sensations with a growing need.

She didn't protest—it was too late for that—instead she applied her fingers to the placket of his shirt. When her hand touched his flesh, the crisp hair covering his chest twined around her fingers.

He raised himself up and pulled his shirt over his head, tossing it carelessly to the floor. Once again his arms enfolded her.

She moved her hand hesitantly across his warm skin, stroking his hardened nipples and moving over his flat stomach and up the sides of his body.

Sam became perfectly still and waited as she explored.

With each touch Reilly became bolder, her fingers spreading and spanning each rippling muscle in Sam's back. His flesh quivered beneath her fingertips and he could no longer remain still, meeting her lips as he lowered his head. They came together with greed, though their greed was that of sharing with each other the fires of their passion—to bring ultimate pleasure to the other.

He stroked her body with the skill of a man who knows a great deal about pleasuring a woman. He left her breathless and begging for more. When he lifted the gown from her body, she shied away and pulled the sheet over her nakedness.

He joined her under the sheet and eased her nervousness with gentle play and coaxed the apprehension from her face. His mouth settled at the juncture of her neck and moved down her chest until his tongue sliced across her hardened nipples. He cupped the sides of her breasts and tongued the aching buds until she was writhing in his arms. His hands moved across her satiny stomach. His fingers coiled in the nest of curls and stroked her gently. She was ready—hot and wet and waiting.

He was hot and hard and ready. He positioned his body and kissed her brow, her eyes, and her nose before his mouth settled once more on hers.

He was probing her femininity when suddenly, to Sam's utter disbelief, his manhood wilted as though someone had thrown a bucket of ice water on his privates. He couldn't fathom something like that happening to him. He probed again. Nothing. There was no life whatsoever in his manhood. Very carefully, he shifted in the bed and lifted the sheet. He had to see this to believe it. Sure enough, his stock and trade was coiled like a sleeping baby against her nest of curls. Sweat popped out on his brow, and he swore long and hard to himself. Thinking he could fix it himself, he moved his hand to the limp member. Nothing.

Reilly didn't know what was happening, but she knew something was going on. "What is it, Sam. Did I do something wrong?"

"No, no, angel. Never you." He wrapped his arms around her and pulled her tightly to him. He cursed himself, his worthless manhood, and his indiscriminate sex life. The one time when making love really meant something to him, he couldn't perform. In an instant all the teasing comments he'd made to Reilly came back to haunt him.

He shifted in the bed. Stacking his hands beneath

216

his head, he studied the sagging ceiling.

Reilly trailed her hand over Sam's chest and beneath the covers, skimming his narrow waist. Gaining courage, she moved her hand over his hip and down the front of his body. Her hand bumped his manhood and stopped. It was soft and warm. Something wasn't right. Earlier his hardness had throbbed against her.

"This has never happened to me before." His voice was low and gravelly. "I guess this is payback for all my misdeeds."

"You sound angry."

"I'm mad as hell, but not at you."

She leaned up on her elbow and kissed him lightly. "Maybe you're trying too hard."

"I can guaran-damn-tee you there is nothing hard around here except my head. Therein lies the problem," he grumbled.

"Well, I'm thankful for your hard head. If not, that fall from the horse could have killed you."

He lifted his hand to her face and stroked the line of her jaw. "Do you always see sunshine when everything seems so dark?"

"My father always told me that if someone gives you a frown, give it right back to them, only turn it upside down."

"Sounds like your father was a very wise man."

"Sam, I don't want you to leave," she blurted out. "Not yet." She flung herself into his arms.

"Hey, what brought this on? Where's the sunshine?" He smoothed the hair from her face and tilted her chin.

"I don't know. I just wanted you to know, that's all."

"I do know, truly I do. But I'm afraid I'll endanger you if I continue to stay here."

"But no one knows that you're alive."

"We don't know that for sure. I know this business

217

with the photograph has you worried. But if the sheriff is satisfied that you don't have any others, I don't think you have anything to worry about."

He couldn't tell her about Mason. And he knew that few men had the deductive powers of Mason Womac, but still there was that chance. Someone might stumble onto the truth. And above all, he didn't want Reilly harmed. "I thought maybe I had worn out my welcome."

"Never," she sighed, moving her hand across the sheet, caressing the outline of his body. Her hand skimmed over his manhood. There was a slight movement beneath her hand.

A delighted smile spanned Sam's face. "So there is some life left in the old fellow. Thank God. I was hoping I hadn't used him up."

Reilly's eyes followed his. The sheet lifted and wavered and lifted some more.

"Come here, angel. We have some unfinished business to attend to."

He was wonderful. Gentle, rough, thorough, loving, maddening. He took her virginity swiftly, making the pain secondary to the throbbing passion ruling her body. The lantern light swirled about the lovers as they embraced. Sam was an instructor, an inventor, an observer, but most of all he was the great lover he claimed to be, and he shared all his knowledge with her.

Nothing else was said about Sam leaving. They were like two children turned loose in a candy shop. They gorged on each other. Reilly's work suffered because she cared more about spending her days with Sam than doing anything else. And there was as urgency about him that drew her to him, as though he knew something she didn't. In her heart she knew their idyllic days were numbered. It would break her heart when it was over, but she didn't dwell on it.

Instead, she gloried in his company. It was like playing house. Only this time it was with real people in a real house. When she was a child, she'd often played house. Only then she'd played alone and her imaginary characters always lived happily ever after. She made up her mind she and Sam would too, even if their *happily ever after* only lasted for a few days.

He was almost the perfect playmate. He was attentive, his wit was contagious, his lovemaking completely fulfilling. But the words she craved to hear never crossed his lips.

They laughed and played and goaded each other until it became a common goal to come up with new and exciting things they could do. Their imaginations were boundless.

As the days passed, the temperature dropped steadily. She and Sam carried wood until the wood box overflowed and each night he'd build a roaring fire. Tonight they had eaten their dinner of thick potato soup and cornbread before its cozy warmth. She carried their dirty dishes to the kitchen and added logs to the fire. She stood before the fire, watching Sam as he shuffled the cards. "You're very good at that."

"I have to be. It's the way I make my living." The lie left a bad taste in his mouth.

"Can you teach me how to play cards?"

"What would you like to learn?"

"Poker."

A leer tilted the corners of his mouth. "Strip poker would be fun."

"I've never heard of it."

"I'll teach you."

Reilly listened intently as Sam explained the game.

Chapter 21

Chug sat at the corner table, deep in the doldrums. As he sipped the weak tea, he watched the men enjoying their drinks. He didn't dare have a drink for fear of the visions returning. He'd been as sober as a judge since that night. Shame had been his constant companion since his encounter with the dead. He'd been so frightened that he'd run all the way back to town. To his utter mortification, he discovered that he'd wet his pants in his flight to reach safety. Even later, it had come to him that he hadn't offered his protection to Reilly. Instead, he'd fled like a scalded dog, worried only about his own hide. Yes, Chug Reynolds was a sorry man, and an even sorrier uncle.

Murdock leaned against the bar, watching the reflection of Chug in the mirror. He'd heard that Chug hadn't taken a drink in days, and he wondered why. The sheriff was like a ferret when it came to sniffing out a person's weakness, and he smelled something that wasn't right. And his gut instinct told him it was something that would benefit him. He had the bartender hand him a bottle and a couple of glasses.

"You look like you could use a drink," Murdock said, placing a glass before Chug and, after uncorking the bottle, he filled the glass to the brim. "Mind if I join you?"

He didn't wait for a reply. He sat down and poured himself a drink and took a long pull on the amber liquor, then wiped the back of his hand across his mouth and smacked his lips. "Ain't nothing like it, 'cept maybe a good woman. And we both know they're as scarce as hens' teeth."

Chug lifted his trembling hand and dipped his finger in the glass. Just before the finger reached his mouth, he shook his head and tossed his hand down in fear. "I can't do it, Sheriff, I can't drink."

"What's wrong, Chug?" Murdock slid his chair close to the frightened man and patted him on the back. "Is it anything I can help you with? That's why I'm here. To help people in need. And you look like you need a friendly ear."

"I seen a dead man, Sheriff," Chug whispered.

This was a damn waste of time, Murdock thought. For once his gut instinct had failed him.

"I talked to him, Sheriff."

"To the dead man?"

Chug nodded his bushy head.

Murdock thought it would be amusing to hear Chug's tale. "Did you recognize the man?" he snickered.

"I sure did. It was the gambler."

"Who? What gambler?" A tingle ran up the sheriff's spine. He was on to something—he could feel it.

"Let me start at the beginning. See I needed a drink real bad, and I was broke. Then I remembered Reilly, my niece. When I lived with her, she had a bad habit of hidin' my bottles when she found them. Well, I figgered she must have a lot of 'em stashed. So I thought that night I'd just sneak in and find me one, just till I could replenish my funds, mind you. I knew most of her hidin' places anyway."

The sheriff wasn't interested in hearing about the

hiding places; he wanted to hear about the gambler. If he didn't interrupt, Chug would drag the story out forever. He nodded his head in understanding and pushed the glass closer to Chug. "Now tell me about the dead man. When you talked to him, did he reply?"

"He shore did. Tol' me I left too many nail ends exposed in his coffin."

"Did your niece talk to him?"

"No, she tol' me it was the whiskey, that there wasn't nobody there."

"You said it was the gambler. You mean Sam Chandler?"

"Yeah, and I know he was dead, cause I took his body to Reilly for her to take his picture."

That bitch. This was getting better all time. Something had happened, and she'd discovered Chandler was alive. He would have sworn the man was dead.

Now he would have Reilly Reynolds just where he wanted her. And he wanted her at his mercy. She was getting too smart for her *britches* anyway, taking that picture of the robbery and not saying anything to him about it. Then she'd sent it back East to some fancy newspaper. If the wrong person saw that picture, it might cause him all kind of trouble. Somebody might get the idea that he wasn't doing his job. If he hadn't seen the telegram, he never would have known. To beat it all, he'd always felt like she was lying about having only the one picture. He wanted to know everything that went on in *his* town. An evil semblance of a smile tilted his mouth.

Once again he patted Chug on the back and got to his feet. "Maybe you're right, Chug. Better lay off the whiskey. Everyone knows a dead man can't come back to life."

After his talk with Chug, the sheriff nodded his way around the saloon and made a hasty departure.

From the adjacent table, a pair of steely midnight blue eyes took a special interest in the sheriff's exit. He shifted his gaze back to the lone man beside him and watched as he traced his finger around the rim of the full whiskey glass. In desperation, the man lifted the glass and slugged down the contents.

Mason had paid close attention to the conversation between the sheriff and Chug. He'd kept a close eye on Chug. Recently the man had had the appearance of someone getting ready to explode. He'd planned to be around when it happened. Now all hell was fixing to break loose. Mason waited a decent interval, then he too made his exit.

Mason pulled his coat around him and eyeballed the sheriff's office. There was a lot of activity going on inside. The sheriff and his deputies were scurrying around like drowning mice. Mason watched for several moments before moving up the street. He passed the darkened studio of Reynolds Photography. Next door at Waters Mercantile, it was also dark inside. He made his way around to the side and up the steep steps to the apartment upstairs. He knocked briskly.

Susan opened the door without looking, thinking her mother and father had forgotten their key. When she saw Mason Womac at her door, it hit her that it was not late enough for her parents to be returning from church. Her breath caught in her throat and her voice quivered when she asked, "Mr. Womac, what can I do for you?"

"I need to get some supplies."

"I'm sorry, we're closed. We'll be open at seven in the morning, if you care to return then."

"You don't understand, I need them now."

"I'm sorry." She fidgeted and ran her fingers along the spine of the novel she was holding in her hand.

"It's important, or I wouldn't bother you."

"Mr. Womac, you have to plan ahead. If I opened

224

the store every time someone needed something, I would get nothing done except running up and down stairs."

"Your point is well-taken. Still, I *would* call this an emergency."

"Mr. Womac." Her voice tingled with exaggeration.

"Miss Waters, a very good friend of yours is headed for deep trouble. A friend of mine is also involved. I'm going to help them in any way I can. Unless you want the glass shattered in your storefront, I advise you to open up for me. Because I intend to get the supplies I need, with or without your help."

"Reilly?" she whispered.

Mason nodded his head.

"Just a minute." She tossed her book aside and grabbed a key from the wall beside the door.

As Mason gathered the things he needed, Susan followed behind him. "Please, tell me what's going on."

"The sheriff knows that Sam Chandler is alive."

"Oh no." She didn't deny his declaration. "What can I do?"

"You're doing it."

"Will they be all right?"

"Sam's no fool. He'll know what to do."

Reilly caught on quickly to the game, and the uncanny luck of the beginner was with her. Soon Sam was stripped to his underwear and socks, while Reilly remained fully clothed. Her chortle of laughter had him threatening to strip her down to her bare flesh just because of her cocky attitude. With a boldness that was uncommon to her, she dared him to carry out his threat. The cards fell abruptly from his hand as he tumbled her to the floor. Amidst bouts of laughter and wet misplaced kisses they endeavored

225

to get her undressed.

The deafening roar of gunfire splintered the quiet and the glass panes of the window shattered, scattering onto the floor. The chairs that Sam and Reilly had just vacated became ridden with bullets. Before Reilly could think, Sam was crawling across the floor. He grabbed the lantern from the table and extinguished the light. The darkness was their haven as gunfire continued to pelt the house.

"We know you're in there, Chandler. You've got two minutes to give yourself up," came the bellowing voice of the sheriff.

"Wonder how he arrived at that number?" Sam asked dryly, moving to Reilly's side.

"Maybe that's as far as he can count," she whispered.

"Where's your revolver?"

"In the dresser drawer."

"I'll get it. You stay here."

"Then you're not going to turn yourself over to them?" She sounded very pleased by her statement.

"Hell will freeze over first." He brushed his hand across her cheek. "Not after all your hard work to save me."

She could hear his smile in the darkness. "You're going to escape, aren't you?"

"I don't have any other choice."

"Will you take me with you?"

"I could never leave you, you know that. But it won't be easy."

"Nothing in my life has ever been easy," she confessed quietly.

"Get some things together. They don't care if they kill us both. It'll just save them a lot of time and paperwork if they don't take us alive."

From the back of the house came the sound of breaking glass as gunfire ripped into the wooden structure.

"Stay down."

"I'm down," she assured him, crawling toward the bedroom.

It was frightening, knowing they were staring death in the face. But ironically there was a peace about her. Until lately, she wouldn't have given Sam credit for knowing about anything except cards and women. Yet some sixth sense assured her that he would take care of her, at any cost.

Lying flat on her back with bullets flying overhead, she hurriedly pulled on her clothes.

Sam had the revolver; she could hear the chamber spinning as he checked the load.

"There's an extra box of bullets in the drawer."

"You take this one, I won't need it."

She knew he wasn't a very good shot, but still, shouldn't he be armed?

The room was dark, but her eyes had adjusted to the darkness enough that she could see his shadowy form as he pulled his carpetbag from the wardrobe. He tossed the first one aside and began pulling things from the other one. She could see flashes of his naked body as he pulled on the clothes he'd taken from the bag.

"Are you ready?"

"Yes, but how?" she answered softly.

"I hope you're not a very good carpenter." He moved a chair to the wardrobe and climbed atop it. He had Reilly firing random shots from the front of the house. He pulled away enough of the sagging ceiling to reach the underside of the roof. When the gunfire was the heaviest, he heaved and shoved until a small portion of the roofing gave way.

"Come on, Reilly."

She unloaded the chamber into the darkened sky, then hustled into the bedroom to join Sam. He helped her atop the wardrobe and tossed their belongings onto the roof.

"We'll wait until they charge the house. It shouldn't be long. They'll think we're either dead or out of bullets. That's when we make our move. The jump won't be bad. Do you think you can make it?"

"Yes," she whispered.

He lifted her until she could scramble through the opening. The night air was cold and the heavens were peppered with stars. She had to clinch her teeth to keep them from chattering. She wasn't sure if it was from fear or from the night air. Sam lifted himself up beside her and wrapped his arms around her. They waited.

It wasn't long until they saw the shadowy figures approaching the house. The men crashed through the front door and the back door almost in the same instant. The noise provided the perfect timing for their escape. She and Sam leaped from the roof and hit the ground in a dead run. When they reached the safety of the trees, they collapsed. Reilly wanted to cry out for joy—they'd made it. They could hear the confusion and the cursing as the sheriff and his men searched the house. Someone lit a lantern. Reilly and Sam watched as the light went from room to room. "Search every inch of this place until you find them. Damnit, I want them found. Do you understand?"

Suddenly, the men rushed from the house and began canvassing the yard.

Sam took her hand and led the way into the forest.

They ran awhile and then they walked. Reilly wasn't cold anymore. Her face was burning with scratches from limbs slapping her in the face. She didn't know how in the world Sam knew where he was going. But he didn't let up as they traveled quickly through the dense undergrowth.

He was like a different person, comfortable and secure with this new position he'd been cast into. Or was it new?

Sometimes when the moon fell through the trees

she got a good look at Sam. Gone was the gambler and every inch of the city slicker. He had a gun strapped to his leg, and he was dressed in black. Even a black kerchief was tied around his neck. And in place of his fine leather shoes were boots. Apprehension rippled down her spine, and she began to question the trust she'd placed in him. Who was this man? And what was she doing placing herself in his care? What had she done?

After traipsing through the woods for hours, they came to a clearing. "We'll rest here before moving on."

She slid to the ground and rested against a tree. "But where will we go?"

"I'm not sure yet."

Suddenly, they could hear the sounds of something moving rapidly through the trees. Scared to death, Reilly jumped to her feet. "What are we going to do now?"

Before she could answer, a man leading two riderless horses burst through the clearing.

"I thought you might be in need of a little transportation," came a dry teasing voice.

"I thought you might show up," Sam answered.

"I brought you some supplies."

Reilly was dumbstruck by the man's appearance and by the conversation unfolding. "Who are you?" she snapped.

"Pardon my manners, Reilly. This is Mason Womac," Sam introduced.

Mason tipped his hat. "Nice to meet you, ma'am."

"But I thought Mason Womac was the man trying to collect a gambling debt from you."

"He's always trying to collect something. I figure this little deal will cost me a fortune."

"No, not really. I had Miss Waters charge it to your account." Mason paused. "And you don't have to worry about her, I'll keep a close eye on her."

Reilly didn't like what she was hearing. Sam didn't have an account at Susan's store. Susan had made that up. How did this Mason Womac know they would be coming this way? What was going on?

Womac dismounted, and he and Sam walked a short distance away, talking quietly. She couldn't hear anything they were saying as she watched them intently. Suddenly a match flared, and she saw Mason's face when he lifted the flame to his cigarette. He looked remotely familiar. From what she could see, he was a handsome man. Why did she think she'd seen him before? For some reason, the thought that she knew him made her feel uneasy. She had to be wrong. He must be a good friend to Sam to go to all the trouble he had. But if that was the case, why had Sam lied to her?

Chapter 22

Sam and Reilly rode slowly but steadily during the night, widening the distance from Castletown and the ruthless men bent on killing them.

Working his way out of difficult situations was nothing new to Sam. When he started a job, he finished it and what Murdock didn't know was that Sam would be back. While working undercover, he was continually putting his life on the line. Even so, he wondered how many more times he could depend on his luck to bail him out. And it was indeed luck that had gotten Reilly and him out of the house alive tonight. Now he had to keep them alive. Sam didn't expect Murdock to begin a widespread search until daybreak.

Sam shivered and buried his neck deep within the collar of his woolen coat. Though the temperature in the mountains was pleasant during the day, at night it dropped considerably, sometimes near freezing. A gust of cold wind suddenly hit him full force in the face. He wondered how Reilly was faring. She wasn't wearing clothing suitable for traveling very long in this kind of weather.

In the moonlight, he could see the outline of her trim figure riding ahead of him. He was damned grateful that she was as good in handling a horse as she was in handling her camera. Another plus in his corner was her ability to fire a gun. If she had been created from the same mold as her friend, Susan, he would have found himself in real trouble. He guessed he had her father to thank for preparing her for the rough times ahead of them.

Reilly had insisted on leading them out of Castletown. During her treks around the countryside shooting landscape pictures, she'd traveled trails that few people knew existed. They were on such a trail now. It would lead them to a place where Reilly said they could rest without fear of discovery.

Yet, he dreaded the moment when they reached it. Conversation would get around to Mason. It had been bad enough that she knew his partner's name, but when Mason struck that damn match, the glow had flashed across his face. He hadn't seen Reilly's reaction because of the darkness. Had she recognized Mason as the outlaw in her picture? If so, how was he going to explain everything and keep his identity as a U.S. Marshal a secret? He also knew she was wondering why he had hidden the clothing he was now wearing. The only thing missing was his marshal's badge, which he kept hidden inside the lining of his coat.

It wasn't that he didn't trust Reilly. If he told her who he was, she'd probably die before she'd give away his identity to anyone. Yes, she was a real Joan of Arc, and he'd be damned if he'd let her die protecting him. So far, luck had been her trusty companion and he'd like to keep it that way. Now, his most important task was to keep her out of Murdock's clutches.

If anything ever happened to her . . . God, he didn't even want to think about it. She wasn't just *any* woman he had to protect, she had become very special to him. When he had made love to her that first time, he'd felt something change inside him. His desire for her had become secondary to a much deeper emotion. If it was love, he wouldn't recognize it. He did know she'd left a burning need inside him that wouldn't let him rest.

Reilly also had a burning need, but it was for the truth. She didn't know Sam as well as she thought she had. All she knew for certain was the way he made her feel—more alive than she'd ever felt in her life.

She shuddered when she thought about their narrow escape. Sam's quick action had surprised her. With unexpected calmness, he had maneuvered them through that volley of fire as though he had done it every day of his life. All along she had sensed a quiet strength about him, but until tonight he hadn't actually shown it. Later, when she'd seen Sam all decked out in his rugged clothing and carrying a gun to boot, she'd thought she had left the house with the wrong person. And then along came this Mason Womac, bringing them horses and supplies. The most surprising thing was that he wasn't following Sam around to collect a gambling debt, but was actually his friend. Tonight when they made camp, she expected to receive answers to the questions she was going to ask.

Again, her mind called up Mason's face as the flame from his match danced over his features. She frowned. She could swear she'd seen him before, and though she sometimes had difficulty in remembering peoples' names, she seldom forgot their faces. He probably resembled someone she had photographed at one time or another. Whatever, she was glad he was Sam's friend, or they never would have made it out of town so quickly.

She wondered what the townspeople would think tomorrow about her sudden disappearance. They had surely heard the sound of gunfire with as many bullets as the men had shot into her house. Murdock would probably tell everyone she had been harboring a criminal and they'd escaped. If Mason didn't get word to Susan that they really had escaped, her friend might think Murdock had already killed them.

The night seemed endless. Reilly could hear nothing but the sounds of their horses' hooves striking the rocky ground. Every living thing had found a warm nook to take shelter from the cold. Every living thing except them. She was so cold she couldn't keep her teeth from chattering. She wasn't wearing gloves and her fingers were frozen around the reins. And where her body wasn't numb with cold, it ached. When she had traveled with her father, they had often ridden horses because the sights they'd wanted to photograph were inaccessible by wagon. She considered herself a decent rider, but she'd spent very little time in the saddle since his death and it was telling on her. She could only hope that in a few days she'd get over the aches and pains.

She could hear the clopping of Sam's horse's hooves behind her. She doubted he was in any better physical shape than she. She'd hoped they would have reached the site by now. Obviously, she had miscalculated the time it would take traveling the trail at night. The shack she was searching for had probably belonged to a hunter. She and her father had found it on their way to Castletown and had stayed there one night. Behind it was a mountain stream filled with trout. It was a shame they didn't have time to linger, for they could catch their weight in fish. But Reilly knew time was valuable. A few hours rest was all they could afford. They'd have to leave at daybreak, if they planned to stay well ahead of Murdock. He would probably have his men combing the area the moment the sun came up.

Finally, they arrived at the shack—what was left of it, that is. One side of the structure had completely collapsed, leaving only the wall and roof around the rock chimney still standing.

Sam drew in beside her. "Is this the place?"

"It was," she said dismally.

Sam dismounted and helped her down. Her legs gave way and Sam caught her up in his arms. "Hey, you all right, angel?"

She rested her head against his shoulder. "No, I'm as cold and stiff as an icicle. What about you?"

"I've felt better," he admitted. "Can you stand now?"

"I'll try, but I'm afraid if I try to straighten my bowed legs, they'll snap in two. It's been a while since I've ridden."

He lowered her to the ground, holding onto her until she felt steady on her feet. "Why didn't you say something?"

"I kept thinking we were almost here. Now that I've seen the place, I'm sorry we didn't stop earlier."

"Maybe it's not as bad as it looks. Let's check it out. We might not be the only ones looking for a warm place."

He pulled out a few matches from his coat pocket, then removed his gun from the holster. Reilly followed him to the doorless entrance. He stopped and lit a match, then they walked inside the room. Picking up a stick of wood, he stirred through the debris, scattering a nest of mice and sending them scurrying in all directions.

He laughed. "Hope you don't mind sharing this place."

With a shivering laugh, she said, "I'd share it with a grizzly if it meant getting warm again."

Blowing out the match, he lit another one and made his way toward the hearth.

"Well, at least we won't have problems getting wood for a fire," Reilly said, picking up several scraps of rotted fallen timber and tossing them inside the fireplace. Sam dropped a match on top of it. The dry wood crackled and immediately burst into flames, sending sparks and smoke up the chimney.

They knelt before the warmth and held their hands toward the fire, rubbing them briskly.

"Better?"

"Getting there," she said, feeling her fingers tingle as the numbness started subsiding.

Sam stood up. "Before I get to enjoying this, I'd better get our gear. You stay here and warm up."

While Sam was gone, Reilly wondered if she should wait until they'd rested before she brought up Mason. No, she wouldn't be able to sleep with all these questions whirling around in her head. He'd expect her to ask him, so she would.

After a couple of trips, Sam had deposited all their belongings inside and said he'd be back after tending to the horses. She mentioned there was a stream out back where the horses could have their fill of water.

While Sam was gone Reilly hastened outside to take care of nature's call. Back inside, she cleared the rubbish from the area in front of the fire. After spreading one of the blankets on the ground, she put the saddle at the end as a rest for their heads. Then she sat down and removed her boots, stretching her legs toward the fire to warm her feet. Unlike Sam, she was not wearing a union suit beneath her clothes. She was frozen down to the bone.

Sam entered and picked up the sack of food that Mason had given him. "Are you hungry?"

"Not really. I'd rather talk."

"Well, here it comes, he thought. Setting the sack down, he leaned against the rock wall to the side of the hearth and crossed his arms and ankles. "All right, let's talk."

She drew the blanket around her shoulders. "First I'd like to know why you lied to me about Mason Womac?"

"At the time it seemed like the best idea." He paused. "Mason's trying to find out who shot me, Reilly. As headstrong as you are, I didn't want you getting the bright idea of teaming up with him and getting yourself in worse trouble than you are now."

"Was he in Castletown when you were shot?"

"Yes. He followed me there." Now comes the hard part, he thought, hoping she would believe what he was going to say next. "You might say Mason has set himself up to be my protector. I can't shake him off." Hell, he hated piling lies on top of lies, but he had no choice.

"He's a drifter. We met a few years ago at a gaming table. Mason's hot-headed and accused a man we were playing cards with of cheating. The man didn't say a word, just jumped up from his chair and went for his gun. The second he cleared leather, I threw my blade and nailed his arm to the wall behind him. In the same instant, he fired and blew a hole through his foot. Anyway, we got the hell out of there in a hurry.

"Well, Mason got the idea he owed me for saving his life. He follows me from place to place, waiting for his chance to save mine. Tonight, I guess he did. If he hadn't brought us the horses and supplies, our chances of escaping would have been slim."

Still puzzled, Reilly said, "All that's fine and good, Sam, but how did he know you were alive to save your life?"

He grinned. "Susan's story didn't wash with him. He came to your house the day of our picnic and saw me outside." Another lie. "He never got a chance to talk to me. I didn't even know he was around until he met us with the horses."

Reilly sighed. "That brings another question to my mind. How did he know Murdock was making his attack on the house tonight?"

He told his first truth. "Chug broke down tonight

237

and told Murdock about seeing Sam Chandler's ghost. Mason was nearby and heard the whole thing. When the sheriff left, Mason knew our lives were in danger."

She frowned at him. "And he knew just where to find us? That's almost too much of a coincidence, Sam. We could've fled in any direction."

Damnit, Sam swore. He felt like he was on the witness stand and facing a hard-nosed prosecution attorney. "He saw us leaving," was all he could come up with, hoping that would satisfy her quick mind.

There was a long pause before she finally spoke. "All right, Sam, everything you've said makes sense . . . I guess."

Her answer spoke volumes. Sam knew without a doubt he hadn't convinced her he was telling the truth.

Thinking the conversation was over and done with, he pushed away from the wall and started to sit down beside her.

"The clothes you're wearing, Sam. You were hiding them from me. Why?"

He gnashed his teeth together so hard, he thought they'd disappeared into his gums. Straightening again, he stared down at her and spoke more harshly than he had intended. "I wasn't hiding them. I just hadn't needed them until now."

"Oh." She frowned. Something still didn't ring true. "You could've worn them the day you brought my camera instead of wearing my father's clothes." She didn't mention the day she'd seen him sneaking back to the house in her father's coat and hat.

"True, but I didn't know whether the sheriff or his men had seen me in them at one time or another. I didn't wear those fancy clothes all the time, Reilly, only in town." Hell, his answer didn't even make sense to him. How could he expect her to believe it?

"I suppose you carry a gun just for looks too. Right?" she asked snidely.

"No, I'd use it if I had to . . . at least I'd try."

He was lying to her, but she didn't understand why. Oh, he was a gambler all right . . . a lover too, but she was beginning to doubt his role as a city slicker. There was something more he wasn't telling her, but she'd let it go for now. She was too tired to even think clearly.

"We'd better get some sleep," she said with a yawn.

"Yeah, good idea," he said, sitting down and removing his boots, thankful for the end of her questions. At least she had not linked Mason with the outlaw in her photograph. Yet. On his way here, he'd figured out explanations for everything except that particular question. He hadn't been able to come up with a good answer.

Lying down beside her, he pulled the extra blanket over them. Reilly scooted close to his warmth, her rounded buttocks nestled firmly against his pelvis.

Sam rested his arm just beneath her breasts and nuzzling her neck, whispered softly, "Are you warm now?"

"I'm getting there."

"Need some help?" he asked, his hand cupping her breast as he brushed aside her hair and kissed her neck.

"Hush," she scolded, "we need to sleep, Sam."

He emitted a long sigh and rested his head against the saddle. "You're right. Good night, angel."

"Sure, what's left of it," she returned.

He stared at the flickering firelight, mentally exhausted from the questioning Reilly had put him through, and the lies he'd had to come up with to answer them. The incident in that saloon had actually happened to him and Mason, but he'd had to change the story in places to suit his purpose. In truth, that was the first time they had worked undercover together. They were lucky to have come through that night alive.

Sam closed his eyes. Damn, he dreaded the day when Reilly learned the truth. And it would come—the day when he pinned on his badge and arrested Floyd Murdock.

Chapter 23

A mental picture of Mason Womac's face suddenly leaped in Reilly's mind. Her eyes sprang open and she almost gasped aloud. Her heart pounding, she closed her eyes again and the picture reappeared. Except this time, it wasn't from behind the glow of a match that she saw him. He was sitting on his horse outside the bank—the day she'd taken the photograph of the robbery.

Blood pounded in Reilly's ears and her chest constricted until she thought she might suffocate. *No, it can't be true. I've made a mistake.* Reilly gave herself a mental shake, not wanting to believe the workings of her mind. As much as she wanted to deny it, Mason Womac and the bank robber were one and the same.

And the man holding her tightly in his arms was Womac's friend and an outlaw too. A mixture of anger, hurt, and fright tore through her insides like sharp claws. Lies . . . lies . . . lies. Was everything about this man a lie? When she thought of everything she had done for him over the past several weeks, she wanted to scream. She wanted to draw from his embrace and slap the fire out of him, tell him she hated him. But she didn't. Instead, she lay there, feeling the steady beat of his heart against her back.

Lord, what am I going to do?

She formed a mental image of Sam in the clothing he now wore and said over and over in her mind: Sam is an outlaw . . . an outlaw . . . an outlaw, trying to force her mind to accept the fact so she could think more clearly.

Bit by bit, the pieces of the puzzle started fitting together. Since Mason was his friend, Sam had probably been in the gang too. On the day of the robbery, he might have ridden out to join them, but someone had shot him before he got there. No doubt, he had intended to change clothes before pulling the job. That would explain why he was still wearing soft leather shoes and a string tie when Murdock had brought his body in for her to photograph. Yet why someone had bushwhacked him, she had no idea. Maybe Murdock had a hand in it; maybe he hadn't. If Murdock was the leader of this gang as she suspected, he might not have trusted Sam. He could have ordered one of his deputies to get rid of him. Neal would be the likely choice since he held a grudge against Sam for stabbing his hand.

Yes, everything was finally making sense. She now knew why Sam hadn't wanted her to clear his name through her photographs. He was protecting Mason Womac. In turn, Mason was protecting him by helping them escape.

Escape. Yes, no matter how many lies he had told, she had to give Sam credit for saving her life. But it was the reason behind his action that made her angry. He was saving her for himself. His lusty nature required constant attention, so what better way to satiate it than to take a willing woman along with him?

All along, Sam had been using her. Any woman would have suited his needs. After all, he couldn't risk going to one of the brothels to get a woman, and why bother when he was wearing down the resistance of the one he was living with? And he had succeeded. Of all the things that had happened, this was the most difficult for her to accept. But accept it she must, and just make sure it never happened again. If she wasn't willing, maybe he'd get tired of her and leave her at the first opportunity.

And when she really thought about it, Sam probably hadn't been sneaking out that day to find his knife, but to meet with Womac. He had purposely riled her and taken liberties with her to make sure she would be out of his way so he could accomplish it. And she had fallen for it hook, line, and sinker.

Now that she knew his true identity, she decided to keep it to herself and use that knowledge to her advantage. If he ever learned that she had linked Mason with the outlaw in her picture, there was no telling what disasters might befall her. Then something Mason had said about Susan hit her like a bolt of lightning. *Don't worry, I'll watch over your friend.*

Oh Lord, how was she going to warn Susan this man was an outlaw! Reilly knew Mason had frightened Susan the first time they'd met. But because he had helped them escape, she would trust him. If Mason started paying Susan the least bit of attention, she might just fall head over heels in love with him. And she'd wind up with a broken heart. Maybe, when they stopped in some town to replenish their supplies, she could wire Susan and warn her. Yet, could she risk doing that when the agent might tell Murdock? After all, he'd gotten hold of her message from the newspaper back East and had read it. No, the only way she could warn Susan was to escape Sam and return to Castletown. But where would she go after that? If Murdock found her, he'd kill her on the spot. There had to be an answer to how she was going to get herself out of this dilemma, but right now nothing came to mind.

Reilly noticed the fire had died down to a dwindling flame. From habit, she almost got up to put more wood on the fire. No, not this time, she vowed. As an outlaw, Sam knew perfectly well how to fend for himself. He'd probably lived in the outdoors as much or more than she had. Also, she had no doubt that he was adept in the handling of a gun. Lord, he'd played his role of a city slicker to the hilt. Well, no more would she wait on him hand and foot. He could damn well take care of her for a while.

Lifting his arms from around her, she turned towards him, and raised on one elbow. She looked down on his handsome sleeping face . . . his lying face. His mouth was slack jawed and he snored softly. Smiling wickedly, she shook him none too gently. "Sam, wake up."

Sam was used to living on the edge, his senses ever alert to danger even while asleep. He came awake with a jolt. In an instant, he had his revolver in his hand and rolled to a sitting position. "Stay down, angel," he ordered, his voice husky from sleep.

"You can put the gun down, Sam. There's no one here but us," she snapped, then added slyly, "Besides, you don't even know how to shoot. Remember?"

"Then why did you wake me? It's still dark."

"The fire's almost out. Don't you think we need to add more wood?"

"Sure, go ahead," he said, settling back down.

Reilly glared down at him. "You do it. I'm freezing."

"Er . . . sure," he agreed, pushing the blanket aside and rising. Picking up some more of the scattered wood, he threw it on the fire.

"Thanks," she mumbled and closed her eyes.

Sam stood by the fire for several moments, watching Reilly sleep. He was wide awake now and knew he couldn't sleep if he tried. He had never required much sleep anyway; a catnap during the day was enough to keep him going. And lately, he'd napped more than usual, simply because when Reilly was at home, they'd make long passionate love, which always left them so replete, they would fall asleep in each other's arms.

He had an idea she was miffed at him. Ordinarily, she wouldn't have even asked him to add wood to the fire. She would've just done it herself. And he'd played the role of the lazy gambler so long, he'd not even thought to offer his help. Maybe she had come to the conclusion that it was going to take both their efforts to survive their dilemma. Also, his actions tonight had probably shown her he was perfectly capable of handling dangerous situations. This change in his character must be confusing to her. Yet, he couldn't tell her a damn thing.

Frustrated, Sam laid back down and, after kissing her softly on her cheek, drew her close to him.

Reilly didn't move and kept her eyes closed. Tomorrow, when they stopped to spend the night somewhere along the way, she knew he would want to make love to her. How could she refuse him without raising his suspicions? She felt the tears squeeze through her closed eyes, wishing she had never learned the truth.

"Reilly, wake up," Sam said, jostling her awake.

With a groan, Reilly pulled the blanket over her head. He heard her muffled words. "Go away."

"You have to get up, Reilly."

"I'm too tired to go to the studio this morning."

Her jerked the blanket off her head. "Open your eyes. You aren't at home, you're in a dilapidated shack, and Sheriff Murdock's probably out looking for us now."

It took a moment for his words to sink into Reilly's disoriented mind, and then she remembered the whole horrid ordeal. She forced her bloodshot eyes open and saw Sam hovering over her. "I was hoping I was only having a nightmare."

"No, it's real. Sit up," he ordered. "I fixed you a cup of coffee before I put out the fire."

"Thanks." Reilly rolled to a sitting position. She grimaced as a dull ache shot through her buttocks and down her legs. "Oh Lord, I feel like a herd of wild horses have run over me. I dread getting on that horse again."

"I'm sorry, Reilly, but you'll have to. We'll take breaks along the way if we can, but it's crucial we get as far away from Castletown as possible today." He handed her the tin cup filled with steaming coffee. Next, he reached into the food sack sitting beside him and handed her a chunk of cheese and bread. "We need to eat. It might be a while before we can stop."

Though she wasn't hungry, Reilly took the food he offered.

As they ate, Reilly studied Sam curiously. She was still having a difficult time dealing with the idea that her lover was an outlaw. He'd stolen people's hard-earned money and perhaps had even killed to gain it. With a pang of remorse, she reluctantly admitted he could be as evil and manipulative as Floyd Murdock. Reilly had thought of herself as an excellent judge of character, but Sam had completely duped her.

"I don't even know you anymore," she said softly, not realizing she had voiced her thoughts until they'd left her mouth.

Sam almost choked on the bite of cheese he was about to swallow. A frown etched his forehead. "What's that supposed to mean?"

Reilly looked across at him and stated boldly, "It means . . . that when you changed into those clothes, you changed into a different person."

"Yeah, I guess I did change a little," he said with a

246

bitter laugh. "It isn't everyday that I have someone hellbent on killing me. Kind of brings out the grit in a man." He paused. "I wasn't ready to die. Were you?"

"Of course not. Forget I even mentioned it," she said, setting aside her empty coffee cup.

His hand gently took hold of her wrist and his other hand tilted her chin. Their eyes met and held. "One thing hasn't changed, angel. I still want you." Leaning forward, his mouth closed over her own and he gave her a slow, potent kiss. A confusing mixture of fear and desire welled up inside her. At that moment she realized the hold he had on her. One kiss and as always, she was ready to surrender.

No, I can't let him make me feel this way, her mind screamed. Yet her body was screaming an entirely different message of its own.

Sam broke the kiss and with a grin that infuriated her, he said, "We'll have time for this . . . and more . . . later."

She clenched her fists and dug them into the ground beneath her as he rose and lifted the saddle. Hoisting it over his arm and shoulder, he swaggered toward the entrance and said, "Come along after you're ready."

Reilly glared at his broad back. "With only one blasted kiss," she muttered, "he managed to make me forget who he is." She rammed her hands through her tousled hair, pressing them firmly against the sides of her head. "It won't happen again. I won't . . . I positively will not . . . let him ever touch me again."

Reilly tugged on her boots and gathered up the blanket, coffee cup, and food sack. Walking outside, she saw Sam adjusting the saddle on her mount. She set down the items near the rest of their gear and strolled behind the shack to tend to her personal needs. When she returned, she only glimpsed his way long enough to see he was already astride his horse.

Placing her foot in the stirrup, she lifted herself into the saddle. Her body cried out against the abuse, but she gritted her teeth and bore it. She looked over at Sam. "Where to?"

"How far's Bodie from here?" Bodie was where he'd told Mason they were going. He knew exactly how far it was, but he wasn't supposed to know such things.

"By train, not far. But by horseback, probably three days, more or less."

"Do you know how to get there? I don't know where the hell we are."

She wanted to call him a liar. He probably knew every town and all the outlaw hideouts in these parts. "We go south," she said with a frustrated sigh. "My father and I stopped there on our way to Castletown. It was a rough route by wagon, but we should make better time on horses."

"Then lead the way," he returned with a smile.

"Where are we going from Bodie?" she asked.

"We'll figure that out when the time comes."

Yes, Reilly thought to herself, and when the time comes, if I can find any way to part company with you, I will.

Chapter 24

By noon, the sun had yet to make an appearance, remaining hidden behind a cloudy gray sky. Rain was on the way. Reilly couldn't believe the absurd thoughts running through her head at probably the most crucial time of her life. She worried about the gaping hole in the roof from where they'd made their daring escape. Uncle Chug would never get around to fixing it before the rain came and ruined everything in her bedroom. The rest of the house would also be in terrible shape since she doubted there was a window left with glass in it. Would Uncle Chug sober up long enough to repair everything? And Lord, what about the livestock? Who would care for them? She hoped Susan would remind her uncle that he had to see to them or they'd starve.

And then there was her studio. Would Murdock destroy her equipment? She recalled all the photographs lining the walls of the room that had belonged to her father, the album that contained pictures she could never replace. Tears sprang to her eyes. If he destroyed those, she would make sure she got the bastard behind bars. Better yet, she vowed he would hear her cheering louder and clearer than anybody else, if he found himself standing on the scaffold with a rope around his neck.

Reilly knew that while Murdock was sheriff, she could never show her face in Castletown again. Somehow, she'd have to prove his guilt on her own. She still had her pictures. Then it dawned on her. She'd forgotten to get them before they left! They were still hidden in her wardrobe. She wondered if Sam had brought along the copies she'd given him. If she got the chance, she'd search through his bag.

"Reilly," Sam called from beside her, "get off the road quickly!"

She didn't have to ask why. She heard the sound of horses' hooves not too far behind them. Veering her mount toward the woods, she rode alongside Sam. They descended a shallow ravine and brought their horses to a halt, listening as the riders galloped past them.

"Do you see them?" she asked breathlessly.

"No, but it was probably some of Murdock's men. If they found the shack, they might've picked up clues that we'd stayed there and discovered the direction we went in. We'll give them time to get a good distance ahead of us before we pull out again."

Reilly dismounted and stretched her back, then did a few knee bends to work out the soreness in her muscles. "At least we're out of the wind for a while."

She felt Sam's hands on her shoulders and her body went taut. "Let me help," he said from behind her, his fingers kneading the muscles in her neck and shoulder. "Relax."

Relax? Oh, how she wished she could! Still, she tried her best because his hands felt so good she thought she might melt into the ground. Too darned good. "I'm better. Thanks," she said, walking to her horse and getting her canteen.

A frown etched Sam's forehead. She was giving him the cold shoulder; she had been ever since they'd left the shack. And he knew the reason. She suspected he had lied to her, and he couldn't blame her. He might have duped someone else with his reckless answers, but not Reilly. She had a mind and eye for detail. Very little got by her that she didn't see or sense.

As Reilly drank from the canteen, Sam removed the sack of food from his saddle bag. He handed her a strip of beef jerky. She chuckled. "I thought I'd seen the last of this stuff when Pa and I settled in Castletown."

"Sorry, but that's all we have. When we get the men off our backs, we can build a fire and cook something decent."

By *we*, Reilly assumed he meant *her*. If a rabbit was crouched at her feet and begging to become stew, she'd starve before she'd shoot it. And if he wanted a campfire, he could damn well build it himself. She *might* go along with picking up the sticks with which to build it . . . but no more. She wondered vaguely why he messed up last night and built the fire at the shack. He'd probably forgotten *she* was supposed to do it. But when it had come to one of them getting up in the middle of the night to add more wood, he'd expected her to do it. Well, she'd shown him.

They lingered a while longer in the ravine until they heard the horses approaching again. This time the men stopped, and they could hear their voices.

"I still don't think they came this way. If you ask me, they've gone toward Virginia City. It's a helluva' lot closer than Bodie."

"If I was them," another voice piped in, "I'd head south, not north anyhow. You know how cold it gits at night this time of year. He ain't fit to take the cold, gambler that he is. And her, a picture taker? Hell, she cain't take it either. Yeah, I'd go as fer south as I could git, Arizoni ifen it was me."

"Look, we're wastin' our damn time," another man said. "Besides, looks like it's gonna rain. Let's

251

get back to the hideout and get word to the boss that there waren't no reason to go no further."

"Sounds good to me. Let's get a move on."

After they left, Reilly turned to Sam. "Sounds like they won't be looking for us in Bodie."

Reilly studied him closely when she said, "They mentioned returning to their hideout. That means they were outlaws, Sam." Like you, she wanted to say. "It's a shame we don't know where it is . . . isn't it?"

Sam didn't blink an eye. "Yeah, but there's little we could do about it now, if we did know. You ready to go?"

"I reckon," she said, looking up at the overcast sky. "I just hope the rain holds off for a while."

Oscar and Neal watched their boss as he paced the office of the jail. Most of the groups that Murdock had sent to search the area had returned to the hideout and sent back the message that they'd not seen hide nor hair of Chandler and the photographer. He walked to his desk and pounded one fist heavily on its surface, nearly upsetting the lantern that sat on it. "They have to be near here, damnit."

"Believe me, boss, they ain't," Oscar said. "The men asked at every home if they've seen them, and checked every abandoned mine and shack within twenty miles of here. Hell, they couldn't have even gone that far without horses."

Murdock scratched his chin where a day's growth of stubble cloaked it. "Maybe they did have horses."

"Yeah, we thought about that," Neal said, "but we don't know where they got them. She only had that one sorry horse and a wagon. It's still at the house. The Waters don't even have a horse, and nobody's reported their horses stolen. It's like they just disappeared off the face of the earth."

252

"Get a message back to Pryor and tell him to hold off on going south. I still think they're right under our noses."

In the gathering room at the hideout, the men had just finished their evening meal, and Saul, the cook, was clearing the empty plates and bowls from the long table. Each man lit a cigarette, and it wasn't long before a thick haze of smoke filled the room.

Mason sat among them, listening to the talk going on around him. He had learned they called their leader, *boss*, making no other reference as to the man's identity. He knew they weren't purposely hiding this information from him because Oscar and Neal had come here often to give them orders . . . from the boss.

Earlier Oscar had brought a message, telling them that tomorrow they'd search the immediate area again. The train was to arrive in Castletown at noon and a few of the men were to keep a close eye on the depot, making sure Sam and Reilly didn't sneak on board to make their getaway. According to the *boss*, without horses, they had no other way to leave town besides the train.

Mason had said nothing, only smiled to himself. The outlaws had so many stolen horses and spare saddles at the hideout, he doubted they would ever realize that two horses were missing. Luck had been with him the night the outlaws had stormed Reilly's house. By the time he had gotten the supplies he'd needed in town and had returned to the hideout, the gang had already pulled out. No one had even known he'd been there. When they'd returned later, he was sharing a bottle of whiskey with Saul, pretending to be irritated at them for running off and leaving him.

Before Sam and Reilly headed out, Mason told him that Cord Lillard had indeed been the man who'd broken into Reilly's house. Worried that Murdock would thoroughly search her house again since no one would be there, Sam had asked him to get the photographs Reilly had hidden beneath the boards in the floor of her wardrobe. Mason immediately returned to the house after they parted and got them.

Mason took a long draw on his cigarette and exhaled, then frowned slightly, wondering how Sam and Reilly were faring. Sam wouldn't have found himself in this mess if he'd hidden somewhere else instead of Reilly's house. Now look where his lovesickness had got him. Mason had tried to warn him by revealing his own painful experience with Elizabeth. He guessed his friend would have to learn these facts for himself.

Mason also had a woman to worry about too—Susan Waters. Yesterday morning, the news about Sam and Reilly's escape had spread through the town like wildfire. Knowing Susan was concerned about her friend's safety, he'd dropped by the mercantile store and waited until they were alone. Not wanting to hang around too long, he'd quickly told Susan that Reilly and Sam had not been hurt during the gunfire, and that he'd supplied them with horses and the merchandise she had given him. He had no idea where they were headed.

As he'd turned to leave, Susan had said, "Hmmm . . . it seems mighty strange to me that you would abet a man who'd cheated you at cards."

He'd known that question would come, but he'd hoped to get out the door before she asked it. Fortunately, a customer had come in, putting a stop to further conversation between them.

Mason was also worried that the sheriff might question Susan about Reilly because of their friendship. Could she hold up under such questioning? Or would she let something slip that might endanger all parties involved, including herself?

Damn, there was no way to get around it. Susan Waters wasn't out of his life yet. She was up to her pretty little neck in this mess and he had to keep an eye on her.

Reilly quickly gathered broken limbs and brush, her earlier vow of forcing Sam's hand to help her diminishing as heavy, dark clouds swirled and rolled over the horizon. It was only an hour or so before dark and she didn't want to be caught in a storm without shelter. When she and her father had camped in the wild, they'd had a tent to keep them warm and dry. Mason had furnished them a small canvas tarpaulin, some rope, and a knife. Sam had left to hunt them something to eat, leaving her with the chore of fashioning a cover to keep them dry. She had nothing but her imagination with which to accomplish this chore. First, before she did anything, she checked his bag for the photographs. They weren't there. Could he possibly have them with him? Surely he wouldn't have left them in his other bag when they fled the house. Lord, if he did, Murdock would've found them.

Giving up her search, she got to work building their shelter. She listened for a gunshot, but heard nothing. In truth, she had thought to hear several. Sam would no doubt want her to think it had taken many misfired shots to get their dinner.

A while later, Reilly finished and stood before their makeshift tent, proud of her accomplishment. She'd drawn a rope from one tree to another and placed the tarpaulin over it, anchoring it on all sides with rocks. Next she'd stacked dead branches against it to camouflage it in case someone should come close to them. Then carrying their belongings inside, she placed them along the sides.

Lingering a moment, she looked around the small

interior. This might have been our private world, she thought sadly. Regardless that Sam was an outlaw, in her heart he was still the man she loved. He had moved into her life with an alarming self-confidence, first taking control of her emotions and then her heart. Turning away from him tonight would be the most difficult thing she had ever done. Could she succeed, or would her own body betray her?

When she came back outside, she saw Sam approaching. "Hey, that's pretty good, angel."

Reilly smiled and then her smile suddenly faded. "Well, I expected you'd come back empty-handed."

"I never saw anything to shoot."

Reilly planted her hands on her hips. "You couldn't *find* anything? My Lord, Sam, there's small game all around us—rabbits, quail, pheasant, only to name a few."

"Yeah? Well, they all hid when they heard me coming . . . except one."

"Why didn't you shoot it?" she hissed.

"It was a porcupine. I didn't think you'd want to spend all night picking out his stickers."

"They're called quills, Sam." Reilly didn't know why she was standing there arguing with him. He knew exactly what they were called and he could probably split a quill from a hundred paces with no trouble at all. "If you *think* you can build us a fire, then *I'll* go get us something to eat."

"I think I can handle that," he said with a thoughtful frown.

With a cheeky grin, Sam watched Reilly stomp away, his eyes fixed on her rear end. *Now that, I could handle just fine.*

She wasn't gone five minutes when Sam heard one shot, then another. He smiled. Ahh . . . it took her two shots.

While he was kneeling beside the sticks he had gathered and building a fire, she returned, dropping

256

two rabbits on the ground beside him.

"I shot'em so now *you* can cook'em."

He stared up at her with a look of astonishment on his face.

Reilly felt like screaming. Instead, she mentally counted to ten, then said in as calm a voice as she could manage, "You do know how to skin them, don't you?"

He nodded negatively. "Sorry, angel. This is all new to me."

Suddenly, they heard the faint rumble of thunder in the distance and darkness was almost upon them. Without a word, Reilly knelt and flopped one of the rabbits on its back. Removing the knife from its sheath, she slit the rabbit and gutted it, then skillfully skinned it. Sam watched her face, expecting to see it flushed and sickly. Instead, her features were so composed, she might have been gutting a pumpkin for a pie. Then he remembered she had removed a bullet from him. Had she been as relaxed then as she was now?

Sam shuddered when she handed the raw piece of flesh to him. "Sure you want to eat this?"

All she said was, "Find two sturdy sticks and skewer this one while I dress the other one."

He grinned at her. "I never could figure out why they call it dressing them. They looked damned naked to me."

As angry as she was with him, his comment brought a smile to her face.

Sam rose and stared down at her for a moment before he strolled away, skinned rabbit in hand. Hell, wasn't there anything she couldn't do? He did admire her though, and actually felt a little ashamed of himself for letting her do all the work. Yet, a gambler would have little knowledge of survival in the wilderness. He had to keep that in mind, but it was damned hard. Again, he suspected she was not entirely taken in by his conduct.

Later, after roasting the rabbits, they huddled close to the warmth of the fire and picked the smoked meat off the skewer. Sam slightly turned his head toward her. Her mouth looked as succulent as the meat she was eating. He felt himself growing hard as he saw her catch the juices that dribbled down her chin with her finger, then slip it inside her mouth. Sam bore this misery of watching her until she took her last bite. Taking the skewer from her hand, he tossed it into the fire.

Reilly turned and looked at him. "Why'd you—"

Recklessly, Sam cupped her chin, his mouth coming down on hers, cutting off her words. His tongue slipped between her parted lips and intimately caressed her own. A small whimper escaped her throat as her body tried to ignore the maddening sensations roiling inside her.

Determined not to let her shut him out again, Sam's kisses became hot, hard, and demanding. Then suddenly he felt her body melt against him as her arms lifted and encircled his neck. Her hands were in his hair, her fingers threading through its thickness, her mouth answering his kisses with an urgency that equaled his own.

The contact of her arching breasts pressed against the hard wall of his chest tormented Sam's lower body with a shuddering need. Moving his hand between them, he deftly freed the buttons of her shirt then pushed it aside. His hand brushed lightly over each bare breast then closed over one firm mound. As he caressed and kneaded her, her hardened nipples felt like hot points of fire stabbing at his palm.

Reilly's breath quickened and her heart pounded as he rolled her nipple between his thumb and finger. A swirling wave of pleasure uncurled within her, spreading a trail of fire that found homage in her loins.

With an anguished groan, Sam released her mouth and gently pressed her to the ground, half covering her with his hard, lean body. His eyes, dark and searing, met the blue fire shimmering in her own.

"God, I want you, angel," he said with a voice ragged and raw with desire. "I want to touch you and kiss you all over. But most of all, I want to feel your hot, wet heat closed tightly around me."

His words intensified the feverish yearning inside her even as a warning skittered through her mind. He doesn't love me. He only loves how I make him feel. I've got to put an end to this now . . . and forever, she thought frantically, her better judgment finally overshadowing her body's weakness.

At that moment, the rain they had expected all day began. Reilly gazed up at him while gentle raindrops pelted her face and mingled with the tears pooling in her eyes. "Sam, please . . . don't do this to me again."

"I wish like hell I could," he murmured shakily.

Releasing a long, discouraged groan, Sam lifted his weight from her and watched as she stood up and ran toward the shelter. *God, could any man feel such pain and keep on living?*

Chapter 25

Inside the tent, it was pitch black and the silence was palpitating with things unsaid. Reilly and Sam sat beside one another, a blanket settled around their shoulders, another one over their laps. Looking through the opening, they could see the spiral of smoke from the campfire and hear the hissing sound the dying embers made. For a moment, Reilly stared at the blackened campfire. Oh, how she wished she could so easily put out the flame that burned in her heart.

Above them, the water beat a rhythmic tattoo on the tarpaulin, and the wind swirled around them, rustling the branches that shrouded their shelter.

A thin mist swam before Reilly's eyes and a big lump rose from her heart to her throat; it was the same emptiness that she'd experienced when she'd lost her father. Except Sam was alive. Somehow she must be brave and overcome the pain and loneliness again.

Sam found Reilly's hand beneath the blanket, and he hungrily closed his warm hand over hers. He felt her tenseness and, when she didn't respond to him, her aloofness caused a pang of remorse to sweep through him. He wanted so much to tell her the truth and bridge the gap between them. In time, she would know, and he clung to the hope that it might not be too late to right the wrong.

Years ago, he and Mason had made a pact. No one must ever know they were partners, except the department that instructed them on their orders. Their survival depended on one another, and to break that pact might jeopardize the life of the other. Until he had met Reilly, Sam had never had a problem with their agreement. He trusted Reilly as much as he trusted Mason, yet his conscience would not allow him to break his pact with his partner. Such an action would only cause bad blood between them if Mason ever learned about it. Yet, in keeping this bond with Mason, he was driving her from him.

Suddenly Sam laid back and drew a ragged sigh. "We'd better get some sleep."

Reluctantly, Reilly lay down beside him and sought to put space between them. Their belongings lined the side of the shelter, so she had no place to go. Lord, how was she ever going to sleep with his body pressed so closely against her?

Sam draped his arm around her waist and ventured to breathe her name. "Reilly?" He wanted to say more, but could not find the words. He wanted her so damned badly, yet she was still avoiding him.

He heard her breath quicken, then suddenly felt her body turn as taut as a bowstring. With a heavy heart, his insides raw like an open wound, Sam released his hold on her and slowly turned his back to her.

Neither slept for a long time, but stared into the darkness, the chasm growing deeper between them, each feeling helpless to do anything about it.

At dawn, the rain began sweeping down in a fierce, steady discharge, pounding loudly against the canvas over them. Unconsciously, Sam and Reilly turned towards one another, seeking comfort and warmth. Her head resting on his shoulder, he breathed in the heavenly scent of her hair, his mind filled with passionate dreams of the woman nestled close to him.

Reilly shifted her body and one slender leg slipped between his hard muscled ones. Desire stirring within them, their bodies moved against one another, and their contented sighs merged as their mouths came together. Their tongues, hot and wet, explored and curled possessively around the other.

Sam came awake slowly. At first, he thought he was dreaming that he was kissing Reilly. But no, she was snuggled close to him, her leg between his, her womanhood pressing intimately against his hardness. As he deepened the kiss, his hand moved between them and, settling it over her breast, his thumb teased her already hardened nipple through her shirt. More, he needed more.

Not once did she protest as he deftly removed each item of her clothing. After removing his own, he wedged her legs apart and moved between her thighs, covering her with his heat.

A deep quivering need pulsed in Reilly's loins. She woke to the feel of Sam's finger sliding between the soft petals of her femininity, and his hot moist mouth sucking on the rigid peak of her breast. Reilly's mind spun dizzily, the hurt and anger she had felt earlier forgotten as a sweet, yet searing sensation unfurled like a fiery banner inside her and spread throughout her body.

Sam didn't question this sudden change in her; he only knew he wanted her more than he had wanted anyone. When she choked out his name, he groaned and took her mouth in a ravenous kiss. Reilly answered him with a need of her own, arching her body against his hand as he plied his fingers to her soft flesh. Spasms of pleasure burst inside her and her hips rocked beneath him.

The storm raging outside was no less fierce than

the tempest that had been unleashed inside the tent. Sam hovered over Reilly. Slipping his hands beneath her buttocks, he lifted her and grazed the hard, silken length of his manhood over her quivering flesh.

I love you, she wanted to scream as she dug her heels into the ground and thrust her body upward to take him within her. *I love you.*

A gust of wind slammed against the tarpaulin and gave the shelter a violent shake.

Poised to plunge deep within her welcoming sheath, Sam froze as he heard the rope groaning and creaking. "Oh God no," came his ragged cry as the rope gave way.

Feverishly aroused, Reilly responded passionately, "Oh God, yes."

Sam collapsed atop her as the wind flipped the tarpaulin to the side, sending the brush and tree limbs on top of him. The rain came down in torrents and found its way between the debris. Cold rivulets of water ran off Sam's back and onto Reilly lying beneath him.

He heard her muttered oaths and felt her hands pushing against his chest.

Sam lifted himself, groaning in agony as the limbs fell away, tearing into his back. "Reilly, are you all right?"

"No, I'm not all right. I'm mad as hell and freezing to boot."

Still between her thighs, Sam settled back on his haunches and saw the tarpaulin within reaching distance. Grabbing it, he pulled it out from under the debris and threw it over them, then covered her with his warmth.

"Darn you, Sam," she snapped, feeling his hard male member throbbing against her belly. "That was a sneaky, rotten thing to do to me."

Her reaction completely took him back. "Hell, it's not my fault the damned thing fell. You should've tied the ropes tighter."

"I don't mean that," she shot back. "I was sleeping, and you . . . you took liberties with me."

Now that bothered him. "Hey, wait just a minute here, angel. I didn't take any damned thing from you. You were giving like there was no tomorrow."

Her pride wouldn't allow her to admit that for most of the night she had fantasized about him making love to her just so she could go to sleep. Instead, the thoughts had only aroused her more. "What did you do with my clothes?"

"Hell if I know."

"Well, get off me so I can find them."

"Forget them, Reilly. As long as it's raining this hard, there's no use in trying to get dressed, and they're probably wet anyway."

"So is this blanket underneath me. Would you mind letting me up?" she snapped.

"What good would that do? The ground's wet all around us. I have a better idea." With that, he wedged his hands beneath her waist and rolled to the side, pulling her atop him. "How's that for quick thinking?" he asked slyly, scaling his hands over her naked back.

His manhood, still rock hard with arousal, was pressed against her groin, reminding Reilly of how close she had come to feeling its pulsing length inside her only moments ago. Her heart raced wildly as she felt his hands sliding downward, then lightly squeezing and kneading her buttocks. "Like this better, angel?"

"Please, Sam, don't," she pleaded.

"That isn't what you said earlier." Smoothing her hair from her neck, he placed his mouth there, tenderly scattering kisses along its length. He touched his tongue to her rapidly beating pulse, then drew tiny circles around it with his tongue. "Tell me you don't want me inside you."

265

Feeling herself sliding toward surrender, Reilly placed her hands on either side of him and pushed herself up. "No, I . . . I don't . . . ever again."

Sam groaned hoarsely as his hands caught her beneath her arms. Bringing her forward, he lifted his head and fastened his mouth over the taut peak of her breast. As he drew her nipple inside his mouth and suckled it, the sensation was almost more than she could bear, the heat rippling through her and centering itself between her thighs.

"No, Sam," she protested, but even to her own ears, her protest sounded weak.

He released her breast and fanning its wetness with his warm breath, whispered, "Liar."

The word found its way into her desire-laden mind. Liar? *He has the gall to call me a liar?* Hurt and anger blanketing one another, she quickly moved off him. Her heart pounding as though she had run a mile, she lay beside him, trying to get her body back into control.

Sam's body trembled and his breathing was ragged when he finally spoke. "Is this the way you really want it to be between us, Reilly?" he asked softly.

"No, but as I said before, Sam, you are not the man I thought I knew. I wonder if I ever really knew you at all."

"Someday you will," he admitted. "Until then, I will do everything in my power to protect you. One day, I'll get Murdock, then you can return safely to Castletown."

She knew better than to press him further. Though he'd said very little, she searched beneath the surface of his words. *Someday you will.* It had sounded like a soft-spoken warning. Someday you will know I'm an outlaw, she finished in her mind.

Reilly sat up. "Speaking of Murdock, we'd better get dressed. I'd hate for him to catch us like this."

"Yeah, you're probably right." He rolled to a

sitting position and fumbled around for his bag. His hand touched his bag and he handed it to her. "Maybe you'll find something dry in here to wear. There should be a change of clothes for both of us."

"Thanks," she said, opening the bag. "Why didn't you mention having these clothes a moment ago?" she asked, rummaging around inside the bag.

He chuckled. "I had some unfinished business to do with a beautiful woman. Any more questions?"

"No," she said quickly, not wanting to broach that subject again.

She removed a pair of his gabardine pants and the beautiful silk shirt she had seen him wearing at her house . . . his city slicker clothes, she thought with irritation. She set them on top of the bag. "They're damp, but I'm glad you had the foresight to bring them."

"Do you need some help?"

"No, I just need to stand up so I can dress."

"I'll hold the cover up for you."

As they both stood up, the rain splashed over their bare feet and legs. The light shone beneath it. Sam stifled a groan as he saw her full breasts and erect nipples before she slipped her arms inside the sleeves of his shirt. Silk against silk, he thought, his eyes caressing the satin roundness of her breasts showing between her parted shirt. God, he'd give anything to be that shirt right now. How long would it take for her to come around? He couldn't imagine going through this hell night after night.

Reilly caught the wicked look in his eyes and a sudden heat suffused her body. She turned away from him and quickly buttoned the shirt. It was way too large for her, but she had never felt anything so wonderful against her skin.

He watched her slide one slim leg into the pants leg and then the other. As she straightened, he had a brief glimpse of the tawny gold hair at the apex of her thighs before she fastened her pants. As chilled as he was, his blood still coursed through his veins like boiling water.

"I need something to hold them up," she said, clutching the additional fabric at her waist.

"I'll get the rope."

"But one side is still tied to the tree. You'll get wet and cold."

"Believe me, angel, right now that's just what I need," he admitted bluntly. "You'll probably hear my skin sizzling when the rain hits it."

Reilly couldn't believe her own boldness as she dropped her gaze below his waist. His hard shaft was thrusting out proudly from amidst the dense dark curls. Her eyes traveled slowly back to his face. One corner of his mouth was turned up in a provocative leer.

"You really are incorrigible, Sam," she snapped.

He chuckled, then flipped up the edge of the tarpaulin and walked outside in the rain. A few moments later he came back inside, dragging the rope in with him. His hair was dripping wet, but this time she didn't dare look down to see if his ardor had cooled.

"Where's the knife?" he asked as a shiver swept through him.

"It's in your saddlebag."

Retrieving the knife, Sam cut off a length of rope and dropped the knife back into the bag.

"I'll tie it around you," he offered.

With one hand, Reilly held up her pants and with the other, held up the cover. As he started to wrap it around her, the shirt got in his way. Drawing up the hem, he brought the ends together. As he started to knot them loosely together, the back of his hands brushed the undersides of her breasts. His hands stilled as he contemplated the idea of sliding his hands up the shirt and cupping her breasts.

"I wonder if it's going to rain all day," she said nervously, not missing the hungry look in his eyes.

Sam mentally shook himself of his carnal thoughts and knotted her shirt. "We can't wait around here to find out. You can bet Murdock won't stop searching for us because of the rain."

"Well, we probably should wear our wet clothes since we're going to get wet again."

Tying the rope around her waist, he said, "I'll cut the tarpaulin into two pieces. That'll help keep us partially dry."

"Good idea. That way, if we ever need it again, we each can have our own separate shelter."

Sam dropped his hands from her waist. "No. We'll need each other body's heat to keep warm. Keep holding that up while I dress."

Reilly knew he was right, but she couldn't chance having something like this happen again. And they had two or three more nights to spend together before they reached Bodie. Lord, what would she do when they reached Bodie?

"Sam, I just thought about something. We don't have any money. What're we going to do when we get to Bodie?"

"Mason gave me enough to hold us over a couple of days," he said, tugging on his pants. "I'll have to hit the gaming tables."

"But . . . but someone might recognize us."

"Yeah, it's a risk, but we don't have a choice." Reaching down in his bag, he pulled out two pairs of socks. He tucked them inside his waist band. "No sense getting them wet. When we find our boots, we'll put them on. Your arms must be tired. Let me hold it while you gather up everything."

Sam followed her around, keeping the cover over her. Fortunately, their boots were dry, but she found the clothes and coats they'd been wearing out in the rain. She wadded them up and put them in the

269

carpetbag. The rain had let up a little, but the sky still showed signs that it wasn't over yet. When they gathered everything in a pile, Sam took the knife and split the tarpaulin hanging over them. Reilly's half fell on her head and she wrapped it as well as she could around her.

Leaving Reilly's side, Sam saddled the horses and packed their gear.

By late afternoon, Reilly was so exhausted and cold, she didn't think she could go any further. The rain spilled endlessly, at times coming down in such thick sheets that she could barely see Sam riding ahead of her. The wind had whipped the canvas wrap from her time and again, and she was soaking wet.

They were traveling along a narrow logging road that cut through the mountain, flanked on the right side by tall nut pines and spruce. The left side dropped sharply and what lay beyond the forest was anybody's guess. With no place to take shelter, they had no choice but to keep going.

Reilly would never know what startled her horse. But as he reared, she noticed with alarm that she'd ridden too close to the edge of the road. Desperately tugging on the reins to pull him to the side, the horse whinnied loudly, trying to find his footing as his back hoof began sliding on the loose earth. Reilly felt her body sliding in the wet saddle and her boot slipped from the stirrup.

Her screams brought Sam to an abrupt halt. Turning in his saddle, he saw Reilly's horse stumbling back onto the road without its rider on its back. A surge of fright went straight to his heart. Dismounting, he ran toward the precipice and looked down. A pair of agonized wide, blue eyes peered up at him from a rain-washed face. Her hands clasped several branches of a shrub that was growing out of the rocks.

"Hold on, Reilly." His plea throbbed with desperation as he quickly left to get his rope.

"It's tearing away, Sam!" she cried out.

In the next instant, the roots pulled from their stronghold. Shock rippled through Sam as he heard Reilly's terrified screams.

Rope in hand, he hurried back, and looking down, saw only the tarpaulin hanging forlornly on the branch she had clung to so desperately.

When he screamed Reilly's name over and over, there was no answer from her. The only answer he received was from the mountains—returning the echo of his tormented voice.

Chapter 26

Dazed, Sam stood stone still on the edge of the cliff, his mind and body numbed by a pain so intense it blinded him. His eyes wet with unshed tears, he searched for Reilly's body down . . . down . . . deep into the woods below him. Then a movement, ever so slight, caught his eye. He blinked and looked again. He could swear he was seeing a leg hanging over a ledge, or did he want to see her so badly that he was only imagining it? He saw the leg move and let out the breath he had been holding. *My God, it was her . . . and she was alive!*

With great effort, Sam tried to choke down the fear rising in his throat. She was so damned close to the edge. God, don't let her roll off, he prayed as he secured the rope around a rock and dropped it over the cliff.

Knowing his tarpaulin would be in his way, he removed it, dropping it down to the ledge. Rope in hand, he descended the sheer face of the cliff, oblivious to the rain that lashed against him. He plucked Reilly's tarpaulin from the branches of a shrub and, dropping it to the ledge, continued down.

His heart pounding furiously, he knelt beside Reilly. She was lying on her back. He could see the faint rise and fall of her chest. Blood streaked the front of her wet shirt. Sharp rocks had ripped the silk fabric to shreds. Pushing the ragged shirt aside, he grimaced at seeing the cuts and scratches that marred her tender breasts and stomach. A long bleeding scratch ran down her rib cage. He wiped away the blood with her shirt; it continued to bleed, but it was not deep enough to be alarmed about. Next, he very gingerly pressed his hands along her ribs until he was satisfied that none were broken.

He checked his surroundings. Behind him was a deep recess cut within the cliff, dry as a bone beneath the overhang. It would make a perfect shelter. Then he looked over the ledge, surprised to see the ground was lying no more than four feet below them, sloping gradually into the thick woods.

He returned his attention to Reilly. "Reilly, can you hear me?"

Her eyes rolled beneath her lids, then barely opened. "Sam?"

Thank God. "You'll be all right now, angel."

"W-Why're you here?"

She's confused. "Where else would I be?"

Her face was scratched and a bluish knot was forming on her forehead. Afraid that she might have broken her neck, he asked, "Can you move your head?"

Very slowly, she nodded, her dazed eyes never leaving his face.

Sam let out a sigh of relief. "Good. Now, where do you hurt the most?"

"J-Just name a p-place, any p-place."

He lifted her arm and squeezed her hand. "Feel that?"

"Yes."

He kneaded her legs. "What about that?"

"Yes," she answered again.

"Reilly, I need to get you out of the rain, but I don't want to move you any more than I have to." He

274

spread the tarpaulin beside her. "With my help, can you manage to lift yourself onto the tarpaulin?"

"I think so."

"Good."

Sam gently caught her beneath her arms. Reilly lifted her buttocks, and he eased her on top of the tarpaulin. Slightly lifting the canvas, he slowly dragged her beneath the overhang into the dry space.

Placing her head in his lap, he drew her close to him. He could feel her body trembling as he rocked her gently in his arms. He tried to think of what he should do to help her. God knew he wasn't a doctor.

A weak moan escaped her softly parted lips. "I'm . . . I'm so cold."

"It's no wonder. I'll build a fire. That should help." Rising, he picked up the other piece of canvas and covered her. "Don't worry, Reilly, I'll take care of you."

Reilly fought for awareness, but her eyes closed, and she carried his words with her as blackness descended upon her.

As Sam gathered up the dry sticks and limbs lying beneath the overhang, he noticed the rain was finally letting up and a mist shrouded the mountainside. He arranged the wood just beneath the overhang as near to Reilly as possible. Fortunately, he still had matches inside his coat pocket. A few moments later he had a decent fire going, hoping the wind wouldn't switch directions and blow the smoke in on her.

Returning to Reilly, he found her asleep. He needed to get her out of her wet clothing. Kneeling beside her, he carefully undressed her. Her legs were in better shape than the rest of her body; the thick fabric the pants were made of had protected them.

After covering her nakedness, he brushed his lips across her forehead. "You just hang in there, angel. I'll be back as soon as I get our horses tended to."

It was then that he remembered he had not tethered

them. He hoped they hadn't run off, or they'd be in a worse fix than they already were. But what in the hell was he going to do with them if they were still around? If Murdock or any of his men happened to travel this way, two riderless horses would certainly draw their attention. Maybe he could find a way to bring them down here with them.

Sam leaped down from the ledge and looked up toward the road as he pushed his way through the thick undergrowth. He stopped as he came upon a path that zigzagged among the rocks and trees that grew along the hillside. Figuring he had nothing to lose, he started walking up it. From its worn appearance, Sam figured the animals traveled it frequently. A short time later he reached the road and felt a moment of relief when he saw the horses standing in the middle of the road.

Because of the rain-slick rocks and pine needles on the trail, it would be tricky to get the horses down, yet not impossible. He had to risk it, but he could only lead one horse at a time.

First, he checked Reilly's mount to see if it had been injured during the mishap. Nothing seemed amiss. Removing their belongings from both horses, he dropped them to the ledge. Untying the rope from the rock, he looped it around the saddle horn. After tethering his mount to a tree, he took Reilly's horse's reins and began the hazardous trip down the mountainside. Several times the horse stumbled, but managed to regain its footing. Then the land gradually began to slope and he reached level ground. Tethering the horse, he made his way back up the hill. Gathering the reins of the other horse, he safely repeated the treacherous route.

Returning to the ledge, he hoisted himself up and put their belongings under the overhang. Then he got the canteen and knelt beside Reilly. Tearing off a strip of her shirt, he poured water over it and cleaned her cuts and scratches. The deeper scratch continued to bleed slightly. Though his kerchief was damp, it was the driest article between them. He ripped strips from along its edges and fashioned a bandage for the wound.

Lifting her head into his lap, he dribbled a small amount of water over her lips to entice her to open her mouth. Her mouth parted slightly. "That's my girl," he said, pouring a little more.

Her eyes opened. She stared up at him with pain-filled blue eyes as she took his offering.

"How do you feel?"

"Like I . . . fell off a cliff," she groaned.

Sam chuckled. "Yeah, and you'll probably feel worse by tomorrow."

"I doubt it."

"Can you feel the heat from the fire?"

"Yes. Thank you."

"Are you hungry?"

"No. I just want to sleep," she said, her eyes drifting shut.

Sam noted lengthening shadows falling over the ledge. Shortly, the night's darkness would settle over them. Taking the rope, he drew it from one side of the ledge to the other and, pulling it taut, tied it around the rocks and made a clothesline. Gathering up the wet blankets and all their clothing, he draped the items over the rope. After adding more wood to the fire, he undressed and placed his own clothes alongside the others. Too exhausted and cold to eat, he settled down beside Reilly, the side of his body touching hers. As cold as he was, he wondered if he had enough body heat left in him to help warm her.

When Sam's eyes drifted shut, he saw himself standing on the cliff, gazing below him, searching for her body. Never had he felt such an aching loss. But when he'd discovered she was alive, he'd felt whole again. He thought back to their times together. How his heart raced when she'd walk into the bedroom. How he smelled her fresh woman's scent still lingering like a cooling mist long after she'd departed. How jubilant he felt upon hearing her laughter or seeing the blush staining her cheeks when he made an off-color remark. How fiery sparks would shoot from her blue eyes when he'd test her temper. Yes, his life had taken on a new meaning from the moment he'd met her.

Yet, she had come into his life at the wrong time. Would there ever be a right time? For him. He had thought about settling down someday, but several years down the road. Damn, he wouldn't let himself love her. She deserved a better life than he could ever give her.

With a sad smile on his face, Sam turned to Reilly and kissed her tenderly on her softly parted lips.

Hot . . . he was so hot. Restless, Sam woke up and kicked one foot out from underneath the cover, relishing the feel of the cold morning air. He heard Reilly moaning and nuzzled her neck. He felt her body shuddering against him. As he pressed his mouth against her cheek, he felt the heat beneath his lips. "Oh God no," he cried out softly.

Leaning to the side, he got the canteen. Uncorking it, he lifted her head and gave her small sips. She drank thirstily until the canteen was empty.

She coughed and her face twisted in pain.

Fear clutched his insides. Did she have pneumonia? He recalled his sister catching the disease one cold winter, and the weeks of near death before she'd miraculously recovered.

He raked his hand through his hair, blaming himself for her sickness. He should have waited until it had stopped raining before he'd set out yesterday morning. Now, they were miles from anywhere . . .

and it wasn't safe for them to stay here. If Murdock had picked up their trail, he would see and smell the smoke from their fire.

Rising, Sam picked out the driest clothing on the line and dressed quickly. The clothing was still damp and cold. He huddled before the fire, trying to get warm before he doused it. He remembered kissing her before he went to sleep. Hell, he couldn't afford to get sick too; Reilly needed him. He strapped on his gun belt, then poured the last of the water from Reilly's canteen over the hot embers.

Dropping to one knee beside her, he raked the damp silken strands from her feverish brow. "Reilly, can you hear me?"

He could see what an effort it was for her to open her eyes. When she did, they stared up at him with a strained, expectant look. "Yes?"

"I know you feel like hell, but we have to leave here. We can't risk staying here any longer and I can't leave you alone."

"I'll be fine," she said hoarsely.

He wished he felt that confident. "I'll get the horses."

He packed their belongings on the horses, then gathering her up in his arms, he eased off the ledge and carried her to the horse. Reilly held the tarpaulin around her as he helped her into the saddle, then mounted behind her. Knowing there was no way he could take the horses back up the trail to the road, he struck out for the woods, pulling Reilly's mount behind them.

Reilly's mind was in a swirling haze. Her body was so sore she felt a jarring pain with each step the horse took. Between bouts of consciousness, she'd catch a glimpse of sunlight and blue sky through the canopy of lofty green branches hovering over them, and hear the wind singing through the trees. Sometime later, she opened her eyes and quickly closed them as the bright sunlight stabbed her eyes.

"I've found a stream, Reilly," Sam said, urging his mount toward the water.

The forest had given way to a mountain meadow where tall grasses swayed gently in the breeze. A narrow stream snaked its way through the valley, the morning sun sparkling like diamonds over its surface.

He drew the horse to a halt and dismounted. Reilly slipped into his waiting arms. Gently placing her in a sunny spot on the grass, he stroked her cheek with the back of his hand. "You're not quite as hot. You must be feeling better," he said anxiously.

She smiled. "Yes, a little. I'm sorry for being such a bother, Sam."

"A bother? After all you've been through with me? If you think about it, I'm the bother. If you'd never met me, you wouldn't be going through this hell."

His statement caused an avalanche of thoughts to tumble through her mind. But one thought stood out more than all the rest. He had not left her alone, but had stayed by her when she'd needed him. He had to feel something for her too, but she wondered if she would ever hear him admit it.

"Will you be all right while I unpack our gear and tend to the horses?"

"Of course, go ahead. The sun feels wonderful."

Sam unsaddled the horses. After quenching their thirst, they moved to the meadow, munching hungrily on the thick tall grass. Returning to Reilly's side, he saw she was sleeping peacefully. He laid their clothing and blankets over the sun-warmed rocks to dry. Then positioning himself on a rock and laying the rifle across his lap, he looked around the area, prepared to shoot anything that moved. Reilly had to eat, and he was tired of jerky and cheese.

God, please don't let her have pneumonia, he prayed fervently. He could only remember praying this hard when his sister was at death's door. He had been too young at the time of her illness to recall how they had doctored her. He could only remember how frightened he was, thinking she might die.

A movement at the corner of his eye caught his attention. Slowly, he turned his head. A mule deer had just come from the forest and was lapping at the water several yards upstream. Poising the rifle, Sam took aim and squeezed the trigger. The bullet hit right on target; the animal's legs crumpled beneath him.

The shot woke Reilly with a start. "Sam!"

Hurrying to her side, he knelt beside her. "No cause for alarm. I only shot a deer."

She managed to smile. "*You* shot a deer?"

He grinned. "Sure did. Of course, it was almost standing right beside me."

She knew better, but kept her suspicions to herself. "I'm proud of you."

"I haven't cooked it yet."

"Sam, I can't eat it anyway."

"I'll fix some venison stock, but it'll be bland because we don't have any seasonings."

"All right . . . I'll try it," she agreed, mainly to appease him. The thought of eating nauseated her.

After Sam removed a few choice cuts of meat from the deer, he dragged the bloody carcass into the woods and covered it with brush and rocks. Still, he'd have to keep a close eye out for predators, knowing the scent of blood might draw them their way.

After building a fire, Sam set the small pan of meat, bones, and water over the hot coals. Skewering a small roast, he placed the meat over the fire. For the next hour, he was back and forth, either checking on Reilly, or turning the meat. After the venison had boiled for a couple of hours, he removed the pan from the coals and set it in the stream to cool. Later he would skim off the fat and reheat it. He hated that it was taking so long to prepare her broth.

Reilly napped off and on throughout the day. Sam periodically doused his kerchief in the stream and wiped her face and neck. She was still feverish, but not as hot as she had been the previous night. But Sam knew that the highest temperatures struck more often at night.

He brought her a cup of the hot broth. At the first taste, she pushed his hand holding the cup away. "Lord, that's awful."

"I know it is, but you need it."

She managed to get a small portion of it down, but suddenly her stomach revolted. Sam supported her as she rolled to her side and retched. The heaving brought such acute pain to her side she cried out in pain.

Sam held her in his arms, stroking her back soothingly. "Oh God, Reilly, I'm sorry."

After a while, she fell asleep. Every so often he'd hear her coughing. It terrified him. He checked the blankets and clothing lying on the rocks and, finding them dry, removed the tarpaulin from her.

Reilly woke up as he was dressing her. "So m-much for modesty, huh?" She coughed and a knife-searing pain shot through her side.

Sam paused in the middle of buttoning her shirt. Her face had wrinkled into a horrible grimace. "Yeah, those days are long over, angel."

"If my body . . . looks as bad as it f-feels, it's . . . it's probably not much to look at anyway."

Sam studied her worriedly as she struggled with her words. "Reilly, the external injuries are minor, and as far as I can tell you don't have any broken bones. But something's wrong, or you wouldn't be running this constant fever."

"Don't w-worry. As a child, I'd r-run a high fever even . . . with a slight cold. Lord, when I had the . . . the measles, it went so high I had convulsions." When she saw Sam's face turn white as a sheet, she scolded herself for her carelessness. She said hastily, "B-But that was the only t-time it ever happened."

"That's nice to know," he said grimly, drawing the blanket over her.

"It's just a b-bad cold. By tomorrow I'll probably be fit as a f-fiddle."

"Sure," Sam said as he stood up. "I've got to build us a shelter."

She nodded and closed her eyes.

Sam stood there a moment gazing down at her, his heart beating suffocatingly in his chest. Bad cold? He doubted it.

Chapter 27

As Sam had predicted, Reilly's temperature soared and her cough worsened during the night. His doctoring skills were damned pathetic, he thought angrily as he wiped her feverish brow with the wet cloth. The word *convulsion* roared through his ears; he worked frantically to prevent it from happening.

It was early morning when Reilly gripped his wrist and with wild-looking eyes cried out, "I'm going to die, aren't I?"

Her remark was Sam's undoing. "And become a real live angel? Hell no," he stormed out, then quickly turned his head. There was no way he could mask the uncertainty and fear that tormented him. "I'll be back in just a minute," he said, rising to his feet and leaving the shelter.

Once outside, Sam took a deep breath and slowly exhaled, trying to get a hold of himself. She's strong, she'll make it, his mind screamed. He walked behind the shelter and took care of his personal needs. He had just finished fastening his pants when she cried out his name. Running back to the shelter, he crawled inside. She was sitting up, clutching the blanket around her neck.

"You're leaving me!"

Sam knelt beside her and, gently gripping her

shoulders, eased her back down. "No, Reilly, I was just outside."

Her bewildered eyes darted here and there over his face as he wiped the hair from her eyes. "Just . . . Just let me die, then you w-won't have to put up with me anymore."

"For God's sake, Reilly, you don't know what you're saying."

Sam drew her onto his lap and held her trembling body tightly against him. "Shhh, go to sleep, angel."

"No, I'm a-afraid when I wake up y-you won't be here."

"I won't ever leave you; please believe me," he said tenderly, pressing her cheek against his chest.

After another spell of coughing, she fell asleep in his arms. Easing her from his lap, he laid her down and covered her. Sam was afraid that if he didn't use this chance to get some sleep, he might get sick himself. He laid down beside her and closed his eyes. When he woke up, he went outside. From the position of the sun, he knew it was almost noon. All that was left of the campfire was a few smoldering embers.

Now that he felt rested, he could think more clearly. He figured it would take a full day of riding before he could get her to a doctor in Bodie, and that would be pushing it since he couldn't travel as fast carrying her. She might not survive the trip, but she for damned sure wasn't going to survive here.

As he struck out to get the horses, he heard a rustling sound in the shrubs to his left. The hair rose on the back of his neck. Sam turned quickly and, in the same instant, whipped his revolver from the holster. Walking slowly toward the thicket, he could barely make out a person crouching behind it.

"Come out of there . . . now," he warned.

The person came quickly to his feet and started running. Sam holstered his gun and crashed through the thicket. Diving toward the man, he grabbed his ankles, tumbling him to the ground.

"God almighty, you're a girl!" Sam bellowed in stunned fascination as he rolled his captive to her back. Not only was she a young girl, but an Indian.

Sam caught a glimpse of a gleaming silver blade as her hand arched toward him. Catching her wrist, he brought it to the ground, trying to twist the knife from her hand. Planting her foot against his chest, she let out a fierce cry and shoved him backwards with all her strength. Leaping quickly to her feet, her lethal blade clasped tightly in her small hand, snapping green eyes glared at him defiantly.

"Look, I'm not going to fight you," Sam said, closely scrutinizing the girl. Green eyes—she wasn't a full-blooded Indian. Also her skin was too light and her hair was a dark reddish brown. Her tall, slender body was clothed in skins pieced together to make a dress. She wore moccasins laced to the knee.

A low, threatening growl behind him interrupted his perusal. Whipping his gun again from the holster, he rolled to his belly, coming eye to eye with a gray wolf. Sharp, pointed fangs were bared to the gum and a long tongue dangled hungrily from the corner of his mouth.

Sam took aim.

"No, Wolf, stay!" the girl called out.

Sam's finger froze on the trigger, a bewildered expression on his face as the girl rushed toward the wolf. Kneeling beside the animal, she clasped him around his neck. "Don't shoot him, please."

"Well, I'll be damned," Sam swore, "now I've seen everything." He slowly got to his feet, his gun still aimed at the shifty-eyed animal.

"He won't attack you unless I tell him to."

"I'm supposed to believe that when he's looking at me like he wants me for his next meal?"

"No, I fed him good this morning," she said

offhandedly as she stood up, her hand still gripping the knife.

"That's encouraging." Sam took a chance and holstered his gun to show her he meant her no harm. "Why don't you put away that knife? In turn, I'm trusting you to keep your wolf at bay."

Hesitantly, she slipped the knife inside the sheathe at her waist, but kept her hand on its hilt.

"My name's Sam Chandler. What's yours?"

She studied him long and hard for a moment, then replied, "Moira."

He smiled. "A very pretty name." Not exactly an Indian name, he added to himself. "I take it you live around here somewhere?"

She nodded.

"I'd like to ask a favor of you, Moira."

"A favor?"

"Yes. In the lean-to is a very sick young woman. If I don't get help for her soon, I'm afraid she'll die. Do you know anyone nearby who might help her?"

Moira's eyes swept his tall, muscular body. He was the most handsome man she had ever seen. "My mother knows healing, but she won't come here. You'll have to bring her to the house. But first I have to ask my father and he isn't home yet. He'd be very upset with me if I brought home strangers without him being there."

"When do you expect him to return?"

"At any time."

Frustrated, Sam plowed his hand through his hair. "I don't have time to wait. Look, if you're afraid I'll harm you and your mother, I'll give you my gun. My rifle's in the lean-to." Sam unfastened his gun belt, and as he held it out to her, the wolf growled and showed his fangs. Sam quickly drew back his hand. "Looks to me like you've got all the protection you need."

After giving the matter considerable thought,

Moira decided she could trust the man. He could have killed her pet in a heartbeat. Sighing, she acquiesced. "All right, Mr. Chandler, I'll take you. We've sighted a grizzly recently, so keep your gun. When we reach the house, I'll take your guns then, in case my father's home. Perhaps he won't be as angry with me if he sees you're not armed."

Returning to the campsite with Moira and the wolf, Sam went inside the lean-to and woke up Reilly. He told he where he was taking her, but her eyes looked so vague he doubted she understood him. After wrapping the blankets around her, he carried her outside.

"Moira, would you mind looking after her while I get our things together and bring in the horses?"

"Sure," Moira said, her green eyes fixed on the tangled blond hair that cascaded over Sam's arm. "She has pretty hair."

"Yeah, she does," Sam answered, a soft smile on his mouth as he looked down on Reilly's pale face.

Reilly turned her head toward the unfamiliar voice. As she tried to speak, she started coughing. Moira saw the helplessness and pain on Sam's face as he held her to him. When the coughing subsided, he urged, "Don't try to talk, angel."

"Is her name Angel?" Moira asked.

"No . . . Reilly."

"She's your . . . your wife?"

"No, but she's very special to me."

Moira didn't miss the tenderness that washed over Sam's face. Her hopes suddenly vanished like smoke. She quickly turned her head so he wouldn't see her jealousy. It was obvious this woman claimed his heart. Perhaps her mother couldn't save her and then he would want her as his woman. Moira scolded herself for such a cruel thought. "My mother will make her well," she said, straightening her shoulders proudly.

289

"God, I hope so," Sam said as he laid Reilly down. He smoothed the hair from her brow. "Everything's going to be fine. I'll be right back."

Her fevered brain brought on her worst fear. He had found someone to stay with her. She clutched his arm. "You're l-lying. You . . . you won't come back."

Sam placed his hand gently over hers and lightly squeezed it. She seemed obsessed with the idea that he didn't want her. "Moira is staying with you until I bring in the horses." With an exasperated sigh, he rose and walked across the rock-laden stream to the meadow.

Moira sat down next to the young woman and, drawing her knees to her chest, critically studied the sick woman's face. She had closed her eyes again, and long, curling brown lashes rested starkly against a complexion that was as pale as her hair. Her full lips were dry and bloodless. Yes, she was very sick, but she would live. She had seen the healing powers of her mother too many times to think otherwise. But Sam would need someone to fill the idle hours while she was recovering from her illness, and Moira intended to be that someone. Also, she wondered at Reilly's suspicion that Sam would leave her. Would he?

A while later, Sam had everything packed on the horses. "Would you like to ride the extra horse, Moira?"

"Yes, we could make better time."

When Sam took her arm and assisted Moira into the saddle, he had no idea how that simple touch sent Moira's heart racing in her chest and sent her stomach to fluttering.

Lifting Reilly, Sam gently laid her across the saddle, then mounted behind her. Drawing her up into his arms, he nestled her head against his shoulder and brushed his lips across her forehead.

Moira's features tightened. "When we get to the

house, you stay back a ways until I tell Mother," she suggested.

"Fine," Sam agreed. "Lead the way, Moira."

An unrelenting sun beat down on them as they traveled slowly through the meadow, the wolf walking alongside Moira's horse. Thinking Reilly was too hot, Sam eased the blanket from around her. Removing his hat, he placed it atop her head to shield her face from the intense rays. His heart wrenched painfully as he gazed down at her. God, was he doing the right thing, placing her life in the hands of a woman he knew nothing about? But what else was he to do? Any doctoring at all was better than what he had done for her.

An array of wildflowers washed the valley with vibrant color while scattered forests gave way to jagged cliffs dotted here and there with pine tree crowns. Beyond these, rising high in the clouds were barren castellated mountains still clad with snow.

Leaving the meadow, Sam followed Moira and the wolf along a path in the woods. In a clearing ahead of them, he saw a thin spiral of blue smoke wreathing up from the chimney of a small log house. Several clucking chickens with their brood of chicks scratched the dirt-packed ground. A scrawny cow and a goat, both tethered by long ropes, grazed the grass that edged the clearing.

Moira reined her horse to a halt and Sam rode in beside her. "Here, you'd better take this," he said, unbuckling his gun belt and handing it to her. Then he removed his rifle from the saddle, and gave that to her too. Moira rode toward the house, the wolf darting ahead of her. Sam counted five children in the yard, either playing or busy at their chores. Moira appeared to be the oldest of the siblings. Like Moira, they wore buckskin clothing that appeared to have been resewn many times.

An Indian woman that Sam assumed was Moira's

mother knelt on the ground, her hands clasping a pestle and working it in a circular motion inside a large wooden bowl.

Sam's attention was drawn toward the house as the hide covering the entrance was swept aside and a small, wiry man stepped outside. Sam shifted uneasily in the saddle. Was this her father? He looked like a throwback from prehistoric days. He carried a rifle, resembling an old Sharp. He wore a rusty black garment, his legs encased in thick blanket leggings and moccasins. He didn't wear a hat and his long hair and full beard were grizzled and matted.

When he saw Moira riding in astride the unfamiliar horse, he stepped down from the porch and walked over to her. After handing her father the guns, she dismounted. As she spoke with her father, the man's eyes stayed fixed on Sam.

Finally, he motioned Sam to ride in. The woman joined her husband while the children gathered around Moira. They all watched Sam with wide-eyed curiosity as he reined his horse to a halt in front of the house.

"Welcome to our home, Mr. Chandler. I'm Cyrus MacDonald. This is Little Fox, my wife. My daughter says yore woman's feeling sickly and you need our help."

"Yes. I'm sorry to run in on you like this. Moira was reluctant to let me come, because she didn't know if you'd be here or not."

"Jest got in. What's her name?" Cyrus asked, nodding toward Reilly.

"Reilly Reynolds. I've done all I can for her, but nothing's helped. She's getting worse. Moira said her mother might help her."

Sam saw compassion in Little Fox's dark eyes as she gazed at Reilly. She was not as old as she had looked from a distance. Her bronze face was a lacework of fine wrinkles and her braided black hair was interspersed with gray strands. She looked back at her husband. He nodded.

"You may bring her inside our house," Little Fox said.

"Thank you."

Turning toward her children, she ordered, "Do your chores and stay outside."

Cyrus handed one of his sons their guns. "Here, I'll take her," he offered.

Sam handed Reilly down to the man, then dismounted and followed them inside the house. Little Fox unrolled a pallet and Cyrus laid Reilly on it. Her eyes fluttered open and darted anxiously from one face to another until they fastened on Sam. "You're here," she said hoarsely.

Kneeling, he brushed the back of his knuckles across her cheek. "I found someone who's going to make you well, Reilly. Her name is Little Fox."

Reilly smiled softly, then closed her eyes.

Cyrus left them, saying he would see that their horses were tended to.

Little Fox knelt beside Reilly. "How long has she been sick, Mr. Chandler?"

"Two days." Sam went on to tell her about Reilly's accident and all that had happened since that day.

"I will do what I can for her. Now, you must leave."

"But you might need me," Sam protested.

"If I need someone, Moira will help me. You will only get in my way. Now go, Mr. Chandler."

Sam stood up and walked toward the entrance. Reluctant to leave Reilly, he never made it outside. Thinking Little Fox wouldn't notice him, he leaned against the inside wall beside the doorway and surveyed the room. Dried bunches of plants were tied together and hanging from several places around the small room. On one wall was a stone fireplace and flames licked at the iron pot suspended over the hearth; an unfamiliar aroma wafted from it. Suspended from the rafters in one corner of the room was the forequarters of a deer. Stretched on the walls were dry skins of various animals. A hand-hewn crude table and bench served as the table. Sam didn't see any beds, only mats rolled against the walls.

Suddenly, it dawned on him that he and Reilly would be sharing this room with the whole family. So much for privacy, Sam thought grudgingly. But what good would privacy do them anyway? Still, Cyrus and Little Fox had to have had their private moments somewhere to have produced six children.

Little Fox glanced over at Sam. "Mr. Chandler?"

"Yes?" he asked, shifting his attention her way.

"Please go outside," she demanded softly.

Sam almost shot back a sharp retort. Hell, it wouldn't do to make her mad. Pushing the hide aside, he stepped outside on the porch.

Resting heavily against the wall beside the entrance, he clenched and unclenched his fists with despair. Surely this damned sickness wouldn't take her from him, not after all she had survived. Yet Sam knew with sickening clarity that death had no respect for people, even someone like Reilly.

Chapter 28

"Where's Sam?" Reilly cried out.

A muscle worked furiously in Sam's jaw at the sound of Reilly's voice. *If she calls for me one more damned time, I'm going in.*

"The young 'ens are givin' yore horses a good rub down," Cyrus said, stepping upon the porch. "They'll bring along yore things in a little while."

"Thanks," Sam said, anxiously pacing the floor. He heard Reilly call his name again. He started for the door. Cyrus stepped in front of him, blocking his way. "She'll let you know if she needs you."

"She's letting me know now."

"I mean Little Fox. She don't like nobody, 'specially strangers, in the room when she's doctorin'."

"Why not?"

"'Cause she ain't got time ta fool with you. Now, if you want her ta help that little gal, you'll wait right here and let her do it. Little Fox knows what she's doin'. We have six healthy young 'ens. That ought ta tell you sumpin'." Walking to the end of the porch, Cyrus picked up a chair and set it down beside Sam. "Now, sit yoreself down afore you wear my durn floor out."

Sam plopped down in the chair and propped his

elbows on his knees, cupping his chin in his hands. "I'm sorry, it's not that I don't trust your wife, Mr. MacDonald. I'm just so damned angry with myself. If it wasn't for me, Reilly wouldn't be in this condition. I pushed her too hard . . . too fast. I should've waited until there was a break in the weather."

Cyrus studied him for a long moment then said, "Yeah, but when the law's tailin' you, you caint wait on the weather ta change, can you?"

"What?" Sam cut his eyes toward Cyrus, thinking he'd misunderstood him.

Cyrus propped his shoulder against the support post and pulled a pouch of tobacco from his pocket. Sticking a wad in his mouth, he chewed it several moments before positioning it comfortably in his jaw.

Sam repeated his question. "Did you just say something about the law tailing me?"

"Yep. I was in Castletown just after you and Miss Reynolds escaped. Heared all about it, Chandler."

"They why are you helping us?"

"Mainly because that girl's father was a good friend of mine. If one of my young 'ens was in a passel of trouble, he'd do the same for me."

Sam looked at him in disbelief. "You knew Morgan Reynolds?"

Cyrus chuckled. "Maybe I ought ta back up a bit. Years ago, before Reilly first come out here ta be with her dad, Morgan hired me as a guide. He wanted to take photographs of places that nobody'd seen back in the East. I traveled with him for quite a while.

"Anyhow, I happened ta be passing through Castletown on my way home and saw his name on the sign over his studio. I went ta pay him a visit, but his place was closed. So, I went next door ta Waters Mercantile Store ta ask where he lived. Miss Waters told me Morgan died a year ago and that Reilly had

296

taken over the runnin' of his business.

"Well, then I learned about the sheriff tryin' ta capture you, but you and Reilly had escaped. I didn't hear nuthin' else because Miss Waters's father come into the store and she clammed up real quick like. In the Gold-Dust Saloon, I heerd the rest. Did you really rob that bank and kill the teller?"

"No," Sam said bitterly, plowing his hands through his hair.

"Didn't think so," Cyrus said, spitting a stream of tobacco juice over the railing.

Sam shrugged. "Thanks for the vote of confidence."

"No, it ain't that I'm that trustin'. I jest know how Sheriff Murdock works. Awhile back, I stayed a few days in a small town in Arizona. Murdock was the sheriff. They was havin' problems with cattle rustlers. Anyways, Murdock brought in this young feller, said he was a rustler and had him hanged. Murdock claimed he'd found the man's brand stamped over another cattleman's brand." Suddenly his eyes turned fierce and a deep scowl lined his forehead. "He was a family man too, with three young'ens. To my dyin' day, I'll never stop hearin' his young wife's screamin' and cryin' when the hangman placed the noose around his neck. Over and over, I kept sayin' to myself, 'Cyrus, that could be you.'

"Well, I could tell the folks there was real upset over it like me, but nobody said nuthin'.

"Then one night I was sharin' a bottle with a drunk in a saloon. He told me he thought the young feller was set up. Said the town had had its share of problems, but things had turned from bad ta worse since Murdock took over as sheriff." He hesitated. "Heered pretty much the same things goin' on in Castletown. Anyhow, you might be guilty, or you might not, but if that little gal in there thinks you ain't, then I'd take her word long afore I'd take Murdock's."

Little Fox interrupted their conversation. "Mr. Chandler, can you come inside a moment?"

Sam looked behind him and saw Little Fox standing in the entrance, an expression of deep concern on her face. Thinking the worst, his heart tripped several beats as he bounded to his feet. "Oh God, don't tell me she's—"

"No, she will be fine once I get her fever down. But she is restless. She keeps saying you are not here. You go in and maybe she will settle down so I can tend to her."

Sam sighed. "Sure, I'll talk to her," Sam said, walking past Little Fox into the house.

As Sam knelt beside Reilly, she gazed up at him, her hand reaching for his face. He felt the heat of her hand as she touched his cheek. "It doesn't matter."

"What doesn't matter, Reilly?" he asked softly.

"I don't care if you're an outlaw," she choked out. "Just stay with me."

Her words tore through his heart. Now he understood her fears. God, she'd made the connection between Mason and her photograph. That's the only thing that would make her think he was an outlaw. He turned her hand and brushed his mouth over her palm. "Ah . . . Reilly . . . my angel, I'm not an outlaw. Please trust me. We've been through too much together for me to ever consider leaving you behind." He smiled. "These people want to help us. We're safe here; Murdock won't find us. As soon as you're well, we'll leave . . . together. Understand?"

He couldn't know if she understood him or not. The fever was taking its toll on her, and in her eyes all he could read was confusion. He squeezed her hand. "Please, lie still and let Little Fox make you well. I'll be right outside. I promise."

Standing up, he walked toward the doorway.

Pausing, he turned around and saw her watching him. "I promise," he repeated as he stepped outside. "I hope I did some good," he said to Little Fox. "I don't know why she thinks I'd desert her," he lied, hoping Reilly had not, or would not blurt her worst fears to Little Fox. "Would you like me to stay with her while you treat her?"

"First, let me see if she will rest, now that she has seen you. I need to be alone with her for a little while and then you can come in as often as you like."

Sam nodded. He knew Little Fox would call him now if she needed him.

When Little Fox left, Cyrus said, "I'm gonna have ta leave again in the mornin'. I'm meetin' a man in Bodie who's hired me to take him and a group of Easterners on a hunt. The hunt ain't till next month, but he wants to get it all planned out afore they get here. If it wasn't already set up, I'd stay. Hate runnin' out on you like this, but I should be back in three days or so. You ought ta still be here."

"I'll be glad to help out in any way I can while you're gone. Also, I'd be glad to pay you for our upkeep."

Sam's offer seemed to insult the man. He said gruffly, "No, I ain't doin' this for the money, Mr. Chandler. It don't take much for us to live on."

"Thanks, Mr. MacDonald. I'm glad you trust me enough to leave me here with your family. Do you leave them alone like this quite a lot?"

"Comes in spurts. Sometimes I go for months without work. But when I'm gone, it can be for weeks at a time. They do fine though. Caleb and Paul learned how to shoot the day they was big enough to tote a rifle. They're good hunters now, so I don't have to worry 'bout nobody goin' hungry or gettin' killed by bears or mountain lions. And any strangers comin' around lookin' for trouble, change their minds when they see our wolf. Only one thing of

299

value I got here that would interest a man no how. My wife and oldest daughters. Wolf's mighty protective over them. One word from them and he'd tear a man apart in a second if he tried to rape one of 'em.''

Sam didn't comment. He knew he could've killed the wolf had his intention been to rape Moira. She had been too eager to take care of him herself with her knife.

"Well, while you're gone, I'll be glad to watch over them too. That is, if you'll return my gun and rifle."

"Caleb has 'em. I doubt the law'll ever track you here, but in case they should, you'll need them."

Reilly slept intermittently throughout the rest of the day. Sam made certain he was always at her side when she was awake. He now understood why she thought he would abandon her. As an outlaw, he'd want to make a fast getaway. She thought she was hindering his escape. Had she realized who Mason was the first time she'd seen him? If so, it was no wonder she couldn't believe all those lies he had told her. How frightened she must be right now. She was depending on an outlaw to protect her, a man she had lost trust in, yet she had no choice but to accompany him. She had given him refuge in her home, so in the law's eyes, she was just as much a criminal as he.

During those times he sat with her, Sam waited anxiously for her to bring her fears out in the open again, but she never mentioned them. He began to wonder if she even remembered telling him at all. He figured it would be better to keep this knowledge to himself; he could not tell her the truth regardless and it sickened him.

He could find no fault with Little Fox's skills. She had assured him that the shock from Reilly's fall,

300

combined with a bad chest cold, had brought on her fever. How she knew this, Sam didn't question. Just knowing she didn't have pneumonia relieved his mind.

Little Fox had applied a poultice made from the inner bark of a white pine to Reilly's cuts and bruises, and to break up her fever, she'd prepared a hot brewed drink of tansy and catnip leves. She gave Reilly this concoction frequently throughout the day.

Early the next morning, Reilly's fever broke. And the first person she saw was Sam. He had slept on a pallet beside her. As he rolled over and saw her watching him, the soft smile wreathing her mouth had taken his breath away.

As he leaned forward to kiss her, she pressed her fingertips over his lips and, with a negative nod of her head, denied him the pleasure. "No, you don't want to be sick too. I'll be well soon."

The only thing that kept him from risking a kiss from her was hearing the encouragement in her softly spoken words. Their relationship wasn't over . . . just put on hold for a while. He would do everything in his power to keep her thoughts channeled in that direction. Somehow, someway, he had to regain her trust again.

Chapter 29

On the fourth day of Reilly's convalescence, Little Fox asked Moira to move Reilly's pallet outside on the porch, telling Reilly the fresh air and warm sunshine would speed her recovery. Her body still ached, but her cuts were healing. She still had a cold, but it was no longer in her chest.

Reilly eased herself down on the pallet and rested her back against the wall. Drawing her knees to her chest, her eyes roamed around the yard. Everyone was busy at one chore or another. Sam was helping the older boys, Caleb and Paul, rechink the gaps between the logs and patch the chimney. She admired Sam for helping the family in any way he could. He'd told her he'd insulted Cyrus by offering to pay him for their upkeep and Reilly's care.

Ruth and Will, the ten-year-old twins, were working in the vegetable garden. Moira was hanging the clothing on the line that Elsa had just washed. and the "big bad wolf" was dozing in the front yard, not the least bit interested in attacking the chickens that were all but stepping on top of him. Looking at that wolf now, it was hard to believe Sam's story about the beast almost attacking him. The wolf looked more like a sheep in wolf's clothing rather than the reverse. Reilly chuckled. She knew there was a comparison somewhere. Sam would have fit the same description until recently. Now it seemed he was the wolf in sheep's clothing. But regardless of what he was, she knew he would watch over her. Much like Wolf watching over this family.

Reilly could only vaguely recall what Mr. Mac-Donald looked like, but she would swear he and the wolf were blood kin. Had she not been delirious with fever, seeing that bushy face and wild-looking hair would have certainly scared her to death. When her fever had broken, she had asked Sam if the man was real, or only a figment of her imagination. Sam had then told her about the unusual family that had taken them in. Cyrus MacDonald was Irish and Little Fox was the daughter of a Shoshone chief. Whether or not they were married was anyone's guess. Cyrus had been a fur trader in the beginning, but when wealthy hunters as far away as England began venturing out West to hunt the bighorns, he found it more profitable to become a scout and guide.

When Sam had told her that Cyrus had been a guide and a good friend of her father, it had stunned her. Then Sam had told her that Cyrus had been in Castletown and had heard about their escape. Because she was his friend's daughter and he had heard enough about Floyd Murdock to know he didn't trust him, he figured the sheriff had set Sam up on false charges. Still, he had no proof that Sam wasn't guilty. All he'd had was Sam's word. Like her, he could never believe Sam was an outlaw.

In truth, Reilly wished she'd never discovered that Sam was an outlaw. That knowledge tormented her. Could she convince him to give up his outlawry? They could change their identities and move far away where Murdock would never find them. Let someone else get rid of Murdock. Perhaps his friend, Mason, or another man out for revenge would do the job for him. But first she must know his feelings for her before she ever made the suggestion.

Still, there were those photographs and negatives still hidden at her house. And where were Sam's copies? To protect Sam from the law, she had to protect Mason too. If someone other than Murdock found those photographs, they'd turn them in to the authorities. Someone would talk for certain and the law would be after Sam too.

Reilly couldn't believe the workings of her mind. Did she love Sam so much that she would go to such limits to protect his outlaw friends? Yes, she would do anything for him. He had to care for her at least a little, or he would not be here with her now. Oh how she wished that could be true, but whatever else Sam might be, he was not a man without a conscience. He might only be staying with her until he felt assured she had completely recovered from her illness. Knowing Cyrus was a friend of her father's, Sam would feel safe in leaving her with this family. She might wake up one morning and find him gone.

The subject of her thoughts came around the corner of the house whistling and carrying a pan of mortar. Sam hadn't known she would be outside today, so he didn't look her way. Setting the pan on the ground, he began chinking the cracks between the logs.

The sun's rays were hotter on the front of the house, and there were no trees to shade Sam as he worked. Sweat rolled down his face and several times he had to stop to wipe it from his eyes. She couldn't see a dry spot on his shirt, and grimaced when she noticed it was one of his nice silk ones. She looked toward the clothesline and saw his rugged, more durable clothing, hanging on it.

That's when she saw Moira approaching with a pail of water and a dipper. She passed Reilly without so much as glancing her way . . . and she knew Reilly was sitting there. Reilly got along well with the rest of the children, especially Ruth and Elsa, but Moira went out of her way to be unfriendly. The only time the girl had spoken to her was when she couldn't avoid it. Finally, Reilly had decided to leave her alone; she couldn't force Moira to be her friend.

Elsa and Ruth loved brushing Reilly's hair, although Reilly didn't know why since it had been forever since she'd washed it. She had seen Moira glaring at the girls when they took up the task. What on earth had she done to Moira that caused her to show such animosity toward her?

Moira set the pail of water on the ground near Sam and filled the dipper. "Sam, would you like a drink?"

Sam turned at the sound of her voice. "Sure. Thanks." He smiled that charming smile that always caused Reilly to melt. "You'll have to hold it for me. My hands are messy."

Reilly noticed Moira move in close to Sam, much closer than necessary. In fact, he had to step back as she lifted the dipper because of the long handle.

When he finished, Moira asked, "I could help you with the chinking and you'd get through faster."

"Thanks, but I'm almost finished. Your brothers probably could use your help though. The bees have riddled the chimney with holes. I'm sure they'd like a drink of that water too."

Reilly could tell by the downfallen expression on Moira's face that she didn't like his suggestion at all. "Mother needs me to help her prepare the noon meal." With that, she turned and disappeared around the house with the pail of water.

If her mother needed her, then why did she offer to help Sam in the first place? Reilly wondered. Had Sam noticed her excuse?

Moira returned shortly and poured the rest of the water into a bowl sitting on a stump. "You can wash up here when you're finished. I'll see you later," she said, stepping onto the porch. She stopped briefly beside Reilly and shot her a killing look before she entered the house.

Now Reilly understood why Moira didn't like her. Her eyes cut toward Sam as he leaned over the bowl and splashed water on his face. Moira was in love with Sam. No, infatuated with him would better describe it. She doubted Moira had met many men or boys being stuck way out here all her life. She could not help feeling pity for the young girl. At sixteen-years-old, this was probably Moira's first experience with the the emotion. Reilly smiled to herself. *She felt it a lot earlier than I did. It took me twenty-four years.* But Reilly knew her own deep feelings for Sam were more than mere infatuation . . . which she had thought it to be in the beginning. She wondered if Sam realized Moira's infatuation. A while ago, he had done nothing to raise the girl's hopes.

"A penny for your thoughts."

Reilly jumped at the sound of Sam's voice. He was standing in front of the porch with his arms crossed over the railing, grinning at her. "You sure are a sight for sore eyes."

Reilly chuckled. "Only because you've been in the sun too long. I look terrible, and you know it. But thanks anyway. Are you finished?"

"Yes, with that section," he said, coming up the steps. "I'll start on the other side tomorrow."

He sat down beside her, his back against the wall, and stretched out his long legs, crossing them at his ankles. His head turned her way. He gazed into her eyes for a long moment. "You know what I'd like more than anything right now?"

"What?" she dared to ask, wondering what kind of ribald answer he'd give her.

"Privacy . . . like we had at your house. For two nights now, I've barely had any sleep."

"I've slept fine."

"Yeah, I would too if I had a cup of that sleeping

307

potion Little Fox gives you. I've never heard the likes of so much snoring, grunting, and snorting going on under one roof in my life. If I didn't know better, I'd think I was sleeping with the pigs. It smells about as bad in there too. I don't think those boys have had a bath in months."

Reilly laughed. "Yes, I'll agree with you there. Have you seen a tub of any kind anywhere?"

"No. I figure they bathe in the lake. I was taking a walk yesterday and found it. It isn't far from here. If I'd had clean clothes with me, I would've taken a bath then." He hesitated as a thought came to his mind. He leaned over and whispered conspiringly, "We could sneak down there later."

"Sneak? With six kids always under our feet? Think again, Sam. Anyway, as much as I'd like to take a bath, I'm sure the water's too cold. I want to get well so we can leave."

"I know. Still, you could go with me."

"No, you should go alone. If they see us leave together, they'll follow for sure to see what we're up to."

"Yeah, I've noticed them watching us closely. They're wondering if we're lovers."

Reilly blushed.

Actually, the only one Sam had noticed watching them at all was Moira, but he didn't mention it. When he was alone, she always managed to find him. Earlier that morning, he had gone to the barn to check the horses. He turned around to leave and there she was, standing right behind him. Right off, he noticed she had unlaced her bodice just enough to give him a glimpse of the upper swells of her breasts. She struck up a conversation with him, wanting to know all about him. She got so close to him a few times, he'd felt her breasts rub against his chest. This seduction coming from a sixteen-year-old girl had shocked him. Then Elsa had entered the barn and

308

told him Reilly had awakened and had asked for him. It was just the excuse he needed to get out of there in a hurry.

Little Fox came outside and called everyone in to eat. "Do you feel like sitting at the table now, Reilly?"

"Yes, thank you."

Reilly saw Moira glaring at her when Sam sat down beside her at the table. Then she remembered that Moira had sat next to Sam during the previous meals. Well, it was time to set the girl straight that Sam belonged to her. At least, make it look like he did, she thought glumly.

Moira told the twins to scoot down and took a seat directly across from Sam. After Little Fox had filled everyone's bowls with venison stew and placed the cornpone on the table, she sat down with them, and Caleb said the blessing. The instant he said "Amen" everyone snatched a piece of bread from the plate.

Reilly thought she had never eaten anything so delicious, thankful that her appetite was returning. She felt Moira's jealous eyes on her, but ignored her. When everybody was having their bowl filled again, Reilly was only halfway finished with her first. She was already so full she couldn't finish the rest. No one talked, and she wondered if that was a table rule, or if they were too busy eating. All was quiet except the sound they made as they slurped the gravy from their spoons.

Finally Elsa said, "Did you remember to tell Papa that tomorrow's your birthday, so he'd get you somethin', Moira?"

"Why bother? He doesn't even know how old I am."

"Yes, he does," Sam piped in. "He told me you were sixteen."

Moira rolled her eyes and the children around the table snickered and laughed.

"Four years ago she was," Paul said, his mouth so full of cornbread they could barely understand him.

Reilly's mouth dropped open in surprise. She had thought Moira looked older, but twenty? She glanced at Sam and noticed he'd stopped chewing and was staring at Moira. Darn him anyway, Reilly thought angrily. Is he changing his mind about her now that he knows she's older? She gave him a sharp nudge in his side with her elbow. Sam blinked and swallowed, almost choking on a half-chewed potato.

Caleb added his two-cents worth. "Pa has trouble rememberin' all our ages. I reckon he's gone so much, he fergets."

Ruth, the ten-year-old, was sitting beside Moira, across from Reilly. She was gazing at Reilly with adoration in her eyes. "Are you older than Moira, Reilly?"

"Yes. I'm twenty-four."

"Hmmm . . . you're prettier than Moira."

"Oh, Ruth, that's not true," Reilly said, feeling the blood rush to her face. She looked at Moira and saw fire glittering in her green eyes.

"She doesn't have long yellow hair like you though. I like your hair better."

Little Fox noted the conversation getting entirely out of hand and rose from her seat. "If everyone has finished, we will clear the table."

While the girls helped their mother, everyone else went outside on the porch.

Sam leaned in close to her and whispered. "Now's my chance for that bath. My clothes on the line ought to be dry by now. Be back in a little while."

As Reilly sat down on the pallet, she saw Paul pull a deck of cards from his pants pocket. "C'mon, Reilly, Will, Caleb, and I'll play ya a game of poker."

One foot on the ground, the other on the step, Sam turned. Reilly saw his mouth split into a wide smile. He stepped back upon the porch and caught her grinning at him.

"The bath'll wait." Then he called to the boys, "Bring those cards over here. Reilly and I'd like to play."

"Hey, that'll be great," Paul said.

They came bounding over and, gathering around Reilly, sat down. Reilly whispered to Sam, "Maybe I'd better watch. All I know how to play is *strip* poker, remember?"

Her remark was his undoing. Sam's gaze dropped to her breasts and lingered. Desire spread through him like wildfire. "Do I ever," he muttered. Then a scowl creased his forehead and, forgetting where he was, he added in a harsher voice, "Damn Murdock for interfering when he did."

"Who's Murdock?" Will asked.

Sam jerked up his head. "Nobody you'd know. Deal the cards."

Reilly covered her mouth to smother her laughter.

When Sam became the dealer, the boys became so enthralled with his fancy shuffling, they wanted him to teach them how he did it. After that, he taught them card tricks and told them to practice on each other.

"That ought to keep them busy for a while," he said to Reilly with a wink. Rising, he left the group on the porch and made his way across the yard though he was unaware that Will was watching him pluck his clothes from the line and saunter toward the lake.

Chapter 30

Kneeling on the bank at the lake, Moira finished washing the last pot and set it in the washtub with the other dishes. Unlacing the ties on the front of her shirt, she scooped a handful of water and doused her neck. As the cool water spilled over her breasts, it felt as though a hand had caressed her—Sam's hand. She closed her eyes as she imagined his mouth on hers, his warm hands and deft fingers touching her, arousing her to a feverish passion. Her desire for him coursed through her thighs and throbbed wildly in her loins.

Moira had lost her virginity at age fifteen, but no one in her family knew it. Since then, she had given herself to several men who had come to their home. Some were strangers; some were acquaintances of her father. They all had told her she was beautiful and desirable, yet only one man had wanted her as his woman. A few months ago he had come to see her again. This time she had almost left with him. If she had, she would never have met Sam.

Moira had never had to compete with another woman for the attention of a man. Though she hadn't truly wanted Reilly to die, she wished she was not recovering so quickly. It was obvious Sam loved this woman, but love was not what Moira wanted from

313

him. She hated herself for her weakness when it came to men. Knowing they needed her excited her and left her feeling replete. And she knew she had to have Sam just once . . . before he walked out of her life with Reilly.

Moira cocked her head and listened to the sound of someone whistling as they came down the path. Sam! Jumping to her feet, she picked up the washtub and ran behind the large boulder to hide. If Reilly was with him, she might find out how much longer they were going to stay here.

If Sam was alone, well . . .

Moira smiled expectantly.

Sam arrived at the small lake and laid his clean clothing on the rocky bank. Unbuckling his gun belt, he laid it near the water's edge. Next he removed his boots and stripped out of his soiled clothes. He stared at the snowcapped peaks mirrored on the surface of the crystal blue lake. The water looked so cold he almost reconsidered his need for a bath. Before he completely lost his courage, he rushed through the cold water. When he was waist deep, he started swimming briskly toward the other side of the lake, feeling a rush of warmth flow through his body. Then flipping around, he swam back, his thoughts on Reilly.

In a few days, she would feel well enough to leave. He wished he could persuade her to stay with Cyrus and his family. Murdock would never find her here. Yet, he didn't want to leave without her. When he'd seen her sitting on the porch, just looking at her made him feel hot all over and it had nothing to do with the sun. He reluctantly admitted his selfishness. He was looking forward to being with her . . . alone.

Sam looked toward the bank, his eyes widening with disbelief when he saw Moira swimming toward him. The only way he could avoid a confrontation was to swim to the other side of the lake again. But then, she'd either follow him there or wait for him to return. Somehow, he was going to have to put a stop to this.

He lowered his feet to the rocky bottom as she met him, glimpsing her breasts before he jerked up his head to meet her broad smile. "Hello, Sam."

"Moira, what the hell are you doing here?" he ground out between clenched teeth.

Her smile faded. "You don't have to shout at me. I thought you might like some soap." She held out a cake of lye soap.

"Thanks," he said, taking her offering. "Now, would you please go?"

"I thought I might bathe too. Don't you want some company?"

"Damnit, Moira, you shouldn't be here. It's just not proper." Sam couldn't believe he'd said that. When had he ever cared if something was proper or not? Here was a naked, good-looking woman, with full, ripe curves . . . and he was not the least bit interested.

"But I'm not proper," Moira returned boldly. Lifting the thick long braid at the nape of her neck, she brought it over her shoulder.

Her eyes held his as she slowly unraveled it. She lowered herself deeper in the water and tilted her head backwards, wetting her hair. When she stood back up, her hair fanned over the water. She smiled sensuously. "You do want me, don't you?"

"If you're not leaving, then I sure as hell am."

A movement on the bank captured his attention. Her youngest brother and sister were picking up his clothing. "Hey, leave my clothes alone!"

The children's laughter carried over the water as they took off running through the woods, taking his clothes with them.

"Come back here, you little hooligans," Sam shouted furiously.

Moira giggled.

Sam glanced at Moira, grateful that her long thick hair covered her breasts. "Did you put them up to this?" he snapped.

"No," she returned huffily. "But I'm glad they did. Now you'll have to stay."

"Then you don't know me very well." As he started around her to go to the bank, he saw Reilly coming slowly down the path. A sickening knot formed in his stomach. "Damn," he hissed.

Moira followed his gaze and smiled wickedly. "Why, what a surprise. Reilly must be feeling much better."

Reilly came to an abrupt halt on the bank and looked across the water, her eyes lighting on Sam and Moira.

With a lame smile on his face, Sam raised his hand in welcome. "Hey, angel, glad to see you up and about."

"I'm sure you are," she said, pasting a pleasant smile on her mouth. Well, he certainly didn't waste any time after learning Moira wasn't sixteen, but a mature twenty. Then again, maybe she shouldn't judge him so harshly. She doubted he had planned this rendezvous. Moira had probably followed him down here. Slowly, her anger began to subside and devilment took over.

She sat down on the bank. "Don't mind me. I'll just sit here and enjoy the sunshine while you and Moira finish bathing. Oh, and Moira? Sam loves to have his back washed."

Hell, what's she up to? "Look, I don't want my damned back washed, all right? Moira might be used to bathing in this ice water, but I'm not." He turned to Moira and in a low threatening voice, said, "Get

316

the hell out of here and get dressed." Then in a much stronger voice that carried over the water, he ordered, "And then, for God's sake, *please* go find my clothes."

"You lost your clothes?" Reilly asked, looking around her, seeing only his gun belt laying beside the boulder.

"No, I didn't lose them. Ruth and Will sneaked down here and took off with them."

And he thought he'd have privacy, Reilly thought, laughter bubbling up in her throat. She rose and picked up his gun belt. "Well, at least they didn't take your gun belt. You can wear it," she teased.

A mental picture of him wearing only his gun belt flashed through his mind. He threw back his head in laughter.

Moira didn't think it was one bit funny. Reilly should be jealous to find them naked together, yet here she was teasing him and he was laughing about it. "I'll get your clothes," she snapped, sending up a spray of water as she stomped hastily to the bank.

Sam turned his head from Moira's nakedness, his eyes still sparkling with laughter. At least some good came from all this, he thought as he washed his hair and body with the soap Moira had given him. God, he hoped Reilly would believe this was all Moira's doings.

Reilly smiled sweetly at Moira as she stepped upon the bank, though she did feel a tinge of jealousy. As clear as the water was, she'd bet Sam hadn't missed any of those luscious curves.

A short time later, Moira left, carrying the tub of dishes. *So, that's why she had been down here.* Knowing that Moira had not purposely stalked him made her feel better. This family was so different from any she had ever known. Since they all slept in the same room, maybe they took baths together too,

317

and thought nothing of it. Except . . . Sam was definitely not a family member. No, Moira knew exactly what she was doing.

"She's gone, Sam."

"Thank God," Sam said, walking slowly through the water.

Reilly immediately jerked her head to the side to avoid seeing his nudity. Lord, as many times as she'd seen him, she'd think it wouldn't bother her. But it did . . . because it stirred up all the wonderful memories of making love with him. Not liking the direction of her thoughts, she shrugged them aside.

Sam stepped onto the bank in front of her, feeling slightly unsteady on his numb feet. "I'm damn near frozen solid from the waist down."

Reilly couldn't prevent her eyes from cutting slightly to the side and peering down at the thick mat of hair at the juncture of his legs. She reddened to the roots of her hair.

Sam followed her eyes and replied brazenly, "Yeah, him too. Might take days for him to thaw out. Of course, with a little help . . ."

Lord, he was back to his old self. She shifted her eyes straight ahead of her. "Sam, stop it." Still, her mouth quivered with amusement.

"Well, in that case, guess I'll have to take you up on your suggestion," he said with a grin.

Reilly frowned. What suggestion? She caught his movement from the corner of her eye. Her curiosity winning out, she looked down again, wishing a hundred times she hadn't.

He'd wrapped his gun belt around him and buckled it, then slid the belt around until the holster covered his privates.

"There. Feels better already. The leather's warm from laying in the sun."

"Shame on you, Sam," she chastised as her eyes

318

locked with his.

"Yeah, shame on me," he repeated with lust in his eyes as he pulled her into his arms. Spreading his legs, he clasped her buttocks and drew her snugly between them.

"Sam, we can't . . . you might catch my cold . . . someone might come—"

"Hey, all I want to do is hold you in my arms. You feel so good and warm against me."

"Well, not so tight, please, my ribs are still sore."

He loosened his hold on her and smiled down at her. "Sorry, I forgot. What brought you down here anyway?"

"Little Fox asked Caleb and Paul to finish their chores and said it would do me good to get up and walk around a bit. So . . . here I am. Wonder what would've happened if I hadn't come down here?" she asked teasingly, though there was a spark of jealousy just beneath the surface of her words.

"Nothing would've happened." He quirked an eyebrow. "Jealous, angel?"

"A little," she admitted.

Her confession pleased him . . . too much. His pent-up passion shot straight to his loins. The thaw had begun. Hell, and there wasn't a damned thing he could do about it.

"She's very pretty."

"You're much prettier."

"She's got bigger br—" She turned red.

He chuckled. "I didn't notice."

"Ha! You aren't the Sam Chandler I know, if you missed that part of her anatomy."

He grinned rakishly. "All right . . . I noticed. Does that make you feel better?"

"No."

His hand came up between them and closed over her breast. "That's enough for me, angel. Any more than a handful's wasted."

She removed his hand and placed it on her shoulder. "This isn't the time for fooling around, Sam."

Her remark could not have come at a more appropriate time. At that moment they heard a loud crashing sound as a grizzly broke through the thick overgrowth of shrubbery.

Chapter 31

Sam shoved Reilly to the side. Turning abruptly, she saw the bear and let out a blood-curdling scream.

Startled and angered by Reilly's scream, the grizzly lifted all eight feet of his massive body in an upright position. Sam saw the long, curved claws on his paws; one blow from that powerful paw could kill a man quickly.

Out of habit, Sam went for the gun on his hip, feeling only bare flesh. "Ah, damn!"

Reacting quickly, he reached at his front and whipped the Colt from his holster. He fired repeatedly, sending the bullets slamming into the thick-skinned beast. The beast growled angrily and kept coming at them. Grabbing Reilly's arm, Sam pulled her stiff, frightened body behind the boulder. At that instant a shot rang from another direction, then another.

Silence followed.

Sam and Reilly slowly stepped out from behind the boulder and saw Cyrus MacDonald walking around the massive heap on the ground, his Sharp posed to shoot again if the huge beast moved.

Sam holstered his gun. "Thank God, you came along when you did, Cyrus. I emptied my gun into him, and the varmint still kept coming."

Cyrus stopped walking and looked at Sam, disbelief marking his features.

Sam had forgotten his nudity and looked down. For Reilly's sake, more than his own, he quickly resituated the holster. He smiled sheepishly at Cyrus. Hell, what else could he do?

Reilly stood stone still, her hand clasped over her mouth, her face so hot from embarrassment it was on fire.

Would Reilly ever forgive him for humiliating her like this? "It's not what it looks like, Cyrus," Sam tried to explain.

Cyrus spit out a stream of tobacco juice, then eyed the bear. "Looks like to me that grizzly come along at the wrong time."

"No!" Reilly blurted out. "You see, the twins stole his clothes and . . . and—"

"Hey, Pa, what's all the shootin' about?" shouted Paul as he came down the path, carrying Sam's clothes and boots in his arms.

Sam had taken all the ribbing he could take and quickly hid behind the boulder.

"Good Godamighty!" Paul swore softly as he looked down on the grizzly. He switched his attention to Reilly. "Did he try to attack you?"

"Yes," she squeaked, unable to say another word.

Paul thought Reilly was trembling because of her close brush with death. "Who shot him? That big son-of-a-gun has been around here for weeks, scaring all the livestock."

"Sam shot him several times, then my lucky old Sharp here finished him off," Cyrus said, patting the stock of his gun.

"There's enough meat on him to feed us for a month. Ma'll sure be glad to have that hide too." Then suddenly he remembered why he'd come down in the first place. "Oh, where's Sam? I brung his clothes."

"Back here," Sam called out.

Paul took Sam's clothes to him and returned. "You want me to skin him now, Pa?"

"In a little while. Reilly says the young'ens was up to mischief. Where are they? I'll bust their butts 'til they won't sit down for a week."

"Oh, please don't, Mr. MacDonald," Reilly intervened. "It was all in fun and no harm done."

They heard a loud angry snort come from behind the boulder.

"He'll get over it," she whispered.

A grin split Cyrus's bushy-haired face. "C'mon, boy, let's get on back to the house and give these folks time to . . . ah . . . get themselves . . . back together."

Reilly knew exactly the meaning behind his remark. She walked around the boulder as Sam was pulling on his pants.

"I don't think I'll ever be able to look that man straight in the face again," she said furiously. "Never in my life have I ever been so . . . so humiliated."

"Well, then that makes two of us. If those little monsters hadn't taken my clothes, none of this would've happened," he snapped, tucking in his shirt. Then he looked at her beseechingly. "I'm sorry, Reilly, really I am."

It helped knowing he was as upset as her. She had never known Sam to be embarrassed over anything. "Oh, what's happened has happened. Nothing can be done about it now."

"I'd feel a helluva' lot better if those youngsters got the whipping they deserved."

"You're probably right, but I didn't think the twins deserved a spanking if Moira didn't get punished for her behavior. Do you think they'll tell their parents about seeing her in the lake with you?"

Sam let out a long sigh. "No, at least not yet. They'll wait until she has something on them first. Then they'll bring it up."

"They learn blackmail at an early age, don't they? Since I was an only child, I never learned that tactic."

"Hell, I did," Sam said as he slipped on his socks. "I even kept a list."

"What kind of list?"

After he put on his boots, he looked at her and quirked one eyebrow. "I don't know if I should be telling you all this. You'll get the wrong idea about me," he teased.

"No, nothing you did would surprise me now. Stop keeping me in suspense."

"All right. Every time I'd catch one of my brothers or sisters doing something bad, I'd write it down in my tablet."

"Did they know about the list?"

"Yeah, so they never threatened to tell on me because I warned them I'd show it to our parents. That worked fine for a short time. Then my mother happened to find my tablet hidden beneath my mattress. Well, she gave it to my father. For every wrongdoing against my siblings that I'd written in that tablet, *I* got a lick." He chuckled. "Oh, he didn't do it all at once. He wanted me to sweat it out for a while. He gave me a couple of hard licks a night for a month or so."

"You must've had quite a long list."

"Yeah, with three of them to keep up with, it adds up in no time."

"That doesn't sound fair, Sam, to punish just you and not the others."

"Oh, they got theirs, too. One lick for every misdeed they'd done, not the combined total like me."

"It's still not right," she protested adamantly.

Sam shifted his weight from one foot to the other. "Yeah, Reilly, it was. I'd hate to think of how many lickings my father would have given me if he'd ever

324

discovered all I'd gotten away with because of my blackmail."

"Well, in that case, I guess you did deserve it."

Reilly turned to leave. "We'd better get back to the house."

Sam took hold of her arm and pulled her to him. "No, not yet. This is the first time we've had a chance to be alone. We should take advantage of it." When she stiffened, he said, "I doubt they'll be coming back."

Reilly silently agreed and allowed him to draw her into his arms.

His voice was raw with emotion as he said, "God, I can't wait to leave this place."

"With the way Moira's behaving, I think we should leave soon."

"Forget Moira. I only want you," he said huskily, his finger tracing the curve of her mouth.

As he lowered his head to kiss her, Reilly turned her head and his lips brushed her cheek. "No, you might catch my cold."

"It's a sorry gambler who never takes a risk," he said, cupping her chin and turning her to face him.

Reilly gazed up at him, her soft mouth parting as he lowered his head and kissed her. Too long, they had denied themselves this pleasure, and what had started as a gentle touching of mouths turned to greediness and fierce possession. Passions flared like a burning torch within them. Her hands suddenly came up from between them and, clasping the back of his head, she pressed her mouth firmly and eagerly against his own.

Sam's hand closed over her breast, all rational judgment leaving him as he felt her hardened nipples against his palm. The only thought that filtered through his desire-filled mind was his error in dressing so soon, as he deftly began unbuttoning her shirt.

Sam heard the giggling first. His hand stilled on the top button.

Reilly heard it next, her hands loosening in the thick curling hair at his nape.

Their lips still touching, yet immobile, their bodies still touching, yet restrained, their heated eyes gazed into one another with a mixture of yearning . . . and alarm.

Slowly, they parted and turned around to see two pairs of eyes staring up at them.

"Pa said fer us to 'pologize to ya," Ruth said, looking down at the ground as she raked the pebbles with her bare toe.

"We're awfully sorry we took your clothes, Sam," Will said, a grin sneaking across his face.

"Yeah, you really look sorry," Sam bristled.

Ruth and Will exchanged glances, then Will said, "Guess we shoulda waited til they come up to the house . . . like Pa said."

"Yeah, now we're gonna hafta 'pologize agin for catchin' 'em kissin'."

Reilly had to bite her lip to keep from laughing.

Sam's temper only softened a little. Had they come a few minutes later . . . well . . . his mind dwindled off. "Look, kids, I accept your apology. Just promise you won't do it again."

"All right, Sam."

Turning them around, Sam lightly smacked them none too gently on their rears and said, "Now get yourself back to the house. Reilly and I'll be along shortly."

The moment they were out of earshot, Sam hissed, "Damn!"

"I couldn't have said it better myself," Reilly said with a laugh. "Let's leave for Bodie tomorrow, Sam." She waited expectantly. If he didn't plan to take her with him, now he would have to tell her.

"Tomorrow?" he asked surprised. "Are you sure

you're well enough?"

She nodded. "Yes, that incident just cured me."

"Then tomorrow it is," he said as he dragged her into his arms again for a long hard kiss.

That night at the supper table, Sam told the family that he and Reilly were leaving early the following morning. No one asked where they were heading, so Sam kept this information to himself. Should Murdock and his gang ever trace them to here, he didn't want one of the children telling them where they had gone.

Cyrus surprised everyone by bringing out a pretty calico dress that he had brought Moira for her birthday.

"Sixteen? Right?" he asked as he handed the gift to her.

"No, twenty, Pa," she said, lifting her eyes heavenward.

"Well, whatever. You can wear it when Jesse comes for his next visit."

She lowered her head shyly. "Thanks, Pa. I will." And this time, she vowed, she would go with Jesse when he asked.

They spent the rest of the evening around the hearth and Reilly listened with interest at the many places Cyrus and her father had traveled. Some of the stories he told made her laugh; others made her almost cry. And after the telling was over, she felt a strange peace steal within her. She didn't feel so lonely anymore. She collected the fond memories of her father and stored them in an empty chamber in her heart. Only one chamber was left to be filled; she'd reserved it for Sam's love.

That night Reilly slept soundly while Sam thought about the days and nights ahead of them. This sudden change in Reilly's behavior toward him baffled him. First, she had shunned his lovemaking, but now, she was warming to him. Why on earth would she want to consort with him when she thought he was an outlaw? She could have stayed here, or chosen to go somewhere else, maybe even back to Philadelphia, but she wanted to go with him. Of course, how could she go anywhere with only the clothes on her back and no money?

Regardless of what her reasons were, he would show her a good time in Bodie. After that, he'd have to figure out what to do with her. Surely there was family somewhere, an aunt, a cousin, a friend, someone that he could send her to live with while he completed his job in Castletown. He knew he could never convince her to return here. Moira would make her life miserable.

And *his* life would be miserable without Reilly, but he had a job to finish. He had to start thinking with his head instead of allowing his desire for her to cloud his judgment. Or someday his epitaph might read: *Here lies U. S. Marshal Sam Chandler, a man torn between duty and desire.* And it wouldn't take much thought on anyone's part to know which one put him in his grave.

Chapter 32

Bodie, California

Reilly sat down on the bed and sighed deeply. She was tired. For her comfort and well-being, Sam had not set a grueling pace to reach Bodie. The remnants of her illness still lingered. She had lost weight she couldn't afford to lose. Not long ago she'd always had an abundance of energy. Now she had to force herself to keep up with Sam. But deep inside her heart where lies couldn't gain any ground, she knew it was heartache that was behind her fatigue. The lies and half-truths that she suspected Sam of telling had taken a toll on her, and she wasn't quite sure how to deal with them. At the moment, she had no choice but to go along with Sam's deceit, because truly she couldn't accept that he was no more than a common thief. Her heart wouldn't let her.

She had gone over everything, trying to come up with an explanation. Nothing fit. If he were the black-hearted scoundrel she'd tried to make him out to be, he would have abandoned her at the first opportunity. Instead, he'd taken such good care of her when she had been sick. Many times, as she'd tossed restlessly in her sickbed, she'd awakened to find Sam at her side, encouraging her to rest and get well. When she pictured him in that light, it was easy to believe he was just what he claimed to be. But when she remembered Mason Womac coming to their aid the night they'd escaped, it clouded her thoughts. And the thing that darkened the cloud even more was the complete turnaround of Sam that night. He'd taken the situation in hand and proved he was proficient in outsmarting his enemy. His dress and manner had changed so rapidly she had a problem dealing with the turnaround. Instead of doing everything for him and watching over him, she'd found herself being taken care of and watched over by him.

Now here she sat in the fanciest hotel the town had to offer . . . while Sam was up to what? Lord only knew what he was doing now. Was he gambling? She knew they had very little money. She was tired and worrying wouldn't solve anything. Maybe if she just shut her eyes for a few moments . . . maybe with a clear head she would be able to think straight . . .

Hours later a terrible racket jarred her awake. She jumped from the bed and stood perfectly still in the middle of the room.

"Reilly?" called a muffled voice. Someone was at the door.

"Sam?" she asked hesitantly.

"Open the door."

She rushed to do as he asked. She opened it a crack and peeked out, still not sure that it was Sam.

His arms were loaded with packages. She swung the door wide and took a couple of the packages from his arms. "Where have you been?"

"Shopping, among other things." He dumped the boxes on the bed and turned to her. "Did I wake you?"

"Yes. What time is it? I must have slept away the entire afternoon."

330

"That's okay, you need to get your strength back. I thought we might get all dressed up and go out for supper. I bought you some clothes."

"How are we going to pay for all this? We don't have any money."

"Don't worry about it. Did I worry when you were taking care of me? Won't you let me do the same for you?"

"I'm sorry, I can't help it."

He lifted his hand and brushed her hair from her face, cupping the side of her head gently with his hand. "We have money, angel, maybe not a lot, but enough. Now quit worrying."

"I'll try."

He tilted her chin and studied her face for several seconds. "Regardless of how it looks, or what you think, I won't let you down. I promise." He leaned forward and kissed her on the tip of the nose. "I want you to see the things I bought you."

His words lifted her spirits and his mood lightened her own frame of mind.

They plowed into the packages like children on Christmas morning. She squealed with delight when he just kept handing her one box after another. Then she laughed even harder at his expression when he was left with only one box for himself. But with a teasing smile, he made a quick trip to the door where he'd left several packages in the hall; this settled the dilemma.

Tears sparkled in her eyes and the breath left her body when she began opening the boxes. A glorious dress in a paisley design with varying shades of burnt orange was made up in a linen-wool combination and trimmed with soft velvet. One shirtwaist of Indian silk had a delicate lace bodice, another was made of muslin and simply pleated. And to go with these, he'd chosen skirts made of foulard and cashmere. Of all he'd bought her, her favorite was a dress of peacock-blue sateen, and a hat with a feather plume that reminded her of a question mark as it drifted over a narrow brim.

Reilly blushed when she noted the care he'd given in the choosing of her undergarments. There were drawers and camisoles of lawn with intricate satin stitch embroidery, yokes of tatting, and ribbons laced through delicate pleats; and silk stockings so sheer she was afraid to touch them. One box even contained a corset. He'd forgotten nothing. Shoes of soft leather accompanied the dresses, and a parasol wildly adorned with lace and flowers added the final touch to her new wardrobe.

Reilly had never owned anything like the assortment spread before her. She could remember her mother dressing in beautiful clothes. And in times past, Reilly had studied the Montgomery Ward catalog like it was a Bible, drooling over the latest fashions. But she'd known she couldn't afford anything. Instead, she'd worn her britches, and used the excuse of her work for her appearance.

Suddenly, she became aware of the silence. She lifted her head to encounter Sam studying her. "What?" she questioned.

"Do you like them?"

"Yes, they're beautiful, Sam. Thank you."

"I've ordered water for your bath. When you're ready, I'll meet you downstairs."

"Where are you going?"

"To the bath house. It will save time. Besides I need a shave and a haircut."

She thought he was perfect just the way he was. But she wasn't about to tell him. She feared he already knew the way she felt about him. Still, she watched his every move as he gathered up his clothes. His moves were smooth and relaxed. No one would ever know by looking at him that they were running from the law.

With his clothes thrown loosely over his arm, he leaned from the waist and placed a kiss on her cheek. "I'll see you in a little while. Take your time."

As he opened the door, a trio of employees entered the room with buckets of steaming water. After they filled the tub, Sam thanked them and gave each a coin.

He followed them to the door and, at the last moment, turned to Reilly. "Enjoy your bath, angel."

"I will."

He winked and pulled the door closed.

Her heart fluttered and the warmth of happiness flooded her.

As she was readying for her bath, she found another package from Sam. It was a selection of bath salts for her bath and creamy lotions for her body to use when she finished bathing. She couldn't believe that man. He knew instinctively how to please a woman. How could she have ever dreamed for one moment that maybe he would want only her?

After piling her hair atop her head, she slid into the water. It was pure pleasure, especially after days of wondering if she'd ever feel such pleasure again. Her eyes drifted shut and her mind swirled with memories. No matter what happened with her and Sam, she would have her memories, and no one could take them away. Not even the sheriff. He might lock her up and throw away the key and he might steal her happiness, but he couldn't take her memories.

As Reilly lay there, an idea came to her like a lightning bolt. Womanly wiles. That's what she'd told Susan to use. What about herself? Maybe a few womanly wiles wasn't so farfetched. She'd bet everything she owned, and she didn't own much, that it had been womanly wiles that had enticed Adam to take the apple from Eve rather than anything else.

Reilly had never given any thought to the resourcefulness of women. But surely it had some merit. Everyone knew men were stronger than women, and it was a foregone conclusion that men were smarter; this was true only became women allowed it. They figured what the men didn't know couldn't hurt them. And wasn't it true that behind all good men was a woman? Had Reilly been missing something all these years? Her mother and father had never had a conventional marriage, not with her father being gone all the time. So Reilly wasn't familiar with the mechanics of give and take between men and women. But she was learning fast. As soon as trouble had struck, Sam had assumed the role of caretaker with ease. If that was his role, what was her role? She had to think about that for awhile.

But for now she would play it by ear. She'd do the best she could to let Sam take care of her, instead of plowing ahead and seeing to everything. Helpless she wasn't, and Sam knew it. Female she was, and the beautiful clothes could enhance that fact. She stepped from the tub and studied her new wardrobe. Before today, she'd only had one dress to her name. She lifted the peacock-blue dress and held it next to her body. The color was a perfect contrast to her blond hair . . . and her imperfectly tanned face. Yes, she would wear the blue.

After laying out each article of clothing she would need, she brushed her hair until it gleamed with life, then coiled it around her head. The loosened strands she'd left unbound curled with a life of their own beside her face.

Dressing like a lady took a lot of doing. But it was fun. Once again, she felt like she was playing house, but deep inside she prayed that it was more than a game.

Sam waited in the lobby, looking out the window. The people hurrying past were the farthest thing from his mind. He was worried. When he was on a job, he'd never had to put anyone's safety ahead of getting the job done. He just did it, he and Mason. He was in a quandary. He couldn't leave Reilly, not after what she had done for him. But he had to get the goods on the sheriff and get this assignment behind him. Hell, this was taking forever. Women! He knew better than to mix business with pleasure. He had to come up with a plan to send Reilly packing, and still protect her from the sheriff until this ordeal was over.

Suddenly, he turned and the breath caught in his throat. *It couldn't be, could it?*

Sam's heartbeat stilled, and the fingers that brushed his hair from his brow were trembling. Their eyes met and locked across the crowded room. Sam was humbled by the dazzling beauty standing before him and moved toward her as though there were weights strapped to his ankles.

Reilly moved closer to the man who disturbed her peace more than she liked to admit. How could she help it? Sam was a handsome man and he had never looked better. Strong, masculine, and utterly captivating. She forgot her fears; forgot the steely determination that drove Sam and frightened her. All she wanted to do was reach his side. She needed to feel his strength beside her.

Their fingers touched and clasped with the desperation each was experiencing.

Sam's eyes caressed her with warmth and longing. He'd seen her lying naked beside him with moonbeams streaking across her golden body. He'd watched her step from the tub, her body sparkling with droplets of water. He'd taken in the visions as

335

though they were his due. But this . . . Oh Lord. He wasn't ready for this.

Sam had never seen Reilly in a dress, and damnit, this just wasn't fair. One moment he was trying to find a way to rid himself of her and the next . . . hell. Now he couldn't bear to think of her being out of his sight. She wasn't playing fair, and it was all his fault. He never should have bought her the clothes. How was he to know she would look so tempting? He should have bought her a couple pairs of denims and been done with the whole thing.

Her golden hair was pulled atop her head, showing off her creamy neck. He wanted to lower his head until he could taste her warm flesh. Squelching his urge, he continued his perusal. Her face was a delight to behold. Her eyes looked at him hesitantly for his approval. Yet they glimmered with the pride of one who knows she looks her best. Her face was flushed with a rosy glow and she smelled heavenly.

She was a vision in peacock blue. He'd definitely made a good selection in choosing the dress. But Sam knew no one but Reilly could have done justice to the garment. Her breasts swelled like twin peaks against the shimmering fabric, and her waist was small enough that he could easily reach his hands around it. From the waist, the dress fell freely with yards and yards to a hem that was nipped and tucked and decorated with tiny bows of the same fabric.

Reilly was making her own perusal, but she didn't get any farther than Sam's broad chest. She hadn't seen him all decked out in his finery since before he was wounded. And that had been from afar. Her eyes kept darting back to his narrow string tie, and her memories wouldn't leave her alone. She remembered the limp string tie lying against his bare neck, and tears sparkled in her eyes.

Sam cupped her chin, and his thumb traced the

curve of her mouth. "Why the sad face, angel? Don't you like the dress?"

She swallowed her tears and smiled brightly. "I love the dress." On a sudden impulse, she hugged him. "I'm glad you look so fit tonight."

They both knew what she meant when she lifted the tie, then watched as it drifted back to its position.

"I think we both look fit tonight," Sam whispered softly. "And we deserve a night on the town."

Chapter 33

People hurried along the streets and boardwalks in different directions; others visited and caught up on the latest killing. Still, others passed the time watching the people.

Sam and Reilly passed the tinsmith shops, saddlemakers, grocers, a Wells Fargo office, and lodging houses. Perched between everything from the pharmacists to the lawyers' offices was a saloon or gambling hall. Business was flourishing in these pleasure dens. Some were permanent structures; some were only tents pitched in haste. The mining boom in Bodie, California had happened suddenly, and everyone wanted to line their pockets while it lasted. They knew it would go out as fast as it had come in.

Word had traveled like a brush fire about the discovery of a rich ore chamber, and the incorporation of the Standard Mining Company. Every gold-hungry miner that could walk, ride, or be carried, flocked to Bodie. Gunslingers and gamblers suddenly called Bodie home. Robberies, fast guns, and killings became the norm.

Decent, hardworking people went about their daily routine, hoping the boom would soon burn itself out. Ministers preached louder and longer about the sins besetting their town, and prayed with fervor that the evil permeating their beloved town would not tempt their flocks. One local minister described Bodie as "a sea of sin, lashed by the tempest of lust and passion." He didn't miss the mark, for ladies of the night in Bodie's red-light district did a rousing business. Sins of the flesh and the taste for spirits ran neck and neck; you couldn't have the one without the other.

Bodie was the perfect place for Sam and Reilly to get lost in for awhile. No one would question another new face; there were so many already.

Reilly couldn't help the excitement that rushed through her. The people seemed to be celebrating, the mood festive and contagious. She squeezed Sam's hand tightly and smiled up at him.

He returned her smile, and once again he had trouble taking his eyes from her beautiful face. His stomach had an odd fluttering that had nothing to do with hunger.

Sam led her through the double doors of an elegant restaurant. Reilly stopped to take in her beautiful surroundings. A waiter, dressed in black with a snowy white shirt, escorted them to a small intimate area, fashionably grouped with matching chairs covered in a delicate damask fabric.

"Your table will be ready shortly, Mr. Chandler. Would you care for a glass of wine while you wait?"

"Wine will be fine," Sam answered, leading Reilly to one of the chairs.

"How do they know your name?"

"I've dined here before."

"Oh," she answered simply, determined not to ruin their night with her mistrust. "This is a beautiful restaurant. I remember places like this from my childhood. When my father was home, we went out to eat sometimes."

The waiter returned with their wine and a tray of

delicately sliced cheeses and oddly shaped crackers. As he placed the food and wine on a small table, Reilly continued to study the room. The windows had padded cornices covered with the same fabric as the chairs. Deep pleated draperies covered the windows, enhancing the intimacy of the room. Starched white tablecloths covered the tables, and a candle was burning in the center of each, its flame dancing and twinkling. Diners filled the restaurant, but no one paid any attention to Sam and Reilly.

When Reilly lifted her glass, Sam put his hand on her arm. "A toast to courage and beauty."

"To courage and beauty," she agreed. Their glasses tingled.

"Why courage and beauty?" she asked after taking a sip from her glass.

"Because you are the most courageous woman I have ever met. I'm impressed every day by your outlook on life, and I've never been easily impressed. You are beautiful beyond compare. Beauty and courage wrapped tightly in the same package is an unusual combination. One I'm not accustomed to."

"I didn't think there was much you hadn't experienced in your adventures."

"There's not. That's why you're so special."

She mulled the word over in her mind. *Special.* That could mean many things. But could it mean what she wanted it to mean?

The moment they finished their wine, the waiter showed them to their table.

This was not the first time that Sam's manners had impressed Reilly. He was a gentleman to perfection. Sometimes she had trouble believing he was the same man who had escaped the sheriff's band of cutthroats and carried her to safety. Indeed, he was—and more. She was determined to make the most of their time together, because when he left her—and he would— her memories would sustain her.

They feasted on prime rib, baby carrots, scalloped potatoes in a thick sauce, and rolls so light they could float from the plate. They enjoyed more wine with their dinner. After a dessert of rich chocolate pie, they had another glass of wine. At one point Reilly accused Sam of trying to get her drunk.

He only laughed and toasted her beauty once again.

Indeed, Reilly was a beauty to behold. Sam couldn't look at her enough. He couldn't figure out what was wrong with him. She was a delightful companion. Her face was flushed with color, and the candlelight reflecting off her hair reminded him of spun honey. Her smile lit the room and her soft laughter was like a melody. What in God's name was the matter with him? He was waxing poetic and he didn't even like poetry. He needed something stronger than a glass of wine. He pushed the glass away in disgust and asked her if she was ready to leave.

Accustomed to his sudden mood changes, she gathered her belongings while Sam took care of their bill.

The temperature had dropped considerably while they'd been inside. When they stepped outside, Reilly shivered all over. Sam was slow and deliberate as he helped her drape her shawl around her shoulders. He caressed the width of her back and the ridge of her shoulder. His warm fingers moved along the column of her neck. His thumb directed her chin and his fingers settled in her upswept hair.

She could feel his warm breath on her face as he lowered his head. Her chest constricted and the blood sang wildly through her veins. She parted her lips and waited.

His arms came around her in a rush, and she thought she heard him swear just before his lips touched hers. She expected no more than a gentle kiss. Instead, it was like two broken hearts melding and mending in a last attempt to right the wrongs of their life. They moved together, two shadows in the darkness until they were one. She clung. He held. They tasted each other. They felt the other's heat and both wished they were somewhere other than the darkened boardwalk in Bodie.

Somewhere in the distance the crack of gunfire split the quiet. They parted and directed their attention to the drunk in the street who was shooting at the stars.

Sam took her hand and they walked the darkened streets, peering inside the windows of the shops. Piano music drifted from the saloons. Sometimes bodies tumbled from a building, arms and fists swinging angrily at each other.

"Can I take you back to the hotel, or would you like to join me in a few games of chance?"

"Sam, ladies don't go into saloons."

"But you'd like to, wouldn't you?" he teased.

She could see his smile in the shadowy darkness. "You know me too well."

"That's just it. No one here knows who you are. You can test the waters so to speak, and no one will ever know."

"You'll know."

"I don't count, because I already know all your secrets."

For an instant her heart felt heavy as the truth swirled through her head. *That's what you think. You don't know that I love you and that I would do just about anything to be by your side. You don't know that I think you are an outlaw, and that if you are, I'll love you anyway. No, Sam, you don't know all my secrets. If you did, you would leave me, and I couldn't bear that . . . not right now. So I'll go with you wherever you want to take me . . . but please don't ask me to leave you.*

"Come on. It'll be fun. You might find that you enjoy it. Besides, I'll take you to a nice saloon."

"I didn't know there was any such thing as a 'nice' saloon."

"Some are nicer than others. Believe me I know. I've been in them all."

"I'll bet you have," she teased. "Okay, I'll go with you. Just promise me when we get inside, you won't abandon me."

"I promise."

After the cool of the night, the warmth of the saloon was like walking into a hot oven. Its appearance pleasantly surprised her; the saloon was brightly lit with a cloud of smoke lingering in the air. Men leaned their elbows on the long bar that ran the length of the room, nursing their favorite drink. Occasionally, they dipped their hands into bowls of popcorn that were placed every few feet on the shiny surface. A large smoke-stained mirror ran the length of the bar, reflecting the faces of the patrons. Seated at tables around the room were men and women alike, some in the midst of a card game where conversation was nonexistent. Still, other men sat with women, talking and laughing. The atmosphere was pleasant enough, but the skimpy dresses the women wore exposed more of their flesh than they covered. Their legs were revealed and covered with stockings that looked like fine fishnet. Some even had lacy garters exposed.

Reilly had to pinch herself to keep from staring, when at one table a "lady" stood beside a man with her foot placed in the chair beside him. Her petticoats draped the back of her leg like a waterfall. When the man leaned forward and ran his hand up her leg and snapped the lacy garter, Reilly stumbled. She jerked her head away. Sam tightened his hold and directed her to a table in the corner. After he seated her, her eyes traveled back to the woman. The man was still fingering the garter. The woman lifted her foot from the chair and slid it down the inside of the man's leg. A white hot heat flushed Reilly's body and a fine sheen of perspiration dotted her brow.

Sam cupped her chin and turned her face to him. "You're staring, Reilly."

"I can't help it. Did you see what she did?"

"I have a pretty good idea." He glanced in the direction that had bound Reilly's attention.

"Is she for sale?" she whispered.

"To whoever has the coin to purchase her time."

"But she's beautiful. Why would she sell herself?"

"They all have a different story. Some have been cast aside by their lovers and left to fend for themselves. It's the only life they know. Others have been convinced that it's a quick way to get rich. For a few it is, but for most, it's a vicious cycle that they can't break."

"Well, I feel sorry for them."

"Don't. They're hard as nails and know what they're doing."

"Chandler?"

Reilly's head popped up, while Sam lifted his head slowly to the man standing beside their table.

"Would you like to sit in on a few hands? We need a fourth," the stranger said.

"Fine by me, if the lady doesn't mind."

"No, no that's fine," Reilly said, when she could control the tremor in her voice.

The man nodded and turned sharply on his heel. Reilly watched him walk away and a shiver scaled her back. He didn't act like he cared whether she agreed or not. He had looked straight through her. He wasn't as big as Sam, but if one could judge a man by his looks—he was a mean man. The immediate thought that ran through her head was the term widely applied to the town toughs—*Bad Man from Bodie*. He fit the bill to a T, but so did the men he joined at the table across the room.

Once again, Sam escorted Reilly across the room. This time, she centered her attention on her destination. She took her seat and didn't utter a word; she was afraid to. The men didn't seem like they would appreciate idle chatter. Once Sam took his seat beside her, it was though someone had pulled a mask over his face. His features became hard and cold. Gone was the teasing glint in his eyes and the carefree manner that he had displayed earlier. When she would have slid her chair away to give him more room, his hand snaked out and stopped her. When she would have questioned him, the slight shake of his head settled the matter. She stayed by his side and watched the game with interest. When she'd least expect it, he would reach out and touch her, sending a volley of warmth rushing through her.

He was by far the most handsome man in the room and Reilly noted quickly the other women boldly appraising him. As she watched the intimate exchanges between the men and women, a heat began to build in her that had nothing to do with warmth of the room.

The bartender brought drinks, and as Reilly sat there, she sipped the amber liquid. At first it burned all the way down, until it settled like a warm coal in her stomach, radiating heat throughout her body.

Sam studied his cards and the other men pondered theirs. The playing became intense. Reilly could hear the man sitting to her left breathing heavy. Another of the players flipped his cards, then studied them again as though in hopes he'd read them wrong the first time. The third man gritted his teeth. But Sam didn't move a muscle. He slouched in his chair and waited for his opponents to make a move. His eyes were like shards of brown marble. In turn, every man placed his cards on the table.

"Gentlemen, I believe this hand is mine," Sam

placed his cards on the table. "Three ladies."

"You son of a bitch, I don't know how you do it, but you do it every time," said the man with the heavy breathing.

Reilly sighed with relief. She'd been afraid something terrible would happen if Sam won all their money.

Sam picked up Reilly's hand and brought it to his mouth. "She's my lucky charm."

Reilly was feeling warm all over and a bit light-headed.

She smiled sweetly.

"You two-faced bitch. What do you mean moving in on my man the minute my back is turned?"

Reilly stiffened in her chair and her face drained of color. The voice came from behind her and rang through her head like gunfire. Was the woman talking to her? She was afraid to look at Sam for fear that he would confirm her fears.

Every head turned, Reilly's very slowly as she expected the worst. She was sure one of Sam's women was challenging her. And she didn't relish the encounter. Everyone waited in anticipation. She could've heard a small pin drop if anyone had the forethought to drop one. There was nothing like a good fight to get everyone's attention and get the juices flowing.

Chapter 34

To Reilly's immense relief, the woman was not talking to her. She was standing nose-to-nose with a heavy set woman at the table behind her. Reilly took a deep breath and patted the sheen of perspiration from her face. She listened to the heated conversation with a new interest.

"You weren't anywhere in sight when I came over here. You're just jealous because Frank prefers my favors to yours."

"Ha! Me jealous of a sow like you? Only in your dreams."

"You take that back, you stringy-headed bitch, or I'll pull out that red mop by the roots."

"You and who else? It's for damn sure you can't do it by yourself."

Reilly's chair rocked wildly as the stringy-headed bitch pushed the sow into her. The fight was on!

Sam pulled Reilly to safety as the scuffle intensified. Chairs emptied and men circled the women, calling out encouragement to their favorite. One industrious soul began hawking odds and taking bets on the outcome. Caught up in the heat of the fray, the spectators emptied their pockets, passing their money to the hawker as they shouted their bets.

The bartender climbed atop the bar and shouted

dire consequences to the brawlers. "If you break the damn mirror again, you'll pay! I have to send all the way back East for a replacement, and I'm damn tired of it!"

Watching the two women fight was like watching the mating of two cats. They bristled and circled each other, hissing until the air was blue with their predictions. Then suddenly they pounced. A lot of hair pulling and clawing took place, but in truth, there were no damaging blows.

The crowd loved it. Their enthusiasm was so boisterous, they never noticed the industrious soul, who had taken their bets, duck beneath the pumping arms and scurry toward the door.

Sam noticed. He'd seen the same ruse used time and time again. He nudged Reilly and nodded toward the culprit. The man's pockets were bulging with money, as were his fists.

"It's a flimflam. He and the redhead will meet later and split the money."

"Oh my," Reilly whispered as she watched the man disappear through the doors and into the night.

Sam smiled at her, his eyes glowing with an inner warmth that sent her heart to pounding wildly. She answered his smile with one of her own.

When she turned her attention back to the women, the fight was over . . . and the redhead was staring Reilly in the face. "You think it's funny, bitch?"

"No, not really. I wasn't paying any attention."

"So, we bore you? Is that what you mean?"

"What I mean is . . . you don't matter to me one way or the other. I don't care what you do."

"You'd care if I slapped that pretty face, wouldn't you?"

Reilly felt Sam against her as he stepped closer. She lifted her arm for him to stay in place. She didn't want him fighting her battles for her; she could take care of herself.

350

"I don't think you can slap me," Reilly answered evenly.

The redhead laughed and brushed her tangled hair from her face. "Honey, there's not a damn thing you can do to stop me. I've dealt with tarts like you all my life. One little slap, and you'd be screaming your head off."

"You think so?" Reilly said sharply.

"I know so."

"Then take your best shot," Reilly challenged.

For an instant, Reilly's boldness caused the woman to hesitate. "Oh, what the hell." She lifted her arm and swung with all the force she could muster.

Reilly was as quick as a bolt of lightning. Her left arm shot out to block the sweeping blow while she doubled up her other hand and swung with the precision of a street fighter. Her fist caught the redhead just beneath the chin.

For a second, a look of surprise flickered across the woman's face, then she was out like a light.

Sam caught the woman before she hit the floor. The look on his face was as surprised as the victim's. He shook his head in wonder as he lowered the unconscious woman to a chair.

"Damn, I wish I'd had my money on the blonde," one of the men called out as a round of applause cheered the victor.

"Drinks are on the house," the bartender called, relieved that his mirror hadn't suffered any damage.

The spectators turned in unison and bellied up to the bar. It was a rare day indeed when the bartender gave away anything, and the patrons planned to take advantage of his generous spirit before he had time to change his mind.

Reilly and Sam were carried along in the crush to the head of the bar. The bartender handed Reilly the first drink. Just what she needed, she thought, her

351

head already spinning like a top.

When the bartender had served everyone, a man in the back of the crowd shouted out a toast. "To the little lady with the iron fist. This is the first time I've ever seen Red when she wasn't spouting off to someone."

Every head turned to the redhead lying unconscious in a nearby chair.

A chorus of cheers followed the declaration.

Steadily, Sam moved Reilly through the crowd and toward the door. They had just about made it when one of the men asked where the man with their money was. He'd won on the fight, and he wanted his payoff. Another man voiced the same thought. They looked around the sea of faces waiting for the man to step forward. It wasn't long before the revelry turned into rivalry. They all wanted to find the little double-crosser. Every table was moved, every nook and cranny inspected. They'd been duped, royally. In the anger and confusion, tempers flared and fights broke out. Friend became foe as the fights ensued. The realization of their gullibility was an embarrassment. They needed to hit somebody, so they hit each other. It wasn't long before a whiskey bottle made it into one of the combatant's hands and went sailing through the air.

The bartender stood there in slack-jawed wonder, watching a small break run from one side of his prized mirror to the other side, like a tear in a woman's stocking, before the pieces broke loose and fell to the floor.

Sam shoved Reilly through the door just as the bartender's bellow of rage erupted. "Out, you sons a bitches! I warned you what would happen if you broke my mirror. Out! This place is closed."

The men bolted through the door like a cattle stampede. For a moment Sam and Reilly watched, unable to believe the men would really leave. When a bottle ricocheted off the head of one of the fleeing customers, they understood the rush.

Reilly didn't mean to laugh; she understood the aggravation of trying to replace the mirror. But she couldn't control her laughter.

"I'd better get you out of here before you get us into any more trouble." Sam hugged her close and walked her up the street.

"Me? I haven't gotten us into trouble."

"Tell me, where did you learn to deliver an uppercut like that?"

"Ha! Impressed you, didn't I?"

"I'm impressed with you every day."

"Several years ago, before my father died, we were at a mining camp photographing the miners. While we were there, my father met a man that sponsored a boxer. They went from mining camp to mining camp promoting fights between the boxer and anyone that had the courage to take him on. Of course, the miners loved it and rallied to take on the boxer." Reilly stopped and turned to Sam.

"I met the boxer and, in some ways, you remind me of him."

"Now . . . I don't know if I like that or not."

"He was very tough on the outside, but a gentle man on the inside."

"Which is it? Am I tough on the outside or gentle on the inside?"

"Both."

"You think I'm gentle on the inside?"

She laughed. "Sometimes. But you would die before you let anyone know it. Anyway, about the boxer. We became good friends and he gave me a few pointers on protecting myself."

"What would you do if some drunk came up to you and wrapped his arms around you?" He acted out the part of the drunk.

She bowed her arms and lifted her knee in the same movement. Her taffeta-draped knee gently nudged his crotch.

"I could get to liking this, angel," he whispered, cupping the back of her leg and holding it against his budding hardness.

"Not if I was serious. I could've hurt you, if it had been my intention. A drunk would've been more concerned with pinning down my arms, and I could've nailed him with my knee."

"Very clever."

"I thought so. I figured that out for myself."

"It makes me wonder, will I ever know the real Reilly Reynolds?"

"Would you like to know the real Reilly Reynolds?"

"More than anything," he admitted as he pulled her into a deserted alley.

Before she could get her bearings, his mouth covered hers. Every thought left her as he swept her into full-blown passion.

His mouth was hot, his tongue searching. He buried his hands in her hair, loosening the pins, scattering them carelessly on the ground. His finger combed her hair until it swirled around them like a blanket. He was filled with the smell of her, the taste of her, and he didn't want to stop. Oh Lord, he didn't want to stop. She was everything he'd ever dreamed about. He couldn't tell her, not yet. But he would show her in the only way he knew.

The events of the evening, the drinks, everything she had seen, the man at her side, and an aching heart, answered his passion with an ardor that took his breath away. She nestled against him, her legs tangling with his, her arms embracing him as she lifted herself against his solid length.

A volley of emotion swirled through her. She couldn't control it; nor did she want to. She was carried on the crest of passion, higher and higher. His mouth took hers with a hunger that left her trembling in his arms. The tiny murmurs of surrender that escaped her throat, Sam absorbed with his mouth. His hands scaled the length of her back and buttocks as he drew her closer, closer.

With passion roiling through him like a fire out of control, he tried to get a grip on his senses. Reilly meant too much to him to take her in the darkened alley. He wanted to take his time and savor the beauty of her body. But how could he quit now? His body was aching for fulfillment, singing with the feel of her in his arms. He tried to take a deep breath and still his rising passion. But his breath rattled from his body and his limbs trembled with desire.

From somewhere deep inside, he dredged up a strength he didn't know he possessed. He held her gently to him and buried his head against her neck. He needed to hold her just a moment more. They stood there in the shadows of darkness and held each other. He lifted his head and kissed her lightly.

"Let's go to our room." His voice was coarse and heavy. He skimmed the neckline of the dress, his fingers leaving a trail of fire. "When we make love, I don't want anything between us."

A tinge of embarrassment colored her cheeks, and she was grateful for the darkness. It hadn't mattered to her where he took her, so long as she was in his arms. When she lifted her hand to smooth her tangled hair, his fingers joined hers, and he brought her hand to his mouth. A sigh of pleasure escaped her, and her head fell forward to rest on his chest.

He took her hand, and they left the darkened alley, walking along the boardwalk hand in hand.

"Do the people of Bodie ever sleep?"

"Eventually."

Lights from the saloons flooded the street, and music drifted through the night air. As they passed one of the saloons, they could see a group of men gathered around a battered piano. The player hammered out his rendition of *Little Brown Jug*, while the group sang. On occasion, it sounded like they were all singing a different verse. Soon the men paired off and began dancing with each other. They faced each other and linked arms, high stepping and swinging each other to the beat of the music.

It was fun and sad at the same time. "They're lonely, aren't they?"

Sam nodded his head. "They're here by themselves trying to make a better life for their families. When they've made their fortune, they'll send for their families, or return home. All they have right now is the company of each other. They make the most of it, to forget how lonely they are."

Reilly knew about loneliness firsthand, and she hoped each and every man found his fortune soon and could return to his family. The sad thing was . . . they didn't understand that their families were their fortune, not silver and gold.

Reilly squeezed Sam's hand and as they continued their walk toward the hotel, neither were aware of the man following them. Entering the hotel, they approached the desk while the man lingered unnoticed nearby, listening as Sam asked the clerk for their room key. As they walked up the stairway to their room, the man turned on his heel and left the hotel with a twisted smile on his face.

Chapter 35

Sam pushed the door closed with the heel of his boot and pulled Reilly into his arms. His mouth found hers, and once again the fires of passion ignited.

Her fingers stroked his face and twined in his dark hair. She had no reservations about what she was doing. She was his for the taking without any promises for the future. Her heart belonged to him regardless of what tomorrow brought. She was tired of trying to figure out this man she loved. Good or bad, she wanted him and he wanted her.

He lifted his mouth and trailed a fiery path down the column of her neck. As he leaned against the door, he carried her with him. His hands eager to feel her warm flesh, he pulled and tugged at the fastenings of her gown. Some of the buttons loosened, others fell unnoticed to the floor. A bit of lace came away in his hand, and it didn't matter.

He pushed the dress from her shoulders and the breath caught in his chest. The moonlight that splashed through the window highlighted her creamy naked flesh. Her breasts rose and fell with every breath as they pressed against the delicate lawn fabric of her chemise. Her nipples were like petals of a flower closing in the darkness, until they were buds that pressed with life against the fabric. He couldn't deny himself the taste of her. He lowered his head and tongued the fabric until it was damp with moisture. He cupped the mounds in his hands, his thumbs swirling around the throbbing buds.

Reilly writhed against him, the sensations surging through her, vanquishing any thought of modesty for herself or Sam. Her hand fisted in the fabric of his shirt and pulled until the buttons scaling the front of his shirt joined hers on the floor. Eagerly, she pushed the fabric aside until it draped his shoulder. He shrugged out of the shirt, letting it drop carelessly to the floor. She buried her face against the springy curls covering his chest and breathed deeply of the clean masculine smell of him. Her tongue darted out and tasted his flesh. His nipples puckered and became hard as she mimicked his play.

She didn't know how it happened, nor did she care, but suddenly her chemise was dangling from Sam's fingers. They came together, heated flesh against heated flesh. She wiggled her hips and peacock-blue taffeta puddled around their feet.

Sam cupped the sides of her head, his thumbs skimming her kiss-swollen lips. His heart was pumping wildly in his chest as his hands moved in unison down the length of her neck before lingering on the fullness throbbing against him. He lifted her breasts in his hands. For an instant, his thumbs stroked her before moving to her narrow waist. Once more, he hesitated, stroking the gentle curve of her hips. His thumbs worked their way through the nest of soft curls and lingered at the juncture of her legs, gently massaging the inside of her legs and skimming the dewy warmth of her womanhood.

Passion swirled through Reilly like clouds racing across the horizon, paralyzing her with emotion. She held her breath, savoring every touch, every sensation until she could bear it no longer. She surged toward him, her body merging with his, their mouths joining in a ravishing kiss that bruised their lips and extolled their ardor. Her hands swept into his shimmering hair, holding him tightly to her.

He scooped her up in his arms and, in a few quick strides, carried her to the bed. After placing her gently on the mattress, he stripped off her shoes. His hands ran the length of her legs until he hooked his fingers in the top of her stockings. Taking an eternity, he eased the stockings from her legs. She could see the fire burning in his eyes and knew his desire matched hers, and marveled at the thought. He sat down on the edge of the bed and began removing his boots. She couldn't stand the separation.

Coming to her knees, she leaned against his back and wrapped her arms around him, settling her hands in his lap. His breath shuddered in his chest, his purpose for sitting on the bed completely leaving him. He covered her hands with his and pressed her fingers into his hardness, moving her hand against him. She nibbled the side of his neck as she rocked against his back. Her naked breasts were feverish with expectancy as they scaled his heated flesh.

Sam fumbled with the fastenings of his pants until they opened. Still clutching Reilly's hand, he guided it to his heated flesh. When her hand curled around his manhood and slowly stroked him, he groaned and gripped her hand tighter.

The sounds coming from his throat enhanced her desire. She increased the motion of her hand as she kissed her way across his broad shoulders. Her hair spilled over his arms and into his lap, the delicate scent enclosing him in a haze of passion. He turned slightly and gathered her in his arms. Breathing her name in a hoarse passion-filled voice, he lifted her and turned her, sitting her atop his lap. His manhood beat against her warmth until she lifted herself to her knees, and his throbbing manhood found its way home. His mouth joined hers in a wild and desperate reunion, the long weeks of pent-up desire surging for completeness. Her ride was short-lived as their release came swiftly and completely. She collapsed against him, marveling at the sheer abandonment of her actions.

He lifted the hair from her neck and replaced it with his lips, whispering his way across her damp flesh. His words excited her anew. With her clasped tightly in his arms, he turned until they were lying side by side. He stripped his pants off and applied his attention to Reilly.

She was so sated she hadn't dreamed there was a spark of desire left in her body. He proved otherwise. Very slowly, he stroked her body, renewing passion's flame. Their lovemaking began gentle and sweet, their desire overcoming all else. It was the same wild abandonment that carried them to sudden and violent release.

They curled together, holding each other. Completely relaxed, Reilly shut her eyes and felt herself drifting to sleep.

She was sleepily aware when Sam kissed her lips and whispered softly.

A few moments lapsed before his words sunk in, and even then she wasn't sure she'd heard him correctly. Her eyes popped open. She tilted her head until she could see his face in the moonlit room. In the shadowy darkness she could see the planes and angles of his beloved face. "What did you say?" she asked breathlessly.

"I love you, angel," he repeated quietly.

At long last the words she'd craved to hear, and she'd almost slept through them. She was wide awake now and wanted to talk about it. But she could tell that Sam was almost asleep. Still, she couldn't resist a few questions; she'd waited too long.

She nudged him gently and asked softly, "Was it so

very painful to say the words?"

"No, it's just that I've never said them before."

"I'm glad."

"Are you?"

"Very."

"Well, what about you?"

"If you're asking me if I love you, I think you already know the answer."

"It would still be nice to hear you say it."

"I love you, Sam Chandler. I've loved you since the day you stepped down from the train in Castletown."

"That long, huh?"

She could see the crooked smile that spanned his face. "Don't get cocky. I haven't decided if you deserve my love or not."

"But I do. No one else would put up with your high-handed ways."

She laughed softly. "Maybe you're right. I do get a bit carried away when I have something on my mind."

"A bit? You're like a mule with blinders on when you get something in that pretty head of yours."

"Pretty head, huh? I think I like that." She snuggled against him and lay perfectly still, pondering his words. The heat from his body soon enveloped her in a cocoon of warmth and security. The memory of his words warmed her insides, filling her with an abundance of peace and hope for the future, their future.

Though Sam slept peacefully beside her, sleep was the farthest thing from Reilly's mind. It was as though his words had opened a flood gate, and she had so many questions. Surely, he would answer them for her now. As the questions rolled through her mind, her eyes became heavy with sleep, and soon she joined Sam in peaceful slumber.

*　　　*　　　*

The bright yellow moon scattered its rays across the town of Bodie, and twinkling stars played hide and seek with the mountain tops as Reilly and Sam slept. His sleep was dreamless; her own was filled with sweet dreams of steepled churches and bridal bouquets.

Farther down the street in the bowels of the red-light district, that was not the case. Behind the closed door of a seedy hotel, Neal coached a woman repeatedly on her speech and her manner.

"You won't have to shout, she isn't deaf. Speak softly and don't swear."

"It makes me want to swear just lookin' at that getup you expect me to wear," the woman protested.

"I'm paying you enough to go stark naked, if that's what I want."

"I'll tell you something, honey, I'd be a helluva' lot more comfortable stark naked than I'll be in that garb," she retorted, tossing her dyed black hair across her shoulders.

"Watch your mouth and your manners, or you won't get a dime."

"Hey, you promised half up front and the rest when the job's done."

"You won't get a dime if you're not convincing."

"Honey, for what you're paying me, I could convince Sam Chandler that I'm his wife."

Neal eyed her full breasts as they pressed against the transparent camisole. He pulled at the front of his pants. "Yeah, I guess you could. Let's run through it one more time and then we'll call it quits."

Reilly was up before dawn. Standing at the window, she watched as the sun peeked over the horizon. Her head was filled with plans. Since they had now professed their love to one another, she had to convince Sam to change his outlaw ways. She wanted them to be free to live their lives without always looking over their shoulders in fear. Would he want to go somewhere and start over? She would talk to him about it. A shiver caused her to rub her hands briskly over her arms.

"Reilly, come back to bed and I'll get you warm."

With a bright smile lighting her face, she didn't waste any time taking him up on his offer.

He cupped her face and his thumb caressed her kiss-swollen lips. "I know you have a hundred questions. I see them mirrored in your eyes. And I promise I'll give you the answers you seek. Your feelings for me have placed you in a delicate situation. But believe me, you won't be disappointed. All I ask is that you give me a little while longer. Just trust me."

She nodded her head.

Her questions went right out her head when he wrapped his arms around her and began to stroke her body, his kisses telling her all she needed to know at the moment.

When Reilly woke several hours later, she was alone. She stretched and rolled over on Sam's pillow, burying her face in it. She could smell his clean scent. It was strange how he had come into her life and changed the whole focus of her being. He meant everything to her. She looked around the room and saw his things neatly stacked on the dresser, the clothes they'd worn the night before folded and lying on a chair.

She got up and padded across the room to the dresser. The water in the pitcher was still warm, so she knew he hadn't been gone long. She hurried with her morning bath and put on one of her new dresses. After brushing her hair until it gleamed, she coiled it atop her head. She had just put the finishing touches to her hair when someone knocked at the door.

"Sam," she called as she flung open the door. "Oh,

excuse me. I thought you were someone else."

A beautiful woman stood there, dabbing at her eyes with a lacy handkerchief.

"Can I help you?" Reilly asked, admiring the beautiful black- and emerald-striped dress the woman was wearing.

"I hope so," the woman said softly.

"Pardon me? I didn't hear you."

"I said, I hope so," the woman said loudly, then dabbed once more at her eyes. "I'm looking for my husband."

Reilly smiled hesitantly. "Well, I can assure you he isn't here."

"But they told me downstairs this was his room." She glanced at the door quickly. "This is room 147."

Suddenly, Reilly didn't like the feelings attacking her heart. She took a deep breath and asked, "What is your husband's name?"

"Sam Chandler." The tears began in full force as the woman spoke. "I've searched for him everywhere. I don't know why he left me. I just have to talk to him. If he tells me he doesn't want me in his life any longer, I'll take the children and return to my parent's home in the East."

"Children?" Reilly gasped. She wanted to cry. She wanted to scream. No, she wanted to hit someone. She wanted to hit Sam Chandler's lying face.

"Sam should return in a little while. If you'll wait for him in the lobby, I'm sure you won't miss him."

"Thank you, you've been a great help."

Reilly watched as the woman walked down the hallway. At first, Reilly had thought the woman beautiful. But on second glance, she was harsh and brassy. Her gown was beautiful and her hat was the latest fashion. But Reilly was sure the hair tucked beneath the hat was dyed and not very well. What did it matter what she looked like? She was Sam's wife. And he had children. He was truly a hard-hearted man, if he could abandon his children. He was nothing like the man Reilly had conjured up in her mind.

The tears began to fall in earnest and her breath came in great heaving sobs. She ripped the dress from her body and tossed it carelessly on the bed. Sam could give the clothes to his next conquest. She was through playing this game of hearts. She was going home.

After pulling on her old denim pants and shirt, she slipped out the back of the hotel and stomped down the alley. She wasn't sure how she was going to get home, but she would figure out something. Their horses were at the livery; that would be her first stop.

But before Reilly reached the end of the alley she came to a grinding halt. Something wasn't right. Her mind was in a whirlwind. Sam had asked her to trust him and at the first opportunity she'd bolted. Why? She'd taken him into her home when she knew he was a gambler. She'd stayed with him when she discovered he was an outlaw. But the moment some woman claimed she was his wife, Reilly took off like a scalded dog. Why? Because her heart was involved and there was nothing she could do about it.

Well, she wasn't leaving . . . not until she confronted Sam. As she turned to retrace her steps she didn't notice the two men converging on her. When they took her arms and turned her around, it was too late.

"One move, little lady, and I'll put a hole in you the size of an egg."

She stumbled when the gun gouged her in the ribs.

"You've got an appointment with Sheriff Murdock. He's real anxious to see you."

Reilly was beside herself with anger for letting her guard down. Sam had been right when he said she was like a mule with blinders on. She was headstrong and reckless. And now she'd put both their lives in danger. She'd run hellbent into the arms of trouble. Big trouble. Now what would she do?

Sam stepped back quickly on the boardwalk as the batwing door of the saloon swung open. A man backed through it, dragging a well-dressed gambler by his booted feet, directing another man to find the undertaker. Bright red blood stained the white shirt of the gambler and, still clutched tightly in his hand, was a knife. After depositing the gambler on the edge of the walk, the man knelt beside the dead man and unlaced his fingers from around the knife.

"Nice knife," he said gruffly, running his finger along the shimmering blade. He slipped the knife inside his jacket. "But you won't be needin' it anymore."

Similar words echoed loud and clear in Sam's ears, causing a chill to run up his spine. *Real nice pigsticker you have here, Chandler, but not much use to a dead man . . .*

Sam's long shadow fell across the man as he stepped forward and paused beside the body. Only then realizing someone else's presence, he looked up and saw the deadly gleam in Sam's eyes.

Nervously, he stood up and faced Sam. "Hey, he came at me with that knife. I had to kill him to protect myself," he said, fearing for his own life.

Not uttering a word, Sam tipped his hat to him and, with a ghostly smile, continued on his way, leaving the man slack jawed and wondering if he'd just seen the devil himself.

The haunting words kept drumming through Sam's head, until they conjured up a picture in his mind. The man was hunkered down beside him as he spoke . . .

"Real nice pigsticker you have here, Chandler, but no use to a dead man."

Feeling the hot sunlight piercing his eyelids, Sam could barely open his eyes. Through his thick lashes, he saw a hand slowly turning the hilt of a knife in his hand, the blade flashing brilliantly as the sun rays bounced off its surface.

"Think I'll keep it as a memento," the man said, chuckling deep in his throat.

As he stood up and pocketed the knife, his large body blocked the bright sunlight, giving Sam a clear view of his enemy's face—the thick-lipped, heavy-jowled face of Floyd Murdock.

He closed his eyes just as Murdock stared down at him. "I had to kill you, or you might've seen my men. Well, I plan to go back to town a hero, because I just killed the leader of the gang." He threw back his head and laughed.

As Murdock's vision and laughter faded from his mind, Sam sighed tiredly, feeling as though he had just returned from a long, unpleasant journey. All along he had suspected Murdock, but there was always the chance that Neal had shot him. Now, he could at least return to Castletown and arrest the bastard for attempted murder. And by now, Mason might already have proof of his other criminal acts.

But . . . what was he going to do about Reilly? For a long while he pondered his dilemma. If he told her he knew Murdock had shot him, and he was going after him, she'd never let him go to Castletown without her. If he just up and left without saying anything, she'd follow him. He finally decided he'd have to break his agreement with Mason. She had to know the truth, or she would never begin to understand why he didn't want her with him. Until he and Mason had Murdock and his outlaws in jail, she wasn't safe.

He figured he could win enough money gambling tonight to take care of her needs. He'd demand she lock herself in her room and take her meals there too.

He didn't want her out on the street alone. He'd wire her immediately after their mission was complete.

Sam slowed his pace, dreading his confrontation with Reilly. He recalled every lie he'd told her, and knew she'd recall them too when he finally told her the truth. Would she forgive him? He'd soon find out, he thought with a grimace.

Sam nodded politely to two elderly women as he passed them. Behind him, he heard one of the women comment, "Why, look over there, Mable. That deputy looks like he's trying to handcuff a woman."

"Well, any woman bold enough to wear men's pants probably did something to deserve it," she said with finality.

Their remarks stopped Sam in his tracks. Snapping his head around, his gaze shot across the street. Though her back was to him, there was no mistaking Reilly's long blond hair and her trim buttocks. Sam's breath came in hard and fast as he saw her twist her wrist free from the deputy's grip. As she hauled her arm back and drew her hand into a tight fist, another man quickly intervened and grabbed her arm. Pinning her hands to her back, the deputy clamped the handcuffs around her wrists.

Sam's heart almost stopped beating when he saw the deputy's face. *Good God, it's Neal!* How'd he get here so fast? His eyes cut to the deputy assisting him. He was a young kid Sam had never seen hanging around the jail. Again, he glimpsed at Reilly, wondering why she was dressed in pants. Another thing bothered him. How had they caught her? She would have never opened the door and let them into their room.

Sam shrugged the thoughts aside as the men roughly gripped her arms and forced her to walk down the boardwalk. Sam resisted the urge to go to her aid, seeing right off what they were about. Marching her through town handcuffed like this was

368

a way to draw attention . . . his attention. Well, they had his attention all right, and they'd regret it.

He'd known they were taking a risk coming to Bodie. Yet, he'd hoped the town was far enough away that if Murdock should learn they were here, they'd be long gone before he could catch them. He'd been wrong. After canvassing all the towns close to Castletown, Murdock had widened his search. Neal had probably been here for days, waiting for them.

Drawing an iron mask over his face to hide the turmoil within him, Sam followed them, his heart in his throat. He thought of the wonderful years ahead of them, holding Reilly in his arms each night, having children by her, feeling a purpose to his life when he woke up in the mornings . . .

The shrill sound of a whistle interrupted his thoughts. He looked ahead toward the depot as the train came to a grinding halt. He watched Neal and the deputy escort Reilly on board, then disappear inside the car.

God, he had to think straight. The life of the woman he loved was in his hands, and if he reacted impulsively, he could lose her in a heartbeat.

Chapter 36

The whistle blew and the engineer brought the train into Castletown with a teeth-jarring halt. A crowd waited in anticipation at the depot. Word had traveled fast that a prisoner was being escorted into town. Shock and disbelief swept among the spectators when Reilly Reynolds stepped down from the train, her hands cuffed and a deputy clutching each arm.

She held her head high and her back straight as she met the astonished faces of the people.

The sheriff stepped from the crowd and took possession of her arm. "So we meet again, Miss Reynolds."

"Not by choice, I assure you."

"I see that being on the run hasn't tempered your smart mouth."

She wouldn't let him goad her into replying. Instead, she bit her lips and watched her step. The one thing she didn't want to do was stumble in front of the crowd. She'd made enough of a spectacle of herself already. As Murdock marched her through the crowd, it hit her that the people weren't gloating over her capture. She saw compassion mirrored in their faces. They despised the sheriff and what he had done to their town.

The sheriff was the only one gloating. He strutted his bulk across the boardwalk and into the jail, pushing Reilly ahead of him. None too gently, he unlocked the cuffs from her wrists and pushed her into the cell. "Home sweet home, Miss Reynolds. Too bad you can't take a self-portrait. I'd love to have your picture in my collection."

"I thought you only collected photographs of dead people."

"The day ain't over yet." He bellowed with laughter at his cruel joke.

Reilly turned her back on his hated face and tried to block his laughter from her mind. She'd gotten herself in a fine mess. But something wasn't right, and she couldn't figure it out. The deputies who had captured her had paraded her all over town before they'd boarded the train. Also, they'd never mentioned Sam and neither had the sheriff. She would have thought that capturing Sam would have been a feather in Murdock's hat. His unconcern was cause for concern.

She'd had a lot of time on the train to think about her actions. What a marvelous thing hindsight was. She'd been wrong, and now it was too late to set matters straight. Her anger and a broken heart had blinded her to everything else. She'd listened closely to the deputies' conversation, trying to learn something. But they had said nothing that would help her. Neal was one of the deputies with whom she was familiar, but the other was just a fresh-faced kid she'd never seen. And he seemed very uncomfortable with his position.

Even now he appeared nervous and ill-at-ease as he leaned against the wall, waiting. But Neal was another matter as he perched on the corner of the sheriff's desk. He watched Reilly with burning eyes. She paced the small cell nervously, trying to control her fear. Finally deciding anger was her best outlet, she sat down on the thin mattress and watched the sheriff. He was leaning back in his chair, clipping the end of a long thick cigar as though that was the most important thing in the world. He was very pleased with himself; she wanted to know why. Before she could think of something to say to wipe the sly smile off his face, the door was flung wide.

Sam walked into the room as boldly as you please, his eyes darting to the cell where Reilly was confined.

She jumped to her feet. "No, Sam! It's a trap!" At last she'd figured out the reason for Murdock's sly smile. She was only a pawn to draw out Sam. He was the one Murdock really wanted.

The sheriff didn't seem overly concerned as he leaned forward in his chair and nodded slightly at Neal. The poor soul had been taking orders from Murdock so long that he had no better sense than to draw his gun on Sam.

Sam's left hand moved so fast that it appeared as only a flash before the shot rang out and the deputy screamed in pain.

"You son of a bitch, you've hurt my hand again."

"Yeah, but this time I got your gun hand."

Before the other deputy could get a shot off, he felt the barrel of Sam's gun grinding against his neck. Hell, he didn't have no dog in this fight, and he'd be damn if he'd risk his life for the sheriff's sake. He didn't like Murdock anyway. He dropped his revolver quickly to the floor and raised his arms into the air. "It wasn't personal, Chandler, I was just following orders."

"Well, you got new orders now. Think you can follow them?"

It was then the deputy noticed the U. S. Marshal's badge on Chandler's shirt. The man gulped loudly before he nodded. "I'm new on the job. But I'm good at following orders."

Murdock was livid. This was not the plan.

Bellowing with rage, he came to his feet. "I have a bunch of idiots working for me. Can't you do anything right?"

"If you want him, you take him," Neal answered crossly, as he wrapped his mangled hand in his handkerchief.

"The game's up, Murdock. We can do this peacefully, or all hell can break loose. Take your pick," Sam advised coldly as he approached the desk.

At last Murdock noticed the badge and his face paled. "Who are you?"

"Sam Chandler, United States Marshal, and you're under arrest."

Reilly gasped and quickly tried to cover her astonishment. She grasped the bars to keep herself upright and watched Sam. He was in his element and she proudly urged him on.

He tossed the ring of keys to the young deputy and instructed him to let Reilly out. "Miss Reynolds is innocent of any charges the sheriff might have dreamed up."

"I'm the sheriff," Murdock shouted. "You can't arrest me."

"You're not above the law, Murdock."

"What am I being arrested for?" he asked smugly. He knew he'd covered his tracks well. There was no way Chandler could pin anything on him.

"Extortion."

"What?"

"You extorted money from the people of this town for protection of their businesses and that's against the law."

"You can't prove a damn thing."

"Unlike you, I wouldn't make the charge if I couldn't support it. I have about twenty business owners that will testify against you." Sam reached across the desk and relieved the sheriff of his gun.

Sam turned to the young deputy. "Before you

lock him up, check him to make sure he's not armed."

On wobbly legs Reilly left the cell and slid into a chair in the corner, never taking her eyes from Sam. *Extortion? That's all they've gotten him for after all the murders he's committed.* It was all her fault. Her capture had forced Sam to finish his job quicker than he had intended.

Murdock was thinking the same thing as the deputy gripped his arm and turned him against the cell bars. Yeah, he'd be out of prison in no time . . . and he had enough money stashed away to start over again.

The deputy frisked him from top to bottom, finding a knife strapped to his boot. Removing it, he handed it to Sam.

Sam turned the knife over in his hand, eyeing his initials carved in the ivory handle. "Turn around, you son of a bitch."

When Murdock turned, he felt the sharp tip of the knife piercing the fold of fat beneath his chin.

"Know who this belonged to?"

Murdock found himself staring into a pair of dark, deadly eyes. He swallowed hard. Beads of sweat formed on his forehead and rolled down his bloated face. He couldn't speak, he was terrified. This man would kill him; it was written all over his face.

"Cat got your tongue?" Sam applied just enough pressure to draw blood.

Murdock flinched and stammered. "Y-Yours. B-But I d-didn't s-shoot you."

"I didn't ask you that, but since you volunteered, we might as well cut straight to the truth."

"I . . . I don't know what you're talking about."

"Sure you do. You saw me that day when you were going to meet your gang after the bank robbery. You thought I was following you, so you laid in wait and ambushed me. Then you devised the story that I was part of the gang that robbed the bank to cover killing me."

"But I didn't kill you."

"No, but you tried. Do you know what they do to people that try to kill United States Marshals?"

Murdock would have shaken his head, but the tip of the knife anchored against his throat stilled any movement he thought to make.

"Okay, lock him up."

The young deputy grabbed the sheriff's arm and made quick work of putting him in the cell with Neal. He slammed the door and applied the key. Just then the front door opened and Mason Womac pushed two men into the room.

"Brought you some more prisoners, Sam. Think you can handle them?"

"I think so."

Reilly couldn't believe her eyes. Standing before her were the three men in her photograph. But Mason Womac was bringing them in. How could that be? He was part of the gang . . . wasn't he? Then she saw the badge on his coat that was just like Sam's. He and Sam were working together. Lord, her mind couldn't take many more surprises!

"Cord's the one who killed the bank teller. And this unlucky bastard didn't pay any attention to the company he was keeping." Mason nudged the man named Pryor. "Didn't anybody ever tell you boys that crime doesn't pay? Especially when you've got a feisty little photographer catching you in the act." Mason pulled the photographs from his coat pocket and passed them around for all to see.

"Definitely not your best side," Reilly quipped to Cord as she looked at the photographs. Now she knew what Sam had done with the pictures she'd given him.

"Hang on to those. We'll need them in court." Mason smiled, knowing the men would sing like birds trying to clear themselves.

"You all have had a busy day," the young deputy said, lifting his arms to encompass the prisoners.

"All in a day's work," Sam supplied, grabbing Reilly's hand and pulling her to her feet. "And I'm not through yet. I've got a lot of explaining to do."

"I bet you have," Mason teased. "You go on and do your explaining. I'll handle the paperwork."

Sam didn't give Reilly a chance to object as he pulled her out the door and up the street to her studio.

When they entered the studio, she wanted nothing more than to collapse into his arms, but her pride halted her. She'd loved him and he'd deceived her.

When Sam lowered his mouth to hers, all he got was a tight-lipped response. "What did I do now?" he whispered harshly. "What's going on?"

"I would think that's pretty obvious."

"Reilly! I know you're angry because I didn't tell you I'm a marshal. But I couldn't. That information could have gotten you killed. You took enough chances as it was."

Her broken heart wept and tears sprang to her eyes. "That's not it," she said stubbornly.

"You mean it's something else?"

"Oh, what's the use? You've always told me you were a lover. But you might have mentioned it to your wife. She's looking for you."

"My what?"

"Your wife," she sobbed as the tears began to fall.

He lifted his hand and brushed her tears away. "I don't have a wife."

She hiccuped. "What about children?"

He shook his head. "No, no children either."

"Are you telling me the truth?"

"I have no reason to lie. I told you the truth the other night. Did you think I lied?"

She shook her head.

"I haven't changed my mind."

She buried her head against his chest and sobbed, "I didn't really believe her after I thought about it," she rambled.

Sam had no idea what she was talking about. But he knew she would get around to telling him in her own sweet time. So he just held her in his arms.

"I just needed your reassurance," she sobbed.

He listened patiently as she told him about the woman.

"You were set up. And after they captured you, they made sure I saw you. I knew what they were up to. It was time to put an end to the sheriff's grip on this town. I set the wheels in motion and Mason rounded up the men involved in the bank robbery. Finding my knife on the sheriff was an extra bonus. I really didn't believe I'd be able to prove he shot me. Although I was sure he had."

"I knew they were trying to draw you out by locking me up. But I never dreamed you would march in there as brazenly as you did."

"Well we don't have to worry about them anymore. Their game's up."

"How did you know?"

"I knew how their minds worked."

"Takes one to know one," she teased. Her heart was filled with such love that nothing else mattered. They were together and she would forgive him anything.

Chapter 37

A lone figure crouched in the darkness, his eyes never leaving the sheriff's office. If he didn't do something tonight, it would be too late. He had no desire to join the men behind bars. If they talked, and he was sure they would, Chandler would be after him. He couldn't stand closed-in places, and he couldn't think of anything worse than being locked behind bars. Yes, he had a plan. Carrying his bag, he crawled to the back of the jail. One stick of dynamite should do the job.

The night was filled with moonlight and sparkling stars. A night for lovers, Susan thought with a flare of hope as she paused outside the jail. Though the shades were closed, she knew Mason was inside. She'd watched the young deputy leave earlier and enter a restaurant down the street. Would Mason be angry with her if she bothered him? She had to talk to him.

Finally, she gathered her courage and, opening the door, peered around it. "Mason, can I talk to you?"

Hearing her soft voice call his name, Mason looked up from his paperwork. "Sure, but I'll come outside." Rising, he looked at the cells housing his prisoners. They were lying on their cots with their eyes closed, but he knew they weren't asleep. They'd warned him repeatedly that the rest of the gang would come to their rescue. Mason knew better, but hadn't enlightened them. He looked forward to seeing their scowling faces tomorrow when their prediction hadn't come true. Earlier, he'd found out that the outlaws had left Castletown immediately after they'd heard about Murdock's arrest.

Mason stepped outside and closed the door behind him. Turning toward Susan, he saw her face bathed in moonlight. Her loveliness took his breath away.

"I know I shouldn't bother you, but I haven't seen you since all the excitement."

He smiled. "You never bother me." At least not in the way she thought, Mason mused as his eyes dropped to her full mouth. "Let's take a walk," he suggested.

"But should you leave the prisoners?"

"We won't go far. Besides, they aren't going anywhere." Taking her hand in his, he led her across the wide alley. They stepped upon the boardwalk in front of the building next door. Drawing her into his arms, he gazed down at her. "Is something the matter?"

"I was worried about Reilly. She isn't at her house."

"No, she's with Sam somewhere. I told him he didn't have to stay, that I'd handle the paperwork."

"Oh . . . good," Susan said hesitantly, nervously toying with the badge he had pinned to his jacket. "So, you're a marshal. I knew you were hiding something from me, but never something like that. I . . . ah . . . guess you're anxious to leave here, now that you've finished your job."

"No . . . not really," he said, his heart in his throat.

For a long moment, his blue eyes intently explored her lovely face. Emotions warred within him as she returned his gaze with a love she had never been able to hide.

They'd spent several hours together since Sam and Reilly's escape, each worried about their friends' fates. He'd suggested they meet secretly in the alley behind her store after dark so Murdock or his men wouldn't suspect anything going on between them. Mason had had his work cut out for him. Trying to make her believe he wasn't a scoundrel and keeping his true identity a secret had been difficult. He'd felt an incredible urge to confide in her, but he couldn't break his agreement with Sam.

"I'll . . . I'll miss you," she said softly, her hand roaming upward to gently stroke his cheek.

Suddenly, a deep yearning welled up inside him, wrenching his heart when he thought of never seeing her again. Susan's caring, gentle, and undemanding ways had rid him of his vow never to put his faith into another woman. Now, he felt an undeniable peace within him.

"Oh God, Susan," he groaned. Enfolding her in his arms, he lowered his mouth to hers. It was the sweetest kiss he'd ever experienced. But Susan didn't want sweet. She wanted fire and explosions of passion. She wanted Mason. She arched against him and parted her lips, enticing his tongue into the soft warmth of her mouth.

Right on cue, a mighty explosion ripped through the darkness, lighting the sky.

Mason broke the kiss with an expletive. "Damn!"

Picking up Susan, he ran toward the street. Looking behind him, he saw Oscar rush from the alley and fall as a shower of debris came down on him and trapped him.

As he lowered Susan to her feet, she clutched his arm and cried, "Oh, my God, Mason, the prisoners!"

Mason stared numbly at the blaze. "I know. And to beat it all, one of their own killed them."

"How do you know?" she asked, puzzled.

He pointed toward the body in the street that was partially covered with debris. "That's Oscar. I guess he knew they'd finger him. He was going to see that they didn't."

"They were evil men," she said sadly, "but to die like that."

Mason turned her in his arms and cradled her face in his big hands, his expression warm and serious. "You can bother me any old time you want, pretty woman."

The color drained from Susan's face as she caught his meaning. If she hadn't come to the jail . . .

Suddenly, Susan clasped her hands tightly behind his neck, her eyes misty with tears as their mouths met in a long, needful kiss.

Inside the studio, Reilly lifted her hips to meet Sam's final thrust. They came together in a fiery climax as the explosion ripped through the jail. "Damn," he swore in a ragged breath. "What now?"

Sam pushed himself from the divan and slipped on his pants. His heart felt like it would burst when he looked out the window and saw the fiery furnace the jail had become. Mason was his first thought. "Oh please, God, no." Before he could make it to the door, Reilly's shout stopped him.

"I can see Mason, he's all right. He and Susan are standing just across the street."

Relief surged through Sam like an overflowing fountain. "I better check it out. I don't know how Mason escaped, but I'm thankful that he did."

Mason and Sam took charge directing the people. Quick work and helping hands soon had the fire out. When the people were confident that all was done, they began to disperse. They had no grief for the men who had tried to destroy their town. "Good rid-